MAY   2002

Icy Sparks

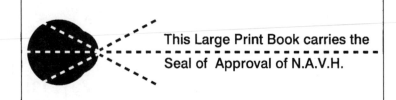

This Large Print Book carries the
Seal of Approval of N.A.V.H.

Icy Sparks

Gwyn Hyman Rubio

G.K. Hall & Co. • Waterville, Maine

10299188

Grateful acknowledgment is made for permission to reprint excerpts from the following copyrighted works:
"Tune Me for Life" from *God the Supreme Musician* by Sri Chinmoy. By permission of Aum Publications.
"Which Side Are You On?" by Florence Reece. © Copyright 1946 by Stormking Music Inc. All rights reserved. Used by permission.

Published in 2001 by arrangement with Viking Penguin, a division of Penguin Putnam, Inc.

G.K. Hall Large Print Core Series.

The text of this Large Print edition is unabridged.
Other aspects of the book may vary from the original edition.

Set in 16 pt. Plantin by Christina S. Huff.

Printed in the United States on permanent paper.

Library of Congress Cataloging-in-Publication Data

Rubio, Gwyn Hyman.
    Icy sparks / Gwyn Hyman Rubio.
      p. cm.
    ISBN 0-7838-9509-7 (lg. print : hc : alk. paper)
    ISBN 0-7838-9510-0 (lg. print : sc : alk. paper)
    1. Tourette syndrome — Patients — Fiction. 2. Grandparents as parents — Fiction. 3. Appalachian Region — Fiction.
    4. Kentucky — Fiction. 5. Orphans — Fiction.
    6. Girls — Fiction. 7. Large type books. I. Title.
PS3568.U295 I25 2001
  813'.54—dc21   2001024918

Para mi compañero, Angel

In memory of Rachel

O Master — Musician
Tune me for life again.
The awakening of new music
  My heart wants to become.
My life is now mingled
  In ecstasy's height.

— SRI CHINMOY

Acknowledgments

I am grateful to the Kentucky Arts Council, The Kentucky Foundation for Women, the Virginia Center for the Creative Arts, and The Hambidge Center for Creative Arts and Sciences for their support.

I feel fortunate to have Susan Golomb as my agent. From the very beginning, she has believed in my work and stood by me. Her relentless faith in my writing has kept me going.

My gratitude also goes to my editor, Jane von Mehren, whose talent, intelligence, enthusiasm, and, above all, calming presence have buoyed me during these past two years. She is a woman of class and kindness.

Thanks to Gabriel Geltzer, Jane's assistant, for being both efficient and pleasant. I am thankful to have received excellent help from Dave Cole, my copy editor, and to have benefited from the artistic vision of Maggie Payette, the designer of my book jacket.

I am grateful for the support I received from the Kentucky Chapter of the Tourette Syndrome Association. Through their loving actions and concern, the members of the Kentucky Chapter demonstrated their belief in the unique essence of every human being. I am most appreciative of my friends Loyal Jones and Father John Rausch for their knowledge and sound advice about Appalachia. Thanks to Isaac and Anna H. Ison for their personal collection of Appalachian expressions, *A Whole 'Nother Language.* I want to thank Lisa Hiner for the hymnals and her lovely rendition of "Gathering Home." To friends far away and to those nearby, I am thankful for their optimistic reassurance along the arduous pathway to publication.

Thanks to the M.F.A. Program at Warren Wilson College for nurturing both my spirit and my mind. A special thanks to the following teachers: Mary Elsie Robertson, for teaching me about courage; Francine Prose, for stressing the importance of humor; Joan Silber, for showing me the value of revision; Stephen Dobyns, for emphasizing the beauty of the creative process; Michael Ryan, for insisting upon concentrated effort; Charles Baxter, for offering hope.

Were it not for Dr. Michael Roy Lyles, for his guidance and concern so many years ago, this novel would not have been written. I will always value his friendship.

My heartfelt thanks go to my brother, Thomas Holt Hyman, for his continuous phone calls of support, and to my aunts, Mitzi Hyman and Dinah Hyman Waterman, for listening to me and encouraging me.

And, finally, I am especially indebted to my husband, Angel Rubio, for his friendship, patience, joyful devotion, and particularly for his thoughtful advice during the writing of this book. His delight in the publication of *Icy Sparks* has been as great as my own. He was the first person to believe totally in my writing; his confidence in my work has remained unwavering throughout the years. My work, my struggles, and my dreams are blessed because our paths are joined.

Prologue

Matanni, my grandmother, said it began deep inside my mama's womb when she was pregnant with me. Mama ate those little green crab apples that grow beside the toolshed. She ate oodles of them, popped them into her mouth like rock candy, crunched, and swallowed one right after another until not one was left to ripen on the tree. "Green apples ain't no baby's nourishment," she said, "but in the beginning they was all your mama could hold down."

No more than a seed myself deep inside her stomach, I had to eat crab apples bigger than I was. I had to take that sour skin into my wee little stomach, grind it down, digest it, and grow. In the darkness of my mother's belly, I ate the tart fruit, so sour on my tongue that it made my lips curl upward, so full of kick that I burped liked a bubble popping. Then, growing into a baby, I burst upon the world. The midwife slapped my bottom, and I croaked so loud that she turned around to see if the legendary bullfrog from Sweetwater Lake had hopped through the doorway. "But it was only you," Matanni said. "Your eyes were bulging from your head, two hard round marbles. Already the blue was tinted yellow.

Your skin was as cold as fresh springwater, slippery and strangely soothing to touch. When the croak sprung from your mouth, your lips were opened wide, stretched not into a yowl but an oval. The croak boomed into the room and slapped against the midwife's cheek. She quickly turned her head, but you croaked again, and she turned back. 'Cold as the bottom of Icy Creek,' she said, leaning over to place you on top of my daughter's stomach. 'Icy,' your mama said, stroking your bald head, and pulling up the quilt with her free hand until only the tip of your head showed. And the name, Icy, stuck," Matanni finished, dropping her head forward till her chin dotted her chest like a period.

Patanni, my grandfather, told me different. "The dynamite in the coal mines done it," he said. "All his life, your daddy was nervous, hearing them veins of coal popping open. Sometimes they exploded; sometimes they just croaked; but the noise always rattled in his brain. The hour you was born, his Chevy was curving along Black Knob Mountain when the coal truck in front of him backfired, blasting rocks down the mountainside. Startled, your daddy jerked the steering wheel to the right and swerved into a covey of quail feeding in the grass. The car slammed to a stop. Wings whooshed through the air, beating plumage and blood against the windshield. Powder-down feathers, like coal dust, flew through the open window; your daddy waved his broad hands in front of his face and closed his eyes; feathers swam around him; they fell upon his hands and seeped into his skin. He leaned back against the seat, breathing

12

heavily, listening to the rocks settle, hearing the far-off rumble of tires crunching stones. He blinked his eyes several times, closed them, then opened them slowly. A dead quail, with squashed beak and smashed wings, stared at him. Your daddy was afraid and tried to open the Chevy's door and jump out, but his eyes were transfixed on the bird's glare, and his limbs were locked like death. Trapped, his eyes tried to escape. They pushed against their sockets, desperate to leap out and run; but try as they might, surging and popping like buoys upon the water, they stayed in place; and your daddy was forced to stay put and behold his future — a dark emptiness foreshadowed in the bird's dead eyes. When he caught sight of his fate, his arms began to shake violently and a bellow tore through his lips. At that very same moment, while your daddy's howl devoured the dusk and his eyes pounded away at the darkness, you — flying from your mama's womb — croaked loudly. In that departing light, your eyes also popped with the truth of what your daddy saw — beaked lips screeching into nothing."

I, Icy Sparks, can't recollect when I was born, but I still remember my daddy — how all his life his eyes bulged forward when he talked, like a dam holding back a flood of words, corking everything inside, so afraid he was of the vacancy left behind should all his thoughts be spoken. I remember how he'd squat in front of the country store, resting on his haunches, talking so quiet that friends would lean over to hear him. The closer they came, the softer his voice grew until suddenly his eyes would protrude like two round stop signs, signaling to friends that they were too near, that he needed to be alone. He had to silence the rumble of dynamite and the thump of dead birds. He needed time to rearrange his insides and summon some quiet. Muffling a scream, he'd simply swallow and create a new thought. Then, another shy sentence would leak through his lips.

My legacy was come to rightly. The good Lord charters a path for each child, and no use comes from fighting against it. My mama died from kidney poison two weeks after she birthed me. From those little green crab apples, she created Icy, the frog child from Icy Creek, and an indigestion so troubled that it gnawed away her system and turned her water as yellow as my eyes. Matanni told me that before she died her urine was the color of acorn squash. "Child, them eyes of yours is her gift to you," Matanni said. "Your mama saw the golden light and sent it back to you. The minute your sweet mama passed into heaven, your eyes turned yellow."

With his eyes popped wide, my daddy died; but, unlike Mama, he didn't see the golden light, just the final scream descending. Patanni found him near Icy Creek. The tin bucket was overturned, its handle clutched in his left hand, the blackberries scattered the length of his leg, his skin puffed up from the stings. The bees so consumed with rage had plunged through his leather boots and bitten the tops of his feet, or so the coroner said. Even so, I remember only his eyes — iced surprise and anticipated horror, saying more to a four-year-old than those thousand pinpricks that covered his body.

I was born a frog child from Icy Creek. From my father, I inherited the fear that resided in his coal-black eyes, and from this fear I've gained wisdom. Fear placed books in my hands and led me to search for the answers. From my mama, I received lush hair, the color of goldenrod, and yellow ocher eyes. My mama gifted me with memory. Ask me to read the Book of Job. Afterward, I'll recite it back to you word for word. From my mama, I grew to see the world through hope-filled eyes. Though hope did not come easy.

Part I

Part I

Chapter 1

On June tenth, I turned ten. The Saturday after my birthday, the eye blinking and popping began. We were eating breakfast. Matanni was sitting across from me; Patanni was at the head of the table. To this day, I can remember my first urge — so intense it was, like an itch needing to be scratched. I could feel little invisible rubber bands fastened to my eyelids, pulled tight through my brain, and attached to the back of my head. Every few seconds, a crank behind my skull turned slowly. With each turn, the rubber bands yanked harder, and the space inside my head grew smaller. My grandmother was studying me, making sure my face had been washed, my hair combed and fastened on each side with the blue barrettes she had bought me for my birthday. While Matanni studied me, I stared straight ahead and glued my eyes, growing tighter with each second, on the brown fuzz above her lip.

"Icy," she said, sipping her coffee, "what are you staring at?"

"Them hairs above your lip," I blurted, extending my arm and pointing at her face. "They're turning gray," I said, jiggling my arm at her nose, "right there."

Patanni, spooning sugar over his oatmeal, snatched up his head and turned toward me. "Calling attention to a person's weakness ain't nice," he said.

"B-but Patanni . . ." I stammered, aware only of the pressure squeezing my head and the space inside it constricting.

My grandfather laid his spoon beside his bowl. "Apologize, Icy," he demanded. "Tell Matanni you're sorry."

"But Virgil . . ." My grandmother reached out and caught his hand in hers. "What the child said ain't so bad. If them hairs turn gray, they won't stand out. Gray is almost white, Virgil, and white matches my skin." She smiled, caressing the top of his hand with her index finger. "It even feels white," she said, releasing his hand, stroking her upper lip.

Patanni pushed back his chair; the legs scraped against the blue-checked linoleum rug. "That ain't the point, Tillie," he said. "Icy, here, made mention of your weakness like it weren't nothing."

"She's just a child," my grandmother said.

"But it ain't respectful," he said.

"She meant no harm," Matanni assured him.

"Icy, what do you say?" Patanni insisted, leaning toward me.

" 'Tain't necessary," my grandmother said,

20

sitting on the edge of her chair, her large breasts weaving over her bowl.

"Icy!" Patanni ordered.

"Icy!" Matanni shot back, looking straight into my eyes.

"Icy!" he began again.

"Icy!" she repeated.

I jumped up. "There ain't no fuzz on you!" I hollered, feeling the rubber bands tug tighter and tighter, sensing the blood in my body pooling behind my eyes, pushing them forward, so far forward that I could stand it no longer, not a moment longer, and, hopping up and down, I bellowed again, "Fuzz is on my eyeballs. It itches my eyes!" Frantically, I wiggled my fingers in front of my face. "They itch!" I screamed, fluttering my fingertips. "They itch!"

Then, unable to close my eyelids or scratch my eyes, I covered my face with my palms and inhaled deeply, hoping that the itchiness and tightness would go away; but instead I felt my eyelids, rolling up further like shades snapping open, and my eyeballs, rolling back like two turtles ducking inside their shells, and the space inside my head, shrinking smaller and smaller until only a few thoughts could fit inside; and, terrified of the contraction, of each thought's strangulation, I threw back my head and cried, "Baby Jesus! Sweet Jesus!"; and, not knowing what to do or how to stop it, I gave in completely to the urge:

Out popped my eyes, like ice cubes leaping from a tray.

Patanni and Matanni just sat there and watched my eyes spring from my head, but a minute later both pretended that everything had passed like it always did each morning. Matanni drank four cups of her mud-black coffee with a squirt of Essie's cream. Patanni finished his one cup, black with six tablespoons of sugar, and I drank my milk. All of us ate our oatmeal. I ladled honey on mine. Patanni preferred sugar. Matanni ate hers unadorned. No one resurrected Matanni's mustache. That one big pop had unleashed all of the tension, and the space inside my head grew large again, plumped up with thoughts. We ate in silence, and I sat calmly, as though nothing had happened.

Still, after that Saturday morning, during the summer of 1956, the urges claimed me. I was no longer Icy Sparks from Poplar Holler. I was no longer that little girl from Icy Creek Farm — our sixty-acre homestead, replete with two milk cows, a dozen chickens, and Big Fat, the five-hundred-pound sow. I was now a little girl who had to keep all of her compulsions inside. Whenever it became too much, after hours of hoarding blinkings and poppings that threatened to burst out in a thousand grotesque movements, I'd offer to get Matanni a jar of green beans from the root cellar, a pantry-sized room dug from a hill not twenty feet from the back door; and, once inside, I'd close the wooden planked door and let loose. Every blink that had been stored up spilled forth. Every jerk that had been contained leaped out. For ten minutes, I'd contort until the anxiety was all spent. Then I'd climb up on the footstool and grab the Mason jar.

With canned beans in hand, heading toward the house, I thought, Secrets are evil, and wondered what secrets my grandparents kept hidden. I listened to the crickets sing. Covered in shadows, their legs contorted deep in the woods; chirping, they gave their secrets away. A wildcat cried, mourning over something forbidden. Down a dirt road cradled between two gnarled, unfriendly mountains, Poplar Holler guarded its mysteries. So far, mine were hidden in a root cellar. Clitus Stewart's were tucked beneath his mattress. Mamie Tillman would throw hers into Little Turtle Pond. Everyone in Poplar Holler had secrets, even the animals, but I — Icy Sparks — knew that mine were the worst.

Chapter 2

If I could catch a ride into town, I went to the movies whenever I could. Immersed in celluloid fantasies, I became a rugged, square-jawed pioneer with a rifle, protecting my land, shooting bloodthirsty Comanches, or I was Running Deer, a Navajo Indian maiden, sitting cross-legged in front of a fire, cradling a baby in my arms. I became Shirley Temple, tap-dancing across the floor, or Joan Crawford, mysterious and dark, scheming for money, plotting out murder. As I sat in the second row of the Darley Theater in Ginseng, I longed to be anyone else. Even Ginseng's Jeanette Owens in her wheelchair seemed luckier than I was. At least the townsfolk pitied her. They thought her brave, rolling through life, a sour grin plastered over her face. Lonnie Spikes, a twenty-year-old simpleton, elicited clucking sounds and slow, pendulous swings of the head. "Poor thing," the townsfolk said. "He ain't got no idea. 'Tis a blessing." Each citizen slackened his pace to let Lonnie stumble by. He'd amble toward the Ginseng Post Office, where he'd sit for hours on the outside steps with his pants unzipped, his tongue lolling from his mouth, his eyes enameled over like those of a corpse.

Clutching a Coke in one hand and a box of Milk Duds in the other, I scrunched back into the brown leather seat, my feet nervously rapping the floor, and waited for *Coyote Sunrise* to begin. The lights blinked three times. Joel McRoy, slouched in the chair behind me, kicked the back of my seat and said, "Icy Sparks ain't nobody's girlfriend."

"Who cares?" I answered, swallowing some Coke and munching ice.

"Peavy Lawson does," Joel said. "He likes you."

I twisted around and glared at him. "I'm only ten," I snarled. "I don't like boys."

"You ought to like him," Joel said.

"How come?" I snapped, tossing back my head, flicking a Milk Dud into my mouth.

" 'Cause he has frog eyes like you." Joel held on to a Chilly Dilly, a long green dill pickle sold at the candy counter.

I slammed the Coke and Milk Duds down on the armrests, one on each side, and jumped up. "You polecat of a dog!" I didn't know if those words meant anything nasty, but I liked the sound of them. "You big fat liar!"

"Your eyes pop out like a frog's," Joel said, waving the pickle around like a baton.

"They don't," I said.

"They do, too," Joel said, thrusting the Chilly Dilly in my direction.

"Liar, liar, pants on fire!" I screamed, losing all composure, pointing my fist at his pickle.

"Shush!" came a voice from a few rows back.

"I seen you, Icy Sparks. I seen you behind Old Man Potter's barn."

"You seen what?" I demanded. "Polecats stink. They ain't able to see."

Joel McRoy rose to his feet, swung his hand upward, and angrily crunched. One-half of the Chilly Dilly disappeared into his mouth. "I . . . seen you . . ." he said between bites, chomping down dill pickle like it was an ear of sweet corn, "jer . . . king, pop . . . ping them frog . . . eyes of yours . . . behind Old Man Pot . . . ter's barn."

"You slimy ole pickle!" I bellowed. "You ain't seen nothing."

"Frog eyes! Frog eyes! Frog eyes!" Joel screamed back.

"Be quiet, you two!" someone warned.

"Liar! Liar! Liar!" I yelled, ignoring the warning, then grabbed my cup of Coke, rocked up on my toes, leaned over, and poured the whole drink, ice and all, over Joel's head. Stunned, he just stood there, a green chunk of Chilly Dilly inside his mouth, swelling out his cheek, a half-eaten pickle gripped in his hand.

"You ain't seen nothing! You just tell lies!" And with these final words, I marched out — knowing full well that Joel McRoy was telling the truth, that the week before when I was out playing tag with him and his cousin, Janie Lou, the urges had gotten really bad, and I had stolen away behind Old Man Potter's barn and let loose such a string of jerks and eye pops that the ground behind the barn seemed to shake.

Not only was I a hoarder of secrets, but — in the space of ten minutes — I had also become a full-fledged liar.

That afternoon, after leaving Darley Theater, I whiled away my nerves and guilt roaming the hilly, winding streets of Ginseng. I passed by the Crockett County Courthouse, the center of town. Farmers in bib overalls were scattered along the brick walkway that led to its four skinny white columns. Red geraniums bloomed on either side of the walkway leading to the entrance graced by a Kentucky flag and a U.S. flag. I continued east on Main Street, walking by the post office only two buildings down, but saw no one sitting out front on its dusty white steps. Adjacent to the post office was the Samson Coal Company — its offices located in a two-story, red brick building. Next came People's Bank, a gray, quarry-stoned building constructed during the 1920s. Three buildings down from the bank on the other side of the street was the Darley Theater, a crimson brick movie house with a marquee in front, where I had told off Joel McRoy. I definitely didn't want to go there; so, instead, I abruptly cut across the street and headed down a steep sidewalk toward the Cut 'n Curl, which was tucked into a corner of Short Street.

When I arrived, I said hello to Mrs. Matson,

the proprietor — a tall, large-boned woman who wore her orange-red hair in tight, short curls — and helped sweep up strands of hair around the chairs and beside the sinks. After I folded towels, picked up scattered magazines, and cleaned the toilet, she gave me a bottle of Coke, so cold that ice clung to the glass while an iceberg floated inside. I sipped the drink slowly, sucking the ice between my lips, feeling my teeth ache from the cold.

Yet all the while, my thoughts were fixed on Old Man Potter's barn. Behind a mound of hay, I had popped and jerked like a caught fish fighting. I had done it all — twisted, contorted, and misshaped my body into a thousand unsightly knots; and Janie Lou and Joel had watched.

I swallowed the last of my Coke and shuddered. "Mrs. Matson, what can I do now?" I asked as she took the bottle from my hands.

"You can get along," she said. "Go find some kids and play."

"But," I argued, "they're at the movies."

"Not all of them, Icy Sparks. Scat, now!" she said, clapping her hands. "It ain't healthy for a youngin' to sit around grown folk all day."

"But —" I persisted.

"But, nothing," she said. "Go outside and play."

Through the glass door, I saw the sunlit streets of Ginseng with its buildings traced in gray, coal's bold signature. Ginseng had always been prosperous. Through coal's boom and bust, it liked to brag on itself. It bragged about Samson Coal and the contracts that kept its miners working even during hard times. It bragged about young Dr. Stone and his brand-new office that stayed busy with soon-to-be mothers, victims of car accidents, miners with black lung, and sick folk who didn't have to travel all the way to Lexington for treatment anymore. It bragged about being the county seat, about having a movie theater and decent schools. It bragged, bragged, and bragged, all the while averting its eyes from the nooks and crannies deep in the hills where life could be hard, where good and bad times depended upon the price of coal and the future plans of the coal companies. Pressing my hands against the glass, I stared at Ginseng Full Gospel Baptist Church, stuck between Willena's Cafe and Dr. Stone's new office, and spotted the Church of the Nazarene, inserted in the tiny space behind Schooler's Funeral Home. In town there was no root cellar in which to hide, no shadows to eclipse my fears. The many churches, squeezed into corners, offered little refuge. They were for righteous, truthful people. As I twisted the doorknob, turning around to wave good-bye, feeling lonely, I remembered Miss Emily. As the sun's warmth burned through the glass and caressed my skin, I knew that Miss Emily would not betray me. Although lately I was too scared to trust anyone, I knew that the child inside her would not turn on me if she caught me jerking. Hadn't her soft, fat arms always sheltered me and kept me warm?

Long before I met Miss Emily, I had heard about her strangeness. At Comb's Restaurant on the river, I had heard the townsfolk gossiping. "She comes by it naturally," they'd say. "Both her parents were fat. Huge tubs of lard." At Margaret's Bakery, I had listened to housewives whispering in superior voices, "She buys three dozen sweet rolls every morning and eats all of them at once." The men at the barbershop snickered and said, "No God-fearing man will marry Miss Emily. If she took to hugging him, he'd be squashed." Women at Stoddard's Five and Dime milled around the lingerie, held up pairs of underwear, snorted, and said, "They don't make panties big enough to cover Miss Emily's broad behind." Then they'd giggle, cup their hands over their mouths, their eyes darting from side to side, and feel pleased with themselves and the unanimity of their attack.

At six, I hadn't understood everything I'd heard, but I had understood the sound of disdain and knew it was mean. In spite of this, I hadn't connected such meanness to the people expressing it, but rather to the one at whom it was directed. So when Patanni first took me to Tanner's Feed Supply and asked me to come inside and meet a really nice woman — Miss Emily Tanner — I had been afraid.

She was in the backroom sorting out corn feed as we had walked through the door. When

30

the bell above the doorway jangled, I had jumped back. "Patanni," I whined, my toes trembling inside my shoes, "I don't want to. Can't I just wait in the truck?"

"I reckon not, Icy," he said, grabbing my hand and pulling me forward. "I brought you over to meet Miss Emily and you're gonna do just that."

"What if she don't like me?" I said, straining in the opposite direction.

"I'll be coming directly," a voice rang out. "I'm shoveling corn."

"What if she don't like me?" I repeated, leaning so far toward the door that my grandfather's fingers popped.

"Doggone it, Icy!" Patanni barked. "Straighten up. The woman ain't no witch."

"But she's fat. Her bottom don't fit inside regular underwear."

"So?" my grandfather said. "What does her bottom have to do with her heart?"

"She eats three dozen sweet rolls every morning," I spewed out. "She's too fat. She could crush a person if she hugged her."

"Nonsense," Patanni said. "Miss Emily ain't crushed nobody."

"But —" I pleaded.

"Shush!" Patanni cut in, holding a finger up to his lips. "Mind your manners."

From the back of the store, I heard wood scraping along a floor and heavy breathing. Suddenly Miss Emily laughed loudly. "What she

31

laughing about?" I asked, tightly squeezing Patanni's hand. "Ain't nobody back there with her."

"Maybe she enjoys her own company," my grandfather said. I swallowed hard and nodded. "Maybe she's a nice woman who likes to laugh."

"Yessir," I peeped.

"Maybe —" my grandfather went on, but stopped short when he saw Emily Tanner, red-faced and sweating, emerge from the backroom. "Hello, Miss Emily," he said, extending his hand.

Ignoring my grandfather's hand, she grinned broadly and said, "Mr. Virgil, I'm gonna hug you instead." Then she lunged toward him, wrapped her huge arms around him, and clasped him ferociously to her chest.

I heard my grandfather groan, saw his head buried in her blue plaid cotton dress, and her face, all bunched up and creased with fat. My heart raced. My palms began to sweat. I could see myself suffocating in Miss Emily's quick-sand of blubber, and I stammered, "Not me, oh no you don't!" Releasing his hand, I inched toward the door and threatened, "You ain't gonna squeeze the life out of me. You ain't gonna squash me." Quickly, I pivoted on my toes and ran.

"I'm gonna hug you, too!" Miss Emily squealed, chasing after me, her flesh crawling forward like a blue-stained snowdrift. And before I realized it, she had snatched my shirt and was pulling me toward her, right into her rotund arms. But instead of moaning from pain, I had groaned from pure delight, cognizant only of her sweet warmth.

Now under a July afternoon's bright skies, with the smell of coal dust tingling in my nose, I headed for Walnut Street, one of the inclines that zigzagged up and down both sides of the courthouse square, passing by Margaret's Bakery, Stoddard's Five and Dime, Denton's Barber Shop, and Danny's Filling Station, to spend the rest of the afternoon in Tanner's Feed Supply.

"Howdy, Miss Emily," I said as I creaked open the screen door, my hand springing up, my fingers fluttering hello.

"Howdy, Icy Gal," she said from the back of the store. Then she turned around from the wire rack where she was arranging packets of seed and held out her arms, so fleshy that the fat flapped to and fro when she moved them.

"I been missing you," I said, throwing my body into those hamhocks, nestling my head between her huge breasts. "I been missing you," I repeated, closing my frog eyes, feeling the tension seep out of me into her surrounding corpulence.

"Icy Gal, where have you been?" She combed my curls with her fingers. "I haven't seen you in weeks."

"Around," I mumbled, my mouth engulfed in gingham.

"You know how I miss you when you don't

visit," she said, placing her square hands on either side of my head, rocking me back, and staring into my eyes. "But I knew you were coming today. Johnny Cake told me you were in town."

"I saw him at the Cut 'n Curl," I said. "He was filling up the Coke machine. I'm sorry I ain't . . ." Then, lowering my eyes, I coughed and corrected myself. "I mean, I'm sorry I haven't seen you in so long."

"Don't feel badly, Icy Gal," she said. She took my hand, and flesh — like warm dough rising — cushioned my fingers. "I've got something for you in the back. Guess what it is." She smiled broadly; her thin lips, a pencil stroke, slit her face.

"A coffee cake?" I asked, knowing full well what Miss Emily had prepared for me.

"No," she said, shaking her head from side to side, her reddish brown hair stroking her chin.

"A peppermint stick?" I ventured.

"Certainly not," she said, and squeezed my hand. "Seems to me after all these years you'd be smart enough to guess what I have for you."

I shrugged my shoulders. "I'm tuckered out from guessing," I said. "I just want to be surprised."

"Get ready. Get set!" she said, still holding my hand. "Go, Icy Gal!" All three hundred pounds of her pulled me through a doorway from which hung a blue velvet curtain. "Now close your eyes," she ordered, trudging forward as I trailed behind. "Okay," she announced, "you can open them!"

As always, teacups, saucers, plates, and miniature silverware were laid out on a small, rectangular table covered with a yellow, pin-striped cloth. " 'Tis wonderful!" I exclaimed, clapping my hands. In the center of the table was a cobalt-blue platter decorated with teacakes, a bowl of sugar cubes, a pitcher of cream, a saucer of lemon slices, and a silver bowl heaped high with taffy. At one end of the table in a doll-sized wicker chair sat Mrs. Possum, a string of baby possums attached to her stomach. At the other end, Gigi, the half-French and half-Persian stuffed cat, was propped upon a leather stool.

Miss Emily lowered herself onto a huge wooden bench on one side of the table while I sat down in a diminutive Queen Anne chair covered in gold satin. "I never would have guessed," I lied.

"Oh, never!" Miss Emily giggled. "But what's different?" she asked.

I scanned the table, hesitated theatrically for a few seconds, then said, "The sugar cubes. We've never had sugar cubes before."

"So right you are, Icy Gal!" Miss Emily said. "So right you are!" She leaned over and removed the tea cozy. "You couldn't have timed it better," she said. "Just a few minutes ago, I put the kettle on to boil. Would you like some tea?" she asked politely.

"Yes, ma'am." I nodded and lifted my teacup.

Miss Emily poured a stream of tea into my cup, then some into hers. "Sugar and cream or lemon and sugar?" she asked.

"Lemon and sugar," I said as she handed me the bowl of sugar cubes and the saucer of lemon slices.

"A tea cake?" she asked, arching her eyebrows.

"Of course," I said.

"Mind if I don't?" she said. "I'm watching my figure."

"Of course not," I said.

"Mrs. Possum, would you care for a cup of tea?" she asked, turning her head in the possum's direction.

"A cup of cream only," Mrs. Possum said in a high-pitched voice. "I don't imbibe in caffeine when I'm nursing. And three tea cakes — please — that is, if you've enough."

"Cream is good for a nursing mother," Miss Emily explained, looking at me.

"That's what Miss Gigi said," I answered, staring back at her, trying to trick and confuse her, wanting to catch her when she threw her voice.

"Miss Gigi?" Miss Emily said, suddenly twisting her neck. "Would you like a cup of tea? After all, you're not a nursing mother."

"Oui, oui," Miss Gigi purred. "I adore the full-flavored taste of tea, with just a hint of lemon." Speaking with a thick French accent, in a smug, self-congratulatory voice, she added, "But I hate children, especially babies."

"A tea cake?" Miss Emily asked, reaching over, holding up the tray.

"See this slim figure?" Miss Gigi hummed. "I didn't get it from eating three tea cakes."

"So what?" Mrs. Possum snarled from the other end of the table. "You got only your prissy body, no man and no kids."

"No babies stealing my strength," Miss Gigi seethed. "No babies leeching from my belly."

"Babies don't leech!" Mrs. Possum growled. "Babies suckle down nourishment."

"Your babies leech," Miss Gigi shot back. "They're parasites, drinking down the vermin you eat."

"I'm warning you!" Mrs. Possum screamed. "Shut that arrogant French trap of yours or I'll . . ."

"You'll what?" Miss Gigi said softly. "Use your brats as switches and whip me till I'm quiet?"

Miss Emily held up both hands. "No more sniping," she commanded. "This is a tea party, not a prizefight." Then, leaning over the table, she asked, "Icy Gal, do you like the tea cakes?"

I nodded, bit into my fourth, and — with a full mouth — said, "Especially these little black things."

"Poppy seeds," Miss Emily explained. "They're little poppy seeds."

Picking one from off my lip, I stared at it on my finger and praised, "They sure are good," as I licked it off.

Miss Emily smiled, stretched herself far over

the table, and raised up the silver bowl piled high with taffy. "My pièce de résistance," she announced. "Icy Gal, will you join me?"

My grin traveled the width of my face. Wanting Miss Emily to see it, I held it until she set the bowl down. Then, not saying a word, I grabbed a handful of pull candy, slipped a glob between my lips, elongated and smoothed it out, and delicately placed the other end between Miss Emily's thin lips. Simultaneously, we both leaned back and watched the taffy grow into a lean, flexible cord connecting the two of us. After which we slowly ate our way forward, coming closer and closer, biting off mouthfuls until we touched noses. Our eyes met, declared love, and we both clamped down, breaking the cord, and swallowed our lumps of taffy.

And although I had not mentioned a word about the jerks and eye pops, I understood, right then and there, that in her heart Miss Emily knew. She was simply waiting for me to tell her.

Chapter 3

The three of us were working in the vegetable garden, a rich patch of ground to the left of the house. Even though it was late afternoon, the sun was still bright in the sky. Years before, my grandparents had cultivated a large garden, at least half an acre, but as they grew older, they decided to make it smaller. " 'Twas too much work before," Patanni said, leaning over, holding the hoe with one hand, with the other ripping out a cluster of weeds intruding on some summer squash.

"Next year, I'm planting even more marigolds and zinnias," Matanni said, plucking a pock-marked leaf off a tomato plant, "to keep away these bothersome bugs."

I whistled through my fingers and pointed at a bunch of wild grass creeping into the green beans. "Way over there!" I said to Patanni. "That grass needs hoeing."

"Ain't nothing wrong with your arm, Icy Sparks," my grandfather said, not making a move.

I moaned, got up from where I had been pulling up milkweed, sauntered over to the green beans, lazily bent over, and tore out the grass. Then, snapping off a bean, I popped it into my mouth. "They sure are sweet," I said.

"I'll cook up a pot for supper," Matanni said. "With some fatback."

"How about some greens?" Patanni asked. "The other day, I seen pokeweed growing in the fencerows near the Tillman place. Since then, I been hankering for a mess of greens," he said. "Pokeweed with spring onions on top, then doused with some of your grandma's hot sauce."

"Some snow on the mountain and some heat to melt it," I said, remembering Patanni's words whenever he ate pokeweed.

"Don't forget your cornbread," Matanni piped up.

"And a few slices of sweet tomatoes," I added.

"Yessir," Patanni said, chopping at the roots of a yellow weed with prickles on its stem. "Ain't no better eating in the world!" he declared, slamming the hoe into the ground. "Excepting for . . ."

"Excepting for what?" Matanni asked, wiping her hands on her apron.

"Louisa's pokeweed," he said, throwing back his head, laughing, his white teeth showing. "That girl almost kilt me."

My grandmother was shaking her head. "Louisa got confused. She did," Matanni said. "Poor girl didn't know the good parts from the bad."

With a faraway look in his eyes, Patanni let go

of the hoe's handle, which wobbled precariously above the loose dirt before plopping to the ground. "In no time, I knowed something was wrong," he said, grimacing, covering his belly with his large hands. "My stomach somersaulting and grinding like it done. The sickness and the vomiting." A smile, wistful and sad, flickered across his lips. "Louisa ate nary one bite, and you were at Stoddard's Five and Dime. I was the only one took sick."

"You weren't the only unlucky one," Matanni said. "Poor Louisa!" she groaned. "She suffered for it, too. Cried and cried. Suffered more'n you. 'Hit ain't normal me not knowing what's good and what's bad and me growing up in these parts,' she said, over and over, till you got well."

" 'Tweren't her fault," said Patanni, walking over to a brown bucket at the garden's edge. "Louisa knowed about garden flowers, but she never cared about wild plants." Dipping his hand into the bucket, he lifted up a Mason jar filled with springwater, unscrewed the lid, and took a swallow. "I tried to learn her, but her eyes would film over like she was dead, and nary a word took root."

"Probably why she ate them little green crab apples before I was born," I chimed in. "She didn't understand they was poison."

Patanni closed his eyes. "When the good Lord took Louisa, He brought us pain." His hand traveled to his chest. "Then He called Josiah home and brought us some more grief. But I reckon I shouldn't complain about getting sick so many years ago," he said, blinking open his eyelids. "I've lived a long time; your poor mama died young."

"She was a good girl," Matanni said, looking at me. "She almost kilt herself nursing your grandpa back. When she done wrong, it was by mistake, never by intention."

Patanni held up the jar of springwater and announced, "Let's toast Louisa, the best damn nurse that ever was!"

Matanni raised her eyebrows. "Virgil, shame on you for cursing!" she fussed, turning toward him.

My grandfather nibbled at his top lip. "Tillie, you know I meant no harm," he said. "God has given us so many tears. Can't I direct a little laughter His way?"

"But Virgil," she protested, "it's been so long since we stepped into the Lord's house."

"Going to church is one thing," Patanni calmly stated. "Respecting God is another."

"I bet Mama never cussed," I said, " 'cause she was more good than bad."

"That girl didn't know bad," Patanni said.

"Then she wasn't at all like pokeweed," I said.

"Oh, no," my grandfather said, "she was a pasture rose, a solitary, sweet pink flower."

The following day, I went hunting for pasture roses. Carolina roses, they're also called, but I liked calling them pasture roses. If they bloomed in Kentucky, I reasoned, shouldn't they be christened Kentucky roses? But if this wasn't permitted, I'd label them pasture roses. Pasture roses belonged to no one and everyone.

I strolled five miles down the dirt road that passed by our farm and came upon Mamie Tillman's land. Dried out and dusty from overuse, an old cornfield lay fallow. Around the edges of the field, I searched for a smidgen of pink, some leftover trace of the June blooming rose, but I found nothing, just beggar's-lice clinging to my overalls. A copse of pine trees stood at the edge of the field; and, wanting to find a cool place to rest, I walked over. In the center of the trees was a small, dark green pond, about twenty feet long and thirty feet wide, which narrowed into a little round pool of water from which jutted the tip of a very large rock. From three feet away, I studied the pond and wondered why I had never come upon it before. Little Turtle Pond, as it was called, had eluded me. Apparently I didn't know every inch of Poplar Holler. This slimy green water and eyelike rock had escaped me.

Suddenly footsteps crunched over pine needles from the other side of the pond. It was Mamie Tillman. The reclusive owner of this land shuffled toward me, her legs moving awkwardly. "Poor Mamie," the townsfolk had said when her daddy died two years ago in a coal mining accident, "she ain't got no one else." Everyone had expected her to leave the area. But, oddly enough, she hadn't. Instead, she had stayed put, living on "Lord knows what," the townsfolk said, leasing out her tobacco patch, getting by alone. Fearful, I scurried behind a large black pine and tried not to breathe.

Mamie Tillman had always been stout, but I noticed that she'd grown fatter. Her black hair was pulled back under a red handkerchief, and she wore overalls stretched over a red cotton shirt. She stopped by the pond's edge and stood still for several minutes. Next, she lowered her arms to her sides, squatted down, and eased herself upon a flat white rock, where she sat with her legs thrust forward.

I sucked in air, stared at her, and tried not to move.

Carefully, she unfastened the straps to her overalls and placed the bib in her lap. She lifted up the shirt, tucked it under her bra, put her big-boned hands over her swollen stomach, and commenced rubbing. Her hands made slow circles over her flesh, then began to swirl faster and faster, harder and harder, until they ground red blotches into her skin.

My mouth dropped open and my eyes widened as a dozen fiery suns flamed over her belly.

Quick as her hands started, they stopped. Mamie Tillman returned her palms to her lap and began to cry — softly and gently — like a young kitten mewing. With every intake of air, her sobs grew heavier, swelled up with anguish, and spilled forth. She threw back her head, half-closed her eyes, and wailed. Great bellows thrashed the air. She cried like this until her voice grew hoarse like a crow's caw.

Crouching behind the tree, I listened and watched as she wiped her cheeks, pulled down her red shirt, brought up her bib, latched her overalls, and pushed herself off the ground. Her wet, red-streaked face made me sad. Her misshapen body was foreboding and ominous. When she gulped down air and said, "Dear Lord, give me strength. I won't make it if You don't," I felt such a sorrow that I touched my own stomach and wondered how Mamie Tillman, who had no husband, could be with child. I was thinking about this, feeling scared and confused, when she turned around, breathing heavily, and ambled up the lonely yellow hill with no pasture rose in sight.

When Mamie had become a gray blotch in the distance, I stepped out from behind the black pine and headed home. The sun was still hot, but starting to slip down. It's tuckered out, I thought, shining on too much pain. Ever since I could remember, Matanni had told me about the pain of bearing children. My own dear mama had grieved three times afore I was born, she had said. God had taken three of her babies. The longest one, she'd carried five months. "After so much pain and sorrow," Matanni had said, "she weren't taking no chances with you." According to my grand-

45

mother, my mama knitted me ten birthing blankets. Five pink ones and five blue ones. Matanni said that if I had been a boy, Mama was aiming to call me Bedloe, because she knew how much Patanni wanted to keep the family name alive. "But you were a girl, and you were named Icy," Matanni had said. " 'Tweren't no other name for you."

I stopped to study a small pink blackberry. Newborn and not yet ripe, it was fragile and delicate. Leaning over, I blew my warm breath against it and watched as it trembled but clung tenaciously to the vine. With any luck, I thought, it'll grow into a big, fat, juicy blackberry. In the beginning, I had been lucky I was conceived the night of the shooting star when Poplar Holler was sprinkled with stardust. Fairy dust, Mama called it. But Daddy called it coal dust after she died. For him, grief and dynamiting had turned Poplar Holler gray.

Squeezing through a honeysuckle hedge, I thought about what Matanni had told me. My mama hadn't acted like Mamie Tillman. She hadn't pulled up her shirt and tried to erase me from her stomach. Instead, she had placed her delicate hands upon her belly and caressed her skin, wanting to protect the baby inside.

"Hit ain't right that your mama never knowed you," my grandmother said. "Hit ain't right that your daddy died so young. They kilt themselves to have you and got none of the pleasure, none of the joy of seeing how you growed up. Such a

46

pretty little girl you've become!"

Mamie Tillman had behaved differently. Beside Little Turtle Pond, I had seen her cry like her heart was splitting, angrily rubbing her belly. With no husband to bring home coal dust and money, she was alone. Only the turtles in Little Turtle Pond, the sweat bees — flitting near the water's edge — and I, Icy Sparks, knew her secret; but we wouldn't tell. No, we wouldn't breathe a word. We, keepers of secrets, had to stick together.

When I rounded the curve, I spotted Matanni and Patanni rocking on the wide front porch, sipping ice tea. Lightning bugs lit up the dusk. Insects and night birds chanted. I noticed the climbing crimson roses that covered the trellis to the right of the front steps and the yellow-orange flowers of the butterfly weed growing from the bald earth beside the corners of the porch. Then, at the edge of the woods, Matanni's pride, the Turk's-cap lilies, six feet high with nodding red blossoms, caught my eyes. Beyond them, even deeper in the woods, the white sycamores shone like lighthouses in the impending darkness.

"Icy!" my grandfather hollered, waving. "Where have you been?"

"Around," I yelled back. "Exploring."

"Ain't supposed to trespass!" my grandmother screamed, her face reddening. "Well, what did you see?" she asked a few moments

47

later, as I planted my feet on the top step, then turned around, my back to them.

"I came upon a pond," I said, sitting down. "One I ain't seen before."

"Where?" Matanni said, loudly gulping down tea.

"In a secret place," I said. "Nearby." I shook my head, my golden hair swirling around my face.

"Child, with that hair of yours, you look like a daisy swaying in the wind." My grandfather laughed and rocked back in his chair.

"A daisy with a secret," my grandmother said.

I pressed my shoes against the step. "Don't you hear them?" I asked, making the rubber soles squeak.

"Hear what?" my grandmother asked.

"My shoes," I explained. "They're telling you where I've been." I squashed my feet into the wood and swiveled them back and forth. "Listen!"

Patanni creaked forward and pointed at my overalls. "Little Turtle Pond," he said, laughing. "That beggar's-lice gives you away."

Matanni jiggled the ice in her glass. "Icy, if you been that far, you must be thirsty. Can I get you something to drink?"

"I'm more hungry than thirsty," I said. "What's for supper?"

"Pinto beans with ham, cornpone, and fried apple pies," she answered.

I sighed deeply and stared at the landscape.

"Sure is pretty," I said. "Like a photograph dreaming."

My grandfather cleared his throat. "But a photograph can't dream," he said.

Extending my arm, I pointed at the empty space. "See how blurry it is," I explained. "It's neither day nor night. Kind of in between."

" 'Twixt day and night," my grandfather said.

"All soft-like," I said. "Like my goose-down pillow. Like the fluff on a dove's breast. Safe, soft, and gray. Bad things shouldn't happen at twilight."

"God don't put much stock in appearances." Patanni clinked his glass on the floor. "Now, Jack-in-the-pulpit is pretty to look at," he went on. "Jack peers up over the edge of his pulpit, protected by that green leaf hanging over him. All summer long, he preaches and preaches until, all wore out, he finally withers away, leaving behind little red drops of blood, a bunch of scarlet berries. If you eat these berries, your mouth and tongue will burn like fire. But if you think Preacher Jack is safe to eat before he withers and changes, you'd be mistaken, 'cause he'll burn you, too. You see, it don't matter how Jack looks. Jack is Jack, all the while."

"Twilight plays tricks," Matanni said. "Sometimes appearances can be deceiving. Remember your daddy died at dusk."

Patanni groaned and stood up. "Yessir," he said, "God keeps on working. In the soft, gray twilight, He took Josiah away."

Looking back over my shoulder, I stared at my grandparents. "I ain't afraid," I said. "Daddy died in twilight, but I was born in it. 'Tis safe for me."

With those words, we headed for the kitchen.

"Our heavenly Father," Patanni prayed after Matanni loaded the table with dinner and we sat with bowed heads and closed eyes, "please forgive us sinners. Find it in Your heart to forgive an old man, who from time to time steals a shot of Satan's poison from the barn. And please forgive an old woman who begrudges Lucy Wester's jam-making talents. She ain't usually so blinded by envy." I opened my eyes and looked over at Matanni, who was biting her lower lip and fidgeting in her chair. "And most important, don't forget about a little girl who has some very big secrets. Amen."

"Amen!" I said angrily, and looked up. My breath came in spurts, and I felt a pounding in my chest. Feeling my throat tighten, I panted, glanced anxiously at Patanni, and said, "You don't need to pray for me!" My cheeks flamed, and the heat shot down my neck. " 'Cause I don't keep secrets, and I don't know what you're talking about!" I jumped up from my chair. It fell backward and thudded against the floor. "I ain't a bad girl. I don't need forgiveness," I said, my eyes filling up, tears streaming down my face. "I ain't bad, and you know it!" I cried. Stunned, Patanni just looked at me. "I ain't bad," I repeated, turning to Matanni, whose mouth trembled and head shook. "I ain't bad," I said again, as tears fell over my lip and my tongue wiped them away. "I thought you loved me," I sobbed, a fresh pool of tears spilling over my cheeks.

All at once, a thousand thoughts and feelings surfaced. *But we do love you,* my thoughts said. *What you do in the root cellar ain't bad. You're not bad,* they told me, *just a mixture. Like the poke-weed.*

I rolled my eyes upward. "Pokeweed," I acknowledged, sniffling, nodding my head. "Pokeweed. Pokeweed. Pokeweed," I said.

"Heavens, child, what's wrong?" Matanni asked, pushing her plate away.

"Pokeweed. Pokeweed," I repeated.

You jerk and pop, but you ain't no tattletale, my thoughts continued.

"Tattletale. Tattletale. Tattletale. Tattletale," I said. "Tattletale. Tattletale. Tattletale. Tattletale," I chanted.

You're a good girl, my thoughts declared. *You won't mention Mamie Tillman's big belly.*

I nodded. "No, I won't!" I said. *I won't say big belly. No, I won't,* my thoughts urged, *'cause I'm a good girl. No, no, no. I'll never say big belly, I'll never say those words.* Frantically, I shook my head; then, before I knew it, before I understood what was happening, before any of my positive thoughts could save me, out slipped "Big belly." Startled, I looked around, hunting

51

for the culprit. "Big belly," my mouth said again. "Great big belly."

"Icy!" Patanni came to himself. "Honey child, what is going on?" he asked, jerking upright.

"Big belly! Big belly! Big belly!" I screamed, repeating what my troubled thoughts said. "Big belly! Big belly! Big Belly!" I hollered, until Patanni rushed forward and scooped me into his arms.

My grandmother jumped up. "Virgil?" she said, twisting her head around like a bewildered chicken. "Virgil, I don't understand."

"Virgil. Virgil. Virgil. Virgil," I said, pressing my face against my grandfather's chest. "Virgil. Virgil. Virgil," I muttered. "Virgil. Virgil. Virgil."

Matanni moaned, was silent for a second, then took control. "Virgil, where's that whiskey of yours?" she asked, scurrying toward the door.

"In Essie's stall." He patted my head. "Behind the bale of hay. Hurry, Tillie."

"Tillie," I said. "Tillie, Tillie, Tillie," I cried.

My grandfather clutched me to his barrel chest. "Icy," he whispered, rubbing my back with his broad hands. "We do love you. More'n anything in the world."

More'n anything in the world, Patanni's last sentence, took over my mind. *World,* his last word, loomed there, large and greedy. The *world* was big, and he loved me *more'n anything* in it. If I didn't repeat *world,* it would grow larger and larger. Soon it would expand and extend itself from the top of my head to the tips of my toes.

Like an enormous parasite, it would live in my body, change into a breathing, thriving, eating *world*, and devour me. So I had to say it. Saying *world* would diminish its power. *Pay homage to the word*, my thoughts told me, *and the world will be satiated.*

Yet after the whiskey seared my throat, I couldn't speak. My mouth burned, and every word that crept to my lips went up in flames. Try as I might, I could only whimper softly. My grandfather, hearing my groans, picked me up and carried me upstairs.

In my attic bedroom, the white wooden beams sloped down to embrace me. The tidy yellow iron bed cradled me, and I felt safe. With one broad sweep, Patanni turned back my quilt and put me in bed. Sitting on the brown braided rug beside me, he stroked my head. I smelled the hot, dark odor of whiskey on his mouth. Over and over, he brought his hand through my hair, combing it back, caressing my temple where the *world* dwelled. "Sugar," he whispered, "don't you worry. Your grandma and me love you. Won't nothing ever change that."

I made a gurgling noise and brought my fingertips to my mouth.

"Burned, didn't it?" he asked.

I nodded.

"I'm sorry. There weren't nothing else we could do."

I gurgled again, shivered violently, and snuggled down under the covers.

"Icy, for the life of me, I can't figure out what brought this on," he said.

I tried to answer, but he shushed me.

"Good girl," he said, still rubbing my head.

I heard the faint clatter of pans downstairs. Then Matanni's tiny feet tapped up the steps. A cup rattled against a saucer, and I saw her round belly and thin legs silhouetted in the doorway. "I got hot milk for you," she said, tiptoeing toward the bed.

Patanni put his hand under my neck, lifted my head, and fluffed up my pillow. "This child's trembling," he said as he took the cup.

Matanni touched my forehead. "Why, Virgil, she's running fever! We got us a case of influenza."

"In this hot July?" Patanni said.

"Stranger things have happened," she said. Matanni scurried to the door and stood there. "Don't you worry, Icy," she finally said. "You'll be well in no time. I promise." Like a humming-bird, she flitted down the stairs. Before I could swallow my first mouthful of milk, I heard the medicine chest creak twice. Once more she was beside me. "Open your mouth," she ordered, dropping two aspirin on my tongue. "Now swallow."

"With some milk," Patanni said, putting the cup to my lips.

"Scoot down." Matanni pulled up the quilt and tucked it under my chin. "Rest now," she said, and kissed my cheek.

"Sweet dreams," my grandfather said, setting the cup and saucer on the floor. "We love you," he whispered, squeezing my shoulder.

Then both headed down the narrow stairs, leaving me alone in the twilight.

That night in my bed, I flew with the fever. God, I felt, was giving me a taste of what was in store for me. Fly right, I kept hearing my grandfather say. So I tried to fly right. I'd open my arms and legs, thrust them out, then bring them back to my sides. Over and over, burning with sweat, I did this, leaving yellow-stained angels on the sheets.

When Matanni touched me, she yelped. Patanni carried up buckets of springwater. Matanni soaked dish towels in the cold water and washed my body, hoping to cool me off, but the water evaporated as soon as it touched my skin.

For three days, I burned. With the heat of a thousand forest fires, I flamed. Like the woodstove, stoked and roaring, I cooked. I was bacon sizzling. When moths brushed against my skin, their wings frizzled. I blazed with Satan's fury and grew red-hot with God's awful love. I burned and burned and burned until my skin withered and my lips cracked. I boiled until my mind dissolved and lost its shape. My thoughts rose upward and evaporated like steam. I burned until there was nothing left. Just Icy Sparks. Ice sparking flames. And no one's tender care, not even my grandparents', could bring me back to me.

Then, one morning, a bright red cardinal landed on my windowsill and chirped loudly. I was drawn to him. His beak smiled, and his eyes twinkled. Then, like scarlet flames, in a whirl of red, he fluttered away, taking all of the heat in my room, all the fire in my body with him.

Weak, I inched up on my elbows and slung my legs over the edge of the bed. When my feet touched the cold floor, I smiled. "Matanni," I said aloud mostly to myself, "what's for breakfast?"

Chapter 4

I felt sweat trickling down my forehead. The hair around my face was wet, but this time it wasn't fever. The tenacious midday heat had turned the grass yellow. Beside the toolshed, the limbs of the crab apple tree drooped. Even the dogwood leaves were brown, curling up like strips of fried bacon. Eager to cool off and forget my worries, I decided to go to the springhouse for a tin cup of cold water when I heard the rumble of tires over gravel. I perched my palms over my eyes and saw whirlwinds of dust and the glow of bright red metal. The red Chevy veered to the left, its back tires screeching, spun onto our rutted driveway, and jerked to a stop at the top of the hill. Miss Emily pounded the horn, poked her head out the window, and yelled, "Icy Gal, come over here and help me."

I squinted into the sun. "I reckon I have the energy," I yelled back, then plodded down the steps and shuffled toward the car.

Miss Emily shoved open the door and extended a barrel-sized leg. "Yesterday, your grandpa dropped by. Said you were here by your lonesome, recovering from the flu. I just had to check in on you."

"Who's minding the store?" I asked, reaching over with both of my hands. I grabbed her left hand and pulled. Swaying forward slightly, she lost her balance and fell back, scrunching again into the seat. "Please try!" I said, wiping my sweaty palms on the front of my shirt.

"Johnny Cake." She brushed her brow with a white lace handkerchief, breathed in deeply, and added, "He loves being important, and I love giving him the chance. Right now, I'm awfully busy with other things, collecting money for the volunteer fire department and helping the library decide what new books to buy."

"Give me both hands," I said.

Miss Emily stretched out both arms. Her palms were slippery with perspiration.

"I'm gonna count to three," I said. "One . . . two . . . three." I jerked back, straining so hard that my face turned beet red, and held firm.

Miss Emily, a huge redwood, oscillated forward, both of her shoes swallowing dirt, then stood upright. "Whew!" she said, shaking. "That was tough."

"I ain't gonna be your walking cane," I said. "I'm too tuckered out."

"I didn't ask you, did I?" Indignantly she tossed back her head, inhaled deeply, and began trudging toward the house. "So you've recovered?" she said, looking at me sideways.

"I ain't got no fever," I said.

"I don't have a fever," she corrected me. "You're from these hills, but you don't have to talk like it. It's time you talked right. Have you forgotten everything I taught you?"

"Of course not," I said. "I like talking hillbilly. Everyone speaks this way."

"Your speech will mark you for life," she snapped. "If you don't change it, it'll hold you back. You won't become the person I know you can be."

As we walked, I could feel my spirits crashing. Miss Emily usually accepted me. Now she was badgering me. "If you don't like me for me, then I don't need this visit," I said.

"Nary a person in these mountains done made it with speech such as this." She smiled and patted me on the shoulder. "Icy Gal, Berea College taught me that there's a time and a place for everything. I'm proud of my roots, but in that great, wide world beyond these mountains, pride — false pride, mind you — is a flaw. It will hurt you. Do you understand?"

"I need to speak right," I said.

"You're smart as the dickens, Icy Gal. Sometimes I forget you're only ten." When we reached the first step, Miss Emily stopped, braced herself, opened her mouth so wide that her lips stretched over her teeth, and inhaled deeply. "Stay close," she said, "or you'll tumble off the edge."

"Ready?" I asked, huddling beneath her armpit.

"Ready," she said, and up we went. The minute we stepped on the porch, Miss Emily waddled over to Patanni's rocker and collapsed. *"Un vaso de agua, por favor,"* she said.

Gigi, the cat, taught me French. Miss Emily taught me Spanish. "From the springhouse?" I asked. "It's very cold."

"In Cuba, we drank piña coladas on the veranda. Even now, my tongue remembers the cold slivers of pineapple and the sweet taste of rum."

"A cup of springwater?" I asked again.

"Delicioso," she said. "The water in town is brown. I've been drinking Coke instead."

"I'll be right back." I sprinted down the steps, raced around the back of the house, and headed toward the old fieldstone springhouse. Lately, Patanni had been hauling buckets of good, clear water from the springhouse because our well water was too muddy to drink. Inside, pooling in front of a brown stone wall, was the spring, my grandfather's pride. I grabbed the tin cup that hung from a nail and dipped it into the cold water. Then I brought the metal rim to my lips and took a long, slow swallow. It was the sweetest water on earth, and I drank the whole cup before refilling it and dashing back. "Here," I said, handing Miss Emily the cup.

She stopped strumming her fingers on the rocker's arm and took it. Closing her eyes, she dramatically brought the cup to her lips and sipped until the cup was empty. "That was exquisite," she hummed, then opened her eyes and draped its handle over the rocker's arm. "You know how to treat a guest." She tapped her yellow shoes against the porch. "Now sit down," she said. "Tell me all about you."

I sat on the floor in front of her. "I'm glad you came," I said. "No one ever drops by."

"Neighbors don't want to get sick," she said, "especially with the flu."

"Even if I'm well, no one comes over."

"Joel McRoy lives down the road, not a mile away," she said. "Why don't you visit him? The road goes both ways."

I made a face. " 'Cause we ain't friends no more." I corrected myself, "I mean, we aren't friends anymore."

She clicked her tongue. "I heard you dumped a Coke over the poor boy's head."

"He brought in on hisself, himself," I said.

"No one, Icy Gal, deserves a Coke poured over his head."

"Joel McRoy did," I said, straining upward. "If you came over here to make me feel bad, then you can get."

Miss Emily put her hands on my shoulders and held me down. "Calm down, Icy Gal! I've heard Joel McRoy's side, but I haven't heard yours. Tell me what happened."

I sat up straight, looked right into Miss Emily's sky-blue eyes, and said, "He called me a name. Like they used to call my daddy."

"What name?" she asked.

I shook my head.

"Icy, you can tell me. I'm your best friend."

"Frog eyes," I mumbled.

"What?" Miss Emily said.

"Frog eyes," I repeated. "He said I looked like Peavy Lawson. That my eyes popped out like his."

"Peavy Lawson?" Miss Emily asked. "I don't know Peavy Lawson."

"He's ugly as a polecat," I said. "Pop-eyed, straggly brown hair, and freckles."

"Well, you've got blond hair and amber eyes," she said. "I can't see the resemblance."

"The likeness is in the pop," I said.

Miss Emily sucked in air, hesitated for a minute, then asked, "I've never seen you. Do you really pop out your eyes?"

I lowered my head and didn't answer.

"Speak up, Icy Gal. Tell me."

"I . . ."

"Come on, Icy."

"Sometimes my eyes pop out," I began, and stopped. Then, before I could think twice, the whole truth rushed from my mouth. "Joel McRoy and his cousin, Janie Lou, caught me behind Old Man Potter's barn popping out my eyes, and I called him a liar and dumped Coke all over his head when I knowed, knew, he was speaking the truth. I admit it. Sometimes my eyes pop out, but they can't help it. I mean, I can't help it. If I don't, my head feels like it'll explode and splatter all over the place." I stopped, ate a mouthful of air, and continued. "I'm popping and jerking and repeating all the time. I can't help it. I hide in the root cellar and do it. I go down to the creek and do it. I did it in Old Man Potter's barn, and I'll probably do it when school starts. I'll do it because I can't help myself, and the whole school will turn against me, and I ain't gonna hang around for that. Do you hear me, Miss Emily? I ain't gonna stay here. No, ma'am! I'll carve me a canoe out of a cedar tree, and I'll sail it down the Kentucky River, then up the Ohio, all the way to Louisville, where they love people who are different." I heaved once, my shoulders shaking, and broke into tears.

"Icy Gal," Miss Emily said, "listen up, you won't have to do that. I promise, we'll find out what's wrong and make it right."

"But you won't tell no one . . . you won't tell anyone?" I asked in a shrill voice.

"On my word of honor," she said, "I'll not mention it to a soul. We'll give you a little time. All children go through phases, little traumas, you know. You might just be going through one. After a while, you'll grow out of it. Now stand up and come here." When I approached, she stretched out her arms and drew me to her, but it seemed that the harder Miss Emily tried to comfort me, the less comfort she seemed to give.

Before leaving that day, Miss Emily had said, "Icy Gal, you don't believe me, but I understand what you're going through. When I gobble down that last sweet roll, I understand. I'm not hungry, Icy Gal, not at all, but I have to eat them all. Another and another and another until the whole box is empty. I could eat all of the sweet rolls in the world, and I'd still want more." She had placed her fat hand on her chest. "The void, Icy Gal. The emptiness in my heart. No amount of food will ever fill it up."

I shook my head and said, "No, it's different. Eye popping doesn't fill up anything. It just causes me pain."

"You think I don't feel pain?" she asked. "You think I don't know what those snotty women say behind my back? 'They don't make panties big enough for Miss Emily's behind.' I've heard every word, every giggle. I've felt every barb. There's only one mirror in my home, and it's covered with a piece of cheesecloth." She pointed at her face and spat out, "Do you think I want to see this hog?" Grimacing, she had slid her plump hands over her body and said, "I'm roasting on a spit in hell."

Nearby was a patch of withered daffodils. I walked over and sat beside the wilted brown stems. Last spring, after the flowers had bloomed, I had tried to prune them with Matanni's sewing scissors. Matanni, catching me through the kitchen window, had rushed outside. "Icy, don't!" she shouted, running toward me. "If you cut them, they won't come back."

"The flowers are gone," I said. "And the brown stems look ugly."

"Pretty and ugly go together," she explained. "A pop-eyed, yellow baby ain't too pretty neither, but I didn't clip you into little pieces and toss you away." Matanni held out her hand, and I gave her the scissors. "Look what you turned into! You was born an ugly duckling but you've growed into a swan."

"Miss Emily was a fat baby. Now she's a fat grown-up," I said. "She stayed the same. So you're wrong. Ugly and ugly go together."

"Don't you like her?" my grandmother asked.

"She's my best friend."

"Then see the pretty part of her," Matanni had said. "Some hearts, Icy, are mean and vicious, but Miss Emily's is sweet and playful."

"Innocent," I had said.

"The heart of a child."

But that day, I didn't believe Miss Emily could possibly understand what I was going through because we were different. Even though she thought our orphaned status made us the same, I knew it didn't. By four, I had lost my parents. Miss Emily was twenty-five before hers died. When I was old enough, I wanted girl-friends who'd ask me to parties and boyfriends who'd take me to the movies. I wanted more than just respect. I wanted acceptance, the wink and nod of approval. In my home, I'd hang a mirror from each wall. I'd look proudly at myself in each. No, Miss Emily had not a clue as to what ailed me. She could stop herself from eating. I, on the other hand, couldn't help what I did. My urges controlled me. Nevertheless, in Miss Emily's eyes, we were the same. She was the orphan of Ginseng; I was the orphan of Poplar Holler. If she had her way, she'd use our strangeness to unite us. She'd be Miss Emily Tanner, the fat woman of Ginseng; I'd be Icy Sparks, the frog child from Icy Creek. Together, we'd become the Orphaned Outcasts of Crockett County. Just the thought of such comparisons made me shudder.

Chapter 5

Monday, the first day of school, took me by surprise. After all my worrying and waiting, it sneaked up on me like a leg cramp in the middle of a dream. Before I knew it, I was putting on my new red calico dress; and Matanni was frying eggs and bacon.

During the previous two weeks, I had kept my impulses in check. My interior thoughts had calmed down; no longer were they arguing the pros and cons of me, transforming themselves into a separate entity, more powerful than I was. No major jerks, pops, or repetitions. I'd get little impulses, but they were more like tics, wee little movements of my neck and head, nothing like my previous goings-on in the root cellar. In fact, they were so subtle that no one noticed them. Still, I was worried. I never knew when the jerks would take over. When they did, people would find me out.

"Go sit down," my grandmother said, as I tapped across the kitchen floor in my black patent-leather pumps with white clip-on bows. My lace-trimmed socks were turned down and skimmed against my shoes. I felt the sharp-edged jabbing of the heel into my right foot and knew that a blister, round as a quarter, was forming.

"I need some help," I said, approaching my grandmother from behind, holding a brush and green ribbons.

"Icy!" she said, stepping back on my shoes.

"Ouch!" I said, and jumped back.

"I can't cook and fix your hair at the same time."

Pouting, I walked over to the kitchen chair and slumped down. "I picked out these green ribbons." I put the hairbrush and ribbons on the table, then flicked the rubber bands that were wrapped around my wrist. "I'm nervous," I added. "It's my first day, and I want to look pretty."

"You got butterflies," my grandmother said. "If you eat a good breakfast, you'll feel better."

I bit my lip. "I ain't hungry," I said. "I'm too scared to be hungry."

"School ain't never bothered you before," my grandmother said, pulling biscuits from the oven. "What's got you in such a tizzy? You've been feeling better for weeks."

I picked up my glass of tomato juice, stared at the thick red concoction, took a sip but — feeling queasy — set it down. "Janie Lou said that the fourth grade teacher is mean," I replied.

"Janie Lou?" my grandmother said, arching her eyebrows.

"You know, Joel McRoy's cousin," I explained.

She nodded. "So?" she said, lifting her eyebrows again.

"So," I continued, "she spanked Prissy Evans last year for picking her nose and slapped Maggie Mullins for nibbling on her nails. Hit her hands with a Ping-Pong paddle. Janie Lou said that she's from Chicago and came all this way to save our minds and souls. I mean, she don't even like it here."

"Nonsense," Matanni interrupted. "You don't even know the woman. You ain't once mentioned her Christian name."

"Her name is Mrs. Stilton," I said confidently. "And she's a Catholic, too," I blurted out, knowing full well that bit of news would worry my grandmother. I looked right into my grandmother's eyes. Neither of her eyebrows was lifted now. She was listening, all right. "She believes in the Pope and practices her singing every day 'cause she's just hankering to go to Italy and audition for the Pope's choir. Even Janie Lou's preacher has heard about her. One Sunday, he warned the whole congregation, 'If you don't watch out, you, too, will be following false prophets and worshiping idols.' Right then and there, Janie Lou knew who he was referring to. Janie Lou calls her Mrs. Zombie. And do you know why?" I didn't give Matanni a chance to reply. " 'Cause her irises are so dark you can't see her pupils. She looks like one of the walking dead."

Matanni blinked twice, shook her head, and scolded, "Don't believe everything you hear!" Then she snatched up a knife and began buttering a biscuit. "Now drink your juice."

"I told you," I sassed, "I ain't hungry."

My grandmother grabbed my plate and marched toward me. "Now, listen up, Miss Icy Sparks. In this here life, we all got things we don't want to do. All of us have our bad days. So don't go taking yours out on me." She plunked down my breakfast. Staring at me were two over-easy eggs, three slices of bacon, and a biscuit.

"I'm sorry," I mumbled, then stabbed an egg with my fork and slowly brought a piece of it toward my mouth. "I'm as jittery as a horse." I choked on the rubbery sliver of egg white, groaned, and spewed tomato juice and egg all over the table.

"Icy, are you okay?"

I shook my head, leaped up, and raced to the bathroom. Matanni chased after me.

"Icy, are you okay?" she asked.

I heaved over the toilet, unable to answer. Then, totally exhausted, I lowered the lid, folded my arms on top of it, and plopped down my head.

"Icy, are you all right?" she asked again from the doorway. "Say something, please!"

I stood up. "I'm okay," I muttered, shuffling to the door. "I feel better now," I said. "Will you braid my hair?" I asked, extending my wrist with the rubber bands wrapped around it. "I want to wear my new ribbons."

Matanni put her hand on my forehead. "No fever," she pronounced. "Just nerves." She took my hand, led me over to the sink, where she turned on the faucet, and splashed cold water over my face. "I don't understand it," she said as she dried my skin. "School ain't never bothered you. By fall, you're aching to go." She combed her fingers through my hair. "Stay right here," she said. "I gotta fetch your hairbrush and ribbons. Don't worry none. We'll make you look real pretty."

I stared at my pale face in the bathroom mirror. My eyes were bleached out and dull. My hair seemed wilted and dead. Like a dead cat's hair, I thought, one that has been dead in a ditch for weeks. Suddenly I understood why Miss Emily hung cheesecloth over her mirror. "If I had me a piece of cheesecloth," I whispered, "I'd hang it up, lickety-split." But I had no cheesecloth and watched dismally as my grandmother, all smiles, scurried into the bathroom and, with hairbrush and ribbons, went eagerly to work.

Peavy Lawson was the first person I saw. He and his frog eyes occupied the first seat of the first row near the door. When I entered the room, he jumped up and waved his hands at me. They looked like frog's feet — greenish yellow, webbed, and slimy. I blinked and looked again, but he had hidden them in his lap. Now he winked at me, his frog eyelids flying up and down like blinds. A wide, thin grin covered his face. I tried to find his lips but couldn't. Frogs, I guessed, didn't have lips.

"Howdy, Icy!" He lisped the *cy*. When he spoke, his tongue — slender and blood red — shot out a full five inches. "Howdy, Icy," he lisped again, the tip of his tongue curling up when he spoke.

I concentrated on my own eyes, tried to sink them way back into my skull, and said, "Peavy Lawson, why don't you jump back into that pond where you belong?"

He popped out his eyes, then rolled them up into his head. "We can jump together," he said.

I snapped my eyes shut — unable to tolerate the sight of him — and blindly shuffled forward. When I bumped into the large wooden desk and heard the class laughing, I opened my eyelids and slid into the first empty seat I could find. The minute Peavy Lawson leaned way over into the aisle, flashing me a huge, froggy grin, I knew that I had picked the wrong desk since I was only a few seats down from him. My face reddened, and I stuck out my tongue. I opened my hands, turned my palms upward, and spit into both. Then, I slapped them together and rubbed them fiercely back and forth, all the while staring into Peavy Lawson's amphibian eyes.

"Hey you, young lady! You're Icy Sparks, aren't you?"

I heard the voice and turned my head toward the classroom door.

"What in the world are you doing?" Mrs. Stilton barked. "I'm beginning to question Miss Palmer's high opinion of you."

I looked at Mrs. Stilton's long nose and her squinty, black eyes and was too frightened to speak. A long quiver started from the nape of my neck and shook me down my spine to the tips of my toes. This ain't no jerk, I thought. This is just plain fear. My desk began to bang against the floor.

"Icy Sparks!" Mrs. Stilton screamed.

I clamped my hands over my ears.

"Remove those hands, young lady!"

I froze.

"Remove them or else!" she warned.

Still, I couldn't move.

"Okay, you asked for it!" she said.

Deliberately, she walked toward her desk and pulled out, inch by inch, the top drawer. In slow motion, she picked up a Ping-Pong paddle, then held it up high for the class to see.

I gasped, but my hands stayed put.

With the paddle held upright in her hand, she strode toward me.

I abruptly closed my eyes, and she disappeared like melting celluloid blotting out an actor when the film projector breaks.

"You think you can make me disappear?" she said.

I pressed my hands against my ears.

"You think you can shut me out?"

My eyelids were tightly shut.

"You think I'm not important?"

I held my breath.

"Well, listen up!" she screamed. "Mrs. Eleanor Stilton is your teacher, and you'd better accept it!"

I bit my bottom lip and sat rigidly still.

Whack! The paddle burned my right hand.

"Do you hear me?"

Whack! It burned my left. Whack, whack, whack!

My ears tingled. My jaw ached.

"Do you understand?"

I tried to speak. Syllables dissolved.

Whack, whack, whack!

My face melted. My hands fell from my ears. My eyes flew open.

"Who is your fourth grade teacher?" the pointed face asked.

"You are," I muttered.

"And what is my name?" the voice thundered.

"Mrs. Stilton," I said.

"Finally!" The voice gasped relief. "Students, this was your very first lesson. I hope you've paid attention."

"Yes, ma'am!" resounded the frightened voices of Mrs. Stilton's fourth grade class. The loudest of which was mine.

By lunchtime, the enormity of my situation had seeped into my mind like the odor of turnip greens permeating the air. I understood that some awful harm was confronting me. From now on, every answer I gave would have to be precise; every word would have to be calculated, ensuring my survival. If I didn't control myself, the urge to jerk, pop, and repeat words would take over, and something horrible — the worst thing ever to happen to me — would occur.

At the table, Emma Richards sat beside me. She held her nose while she slipped a smidgen of turnip greens into her mouth. "I can't taste them this way," she said.

"Don't eat them," I told her.

"I gotta," she said. "Mrs. Stilton heard me telling Sallie Mae how much I hate this stuff, and she said I had to eat all of it. Every mouthful of it, she told me. I seen what she done to you."

"Then you best eat up," I said, forking down mouthfuls of greens, hoping to show Mrs. Stilton what a good girl I really was. When she passed by my plate, it would be sparkling clean. "I like greens," I said, shoveling more into my mouth. "Pokeweed, collards, mustards. Patanni said that I'm like Essie, our milk cow, 'cause I like greens more'n meat."

"I like chicken and dumplings," Emma said. "That's about the only thing I really like, except for candy."

"I like pull candy," I said. "Miss Emily Tanner makes the best in the world."

"It's too gooey." Emma made a face. "I like

proper sweets like those chocolates in Valentine boxes."

I stuffed more turnip greens between my lips and, with a full mouth, proclaimed, "I like blackberry cobbler. My grandma makes the best."

A hand tapped my shoulder, and I glanced up. "You like what?" Mrs. Stilton asked.

"I like vegetables," I said, with the glob of greens mashed in my mouth. I smiled and tilted my plate upward so that she could see how clean it was becoming.

Mrs. Stilton popped me on the shoulder. "You're talking with your mouth full," she said, "and ruining everybody's meal."

I quit smiling, closed my mouth, and swallowed. "Patanni calls me a cow," I tried again, " 'cause I like vegetables more than meat."

"Then you'd be called a vegetarian," Mrs. Stilton said, "and that's not healthy."

"That don't . . . mean . . . I — I don't . . . like meat," I stammered. "If someone gives me meat, I'll eat it. I ain't spoiled. There is hungry people in China."

"There are hungry people in these parts," Mrs. Stilton said.

"Yes, ma'am," I conceded, "there are hungry people all over this country."

"Not in Illinois," Mrs. Stilton said, wheezing air through her nose. "We don't have hungry people in Chicago."

I vigorously shook my head. "Oh, no!" I said.

"Chicago doesn't have any hungry people."

"Finish your ham," Mrs. Stilton ordered, pointing to the pink square on my plate. "You need some protein."

I smiled again, stabbed a piece of ham, and poked it into my mouth. Mrs. Stilton nodded and continued her walk down the aisle.

"That was close," Emma Richards said.

I kept on eating, cutting my ham into little cubes, popping them between my teeth, chewing, and swallowing. I ate my cornbread and also the little packet of saltines on my tray. I didn't know what the crackers were for, but I ate them anyway, then I downed the cherry pie and drank my carton of milk. Pleasing Mrs. Stilton was going to be hard work, I thought. Good grammar, manners, and answers all of the time. "Whew!" I said, wiping my forehead. And school had only just begun.

Chapter 6

The weeks at school passed with Mrs. Stilton's eyes following me. Her gaze accompanied my every step, and I felt like she was a sleek black panther, ready to pounce.

"Don't press down so hard!" Emma Richards whispered to me from across the aisle. "You gonna make a big hole in your paper."

"I'm nervous," I whispered back, looking up to see if Mrs. Stilton was sitting behind her desk. She wasn't. "That woman's always studying me," I said.

Emma pursed her lips and twitched her nose. "That ain't true," she said prissily. "Your mind is just playing tricks on you."

"Then how come she's all the time catching me at something?" I asked her, ferociously erasing the *t* in *today*. "How come I'm the one who gets in trouble?"

"Well, you ain't the only one." Emma Richards screwed up her face and simultaneously shrugged her shoulders. "She gets mad at Lane, too."

"Lane Carlson." I poked out my tongue. "He

don't count. That big sissy deserves everything he gets."

From the back of the room came a high hysterical giggle — Lane's.

"If a sissy touches you, you'll turn into his opposite," Emma said, looping the tail of her *y*.

"I don't believe you!" I said a little too loudly, my eyes instinctively scanning the classroom. Mrs. Stilton still nowhere in sight.

"If Lane Carlson rubs against you," she said, clicking her tongue against the top of her teeth, "then you'll change into a tomboy."

I made a burping noise with my lips. "Well, that don't scare me none," I told her, tossing back my head, " 'cause I already do tomboy things."

Emma slid her paper over to the edge of her desk. "Look at mine," she said. "Ain't my penmanship fancy?"

"Them curlicues look like vipers," I said. "Like little baby snakes." I stretched out my neck, thrust my tongue between my lips, moving it sideways, and hissed liked a snake.

Emma ran her tongue along her top lip. "You might even grow a mustache," she shot back. "It'd come out yellow to match your hair."

I pressed my index finger against my mouth. "Shush!" I warned her. "You're gonna get me in trouble."

Snatching her paper away from the desk's edge, Emma daintily crossed her feet — one ankle over the other — and sighed loudly.

I sighed also, even louder. "You best learn to write like me," I said, pushing my paper in her direction, glancing down, and realizing, too late, that my handwriting was a disgraceful mess. Black smudges all over. A big hole right through the center. "At least my penmanship ain't scary," I said. "It don't look like a bed of baby copperheads ready to bite. It's —"

Mrs. Stilton's grade book crashed down.

I jumped, watching my paper disappear beneath its black cover.

"Icy Sparks, do you think you can write and talk at the same time?"

I nodded, then retracted, urgently shaking my head.

"No, I don't think you can, Miss Sparks!" Mrs. Stilton's eyes were on me, greedily eating a hole right through me. With her fingertips, as though my paper were dirty, she slipped it out from beneath her grade book and lifted it up high for the class to see. "A hole!" she announced. Then, like a magician, she withdrew a pencil propped behind her ear, aimed it at my paper, and poked it through the gap I'd made when I erased my *t*.

The class laughed. Above them all, I could hear Lane Carlson's high-pitched snickering.

"Emma," Mrs. Stilton said, "would you please show the class your work?"

"Yes, ma'am." Emma rose, stood in the aisle beside her desk, and held up her paper, shifting it from side to side so that everyone could see.

"Now turn around," Mrs. Stilton ordered her. "I want the students in the back to get a look."

"Lucy, what do you think of Emma's work?" Mrs. Stilton said.

"It's pretty," Lucy replied, grinning.

"And you, Irwin?" Mrs. Stilton said. "What do you think?"

"I like all them lassos," he said. "They remind me of cowboys."

"And what do I think of this?" Mrs. Stilton asked, still clutching the pencil, waving it back and forth, my paper flapping through the air. "I'll show you," she said, walking toward her desk, the eyes of every student shifting to the trash can. "This is what I think of sloppiness," she said, ripping my paper off the pencil, crumpling it up into a tight little ball before tossing it into the wastebasket.

Stiff in my seat, I shoved my feet against the tiled floor, trying to control the little tremors that were beginning in my legs.

"I got my eyes on you," said Mrs. Stilton, pointing at me, her fingernails inching outward like claws. "And, little girl, don't you forget it." Whereupon she turned her back to us and, with chalk in hand, began putting on the blackboard a string of math problems — neatly lined up and perfectly spaced apart.

Emma Richards giggled as she sat back down, but the rest of the class was silent. Not even Lane Carlson squeaked. Suddenly, across the aisle from me, two seats down, Peavy Lawson

81

made a lisping sound. "Icy," he whispered, his voice low, his eyes bulging, "I like your handwriting best." Breaking a smile, he picked up his paper for me to see: it was a black-smudged mess, riddled with holes.

The only thing I could do was fold my arms on top of my desk and hide my head inside them.

Chapter 7

Mrs. Stilton cleared her throat. In my mind's eye, I saw her neck stretching up like a chicken's and imagined her Adam's apple bobbing up and down. After lunch, she had instructed us to put our heads upon our desks while she read to us. "From now on, we'll do this every day," she said. "It'll help with your digestion." From the satchel beside her chair, she had pulled out a book. This is a good sign, I thought, nestling farther down in my seat, closing my eyes.

Last year after lunch, Miss Palmer had also read to us; she had read *The Secret Garden*, *The Little Prince*, and other books. It was my favorite time during the day, even more enjoyable than recess because all I had to do was listen.

" 'The Lottery,' by Shirley Jackson," Mrs. Stilton began. She read to us about a peaceful little town, not unlike Ginseng, where every summer the townsfolk gathered together in the square to participate in a drawing. So this will be a happy story, I decided, wiggling my toes, feeling them relax inside my patent-leather shoes. Janie Lou had told me that St. Michael's

Church in Dewberry, where Mrs. Stilton worshiped, had bingo every Saturday. "Catholics
love gambling," Janie Lou had said. So suddenly it seemed right and proper that Mrs.
Stilton would be reading a story about a lottery.

In the story, the children were the first ones to
come to the square. They were out of school for
the summer and had too much free time on
their hands.

Clearing her throat, Mrs. Stilton lowered the
book, looked up at us, and asked, "Class, does
this little town sound familiar?" I lifted my head
slightly above my folded arms and saw an eerie
smile creeping over her face. "Does this little
town sound familiar?" she repeated.

"Yes, ma'am," the students said.

"Yes, ma'am," I mumbled, saliva painting my
arm.

"Why?" Mrs. Stilton asked.

"Because it's small, like Ginseng," Lucy
Daniels said.

"What else?" Mrs. Stilton asked.

"Because it has coal and farmers and trac-
tors," Irwin Leach said.

I wondered if Shirley Jackson was from a
small Kentucky town. I sat up and raised my
hand. Ginseng was bigger than the town in her
story; but still, they were alike.

"What is it, Icy?" Mrs. Stilton said.

"Is Shirley Jackson from Kentucky?"

Mrs. Stilton scowled. Ignoring me, she said,

"Class, I just wanted to see if you were paying attention."

I'll have to be more careful, I thought, again resting my head in my arms. Mrs. Stilton was reading to us, but that didn't mean she had changed.

I closed my eyes again, and my mind drifted off, conjuring up my own fantasies. Ginseng could have its own drawing, and it would be fun! Grand, even! Much better than the one in the story. A convertible from Don Scoggin's Used Car Lot would go to the winner. In my mind's eye, I saw the whole of Ginseng gathering around the courthouse on a clear, sunny morning. Matanni and Patanni were there, along with Miss Emily. Even Mamie Tillman was present. She was smiling, and her stomach was flat. Mayor Anglin, who was in charge, put his finger to his lips and hushed the crowd. "Citizens of Ginseng, I now declare the drawing open," he said in a serious voice.

I fancied myself waiting for the winner's name to be called. Nervously, I stood on one foot, then the other, not expecting to win. Never had my luck been good. Still, I was hopeful. I imagined Matanni and Patanni with their fingers crossed and saw Miss Emily, holding her breath. Slowly, Mayor Anglin lifted the top off an old cracker barrel, inserted his fat hand inside, swished around the slips of paper, and dramatically selected one. His face contorted as he held the slip — arm's length from his eyes — swallowed deeply, and grandly announced, "The winner of this year's Chevy convertible is Miss Icy Sparks!"

Feeling light-headed, I slumped forward.

"Come on up here!" he yelled with a broad wave of his arm.

Patanni grabbed me under the armpits and pulled me up while Miss Emily retrieved an ice cube from her cup and pressed it against my forehead. Quickly, I revived. With my head held high, I walked forward, stopping reverently in front of Mayor Anglin, and extended my palm.

"Congratulations!" he said, before dropping a set of silver keys into my hand.

Eagerly, my fingers wrapped around them.

All at once, my baby-blue convertible was whipping around mountain curves. With my blond hair streaming behind me, I drove like a champion, the fourth grade class chasing after me, yelling, "Icy, can we go? We want a ride, too." I was picturing all of this — feeling the cool wind against my face, basking in the adulation of my classmates, delighting in my new-found luck — when, out of nowhere, Mrs. Stilton coughed and brought me back. Her powerful voice was describing a woman in the story who had forgotten what day it was. When she finally remembered, she came running to the square. That woman is just like me, I decided. I wonder if she's headed for trouble. She forgets time like I do when I'm out exploring. But at least I don't keep all of Ginseng waiting, just Matanni at suppertime.

Fascinated, I listened as Mrs. Stilton continued. Her voice began to weave in and out like a distant echo in my head. Abruptly, she quit reading. For ten seconds, she was quiet. Then, in a determined voice, she carefully pronounced the last two words in the sentence: "humorlessly and nervously," she read, twisting her mouth as though exercising her lips. She lifted her giraffe neck and surveyed the room. "Humorlessly and nervously," she repeated emphatically. "Children, you must remember those words," she said, scrutinizing the students up front. "Now, what words are they?" she asked.

"Humorlessly and nervously," those up front responded.

"What words?" she demanded.

"Humorlessly and nervously," the whole class said.

But not me. I kept my mouth shut. *Humorlessly* and *nervously* were already stuck in my mind. Unlike the others, I didn't need to repeat them. The minute I heard both words I knew they were clues. Ominous clues hinting at disaster. It was then I realized that Mrs. Stilton meant to teach us a lesson. She meant to teach me a lesson, and — out of all the stories ever written — she had chosen this one, a story about a town just like Ginseng, to do so. Horrified, I listened, dreading each word as the story unfolded.

Eager to hear what would happen next, every fourth grade head — but mine — shot up. Craning their necks, they leaned forward. But I didn't. Instinctively, I tucked my head between my arms, recoiling from the striking distance of her words.

Before I knew it, my mind was like a movie running backward. The baby-blue convertible moved faster and faster in reverse, its tires sucking in the dust. My body bolted from the seat and flew into the crowd. My fingers burst open, sending the keys upward, toward Mayor Anglin's open hand. Faster and faster, my mind raced. Rewinding all the way back, until the drawing was about to begin again.

"And the winner of this year's prize is Virgil Bedloe!" Mayor Anglin announced. "Virgil, come get your blackberries."

"Blackberries?" I said, looking puzzled, turning around, trying to find the car. "That's the prize?" I reached out to touch my grandfather's hand, but he wasn't there. Instead, he was moving slowly toward the courthouse steps where Mayor Anglin stood. An old tin bucket with a familiar dent in its side was now sitting on top of the cracker barrel; it was overflowing with plump, juicy blackberries. All of a sudden, I heard a faraway buzzing noise and the tin bucket quivering. Ever so slightly, its bottom thumped against the wood. The glossy skin of the blackberries trembled in the sun. Frightened, I put my hands over my eyes. Black and white dots seeped through the cracks between my fingers, but still the buzzing grew louder. Louder and louder, it became. As loud as a hive of swarming bees. And even though my eyes were covered, I could clearly envision them — a thousand golden specks wrapped in black — an ear-splitting buzz, consumed with rage. No, Patanni! Don't take that prize! I thought.

I jerked my head upward. The smiling faces of my classmates alarmed me. Don't they understand? I thought, as my heart beat wildly. Why are you listening to her? I wanted to cry.

"Class, I'm getting to the end," Mrs. Stilton said, raising her head, staring at us. "Everyone better be listening."

Agitated, I twisted around and spotted Emma Richards's big brown eyes, unaware, cheerful, her lips primly upturned. Naturally, she didn't understand. I twisted again and saw Peavy Lawson's froggy eyes. He didn't have a clue.

I shook my head. The faint trace of a whisper was forming inside my skull. Fearful, I listened closely and thought I heard Patanni talking to the crowd. "I don't deserve this prize," he said. "It belongs to Icy. Icy is the winner."

Please, God! I thought. I don't want to win!

Clamping my lips together, I held in my breath. Emma ain't had a chance, let her win, I said to myself. Lucy Daniels should be the winner. See that smile on her face? Look at Peavy Lawson, grinning over there. He loves blackberries. And so does that sissy, Lane Carlson. Let him be the winner. But not me!

I stared at my classmates; their faces swelled with anticipation; they didn't understand. My hands began to sweat profusely. The veins in my temples throbbed. A grinding panic rushed over me.

" 'Letuuzzzzzz finuzzzzzz,' " Mrs. Stilton buzzed.

Her voice rose to a high pitch and whirred against my ears. Terrified, I scrunched down in my seat. Emma Richards snickered and pointed at me.

Folding my arms on my desk, I buried my face inside them and imagined Patanni coming toward me. "It's yours," he said, holding out the tin bucket, gripping its handle. "All yours!" Flinching, he took another step closer. That's when I saw them — the thousand pinpricks covering his body. Behind him, a black cloud hummed hysterically. Undulating, ever so subtly, it changed shapes — snakelike at first, then round like a giant hotcake, zigzagging past him, descending, blotting out Mayor Anglin and the courthouse steps.

No, Patanni! Put it down! I thought. I don't want to win!

Hide! my thoughts yelled. *Protect yourself!* they demanded, as I pressed my knees against the desk, swatting the air with my hands. *Frog eyes!* my thoughts buzzed. *Crazzzzzy!* they hummed. *Little Miss Frog Eyes!* they droned.

"All of you hate me!" I spluttered into the desk top, my lips tingling against the wood.

Right then, a book slammed down. "Icy Sparks!" Mrs. Stilton warned. My knees shot up. The desk rattled on the floor. "Can't you be still?" she said, jerking out her desk drawer. With a thud, the drawer closed shut. "Are you crazy?" Her footsteps clicked toward me. "I'm warning you!" she said, slapping the Ping-Pong paddle against her hand.

"I don't want to win," I said, trembling.

Her footsteps thumped closer and closer. "Are you crazy?" she repeated, coming to a stop beside me.

I felt her hot breath on my skin, her face inches from my neck. The paddle crashed against my desk top. My body shuddered. "Why me? Daddy, why me? Why not them?" I groaned, strangling my head with my arms.

"You *are* crazy!" she hissed.

"No! No!" I said, moaning. "Why me?" I cried, feeling the burn of the paddle against my skin. "My God, Daddy, the stings . . . the stings," I muttered, accepting my fate.

Mrs. Stilton took me to the nurse's station, which was a little room beside Principal Wooten's office, and told Nurse Coy that I had become hysterical during reading time and fallen out of my desk and onto the floor. "Look at those red blotches," she said, pointing to the marks on my arms. "This child isn't normal." She shook her head and glanced down at her watch. "I must get back," she said with syrupy concern. "My children need me."

Nurse Coy, who wasn't really a nurse but had

once worked as an aide at a nursing home in Harlan, gently squeezed my hand in her wrinkled, clawlike fingers, walked me over to the day couch, and told me to lie down. I did so obligingly. I would have done anything to stay out of class and away from that lying, Pope-craving, Chicago-born maniac. I knew that I hadn't behaved exactly right, but I also knew a fall hadn't caused those crimson smears on my skin. Only five minutes ago, I was Mrs. Stilton's prey. Through me, she had played out her fantasies. She had whacked my skin with that Ping-Pong paddle of hers; each whack, a hornet's sting.

"Would you like some Coke?" Nurse Coy asked. "A little Coke will help."

"Yes, ma'am," I murmured.

Nurse Coy patted my arm, which dangled over the edge of the couch, and hobbled out the door toward the cafeteria, where she kept cases of Coke in supply. On her way, I overheard her talking to the janitor, Mr. Sedge, one of the few Negroes in Ginseng. "Dooley, would you like some Coke?" she asked.

"No ma'am," he said. "Remember, you give me Coke a little while ago? I thank you, though."

Nurse Coy laughed awkwardly. "I remember now," she said. "I fixed you a Coke with ice."

"Yes, ma'am," Dooley said. "Coke with ice. On a hot day like this, it sure tastes good."

"Icy Sparks is in there," she said. "I'm on my

way to fix her some Coke. That's why I asked if you wanted some."

"I know you didn't really forget," Dooley said.

"Coke is the best medicine," Nurse Coy said. "It'll cure a stomachache and ease the pain of a headache. Headache, bellyache, and heartache," she explained. "I wish I had invented it."

"I bet you do," Dooley said. "If you did, you'd be a rich lady by now."

Nurse Coy laughed again and padded down the hall. I closed my eyes and tried to calm down. After getting banged about, my confused mind was tired and my thoughts were mostly quiet. Still, every so often, the battle inside myself would rouse, and I'd think, Icy Gal, this is war! Mrs. Stilton is the enemy, and she deserves a good battle.

All the way home, rigid in a seat at the back of the bus, I focused on revenge. Icy Gal, get out your bombs! I wanted to yell. Tit for tat. Raise high your just battle cry! In my mind, I relived every wrong that had been inflicted upon me since the first day of the school year. Mrs. Stilton had never liked me. All of her words had been barbs — sharp, little stings in my skin. Images of her ugliness marched through my mind: her neck, as long as a giraffe's; her black hair with its tight curls, like a top-knot on a poodle's head; her rigid spine, as flat as a cockroach's back; her eyes, black and slitted like a woodpecker's. She was ugly, all right! And I had the right to hate her. Just cause, I reassured myself, my fingers trembling with resentment. An eye for an eye. A tooth for a tooth. A payback in spades, I thought, red-hot anger boiling in the pit of my stomach. Deserves what's coming to her. Deserves my wrath, I persisted until I was almost hugging my hatred, loving and accepting it as an integral part of me when, out of no-where, a truth — more powerful than the fury I was feeling — burned through me and brought me to my senses: from now on, my rage would fuel impulses too horrible to contemplate.

"Oh, no!" I whimpered, as energy seeped from my pores. "Oh, no!" I cried, clutching my shoulders, curling up in the seat. While the other children chatted and laughed, I whispered, "Dear God, protect me from my anger." When Emma Richards giggled with Lane Carlson, I thought about my future and begged the Lord to help me. All the way home, I prayed. When the bus rounded the curve, bumped down the road to Poplar Holler, and stopped in front of my house, I could no longer deny the truth: all the Cokes in the world wouldn't cure this monstrous anger, growing steadily inside me.

"How was school?" Matanni asked as I slouched through the door.

I dropped my satchel on the floor and slumped down on the sofa. "I got sick," I said. "I spent the afternoon in the infirmary."

"Well, I declare!" Matanni said, coming toward me with an open palm. "Why, you're cool as a cucumber!"

Nervously, I looked down at my arms; the blotches, thank heavens, were gone. "I ate too much for lunch," I said, "and got a bellyache."

Matanni sat down at the other end of the sofa. "Lie back and give me your feet," she said, patting her thighs. I plopped my feet in her lap. She unbuckled my shoes and slipped the socks off. "Child, your feet are swollen," she said, and began rubbing my skin, sliding her fingers up and down, from the tips of my toes to my heels. "They're hot, too."

"Maybe I should stay home tomorrow," I said, sighing. "My feet need to rest."

"You wore tennis shoes all summer," my grandmother said. "These feet are just aching to get out of those school shoes."

"Can't I stay home?" I asked.

Matanni ran her fingers over my toes. "Icy, what's wrong with you?" she said. "You used to be so happy at school."

"A person can't be happy all the time," I said.

"That's a fact," she replied, "but, Icy, you can't go around avoiding things."

"Daddy did," I said.

"Your daddy didn't like working in the mines," Matanni said, "but he never stopped."

"Well, he should have," I said. "He should've had more fun before he died . . ." I swallowed hard and whispered, "Before he died that awful way."

Matanni was quiet for a second, then took a deep breath, and said softly, "Child, your daddy's up in heaven now." She tilted back her head, her eyes looking upward. "Up there with your sweet mama. Their spirits are happy and whole, sugar darling. All of the pain in their bodies was left behind."

"Are you sure?" I asked.

"Without a doubt," she said firmly, staring into my eyes. "I reckon the only thing that could make them happier is knowing you're happy, too."

I turned over and buried my head in the red-flowered pillow.

"How do you feel now?" my grandmother asked, tickling the soles of my feet.

I pressed my face into the pillow and tried not to giggle.

"I hear you," Matanni said. "If that's a giggle, you ain't too sick."

I shook my head and giggled louder and louder as Matanni teased each foot.

Chapter 8

The next day I readied myself for school. At five in the morning, I rose and stood in front of a small oval mirror that hung above the white dresser in a corner of my bedroom. For forty-five minutes, I stared at my reflection and prepared my face. Every day from now on would have to be planned. All my spontaneity would have to be subdued. Miss Emily had always said, "Icy Gal, I love your energy. I just love how you play." But today my playfulness would go into hiding. Control would become my new calling card. I breathed in deeply and threw back my head. Then I sucked in my cheeks and tried to sink my eyes. My eyes appeared smaller, more sunken in. In fact, they even seemed a different color — less yellow, more earth-brown. Next, I wiggled my jaw several times, clamped down my teeth, and tried to freeze the stern look that had settled into my chin. But when I whispered at the mirror, my real face broke through, and once more I was Icy Sparks — playful girl. I brushed my hair so long and hard that little, distinct rivulets of yellow trailed down my back. Then I twisted it into a ponytail and straitjacketed it with a rubber band. Finally, from the wardrobe, I selected my ugliest, plainest dress — dingy brown with no frills — and scruffed-up brown loafers to match. I dressed carefully, making certain that even my underwear was yellow and old. I would make myself solid, dark, and impenetrable like the trunk of an old tree. From now on, this would be me. It would camouflage the urges that lived inside me, fence in the rage that triggered these urges, and cordon off my fear. No one ever again would see the real me.

"You sure look drab," Matanni said when I sat down at the table. "Put on that pretty blue dress I bought you!"

"Peavy Lawson's giving me the eye," I answered. "I don't want to encourage him."

"That getup ought to change his mind." She laughed. "Now eat up, you hear?"

"Yes, ma'am," I said, my bland face crunching on shredded wheat. The mask is working, I thought. It'll protect me.

"I like your dress," Peavy Lawson said as I walked through the classroom door.

With my new face, emotionless as a corpse, I walked right by him. "Thank you," I said matter-of-factly, knowing that frogs — like him — were sincere. They didn't lie.

"I like your ponytail," he said.

I sat down — this time not bothering to thank him.

Mrs. Stilton glanced up from her roll book. "Aren't you the pretty one?" she said. "Dressed all in brown."

"Thank you," I answered.

A smirk had settled into the corners of her lips. Laughter played in her eyes.

"You look pretty, too," I lied with a straight face. I hated her poodle hairdo and her red polka-dotted dress.

She cooed, "What a nice thing to say!"

I breathed a sigh of relief.

She eyed me, sneering slightly, and said, "It'd be really nice if you meant it."

"But I do mean it." My rigidity began to disintegrate. Panic was pushing in.

"No, Icy, I don't think so." She picked up the little bell on her desk and rang it. "Now, class," she announced, "does Icy Sparks really think I look pretty?"

Emma Richards smiled and said, "But you do look pretty, Mrs. Stilton."

"That's not what I asked," Mrs. Stilton said. "Does Icy Sparks really think I look pretty?"

Emma Richards didn't answer.

"Only Icy knows for sure," Lucy Daniels said.

Lane Carlson tittered nervously.

"Icy lies sometimes," Irwin Leach said. "She called me stupid when I told her Harlan was the capital of Kentucky."

Peavy Lawson raised up in his chair. "Icy Sparks don't lie!" he said.

"Hold on, class!" Mrs. Stilton said, raising her

hands. "I heard a little story once — about a Coke being dumped over poor Joel McRoy's head."

I took several steps forward. "Please, don't tell it!" I begged. "If you don't, I'll tell the truth."

She nodded and folded her arms in front of her.

"N-no . . . I . . . don't . . . think . . . you . . . look . . . pretty," I stuttered. "I . . . can't . . . stand . . . red . . . polka-dots."

"Thank you, Icy," she said coldly. "It takes courage to speak the truth. If you're going to lie, it's best to stay quiet. Class, did you hear that?"

"Yes, ma'am," the class said.

"Repeat," she demanded.

"If you're going to lie, it's best to stay quiet," the class responded.

"Thank you!" Mrs. Stilton said. "Icy, here, is good for a lesson a day."

"Thank you!" the class repeated. "Icy, here, is good for a lesson a day."

"No, not that," Mrs. Stilton snapped. "You don't have to repeat that."

The class was silent.

I tightened my jaw, pressed my lips together, and narrowed my eyes. I threw back my head and stood up straight. I popped out my eyes, a huge bullfrog pop, shook loose my stiff face, opened wide my mouth, and said, "Were you telling the truth when you said I looked pretty?"

Mrs. Stilton grabbed the top of her desk and

leaned forward. Between clenched teeth, she spat out, "Listen here, little girl, I don't lie. You understand?"

My courage failed. I nodded.

"Mark my words! If you ever — again — call me a liar, I'll have you expelled."

"Yes, ma'am," I said.

All the while, I stared at the purple veins on her forehead, throbbing heartbeats against her skin, and thought: So demons have hearts.

After school, I decided not to take the bus. Instead, I ran all the way to Walnut Street to see Miss Emily at Tanner's Feed Supply. CLOSED FOR INVENTORY said the sign out front when I got there. "Miss Emily! Miss Emily!" I yelled, banging on the door. "Hey, Miss Emily!" I was about to run around to the back of the store where she kept the supplies when I spotted her round face, her breath fogging up the glass.

"Icy Gal!" she greeted me, unlocking the door, the bell above it jingling. "To what do I owe this visit?"

Johnny Cake's voice came from the back, "Miss Emily, you want me to sort out these left-over bulbs?"

Miss Emily cupped her dimpled hands around her mouth. "Go ahead," she hollered. "I'll put them on sale for late planting."

Johnny Cake screamed back, "Yes, ma'am!"

"Now let me take a look at you," Miss Emily said, closing the door behind her, holding me at arm's length, looking me up, then down. "What's wrong, Icy Gal?" she said. "Are you doing any of those strange things we talked about?"

I shook my head. "That's not it," I mumbled.

She took my hand and led me over to the counter where the cash register was. "What, then?" she asked me. Beside the counter was Miss Emily's favorite chair, a brown leather La-Z-Boy. "Get yourself a stool," she told me, while she eased her massive body onto the plush leather seat.

I grabbed a stool from behind the counter and slid it over the floor until it rested beside Miss Emily. I hiked up my left foot to the first rung, swung my other leg over, and, straddling the top, sat down.

"Johnny Cake!" Miss Emily shouted. "How's it going back there?"

"You got one whole case of tulip bulbs," he called out. "And two of daffodil."

"That's good," Miss Emily said. "Just keep on sorting."

"I didn't know it was inventory day," I said, my head slung down. "If you're too busy, I'll go."

Miss Emily reached over and squeezed my hand. "Whatever day it is, Icy Gal, I always have enough time for you. You know that, don't you?"

"Yes, ma'am," I replied, lifting my head, looking sideways at her.

"So tell me, why did you come to see me?"

I cleared my throat.

"My curiosity's getting the best of me." Gently, she popped the top of my hand. "Come on, now. Speak up!"

"Well . . . well . . ." I stalled.

Impatiently, she drummed her fat fingers against the armrest. "Well, what?" she asked, annoyed.

"I told another lie," I confessed. "Not like the one I told Joel McRoy. It was a different kind of lie, but still it made my teacher mad. Real mad."

Miss Emily pulled at her ear. "Well, Icy Gal, I can't say I blame her. You're not supposed to lie."

I scrunched up my nose and glared. "Well, she lied, too," I fumed. "She can lie with the best of them. She's the biggest liar in Ginseng. In Kentucky, if you want to know. Why, she's the biggest liar in the whole United States!"

"Just because she lies doesn't mean you should," Miss Emily said.

I pressed my middle finger against my forehead, breathed in deeply, and thought for a second. "Lies are tricky," I said. "Everybody lies sometimes. You know, to spare a person's feelings."

"That's called a white lie," Miss Emily explained. "A little white lie."

"Yes, ma'am," I went on. "What I told Mrs. Stilton was a little white lie. When she said I looked pretty, I said she looked pretty back. But, truth is, she didn't mean what she said any more than I did. We both lied. The difference between us is she lied to hurt my feelings, not spare them. While all I did was lie to save my hide."

Miss Emily shifted her weight. Beneath her, the leather whined. Leaning way over the armrest, she ran her index finger down the length of my nose. "You know what?" she said, winking.

"What?" I asked, returning the question.

"I think you don't like this teacher of yours."

It didn't require much brain power for Miss Emily to figure that out. "That's the word with the bark on it," I sassed.

"So why don't you?" she said, eyeing me.

"Like her?" I asked.

She nodded, the fat on her chin bouncing against her breastbone.

" 'Cause she's mean," I said flatly. "She doesn't just tell lies. Her whole self is a lie."

"How's that?" inquired Miss Emily.

" 'Cause she pretends to be syrup," I explained, "when she's nothing but vinegar."

"Don't you sometimes pretend to be someone you're not?" Miss Emily opened and closed her mouth like a trap.

I arched my back and aimed my eyes at her. "If I pretend," I responded angrily, "it's not 'cause I want to hurt somebody."

"So you're saying Mrs. Stilton means to hurt?"

"Yes, ma'am," I said firmly. "Everything she says is hurtful. Every look she gives me is mean. She lets me know every day of my life just how much she hates me."

"And do you hate her back?" Miss Emily calmly asked.

I froze my face for a second, all of my anger solidifying in the taut pull of my features; then, unflinchingly, I stared right into Miss Emily's sky-blue eyes and spit out the truth. "I hate her with all my heart!"

"Well, then," Miss Emily said, her demeanor unruffled, "we've got a problem." I nodded, my lips shut tight. "You don't want to exchange your sweet nature for hers."

"No, ma'am," I muttered, shaking my head, "but it's hard. She makes me so dag nabbed angry."

"Sure, it's hard," Miss Emily conceded. "But no one ever said being good was easy."

My lips began to tremble. "Then I guess I'm about the worst person you know."

She pushed herself up with her huge arms. "Icy Gal," she said, pointing her finger at me, "to me, you're the best." Then, before I could tell her how much I loved her, she was pounding across the floor. "Now, how about I take you home?" she went on. "Your grandma must be worried." Poking her head through the doorway, she gave Johnny Cake a dozen more things to do. "You're the finest assistant manager I've ever had," she told him, waddling back to the counter, plucking up her car keys.

"Why, Miss Emily, you're gonna give me a swelled head!" he gushed.

"Icy" — Miss Emily motioned me over, the

keys still cupped in her hand — "have I ever told you how hard Johnny Cake works?" She didn't wait for me to answer. Instead, she put her arm around my shoulders and answered her question for me. Miss Emily didn't know how to lie; I knew — without a doubt — that every good thing she said about Johnny Cake was true.

Chapter 9

"Matanni," I yelled, racing in from school, my anger so intense I thought my body would ignite and burst into flames. "I'm going for a walk!" Before she had a chance to say howdy, I was out the door again — running. In the cool October afternoon, still wearing my school clothes, I sprinted over the hills like a runner on the Ginseng High School track team. Although it wasn't cold, I ran so hard I felt blood rising in the back of my mouth the way it felt when I ran on a very cold day. As I moved, the sturdy edge of my left shoe cut into my skin, and with each step I endured a stab of pain, but I didn't care. If the pain diluted my anger, it didn't matter if a blister the size of a silver dollar formed on my heel.

Throughout September, my anger had grown bigger, more unruly each passing day, until it was determined to get out. In Mrs. Stilton's classroom, it escaped in little gestures directed her way — a pop here, a jerk there — each time she had issued an order, usually when her back was turned. The minute I got home, so much rage was shoving against the backs of my eyeballs I feared they might fly out. So I had run.

I ran until my dress was drenched in sweat, until the balls of my feet ached, until I could barely breathe. I ran until I came to Icy Creek, where I collapsed on the bank. Through the sieve of multicolored leaves, I looked up at the sky, listened to the rumble of water, and prayed. "Dear God," I whispered, "please help me." A squirrel was gathering nuts a few feet from where I lay. Every so often a bird twittered, and once I spotted the white fluff of a rabbit beyond the creek in the woods, but try as I might, I recognized no sign from God, no gesture to let me know that He heard me. But then I wondered how any god could love me. Who could hear my prayers above the turmoil of my jerks and pops? Who could see the real me through the wall of angry urges that set me apart? Miss Emily didn't know who I really was; she was blinded by too much love. And if my grandparents knew the truth, I was certain it would kill them. My mother had been as sweet as a pasture rose. "That girl didn't know bad," Patanni had said. And my father had been hardworking. Honest, he always was. Whenever he popped out his eyes, he had done it right in front of people. There was no running away, no hiding in a root cellar for him.

"Hit ain't right that your mama never knowed you," my grandmother had said. "Hit ain't right that your daddy died so young. They kilt themselves to have you and got none of the pleasure, none of the joy of seeing how you growed up." None of the joy of seeing me grow up, I thought, rolling over, feeling the cool moss through my dress. "None of the shame of seeing how disgraceful I've become," I said, burying my head in my arms, my eyes avoiding the sky, God's dwelling place. "Hit just ain't right," I said, sobbing so loudly that not even the thunder of Icy Creek could drown me out.

As the light started to fade, I eased myself up, wiped the strands of moss off the bodice of my dress, and headed home. It was nearing suppertime. I knew that Matanni would be cooking, waiting for me to set the table. Weary from the run, exhausted from crying, I felt depleted. Tonight, perhaps, I wouldn't have to dash to the root cellar and vomit forth every pop, jerk, and thought that had demanded repetition during the day. Tonight I wouldn't be forced to cast wild, unfettered shadows in the candlelight against the root cellar walls.

When I banged through the front door, my grandparents were sitting in the parlor. Matanni was putting a new hem in an old dress of mine. Patanni was dozing in his chair. "I'm sorry I'm late," I apologized, whisking into the room. "Time got away from me."

Matanni didn't say a word. With pins between her lips, she continued to sew. Patanni moaned and opened one eye, then closed it again.

"I said I'm sorry."

"Sometimes saying it isn't enough," Patanni said, his eyes still shut.

Matanni took the pins out of her mouth, cocked her tiny head to one side, and said, "We waited for you. Must have waited an hour. The fried chicken got cold."

"Your grandma works hard," said my grandfather wearily. "By six o'clock, she'd like to be finished with everything."

"I know," I muttered, my anxiety increasing. "I'm sorry, really sorry."

"We raised you to be considerate," Patanni said. "To think about other people's feelings."

"But lately you've been thinking only about yourself," Matanni added, nodding in the kitchen's direction. "Your supper's in the warming oven," she said. "I saved a drumstick for you."

"I wanted two," Patanni said, "but some of us ain't as selfish as others."

"That's right, Icy," Matanni threw in. "Some folk put others before themselves."

I turned my hand into a fist and popped it against my palm. "I said I was sorry," I shot back. "What do you want me to do? Go to prison? Hang myself from the big oak out back? Scrub the floors with a toothbrush? Lordy sakes, it ain't like I killed somebody!"

Matanni readjusted her glasses. "It's okay, Icy," she said, returning to my dress. "Now go on. Eat your supper before it gets too late."

Patanni stretched out his long legs. "Ain't you got homework to do?" he asked as I walked by.

Immediately I came to a halt at the kitchen doorway.

"Homework?" he repeated, emphasizing both syllables.

I gritted my teeth, heard the sound of them grinding into calcium, digging deep, down toward the nerves. Groaning, I bit the inside of my cheek. "Lordy mercy!" I exclaimed, tasting a drop of blood. "Dag nab!" I said, at that moment remembering. "I left my assignment back at school."

Patanni shifted in his chair, his boots scraping against the floor. "Icy," he said, in a voice filled with judgment. "What will your teacher think?"

Quickly I turned around, and in a desperate effort to channel all of my anger into one movement, I extended my arms, pressing my hands on each side of the doorframe, and shouted, "I don't give a dang what she thinks!" Then, unable to tolerate the tension a moment longer, I pivoted back around, dashed through the kitchen, out the back door, and headed for the root cellar.

Inside its dank walls, I lit the candle that I kept on an empty shelf, hurled the door shut and latched it, and was about to inflict my fury against the block wall when my shadow suddenly caught my eye. Strangely, it had changed. I had grown taller, my body curving upward, the top of my head sliding down the ceiling. I touched my nose. The daintiness and smallness were gone. Like Pinocchio's, it was longer. Its tip end pointed, almost sharp. When I opened my mouth, it seemed as though all the darkness of the root cellar was being drawn into it. I grimaced, and my lips knifed downward, like a scythe harvesting harsh words. Frantic, I felt my eyes. Once immense, they had shrunk to slits. Two tiny cuts in my face. No longer were they the windows to my soul; they were not wide enough for light to shine through, not generous enough to emit it. I shook my head. "Oh, no!" I said, my curls, corkscrewing furiously. Moaning, I lifted my hands to cover my face and watched, horrified, as they expanded, inch by inch, turning into large, round shapes — durable and thick as my grandmother's iron skillets. Immediately I jumped back. "Oh, Lord!" I cried, my arms zooming out, the movements, exaggerated yet quick. "God, no!" I protested. Twirling like a funnel cloud, I longed to spin myself out. Eat my hate up. "Hateful!" I screamed. "I am hateful!" I yelled. My fingers twitched; my left hand whipped forth like a Ping-Pong paddle and slammed against my cheek. Stinging, my face jerked to the right. Then my right hand whooshed forward and hit my other cheek; my face snapped to the left. Over and over, my hands inflicted pain, first one cheek, then the other, until my face burned from the blows. "Oh, God!" I cried, whirling frenziedly. "Sweet Jesus!" I moaned, feeling the weight of God's sky upon me, my body trembling under what I feared was His heavy, horrible sign.

Chapter 10

"Icy, you're gonna get caught," Emma Richards said one day during lunch. "Everybody sees you copying her, making fun of everything she does. One day she's gonna turn around from that blackboard and catch you."

"I can't help it," I said, chomping into an apple. "When Mrs. Stilton flicks out that tongue of hers, my tongue has a will of its own. It's gotta do the same. When she screws up her ugly lips, my lips just naturally screw up, too."

"You're gonna get us all into trouble," Emma said.

I chewed my apple and swallowed. "I can't help it," I repeated. "When she whacks Peavy, my hand can't stop itself." I spread my fingers apart and whacked at the air.

"You're scaring me," she said. "If you don't quit, something bad is going to happen. I can feel it."

I put down my apple and looked straight into Emma's eyes. "I can't help it." I heard the tremble in my voice. "I don't want to. It just happens."

Emma Richards glared at me. "If you don't

quit," she said, "you're gonna turn the whole class against you."

"Why?" I asked.

Her face turned white, and her jaw stiffened. "Because when Mrs. Stilton's mad at you," Emma snarled, "she makes all of us pay."

"But I'm the only one she hates," I said.

"Peavy Lawson gets smacked 'cause he likes you," she said. "I already told you about Lane Carlson; his hands will be next."

"Lane ain't no friend of mine," I said angrily.

"He talks about you all the time," she said. "He's always bragging on you. I promise, afore too long, she'll whack him, too."

"You're wrong!" I said. "Lane Carlson ain't talking about me. I ain't heard a peep out of him!"

"Something bad is going to happen," she warned. "I can feel it."

Mrs. Stilton walked by. I nudged Emma with my elbow. "She worships idols," I whispered.

Emma raised her eyebrows and shrugged her shoulders.

"She thinks she's a great singer," I said. "This summer, she's going to the Vatican and audition for the Pope."

"You're a troublemaker," Emma sneered.

"She's selfish," I said. "She wouldn't give a hungry old man a piece of cake."

"You're a liar," Emma snapped.

"At night, she turns into a redheaded woodpecker."

"You're making that up," Emma said.

"No," I said, "it's the truth. She hops up and down the trunks of trees, always hungry, looking for something to eat, working hard for her food."

"Liar!" Emma said.

"No, really!" I protested. "I got this book at home, all about her. In it, there's this one story about a mean old woman who wears a little red cap and a long black dress. She drapes this white cape around her shoulders. And since she's always baking, she wears a white apron cinched around her waist. She bakes, bakes, and bakes. She bakes enough cakes to fill up every shelf in Margaret's Bakery, but she's so mean and stingy that she won't share them with anyone. When a poor, hungry old man asks her for a bite of cake, she makes excuses. 'This cake is too big,' she says. 'And this one's too little.' That's how mean she is! She won't share nothing with nobody. At the end of the story, though, she gets her comeuppance. All of her clothes — that little red cap of hers, her black dress, and her white cape and apron — all of them turn into feathers. And guess what bird she turns into?"

"I don't care," said Emma flippantly.

"A woodpecker," I said. "A woodpecker from Chicago," I added. "And she spends the rest of her life looking for bugs with those dark, squinty eyes of hers and drilling holes into trees with her mean, sharp beak."

"Sure!" she growled.

"It's the truth," I said. "The story's called, 'The Old Woman Who Wanted All the Cakes.' Miss Emily Tanner gave me the book, and she's an expert on everything."

"She's an expert on eating," Emma scoffed. "When she hugs you, she squeezes the life right out of you."

"That ain't true," I said indignantly. "She hugs me all of the time, and I'm still breathing."

"That's too bad," Emma said. "The longer you breathe, the longer you'll lie."

"I'm not a liar!" I said.

Emma Richards tossed back her head. "Mrs. Stilton ain't no woodpecker, and you know it."

"You wait," I finished. "One day, when we have white cake for lunch, I'll ask her. I'll say, 'Mrs. Stilton, if a hungry old man came up to you and asked you for a bite of cake, what would you do?' You mark my words, Emma Richards, Mrs. Eleanor Stilton will answer, 'If he wants some cake, he can bake his own.' "

After lunch the next day, while Mrs. Stilton read to us, I fell into a daydream and imagined her living as a woodpecker in the black pine near Little Turtle Pond. Her nose had turned into a hard, pointed beak; she was drilling into the pine tree hunting for a little piece of white cake, her tail feathers, stiff and proper, her little dark eyes spiteful and greedy. Mamie Tillman sat on the ground with her back leaning against the trunk and her stomach ballooning over her

117

pants. Every so often, she'd throw up her arms. "Please, Mrs. Woodpecker," she'd beg, "me and my baby is hungry. Could you spare us a bite of cake?"

But the woodpecker wasn't touched. "If you want some cake," the bird trilled, "bake one yourself."

I was enjoying my reverie when Mrs. Stilton plopped down the book she was reading, breaking the spell.

"Now, class, in honor of Halloween," she said sweetly, "I've got a treat for you." Then she walked primly to the back of the classroom, opened the closet door where supplies were kept, and stepped inside.

The whole class waited anxiously. Peavy Lawson tapped his fingers against his desktop. Emma Richards rocked back and forth. Lane Carlson giggled. Lucy Daniels wrapped a strand of her brown hair around her middle finger and whispered something to Irwin Leach. Never before had Mrs. Eleanor Stilton treated us to anything.

"Probably some poison," I whispered to Emma, who sat across from me.

"Hush!" she said.

"Toads and black cats."

"Troublemaker!" she sneered.

"Toadstools," I said.

"Liar!" she said.

"Poison pokeweed," I said.

"Shut up!" she warned.

"Jack-in-the-pulpit. Jack's little red berries."

"Zip it up!" she threatened.

"Hemlock," I was saying, when the closet door creaked open.

"Class!" Mrs. Stilton said.

Everyone became quiet.

"Children, please close your eyes," she said.

When I heard her switch off the lights, I opened my eyes. A constellation of flickering lights floated toward the front of the room. Fearful, I closed them again and was trying to figure out what I had just seen when I heard another clicking sound.

"Now open your eyes," Mrs. Stilton said.

A huge rectangular cake with orange frosting and yellow, lit candles glowed on top of her desk. Neat little rows of candy corn decorated the sides.

"All right, class," Mrs. Stilton said. "There are twenty candles for twenty students. Each of you gets to blow out one."

We all stood up.

"Trick or treat?" she asked, as we filed toward her desk.

"Treat," I heard them say as they pressed forward.

"A slice for each of you." She put a piece of cake on Emma Richards's plate.

"A big treat!" they said at once. "Thank you!" they said, and clapped loudly.

A trick, I said to myself, a cake laced with poison.

But, later on that afternoon, not one student suffered from a stomachache, not even Peavy Lawson, who ate three slices. No one was sent home, and no one died. That October thirty-first, Mrs. Stilton had cast her spell. When class was over and we marched out to catch the bus, Emma Richards refused to walk with me. The minute I'd swallowed that slice of Halloween cake, I'd sealed my fate and turned into a liar before Emma Richards's eyes. On the bus ride home, I overheard her talking to Lucy Daniels. "Icy thinks she's so smart," she said. "Smarter than the rest of us. But Mrs. Stilton sees right through her. That's why Icy hates her."

By the time I got off the bus, she wasn't talking to me and had convinced everyone else not to talk to me, either.

The next day, even Peavy Lawson began ignoring me. No longer did he want me for a girlfriend.

Whenever I walked down the hallway, my classmates would press their backs against the wall, melt into the plaster, and part like the Red Sea. When I mimicked Mrs. Stilton, they pretended not to notice. Like turning off a leaking faucet, they began to turn me off. Having lost my ability to astonish, I had lost my identity.

At home, in the darkness of my bedroom, I hugged my shadow. "Nobody will be your friend," Joel McRoy had once said, and now I knew he was right. Miss Emily was right, too. Cut off from the world, different and alone, we were just alike. Terrified, I withdrew even more, too proud to talk to my grandparents, too disconcerted by Miss Emily to talk to her.

Chapter 11

Patanni was sitting on the porch in his huge rocker about to cut into a piece of pumpkin pie when Matanni pushed through the door with a bowl of whipped cream in her hands. "Virgil, I told you to wait," she scolded him. "I made some topping for that pie." Before he could say a word, Matanni had scooped up two huge spoonfuls of whipped cream and plopped them on his plate.

"This is the part of Thanksgiving I like best," Patanni said, swallowing a mouthful, leaving an outline like shaving cream around his lips. He licked it off with his tongue and smiled.

"I want a dollop on mine, too," I said, shoving my plate at my grandmother from where I was sitting on the step.

"Ain't you having none, Tillie?" Patanni asked. "You been cooking all day, but when it comes to eating, you turn shy."

"Oh, don't worry about me none," she said. "I've been tasting." Matanni sat down, put the bowl on the floor beside her rocking chair, and sighed. "These cool November days sure do feel good," she said.

"Especially after cooking in a hot kitchen," Patanni reasoned, finishing the last of his dessert with a gulp and a loud belch.

Matanni slapped the armrests of her rocker. "Virgil!" she warned him. "Quit that!"

"Just showing my appreciation," he said.

"Well, appreciate a little less!" she snapped.

"Bossy, bossy, bossy! When you go to acting like that," Patanni said, leaning over, placing his plate on the porch floor, "you put me in mind of your cousin."

"What cousin?" I asked, forking up another mouthful.

"Cousin Acorn," Patanni replied.

"She died before you was born," Matanni said, "but she weren't so young when she went." Matanni made a *tsk*ing sound. "Odd, ain't it, how little we talk about her?"

"Acorn was a strange one," Patanni said.

"Came to it rightly," said Matanni, "with Uncle Buddy moving around so much. With Mary being the way she was." Matanni rocked back. Pressing the balls of her tiny feet against the floor, she kept the rocker in position. "She's outstripped us and gone," my grandmother said, "so let's not speak unkindly of her now."

"How was she strange?" I asked, steadying my clean plate on my knees.

Patanni pressed the edges of his hands together, turning them into a bowl. "She gathered up animals the way a squirrel gathers nuts," he said, swishing his hands from side to side.

"We called her Little Acorn on account of it," Matanni added. "Whenever she found a hurt animal, she'd bring it home. She had the usual dogs and cats and even rabbits, squirrels, and birds."

"Fed those baby birds a mush of earthworms," Patanni said. "And how about that raccoon?"

"About drove Buddy and Mary crazy," said Matanni, shaking her head. "Tending to all sorts of critters. Making everyone do her bidding," she went on. "But it was the monkey that was the last straw."

"Monkey?" I said, plunking my plate on the step.

"A tad strange," Patanni said, nervously reaching down, picking up his empty plate.

"Are you wanting more pie, Virgil?" Matanni asked.

"No, couldn't eat another bite," he responded, still fiddling with the plate.

"It was all a little queer," Matanni continued. "Acorn seen this baby spider monkey at the big state fair in Louisville. The minute she laid eyes on him, she had to have him. Said he was sick. Said he was losing his hair. And the truth be known, he was acting puny.

"Bought him, she did. With the few dollars she had saved up for the fair. It didn't matter what her parents said or how they tried to put their foot down; she did exactly as she pleased. Bought a sick, ailing monkey that nobody wanted.

"Stuffed him inside her lunch basket. The whole way back on the train the poor little critter was quiet — being that he was so sick. 'You best keep that dirty animal in the basket,' her mama threatened her, but when they got off the train in Maysville, she pulled that monkey out like he was some grand prize and showed him off to everyone. Poor Mary!" Matanni threw back her head and laughed loudly. Her feet left the porch floor, and the rocker lurched forward. "She was horror-striken! That's what Uncle Buddy said."

"And before anyone knew what had happened, there was a monkey in the house — not in a pen out back," Patanni said. "With Acorn telling everybody what and what not to do."

"Now, mind you, Icy," Matanni said, pointing at me, "we're not talking about a spoiled child. This was an almost grown, fifteen-year-old young lady who should've been thinking about beaus and high school basketball games."

"There's more to life than boys and games," I said. "That's not so strange."

" 'Twas strange seeing a fifteen-year-old cradling a mangy-haired monkey like he was a youngin'," Matanni asserted. "Odd, how she loved that ugly thing."

"And he kept on losing his hair. Scratching and scratching until it was coming out in handfuls. Until he looked like a newborn pink possum," Patanni said.

"All shriveled up." Matanni had a faraway

look in her eyes. "Kind of sad, really."

"Did the monkey get well?" I asked.

"A little cornmash whiskey saved the day," Patanni said. "Uncle Buddy . . ." Patanni hesitated for a second, then turned and looked squarely at my grandmother, "was known to keep a Mason jar or two out in the barn himself, and Cousin Acorn got the crazy notion of getting that monkey drunk."

"Whiskey sure helped me feel better when I was sick," I said. "You wouldn't want folks calling you strange just 'cause you gave me whiskey."

Matanni paid me no mind. "Cousin Acorn fed that monkey moonshine with an eyedropper," she said. "Kept that monkey so drunk he couldn't scratch."

"As soon as that monkey showed some sign of improvement, Cousin Acorn didn't waste no time. She had all the family taking turns with that eyedropper," Patanni said. "That monkey stayed dog drunk."

"But it cured him, didn't it?" Matanni said.

"Stopped losing his hair," Patanni said, "but Buddy told me that later on he died of a bad liver."

Right then, my grandparents started guffawing at the top of their lungs. Both of them were laughing so hard that Patanni's plate slipped out of his hands and fell with a thud to the floor. "You-all are teasing me, aren't you?" I asked them.

Rising from her rocker, Matanni picked up the plate and inspected it for cracks. "Everything we've told you is true, Icy," she said, "but we shouldn't be laughing at Cousin Acorn's expense. Truth is, she lived a pitiful, lonely life. No husband. No children. And no friends."

"Peculiar, she was," Patanni said.

"A house full of animals till the day she died," said Matanni.

"As far as I'm concerned," I stated, vehemently, "animals are nicer than most people. Much nicer than those fair-weather friends I have to spend time with."

"If you don't want to be alone," Patanni corrected me, "you best start thinking better of your classmates."

Grabbing my plate, I stood up angrily. "From now on," I announced, "alone is what I intend to be."

"We'll see how alone you feel on that crowded bus Monday morning," Matanni finished.

Chapter 12

The first time I croaked at school, no one — except for Lane Carlson — heard me. It happened during recess. The girls were jumping rope. The boys were shooting hoops. Miss Palmer, my old third grade teacher, sat in a chair by the wide double doors and watched us. I was swinging in the rope swing that hung from the maple tree, throwing out my legs and pulling them in, whooshing forward and backward. While I swept back and forth, I looked at the fall foliage — the red, yellow, and crimson leaves — smelled the sweet, sharp odor of burning wood, and sang "Greensleeves." All the while, the sound of my voice soothed me.

Lane Carlson sat on the other side of the maple tree, drawing pictures in the brown dirt with a stick. Twice, I glanced down to see what he was drawing. Silly stick figures, I thought. But then, Lane Carlson had always been silly. A prissy sissy, he seemed like a caricature of what he thought a girl should be, except that he had gotten it all wrong, and now it was too late. His father owned a gun shop and was the best shot in Crockett County. His younger brother was as tough and mean as Lane was girlish. "Mabel pampered him too much," the townsfolk said. "She wanted her first to be a girl." Mothers didn't want their sons to play with him. Even girls found him too high-pitched and hysterical. He was a misfit long before I became one. A year ago, before all my own problems started, during one of our afternoon tea parties, Miss Emily had given me some advice. "Look at life from Lane's perspective," she had said. "He only wants to fit in. He just doesn't know how." At the time, I hadn't answered her. Swinging high above his head, catching a glimpse of his stick figures in the brown earth, I now felt ashamed.

Then, as always, the bell rang. Lane Carlson abruptly stood up, cupped his hands around the corners of his mouth, and yelled something at me. I stretched out my legs and slammed my shoes like brakes into the dirt. Lane stepped forward, holding his index finger high in the air.

I felt uneasy. "It's time to go in," I said. "What do you want?"

He shook his finger at me. "Look!" he shrieked.

"What?" I said, coming closer.

"Make it go away," he said.

"Make what go away?" I asked, irritated.

"This," he answered and poked his finger into my face. "The wart." He giggled. "Frogs cause warts," he said, laughing hysterically, jabbing his finger at me.

"Get away!" I screamed, hitting his hand.

"You're a frog," he said. "If you can cause warts, you can make them go away." He pushed his finger toward my mouth. "So bite it off!" he demanded, thrusting the wart at me. I jerked back. "Eat it like you would a fly!" I twisted my head. "You're a frog!" he squealed. "You can do it!" he screeched, and triumphantly shoved his finger against my clamped lips.

Ferociously, I bit down. Blood spurted forth.

Astonished, he jerked back his hand and looked down at his bloody finger. "You bit me, you bit me," he moaned.

"I'm sorry," I said, "but you made me mad." Shaking my head, I wiped the blood on my shirtsleeve.

He lifted his hand and held up his hurt finger. A moment later, a smile slid across his face. "You did it!" he said. "You made the wart disappear!"

Wide-eyed, I stared at him.

"I'm a sissy. You're a frog witch." He came toward me with his arms outstretched. "Don't you see?" His voice was urgent. "Nobody likes us. Now we can be friends." He flung his bony arms around me. "What do you say?" he said, squeezing tightly.

"CRO-OOO-AACK!" I bellowed at the top of my lungs.

Startled, he flinched spasmodically and jumped backward.

"CRO-OOO-AACK!" I repeated. With my

eyes popped out and my head tossed back, I croaked loudly until the second bell rang.

When we filed in from recess, I kept my head down. Lane Carlson tagged behind me, tugging at my shirttail, giggling. Blood stained the front of my shirt and sleeves. Blood covered his hand. We looked as though we had been fighting, but no one would believe that. Again he pulled the bottom of my shirt.

"What?" I hissed from the corner of my mouth. "What do you want?"

"To be your friend," he whispered back.

I turned around, looked at his pitiful eagerness, and — in an effort to hush him up — relented. "Okay," I said.

Red blotches flushed over his cheeks. He tittered and giggled shrilly.

Adamantly, I shot him a look and pressed my finger against my lips. He gulped once. Then no more wild hyena laughs escaped from his mouth.

So Lane Carlson is going to be my friend, my only fourth grade friend, I thought wistfully.

As we marched into the classroom, Mrs. Stilton, who stood by the door, stopped us. "What happened?" she said, grabbing our shirts, pulling us over.

"We . . ." we both began at once.

Then Lane, in a mannerly voice, said, "Icy was swinging too high and fell back. I caught her." Proudly, he held up his finger.

"Are you hurt?" She pointed at the blood.

"We're fine," he said. "I cut my finger. That's all." He waved his finger from side to side. "Icy, here, stopped it from bleeding."

"Really?" Mrs. Stilton said.

"She wrapped her shirttail around it," he explained.

"Yes, ma'am," I said, lifting up my shirt.

Mrs. Stilton clicked her tongue, mumbled something, then said, "Both of you go to the bathroom and wash up. I'll give you five minutes."

Off we went down the hallway. As I rounded the corner, heading for GIRLS, I saw that Lan was following me. "You're a boy!" I said. "Use the other one."

"Oh, yes," he said with a giggle, twirling around.

"By the way," I said, tugging at his shirt, "thanks!" I opened the heavy bathroom door and, smiling broadly, went inside.

A few days later, while we were discussing Costa Rica during our geography lesson, Mrs. Stilton glared at me; and immediately my anxiety began to rise. Thinking that she might detect trouble, I kept very still and made the most of my anonymity. While Sherman Murphy read a paragraph from the textbook, I tried to blend into the classroom. The minute he finished reading, Mrs. Stilton asked, "What is the capital of Costa Rica?"

Emma Richards raised her hand. "San José," she said in a tidy little voice. "And the capital of Guatemala is Guatemala City," she added, beaming. We had studied Guatemala last week.

"Very good," Mrs. Stilton said. "Class, what language do they speak in Costa Rica?"

Emma Richards raised her hand again.

I looked at her appeasing face, and a sliver of dislike cut through me. I inched my hand upward.

"Yes, Emma." Mrs. Stilton nodded and smiled at her.

"They speak Spanish in Costa Rica," Emma said.

"Excellent!" Mrs. Stilton praised.

Red-faced, I shot my hand up.

"Yes?" Mrs. Stilton said.

"Hablan español en Costa Rica," I said, remembering what Miss Emily had taught me.

Mrs. Stilton squinted at me, tilted her head, and announced, "Listen up, class!"

A beginning of a smile flickered over my mouth.

"Icy Sparks wants to show off," she sneered.

Flushing, I fiercely bit my bottom lip and knotted my hands together.

"Icy was too young when she learned Spanish," Mrs. Stilton jeered. "That's why she gets confused and speaks improper English."

I caught my breath. Warm anger rushed through me. "I might be from the hills," I said bravely, breathing in. "But I don't talk like it.

133

Your speech marks you for life," I said. "If you don't speak good English, people will hold it against you, and you won't get a chance to better yourself."

"Now, where on earth did you hear that?" Mrs. Stilton asked. "Those aren't your words, Icy Sparks. Who taught them to you?"

"No one," I said. "I can come up with my own words. I don't need no one, I mean anyone, to teach them to me."

"You're lying, Icy Sparks," Mrs. Stilton said. "Remember what I said about lying?"

"I don't lie," I said, thrusting out my chin. Rage flamed over my cheeks.

"Oh, yes, you do, little girl," Mrs. Stilton growled. "You're known for your lies."

"I am not!" I said vehemently.

"What about calling me a woodpecker?" she said. "Telling poor Emma here that I'm so stingy, so mean, that God punished me and turned me into a woodpecker."

"That's the truth!" I said defiantly. "I've seen you in the woods behind our house. I saw your pointed nose turn into a beak. I saw your squinty eyes become woodpecker eyes. You bored your way into our birch trees."

"Then why do I look like this?" she said, holding out her dark blue skirt, swirling slowly around. "Class, do I look like a woodpecker?"

"No," the class said.

"Emma, do I look like a woodpecker?"

Emma pointed at me and snickered.

"Peavy, do I look like a woodpecker?"

Peavy shook his head.

"Sherman, what do I look like?" Mrs. Stilton asked.

"Like our teacher," he said. "Like Mrs. Stilton."

"Lucy?" Mrs. Stilton said.

"You look like our teacher," she said.

Mrs. Stilton pushed on. "What do I look like, Ronnie?"

"A pretty teacher in a pretty blue dress," Ronnie Halcomb answered.

"Lane?" she asked, cupping a hand over her eyes and looking toward the back of the room. "Lane Carlson, what do I look like?"

He wouldn't answer.

"Cat got your tongue?" she asked.

Lane nervously tapped his feet against the floor.

"Answer me, Lane Carlson! What do I look like?" Her voice was sharp and furious.

Abruptly, Lane stopped tapping his feet, leaned forward, and jumped up beside his desk. "You look like a woodpecker," he said boldly. "A redheaded peckerwood."

"See!" I said, standing up, too. "I'm not a liar."

Mrs. Stilton threw the textbook on her desk. "Sit down, you two!" she warned through pressed lips. "I know troublemakers when I see them." She jerked open her desk drawer and snatched up the Ping-Pong paddle. "You're misfits," she said, stomping around her desk, thudding down the aisle. "You're weird," she said, waving the paddle in the air. "A sissy and a frog," she said, coming toward me. "A sissy and a frog," she repeated, banging the Ping-Pong paddle against my desktop. "A lying, pop-eyed frog," she sniped. "Frog," she said, and smacked the paddle against my arm. "Frog," she repeated, whacking me again.

I tilted to the left, felt my legs crumbling beneath me, and was about to slump down when — out of nowhere like a whirlwind — the urge rushed through me. Bewildered, I grabbed the back of my seat, steadied myself, popped out my eyes, threw back my head, and bellowed, "CRO-OOO-AACK!" Hopping up and down on the tips of my toes, my desk knocking against the floor, I roared, "CRO-OOO-AACK! CRO-OOO-AACK!"

Lane Carlson giggled and shrieked hysterically.

"CRO-OOO-AACK!" I grunted again. "Shit! Piss on you!" I hollered. "You mean ole bitch!" I yelled, and pounded my feet. "Piss on you!" I shouted, violently jumping beside my desk.

Mrs. Stilton looked wildly around her. "You're both crazy!" she screeched. "Crazy!" she screamed, then dropped the paddle and stomped out of the room.

When she returned with Mr. Wooten, the principal, Lane Carlson was still shrieking and I was still cursing.

"Piss on you!" I bellowed. "Piss on you!"

"It's ungodly," Mrs. Stilton said, pointing at me, looking around at the others, who sat stunned and mute.

Mr. Wooten shook his head, calmly strode over, put both of his hands on my shoulders, and in a firm voice said, "Icy, hush now! Get hold of yourself."

"Piss. Piss," I said.

Mr. Wooten put his fingers to his lips, turned toward Lane, and shushed him.

Immediately Lane quit shrieking.

"Now go sit down," he said quietly.

Lane did as he was told.

With his left hand, Mr. Wooten motioned to the door. "I'll handle this," he said, gently grabbing my hands, rubbing them with his square fingers, pulling me out into the hallway.

"Mean ole bitch!" I moaned, my voice growing weaker. "Shit! Piss!" I said softly, closing my eyes, hearing the door snap shut. "Shit!" I groaned. "Pisssss. Pisssss," I sputtered, like an engine giving out. "Pi . . . ss. Pi . . . ss. Pi . . . ss," I stammered. "Pi . . ." I began again. "Pi . . . Pi . . ." I stuttered until, completely exhausted, I stopped and was quiet.

"Good girl," Mr. Wooten said, nodding. "That's a good girl." Picking me up, he folded me in his arms and said, "Icy, you need to rest. I'm going to take you home."

Before I knew it, with my head on a pillow and a cotton blanket over my legs, I was lying down in the back seat of Mr. Wooten's Buick. It was new and smelled like freshly cut cedar.

"I need to talk to your grandparents," he explained. "Have you told them about these spells you've been having?"

"No, sir," I said. "I told Miss Emily Tanner. But she said I shouldn't worry. They'd probably go away."

He glanced at me in the rearview mirror. "You have to tell your grandparents."

"I'm afraid to," I muttered. "I don't want to disappoint them."

"But you must," he said firmly.

"I know," I said in a weary voice.

"Rest now," he suggested.

"Yessir," I mumbled, tightly shutting my eyes, seeing only the white splotches of sunlight that flew against my eyelids. "I'm kind of tired," I said, and felt myself sinking. I longed to sleep and never wanted to pop, repeat, or curse again. I wanted to dream in a place where pasture roses bloomed and goodness thrived, but just as I was falling asleep, the Buick lurched to a stop. As I opened my eyelids, I saw through the window the oranges, yellows, and reds of fall, our white clapboard farmhouse with its red metal roof, and heard the whine of the front door and my grandmother's voice.

"What brings you out this way?" she said as he opened the car door.

"I got a sick girl here," Mr. Wooten explained, "in the back seat."

"Oh, my!" my grandmother said, scampering down the steps over the rough yard. When the rear door opened, I saw the worried look on her face. "If you don't mind, please bring her inside," she said as he leaned over, slid his arms under me, and lifted me up. "I'm going to fetch Virgil."

"Gosh darn!" he said under his breath, rising too soon, banging his head against the doorframe.

But Matanni didn't notice. "Put her on the sofa," she said, already scurrying away. "I'm going to the barn to get Virgil."

My head was resting in Matanni's lap, and Patanni was rubbing my feet. Mr. Wooten sat in my grandfather's easy chair — red and brown plaid with patches on both arms. Too tuckered out to tell my side of the story, I listened while Mr. Wooten spoke. "I've never heard her talk this way before," he said.

My grandmother shook her head. "Heavens, no!" she exclaimed.

"She comes with me to town," my grandfather said, "and spends time at Margaret's Bakery, but she wouldn't hear nothing bad there. I've caught her at Harry's Garage. No telling what Chiggar and Frank talk about. Once I found her at the barbershop. A bunch of old codgers, getting their whiskers shaved and their hair cut, cussing up a storm."

"This was foul language," Mr. Wooten said.

"No garden-variety curse words."

"Oh, my," my grandmother said, stroking my forehead. "I don't understand. Icy's never talked that way."

"Never a problem," my grandfather said.

With her hand beneath my neck, Matanni raised my head, bent over to look into my eyes, and asked, "Sugar, why?"

I fluttered my eyelids. My voice broke. "I don't know," I said weakly. "The bad words just take over. Even when I try to stop myself, I can't."

Mr. Wooten rose. "Icy needs to rest," he said, putting an arm around my grandmother. "She needs to stay home tomorrow and think about what she's done. When she comes back to school, I know she'll be herself again."

At that moment, my face crinkled up and I began to cry. Like a waterfall, the tears washed down my cheeks.

When Principal Wooten left, I retreated to the safety of my attic room, where on notebook paper I composed a letter to Miss Emily.

Dear Miss Emily,

How are you doing? I know it's a busy time for you at the store, but I miss you. Since last I saw you, only bad things have happened. Remember when I told you about the urges? Well, I've done all of them in front of my classmates. Even some I didn't know about. Now, they all hate me, especially Mrs. Stilton.

Miss Emily, I sure do want to see you. I feel so alone. Please come see me soon.

Love,
Your friend, Icy Gal
xoxoxoxoxoxoxox

I folded the letter into thirds, the way Miss Emily had taught me, and sealed it in an envelope. Next, I addressed the envelope and put it on my nightstand. Tomorrow, I would ask Patanni to take it with him. He was going into Ginseng and could, I thought, drop it by Miss Emily's house. I rolled back my quilt and eased into bed. I desperately needed someone to talk to. Without Miss Emily, my anonymity was complete. Closing my eyes, I felt the darkness, like loneliness, envelop me. Fitfully, I slipped into sleep.

I am hanging suspended in midair. Like a puppet, my arms and legs dangle loosely. Exhaustion drags down my eyebrows and the corners of my mouth. Darkness flows around the contours of my body, avoiding my skin. It seems that nothing wants to touch me. "You were restless," my grandmother says, "even in your mama's womb." In an instant, my left arm whips out. My right leg kicks at the emptiness. "Louisa always knew you'd be different. She said that you were too eager to be born."

All of a sudden, my arms and legs begin to scramble frantically. My lips and eyebrows turn up-

141

ward, energized. Around and around I twirl until the darkness begins to whirl with me, losing its round shape, oozing, splashing, jetting me forth.

In the soft light of morning, I am born. Dancing through the air, my movements are delicate and graceful. A welcoming sparrow pecks me on the cheek. A butterfly caresses my lips with its wings. Gnats, June bugs, and dragonflies dip down to taste the sweetness of my skin. I am wrapped in wings. It seems that everything longs to be near me.

The following morning upon awakening, I stretched and yawned. Nebulous time, those moments between sleeping and waking, engulfed me; and, for a split second, I thought that my dream was true, that I had been born again as graceful as a gazelle. But then the second passed, and I was Icy Sparks, trapped in reality, a time which would last forever. Hurriedly, I put on jeans and a red-striped shirt, raced down the stairs, and stopped my grandfather at the door. "Patanni," I said, tugging on his sleeve, "please take this. It's for Miss Emily."

Nodding and mumbling, he slipped the letter into his shirt pocket and shut the door behind him. I crossed my fingers, closed my eyes, and imagined a big hook plunging into the endlessness of time's straight line and jerking it up. With one humongous tug, present time would be altered, and another, better time would be born.

Throughout the weekend, I marked time,

waiting for Miss Emily's visit. When she didn't come, I invented excuses for her. Naturally, she'd be busy raising money for the volunteer fire department and picking out books for the library to buy. And even though she didn't go on dates and wasn't invited to social events like baby showers and weddings, she was always on some committee or other, running the show, acting official. As always, fall was a busy season at Tanner's Feed Supply. The farmers stocked up for the winter ahead. Johnny Cake would be tending his family's farm; all the work in the store would be left for Miss Emily to do. Of course, before the first frost, when the ragweed flourished, she always felt poorly. The rims of her eyes turned red; her nose watered constantly; her head ached. Often she was too tired to do anything after work. Still, though, on Sunday morning, I clung to the hope that maybe she'd visit.

When she didn't show at suppertime, I felt more alone than ever. "Patanni, did you take my letter to Miss Emily?" I asked, spooning some corn pudding into my mouth.

Without looking up, he just nodded.

Throughout the rest of the meal, I caught him studying me. In response, I averted my eyes, avoiding the displeasure I thought I saw in his face. I didn't want to see how much I had let him down. For it seemed that I had disappointed everyone, including Miss Emily, and it was only right that now I should pay for it.

Chapter 13

"This will be your new classroom," Mr. Wooten said as he led me to a small supply room adjacent to Nurse Coy's infirmary. He unlocked the door, eased it open with his foot, and flipped a switch. The room lit up. Against the walls on three sides were bookcases, cluttered with materials — chalk, erasers, paper clips, construction paper of all colors, staplers, tape, tin coffee cans filled with scissors, folders, boxes of pencils, stencils, clear glass bottles of glue, rulers, puzzles, books, bandages, gauze, and bottles of disinfectant. Mr. Wooten pointed at a desk. "See, we've brought your desk inside and cleaned off a shelf for your books. Mrs. Patterson, from fifth grade, will be your teacher. She'll spend the lunch hour with you."

"I'll be by myself?" I asked.

Mr. Wooten laughed and lightly squeezed my elbow. "Nurse Coy is next door." He knocked on the wall. "I'm a few yards away."

I nodded.

"You need some time to yourself," he said, "to think. It's only for a few weeks, just to see how you do, Icy. Then you'll go back to Mrs. Stilton's class."

I shrugged.

"Really, Icy, it's not so bad. Look at the books we got you." He walked over to a shelf and motioned for me to follow.

My textbooks and twelve others lined the shelf. At home, fifteen books rested in my small blue bookcase with its four sagging shelves. At Christmas, on Valentine's Day, or on my birthday, Miss Emily would bring me a book. I hadn't read them all because some, as Miss Emily said, were beyond my years, but I'd get to them eventually, she always insisted. Now I had twelve new books to choose from, twelve more books to eventually get to. Mr. Wooten touched each book and read the title. "*Little Women, Little Men,* and *Spinning-Wheel Stories* by Louisa May Alcott," he said. "*The Wonderful Wizard of Oz* by Lyman Frank Baum, *Cabbages and Kings* by O. Henry, *The Call of the Wild* and *White Fang* by Jack London." He stopped and took a breath. "*Anne of Green Gables, Emily of New Moon,* and *Jack of Lantern Hill,* all by Lucy Maude Montgomery. *The Raven and Other Poems* by Edgar Allan Poe. And finally, *Tarzan of the Apes* by Edgar Rice Burroughs. Well, Icy, what do you think?" he asked, turning around to face me and plopping his square hands on my shoulders.

"They look hard," I said.

"Mrs. Patterson will read the difficult ones to

you," he said. "Some of them, though, you can handle yourself."

"It'll take a year to read them all," I said.

"You don't have to read every one of them." Mr. Wooten was laughing again. "Just read what you can, all right?" He patted my shoulders. "See that little blackboard in the corner?" he asked.

I looked up at him and smiled.

"You can write on it whenever you want."

"Anything?" I asked.

"Whatever you want," he said. "Your thoughts, your ideas, your dreams, anything."

I turned to face the window. "Can I go outside?" I asked.

He cleared his throat. "After recess, when everybody else comes back," he said. "You'll have the swings all to yourself." He grinned broadly; his full lips stretched into half-moons. "Icy, we have to do this, understand?"

"Yessir," I said, "I'd better behave or else."

"Or else what?" His voice was concerned; his smile had disappeared.

"If I don't act right," I said, "something bad is going to happen."

He shook his head. "Not true," he said. "Nothing bad is going to happen. Be a good girl and do what I say. Then everything will be fine."

I walked over to the desk. The initials CW were carved into the upper right-hand corner. A blue ink stain zigzagged down the front. It was mine, all right. "What do you want me to do?" I asked.

Mr. Wooten retrieved a slip of paper from his coat pocket. "Read chapters eight, nine, and ten in your geography book and answer all of the questions at the end of each chapter. Then grab a book from the shelf and start reading."

"Any one I want?" I asked.

"Sure," he said, smiling. "Mrs. Patterson will be here before you know it. Oh, by the way . . ." He tapped his fingers against my desk. "Think hard on what you've done."

"Yessir," I said.

"And if you need anything, poke your head through the door and holler."

I grinned and opened my mouth to say more when he twisted the doorknob and strode through, leaving me all alone with my books.

Two hours had passed when I heard voices and laughter outside. Rising from my seat, I walked over to the window. In the distance, a group of boys were banging sticks against the white picket fence that encircled the fish pond. Then a voice called out, "Look, it's the big, orange one! It's Jonah!"

I squinted into the sunny, hazy day. Light glinted off the bars of the jungle gym. The swings whined. I pressed my nose against the window and stared at a boy, glowing in the sun in front of me. He pirouetted like a ballerina, twirled within my line of vision, then disappeared. Again, he circled nearby. I made a tight fist and rapped against the glass, but he ignored me. I tried to make him out through the sun's glare but couldn't. Once more, I rapped against the window, but he continued to spin like a top. Then, frustrated, using both fists, I pounded the glass. "Hi, there!" I yelled at the top of my lungs.

On a dime, he came to a stop and turned toward my voice. *"Icy!"* he screamed in surprise.

"Lane!" I yelled back.

"Icy!" he repeated, running over to the window, tapping it wildly.

"Lane!" I shouted.

Then, suddenly, we both began leaping up and down, our heads bobbing, our fingers traveling over the window.

"But I thought you were at home," he said, all at once standing still.

"No, I'm here," I answered.

He cocked his head jauntily to one side; a clownish grin covered his face. "Where?" he asked.

"In the supply room," I said.

"By yourself?" he said.

I nodded.

His fingers sashayed over the glass. "Oh, we're going to have so much fun!" he squealed.

"How's that?" I asked. "I'm not allowed to play with any of you."

"At recess," he said, "we'll talk. Right here. Right now. Right through this window."

"You think?" I asked.

"Oh, it'll be fun," he added. "The two of us inventing new ways to play. The two of us against the world."

"The two of us against a woodpecker," I said.

"A redheaded peckerwood," he said loudly, just as the second bell rang.

After my recess was over, I looked around my room. Bandages sat beside rulers. Staples and paper clips were scrambled together in the same box. Red sheets of construction paper were shuffled among sheets of blue. Bottles of glue tumbled over stencils. Crayons were scattered along each shelf. Carbon paper dirtied onion-skin paper. Rolls of toilet paper were stacked against the wall. All of this clutter bothered me. Such visual disorder disturbed the silence in the room and upset my mind. My thoughts began to taunt me. Curses shrieked inside my head. Frantic, I slid to the floor and pressed my hands against my lips. Broken pieces of chalk rested beside whole sticks. Coloring books were piled with textbooks. Tightly, I closed my eyes and shoved a fist into my mouth. Angry thoughts pushed against my skull; swear words filled my throat; and I was about to curse loudly when an idea burned through my brain and, like a swallow of whiskey, soothed me: Bring order to the room, and you'll bring order to your mind.

Quietly, I rose. From now on, red construction paper would be stacked beside boxes of red crayons. Red pencils would come next. Red with red. Yellow with yellow. Red and yellow mixed produced orange. Orange would be third. Orange with orange. The disinfectant was orange. Therefore, I set it beside the orange crayons. Since the black stencils were trimmed in orange, I put them next to the disinfectant. The rolls of toilet paper, in orange wrappings, were lined up next to the stencils. Pencils with orange erasers were plunked into a peach-colored coffee cup because everyone knew that peach was just lukewarm orange. And so on and so on, my logic unfolded until my supply room was in perfect order, until it resembled the root cellar back home, where the canned red beets sat next to the strawberry jam and the green beans rested beside the collard greens, where every jar was color coordinated and the room was a palette of harmonious color. Stepping back and admiring my handiwork, I knew that I had hit upon the answer. I could organize my surroundings and also organize my mind.

It was Saturday. As usual, I was running in the hills beyond our farm to spend my anger; and, becoming tired, I decided to rest behind the black pine near Little Turtle Pond. I felt a slight tingle in my left foot. Not knowing if it was the start of a twitch or a muscle spasm, I stretched out on the ground and rolled my leg from side to side, pine needles crunching against my jeans. The pine trees against the cool November sky seemed orderly. Only a few leaves remained on the oak trees. The jimson weed, milkweed, and burdock were gone. Uncluttered, the land-scape was tidy, appearing as if the flora had been penciled in. Rolling my head on my shoulders, I looked at the stripped field, unruffled as a sheet, and enjoyed a calm I hadn't felt in days. Nothing stirred. The water was smooth and tranquil; the rock eye in Little Turtle Pond seemed to be looking at me; the trees were motionless; the animals were tucked away and quiet. Nature, I felt, had mastered her handiwork. A feeling of relief swept over me, and I was on the verge of leaning over and grabbing the tips of my toes when — out of nowhere — came the sound of footsteps.

Quickly, I jumped up and hid behind the pine's thick trunk. In the distance, wearing a green patterned dress, Mamie Tillman was marching. Her body was much thinner. Her stride was measured and sure. Every few feet, she zigzagged abruptly, either left or right, all the while moving precisely, almost mechanically, like a soldier during a drill, following, I realized, the old path leading from her place to the pond.

When she entered the woods, her movements became more trancelike, her face as emotionless as a mask. There was, I recognized, a uniformity to her, a symmetry in the way she blended into the background. Beautiful order, I thought, touching the pine's old, weathered bark, realizing that for the first time in a long while my hands were twitch-free.

But as Mamie drew closer, I saw her differently. Deep lines cut into the corners of her mouth, and her raw, red skin was damp with sweat. Though I knew she was a young woman — twenty-eight, I'd heard Matanni say — she had aged ten years since I last saw her. Sprinkles of gray ran through her dark black hair, unkempt and straggling down her back. And in her large, dark eyes there was a sadness so deep it seemed to eat its way through her. Strangely, she was cradling a burlap bag in her arms. Every so often, she rocked it to and fro.

When she got to the water's edge, she extended her arms, leaned over, and gently placed the bag in the water. In the cool, eerie silence, it floated for a second, then, with a little sucking sound, slid under.

A moment later, she held out her arms. For an instant, I feared that she was going to throw herself into the pond, too. But instead, with her arms outstretched, embracing the air like a lover, she fell gracefully to her knees. Leaning over, she gently kissed the water. For several minutes, with lowered head, she stared down. Then, as if something inside her were prying itself out, her lips suddenly twisted, and she moaned — a low, anguished cry, the purity of which seemed to transcend sound. Scrambling to her feet, she threw her arms across her chest and, bending over, began to run. She sprinted wildly — zigzagging through the trees — her hands still clutching her shoulders. Her worn boots tore through brambles. Her hair snagged on twigs. And like a madwoman, she faded up the hill.

Trembling, I glanced around me. The woods were not the same. Order, it seemed, had dissolved, simply evaporated into the air like mist. The pine trees were gnarled. Their limbs, twisting upward, pointed accusingly at the sky. Even the stillness of Little Turtle Pond had changed. No longer serene, its quiet water had become frightening, smooth like a shroud, final as death. "Help me!" I whispered, running toward the pond, my hands swishing through the cold water. But my fingers touched nothing. The burlap bag was gone. It had vanished into darkness.

Chapter 14

"Icy," I heard Mr. Wooten say from the door-way.

Startled, I turned around. Over the past week, I had been nervous and afraid.

"What were you thinking about?"

"Nothing," I said, fearing that perhaps my voice carried and that earlier in the week he had overheard me. Whenever Mrs. Patterson had come to see me, I had been polite and attentive; and, when alone, I'd tidied up my life. Yet, during those moments when Nurse Coy had been out, I had not remained calm but had changed instead into my former self and vented every one of my stored-up urges. My body had contorted into hideous shapes. Foul words had bombed from my mouth, and I had proceeded to tic, croak, and curse until all of my demons were purged. "Didn't seem like nothing to me," he said, coming inside and looking around. "Something seems different." He arched his eyebrows and looked puzzled. "The room is changed."

I stood very still. Sadly, it now seemed that

my makeshift classroom could not really calm me. Somehow, the colors weren't right. Peach conflicted with orange. The forest-green erasers didn't match the lime-green rulers. One yellow was more mustard than the other.

Mr. Wooten walked over to the shelves. "Why, you've straightened up everything!" he said.

"Yessir," I replied. "And I've been reading, too," I said. "Those books by Louisa May Alcott. Did you know my mama's name was Louisa?"

He nodded, a slight smile on his lips. "Which one of hers do you like best?" he asked.

"*Little Women* is really good," I said. "Plus women and Wooten both start with *w*'s."

"What's that?" he asked, squinting at me.

"Women and Wooten," I explained. "They both start with *w*'s."

"Oh," he murmured, stroking his forehead, walking back and forth in front of the shelves. "You've been working really hard," he said, frowning. "But I don't quite understand." He stopped in front of the rolls of toilet paper and picked one up.

I held my breath. Order's fragile, I thought.

"But why is this next to the stencils?" he asked.

I bit my bottom lip; chaos was about to take over.

With the toilet paper in his hand, he headed toward the far corner of the room. "We stack it here," he said, placing the roll on the floor.

"No," I mumbled.

"What did you say?" he asked me.

"No," I repeated loudly.

"No, what?" he said, glancing up.

"You're breaking the pattern," I said. "It can't go there."

Slowly, he walked toward me. "What pattern?"

"The oranges," I explained. "They go together."

He stared at the shelves. "Okay, I see." He laughed. "But we can't have toilet paper next to stencils. It doesn't make sense."

I lunged past him. "No!" I yelled, racing toward the corner of the room. "You can't!" I snatched up the roll of toilet paper.

"Icy, honey, it's no big deal," Mr. Wooten said. "Just leave it there."

"No!" I screamed. "You're ruining everything!"

"Icy!" he said firmly. "Put that down."

"No!" I bellowed, fiercely clutching the roll. "I won't let you."

Calmly Mr. Wooten approached me. "Icy," he reasoned, "it doesn't matter."

"No!" I backed away, waving the roll above my head. "You can't have it!"

"I don't want it," he said, reaching out. "I just want you to put it down."

"No!" I lowered my arm and pressed the toilet paper against my stomach. "Shit! Piss on you!" I screamed, crouching down. "Son-of-a-bitch, it's mine!"

Instantly, Mr. Wooten bent over and shoved his hands beneath my armpits. "Icy, stand up this minute or else!" he ordered.

"Piss on you! Piss on you! Piss on you!" I yelled, rolling myself into a tight ball, the toilet paper still jammed against my belly.

"Get up this minute, Icy Sparks!" he demanded.

"Shit! Shit!" I said. "You mean ole son-of-a-bitch!"

"That does it!" Red-faced, Mr. Wooten jerked me upward.

"What you gonna do!" I shouted, stabbing him with my elbows. Groaning, he let go of me, and I broke away. "You gonna make me pay!" I screamed, racing toward the supply room door, gripping the toilet paper with both hands. "You gonna make me pay! What you gonna do?" I flung open the door and dashed out. "What you gonna do?"

Mr. Wooten chased after me.

Sprinting down the hallway, I shoved open the double doors and pushed through. "Throw me in the fish pond! Drown me! Drown me!" I cried, running around the building. "Throw me in and drown me!" I said, darting toward the fish pond, reaching the picket fence, and scrambling over.

"Icy, don't!" Mr. Wooten yelled.

But his words came too late. I had already jumped into the cold water — this black, wet universe which God, at Little Turtle Pond, had shown me.

Part II

Chapter 15

Bluegrass State Hospital, a residential facility on the outskirts of Lexington, was a five-hour drive from Poplar Holler. The minute I saw the guard shack and adults roaming the grounds like they were lost, I knew that my premonitions had come true. This would be the worst fate to befall me.

The dormitory, where the children stayed, was called the Sunshine Building, appropriately named, given its yellow stucco walls and brown-tiled roof. L-shaped and one story, it seemed more modern than the other buildings. In fact, the Sunshine Building stood out like a new car among old, used ones. Located to the left of the Administration Building, it was surrounded by a chain-link fence. Two swingsets, three see-saws, and a sandbox were scattered about the front and side yards. According to Mr. Wooten, the Sunshine Building was something of an experiment. While the rest of Bluegrass State Hospital was run like a hospital, the Sunshine Building, set apart with its own small staff, was supposed to be different. "It doesn't have as many doctors and nurses," Mr. Wooten had told my grandparents. "Too much of that is bad for children," he had explained. "The people who'll take care of Icy will act like family." My grandparents had understood and liked this idea. It was one of the many reasons why they had even considered bringing me to this place. After all, not even the befuddled Dr. Stone had hesitated for a moment. "She must go to Lexington," he'd said.

As we walked up the sidewalk to the front door, I saw children of different ages playing. Two girls in plaid jumpers whisked by me. One clutched a rope. The other a ball. "But I don't want to play ball," the one with the jump rope whined. "We did that yesterday."

A boy with auburn curls and green eyes sat cross-legged beneath a huge oak tree. A notebook rested upon his outstretched knees. In his hand, he grasped a pencil; and, with pursed lips and knotted eyebrows, he drew a picture. A large boy, with a dark crewcut, a boulder-sized face, and a stony jaw, marched from the swingset to the seesaw and back again. He looked older than the one who was drawing. Deep lines of determination were etched around his mouth. Over and over, he retraced his steps. A girl whose face I couldn't see was corkscrewed in a wheelchair near the sandbox. Her dull brown hair bristled out from her head like a mass of Brillo pads.

Beneath a maple tree, to the left of the sandbox, was a young girl lying twisted upon a bright green mat. Although she was on her stomach, her limbs were taut and rigid. While her neck and arms jerked to the right, the rest of her body pulled to the left. Every so often, her arms would hit against each other; her legs would knock. Then she'd lift her head, spasmodically wrench it to one side, and grin deliriously — her dark black hair spiking from her head like needles. I shuddered just looking at her, but then an even worse sight caught my eye. A blond-haired skinny boy, not more than eleven, perched on the top of a sawed-off telephone pole, began twittering and chirping like a bird. With one long leg curled upward, he flapped his elbows from his sides like wings. "Chru . . . chru . . . chri . . . chru," he sang, crouched down, his head bent, his blond hair the yellow breast of a bird.

Oh, Lordie! I thought, staring intensely at him, feeling more alone than ever, thinking that even among misfits I wouldn't fit in. But then I heard laughter, and the two girls in plaid jumpers ran by me again.

"See, it ain't so bad," Patanni said, as if on cue. "You'll make some new friends here."

Matanni put her arms around me and squeezed.

Mr. Wooten nodded, thumped down the suitcases he was carrying, and pressed the buzzer beside the door. A young woman with soft blond curls warmly greeted us. "You must be Icy," she said, smiling. "We've been waiting for you."

163

"Yes, ma'am," I muttered.

"Mr. and Mrs. Bedloe?" she asked, nodding at Matanni and Patanni.

Patanni extended his arm and shook her hand. "We're Icy's grandparents," he said.

Before she could ask who the other gentleman was, Mr. Wooten stepped forward. "I'm Charles Wooten, the principal at Ginseng Elementary, Icy's school."

"And I'm Maizy Hurley," the young woman said. "I'll be taking care of Icy." She winked at me and took my hand. "I bet we'll become really good friends."

"Yes, ma'am," I muttered, stumbling through the huge front door.

We walked down a black-and-white-tiled corridor, so brightly lit that I squinted my eyes against the glare, passed by several office doors, and entered an enormous living room. An over-sized bookcase stood just inside the entrance, to the left of the door. Green and yellow plaid sofas lined two adjoining walls. Cane-backed chairs circling a round wooden table stood catty-cornered from the sofas.

"This is our dayroom," Maizy said, then pointed to the far side of the room. "And we eat our meals over there," she explained, walking toward a long table covered with a bright green tablecloth. In the center of the table was a bowl of mustard-colored chrysanthemums. "Right now patients are napping in their rooms, or else they're playing outside," she went on. "When the place is quiet, it's easier for a new person to settle in, don't you think?"

All of us nodded.

"This building isn't as old as the others," observed Mr. Wooten.

Maizy Hurley grinned. "Right you are," she said. "Until two years ago, we didn't have a children's wing, but the powers that be in Frankfort — thank heavens — finally saw the light."

"It's nice," my grandmother said. "Very clean."

"Our nicest building," Maizy said, abruptly twisting to the right. "Follow me," she said, heading out the door, rounding a corner, and scurrying down another hallway. Quietly, we filed behind her, walking down the longer leg of the L-shaped building, passing doors of different colors, until we reached the next to the last door, white with 13, painted in bright red at the top.

Land sakes, I thought, staring at the 13, feeling a tic coming on.

"Room Thirteen brings good luck," Maizy said, as though reading my mind. "Every child who stays here goes home early."

"How early?" I asked nervously.

"Within three months," she said.

I gasped.

"Three months ain't so long," Patanni said. "You'll see how fast it goes by."

Maizy took a key chain out of her pocket, fingered through a tangle of keys, then popped one into the lock, and twisted the door knob. The door to Room 13 swung open. Curtains, covered with nursery rhyme characters, hung from the windows. Old Mother Hubbard, Little Boy Blue, Little Bo Peep, and Jack and Jill danced in front of me. The walls were light blue, and a dark blue bedspread covered the mattress. A little pink dresser with an oval mirror was beside the bed, and a rocker, painted red, white, and blue, stood in the center of a fluffy blue rug. "How do you like it?" Maizy asked, looking at me.

I felt the tic subsiding. "It's nice," I said, relieved.

"Very nice," Matanni added.

Mr. Wooten set down the suitcases. "Colorful," he said, huffing out of breath.

"I like it," Patanni said.

"We have fourteen rooms in all," Maizy said, "but only eight of them are filled right now. Patients come and go, you know. Some of the kids who don't have parents stay here longer until space opens up in a permanent care facility. But that's not you, Icy," she said, staring into my eyes. "You'll be here only for a little while."

I smiled at her gratefully.

"How many people work here?" Mr. Wooten asked.

"A whole lot of people work at Bluegrass State Hospital," Maizy said. "Around a hundred and twenty, I think. But Sunshine Building has only five daytime staff members." Maizy held up her right hand and wiggled her fingers. "Of

166

course, care providers are here at night when we go home, but the kids don't really get to know them." Maizy caught her breath. "Let's see," she continued. "Seeing as I've been here the longest, I've been designated the top aide, but like the others, I end up doing a little bit of everything. Everything, that is, except cook." She tossed back her head and laughed; dainty little giggles sprung from her throat. "The kitchen staff in Hickory prepares the food. They send it over, then we serve it up."

"Who's we?" Mr. Wooten asked.

"Wilma, Delbert, Tiny, and myself," replied Maizy.

"Are they aides like you?" he inquired.

"Wilma and Delbert are," Maizy said. "But Tiny's a nurse. He got his training in the military. So along with everything else, he gives out the meds . . . the medications," she said, correcting herself. "And then, of course" — she held up her index finger — "there's Dr. Conroy, who keeps us all in line."

"Five altogether?" Mr. Wooten said.

"That's right," Maizy said. "There are five of us."

"Good," Mr. Wooten said. "You'll have lots of time for Icy."

"The sooner you fix her," Patanni said, winking at me, "the sooner she gets to come home. Mind if we unpack?" he asked, pointing at the suitcases.

"Of course not," Maizy said, walking toward

the door. "When you're finished, I'll fetch Icy a big bowl of ice cream. This way she can enjoy herself while we — grown-ups — meet with Dr. Conroy."

When she had gone, Matanni grabbed one of the suitcases and plopped it on the bed. "Ice cream sounds good to me," she said, unlatching the top. Smiling, she pulled out two small patchwork pillows. "I made these for you!" she said, putting them beside each other at the head of my bed. "Now, don't they brighten up the place?"

"Ain't that Around the World?" I asked, recognizing all the colors of the quilted pattern.

"Sure is," she said. "For folks like us, traveling to Lexington ain't much different than traveling around the world."

"This is the first time you've put a quilt pattern on a pillow," I said.

"Well, then, what do you think?" she asked.

"I like it," I said. "The pillows are pretty. They look like baby quilts."

"I aim to please," she said, hanging my dresses in the small closet on the far side of the room. She nodded at Patanni, patting the mattress with her tiny hand. "Put it here," she said. Patanni lifted the second, much larger suitcase and swung it on top of the bed. "Help me out some," she said, and they both carefully began to unpack it, arranging my underwear, blue jeans, and blouses in tidy piles in the little pink dresser.

Patanni had also brought my books. Since

there was no bookcase, he stacked them on the floor beneath the window that was adjacent to my bed.

"I brought these for you," Mr. Wooten said, handing me a thick, heavy dictionary and *Little Women*. "I reckon Ginseng Elementary can spare them."

"In a few weeks, we'll return," Patanni said, standing up, studying the straight line of each stack. "They want you to get used to the place, so they got rules. We ain't permitted to write, telephone, or come before then. In the meantime, you best be pretty and patient; and, as dear as the day comes, we'll be back."

"You know," Matanni said, her voice cracking, "we'll be thinking about you. Ain't a day will pass that we won't be missing you."

Although I was starting to miss my life back home, even the sight of Peavy Lawson, I didn't start crying until I swallowed that first spoonful of strawberry ice cream. One deep sob shook my shoulders, and a large teardrop slid down my cheek, cascaded over my chin, and plunked against the inside of my bowl.

As I was scraping the bowl for the last taste, Matanni, Patanni, and Mr. Wooten returned.

"We want a kiss good-bye," my grandparents said. Matanni opened her arms. Patanni did the same.

I looked at them, hesitated for a second, then reluctantly stood up. "If I hug you, you'll leave," I said.

"Icy, we gotta leave," Patanni said. "They won't let us stay."

"But you'll visit me, won't you?" I asked.

"Ain't nobody gonna keep us away," Patanni said. "Now come over here." He motioned me over. "I wanna squeeze some love into you."

With a heavy heart and quivering lips, I went to him, wrapped my arms around his waist, and screwed my face against his stomach. The buttons on his shirt pressed into my forehead. Squeezing him tightly, I inhaled his earthy smell and whispered, "Patanni, I love you."

"Me, too," he said.

With both hands, Matanni tapped her chest. "What about me?" she asked.

Twisting around, I rose upward on my toes, forced my head between her breasts, and took in the warmth of her skin, the softness of her plump, compact body.

"My darling girl," she said. "You was the light of your sweet mama's life. You're the reason for ours."

I gulped down tears and was seconds away from pleading — *Please, don't leave me here!* — when Mr. Wooten said, "Icy's a tough little trooper. She'll get along just fine. Won't you, Icy?"

I glanced at Mr. Wooten. Concern had darkened his face, and his eyes seemed to say, Don't make this any harder on them. So, without shedding a tear, I hugged my grandmother tightly and stepped away from her.

Mr. Wooten brightened and sidled up beside me. Then he tapped his cheek, leaned over, and asked, "How about a kiss, too?"

My lips brushed against his skin. I could feel the tears coming, so I closed my eyes and lowered my head. With my heart splintered into a thousand pieces, I was mumbling. "Don't worry about me none. . . . I'll be fine. . . . I'm okay. . . . I'll see you all real soon. . . . Maybe next week. . . . Don't you worry about . . ." I heard a car door slam. Startled, I raised my head, my eyelids jerked open. "Matanni! Patanni!" I cried. "Matanni! Patanni!" I yelled. Panicked, I ran to the door, flung it open, and dashed down the hallway. "Don't go! Please, don't leave me here!" I begged, pressing my face against the pane of glass, catching one last glimpse of them. Huddled together in the back seat of Mr. Wooten's Buick, the two intertwined silhouettes slipped past the guard shack, glided through the iron gate, and faded into the distance. Soon they would blend into blue-misted mountains and disappear.

From the end of the hallway, a voice called out my name. Then a patter of heels clicked to a halt behind me. Immediately I turned around and saw Maizy Hurley, breathing rapidly, with her hands on her hips.

"They left," I said, sniffling back tears.

"But they'll be back," she answered. "Now come along," she said, smiling. "I want you to meet someone special."

With my hand in hers, Maizy led me to the dayroom. "This is Rose," she said, releasing my fingers, squatting beside the strange young woman I had seen earlier. She was still lying on the same green mat and was just as twisted as before. "Say hello," Maizy suggested, running her finger alongside the young girl's cheek.

"Hi, Rose," I said, attempting a smile.

"Rose has cerebral palsy," Maizy explained. "She was born like this. She can't talk, but I think she understands every word we say."

I looked closely at her. This time Rose was lying on her back, and I could see her coal-black eyes as they darted back and forth. "Hey, look, she smiled at me," I said, pointing at her thin-lipped mouth, the corners of which appeared to curl upward.

"Of course she did," Maizy said. "She understands. I just know she does."

"Does it hurt?" I asked, scrutinizing her knotted body, which seemed always to fight against itself.

"I don't think so," Maizy said. "But who knows, really? She can't tell us how she feels."

"She must feel lonely," I said.

"Very, but she's such a joy."

Rose gurgled, and drool slid down the corners of her mouth.

"Oh, Rose!" Maizy cooed, plucking a handkerchief from her pocket. "My sweet baby," she whispered, leaning over and wiping off the saliva. "You're such a dear heart!" She patted the

172

spikelike strands of Rose's shorn black hair. "Such a sweetie," she said.

Staring at those black bristles, that idiot smile, and that fresh spittle, I was filled with pity and revulsion. I'm not like her, I thought. I'm not one of them. "No," I said, scuttling back, "I don't want to meet anyone!" And with these words I turned and ran out the door, down the hallway toward my room, with the number 13 scrawled ominously in red across the top.

"I thought you might like some supper," Maizy said, entering before I could answer. "Is it okay if I put the tray here?" she asked, nodding at the nightstand. Two hours had passed, and I was hungry. So I shrugged, and she put down the tray. "May I sit down?" she asked. I shrugged again, and she sat beside me on the edge of the bed. "I know you're scared," she said, looking down.

I shifted my weight to my left side, and the mattress springs squeaked beneath me, but I didn't say a word. In the space of two hours, I had already vomited forth every tic, jerk, and croak that had been rumbling inside me.

"No one is going to hurt you," she said. "We just want to help."

I lowered my head.

"Every child here is different," she continued. "No one is better than anyone else. Do you understand?"

I could feel my face turning red.

"I understand why Rose frightened you. She looks strange. But after a while she'll grow on you, and you'll come to love her. Mark my words, you'll learn to love her as much as I do. I know you, Icy Gal!"

My body jumped, the mattress groaned loudly. "Where did you hear that?" I asked.

"What?" she asked, crinkling her eyebrows.

"I-Icy G-Gal," I stuttered.

"I just came up with it," she said spryly. "Why? Don't you like it?"

"I . . . I . . . I guess so," I said. Then, breathing in deeply, I regained my composure, smiling ever so slightly.

Maizy stood up. "How about some food?" she asked, pointing at the nightstand. "You can eat in here tonight, but tomorrow you gotta eat with the others."

It was not until she slid the nightstand in front of me that I looked at the tray and saw the meal — a shriveled brown hot dog on a bun, a bag of peanuts, a thumb-sized dill pickle, a chocolate cupcake so dried out that the frosting had lost its gloss, and a small glass of milk.

Chapter 16

A noisy banging woke me. My eyes flipped open, and my body snapped upright.

"Rise and shine!" a high, nasal voice announced loudly. "It's time to get up!"

Rubbing my face, I looked frantically around the room. That red, white, and blue rocker wasn't mine. My heart began to pound. The fluffy blue rug didn't belong to me. I bit my bottom lip. Matanni hadn't sewn those curtains. She would never buy such silly-looking material. Bewildered, I touched my eyes.

"Hey, in there! Do you hear me?" the nasal voice said.

I slid off the edge of the bed, spotted my suitcases in the far corner of the room, and finally realized where I was. "Yes, ma'am," I said wearily.

"The bathroom's down the hall," the voice said. "Grab some clothes, go take a shower, and get dressed. Breakfast will be served in the dining room. Got it?"

"Yes, ma'am," I yelled back.

"Yessir," the voice demanded.

I was silent.

"Yessir," the testy voice repeated.

I didn't make a sound.

"Yessir," the voice demanded again. "I'm a he, not a she."

Anxiety tickled my throat. "Yessir," I stammered. "I heard you, sir. Grab some clothes, go take a shower, and get dressed."

"That's more like it, Icy Sparks," the voice said. "From Ginseng to Sunshine. From schoolgirl to inmate. Your life is changing."

"Yessir," I replied vigorously.

"Icy Sparks," the voice continued, "do you realize that you've hit the jackpot, won the lottery, caught the big one? Icy Sparks . . ."

"Yessir," I said.

"The big time. The big house," the voice said.

"Yessir," I answered, confused.

"Grab some clothes, go take a shower, and get dressed," the voice said. "The boss wants to see you."

"Delbert," another voice yelled, "get a move on it! We need some help with breakfast."

"I gotta go," Delbert said. "Wilma calls. You're on your own."

My thoughts rushed from my brain, scrambled down my neck, skimmed through my fingertips, and sloshed inside my stomach. Then they raced toward my hips and sprinted into my feet. My head felt fuzzy, and my toes trembled. For the life of me, I couldn't understand what had just been said to me or what I was supposed to do. Dazed, I meandered over to the little pink dresser and slipped open the top drawer. I reached for a pair of cotton panties, walked over to the closet, snatched the nearest hanger, upon which was draped a yellow-flowered dress, and headed for the bathroom.

I was alone. Matanni couldn't braid my hair or button the back of my dress. So the top two buttons were left undone. She couldn't pinch my cheeks to give them color. So my skin was parchment pale. She couldn't kiss me to give me courage. So I shuddered when I entered the dayroom and saw the odd group of children who lived here with me.

Maizy Hurley was hovering over an adolescent girl with chalk-white skin and empty blue eyes. Through her wispy thin hair, I could see patches of dull white scalp. Her large mouth was contorted, stretching from one side of her face to the other, yet her expression was both angry and vacant. Gripping a spoon filled with oatmeal, Maizy slowly brought it to the girl's mouth, which at once opened wide, revealing four sharply chiseled teeth, two at the top and two at the bottom, and a mass of bright pink gums.

"The Mouth ain't gonna eat real food," a fat woman at the other end of the table said. "The Mouth wants skin and bone."

"Her name is Mary," Maizy Hurley said through clenched teeth. "I wish you'd call her by her Christian name."

"I don't give a hoot what you wish," the woman said. "You're just an aide, no better than the rest of us."

"Everyone deserves some respect," Maizy said, glancing up and spotting me near the doorway. "Icy," she said, "this is Mary. She lives in Room Nine."

With her mouth opened wildly, oatmeal spread over her gums like paste, Mary lunged forward, spewing her breakfast all over the table.

"Hel-l-lo," I stuttered, hopping back.

Maizy anchored a hand on Mary's shoulder and pressed down. "Come on in, Icy," Maizy said, leaning forward. "Grab a chair!" She pointed to an empty chair at the end of the table. "Sit down and eat some breakfast." Maizy paused as Mary began to bellow, her pink gums vibrating. "You've got to see Dr. Conroy at nine."

"Yes, ma'am," I said, cautiously inching forward and sitting down.

"Wilma," Maizy said, turning toward the fat woman. "This is our new girl, Icy Sparks."

"Howdy," Wilma snorted.

Staring at Wilma's face, round and puffy, punctuated by two black eyes that raced back and forth like cockroaches beneath thick lenses, I suddenly realized that I was looking at the ugliest face on earth. Tiny pimples covered her skin, and a dull pink scar zigzagged over her right cheek. Black, oily, stringy hair fell limply against her shoulders. A dark, bushy mustache thrived above her lip; but, for all of her hair, she strangely had no eyebrows. If I hadn't heard her name and eyed her closely, spotting breasts that hung down like bags of corn feed, I would have taken Wilma for William.

"Hello," I said, picking up a sweet roll.

"Tiny's bathing Stevie," Wilma sneered. "He had another b.m. He ain't been here but one week and already I've smelled enough of his shit to last me a lifetime." Wilma headed toward Rose, who was awkwardly strapped into a wheelchair. "You need to mark it on his chart. From the stink, you could tell what he ate last night. No more hot dogs for him."

"Rose needs to finish her milk," Maizy said. "I've already fed her a big bowl of oatmeal."

"Anything for Rose," Wilma said. "Anything for your precious Drooler."

"Please, Wilma!" Maizy's voice was tired. "At least not in front of me."

I looked at the sweet roll in my hand and reluctantly took a bite. It was stale and tough. Chewing, I turned to look at Maizy, who was still spooning mouthfuls of oatmeal between Mary's lips. After each gulp, the girl howled and her mouth stretched open. I swallowed — whole — the lump of roll and tried to take another bite, but my stomach heaved, and I couldn't. Immediately Miss Emily popped into my mind. She'd lose weight here, I thought. No way she could eat three dozen of these. Picking up my napkin, I spit out the mouthful of roll. In my mind's eye, I saw Matanni's buttermilk biscuits with thin slices of country ham sandwiched between each one. Right now she'd be sipping another cup of coffee. Patanni would be in the barn milking the cows, talking sweetly to them like members of the family.

"Where's Delbert?" Maizy asked.

Wilma grimaced, and I marveled how someone that ugly could make an even uglier face.

"He's taking the others to music," Wilma said.

"Oh, yes," Maizy said. "I forgot about music therapy this month."

" 'Cause you're too busy finding fault," Wilma snapped.

Maizy's jaw tightened. She wiped Mary's face, grabbed her firmly by the forearm, and led her over to the sofa, where she sat her down. "Are you finished?" she asked, glancing over at me, smiling.

"Almost," I said, downing my milk.

"Well, come on," Maizy said. "Dr. Conroy is waiting for you."

I pushed back my chair and stood up, tottering a little to the left, grabbing the top of the table for support. Then I steadied myself, inhaled deeply, and said, "Okay, I'm ready now."

Dr. Conroy's office was tidy. Never before had I seen such a neat room — a place for everything, everything in its place. Even after I had color coordinated all of the items inside my supply room at school, it hadn't been as trim as

Dr. Conroy's office. Such orderliness left me feeling both impressed and afraid. Papers were stacked in little piles and placed inside wire baskets. Red pencils stood in a red plastic container that had PENCILS written across the front. A wire bin labeled IN sat on a metal shelf beside the desk. Another labeled OUT sat next to it. A bookcase filled with textbooks covered one wall. One shelf, I noticed, held books with titles like *Behavior Difficulties of Children*, *Early Infantile Autism*, *Child Development*, *Journal of Mental Deficiency*, and many more titles with strange words printed on their spines. Along the middle shelf were twenty volumes all with the same name, *American Journal of Orthopsychiatry*. Manuals on policy and procedures lined the two bottom shelves.

"Dr. Conroy, this is Icy Sparks," Maizy said.

Jittery, I turned my eyes toward Dr. Conroy and stepped forward.

"So nice to meet you, Icy," the doctor said, reaching out, taking my hand, and shaking it.

Like her office, Dr. Conroy was efficient-looking in her white doctor's jacket, compact and tidy. My eyes traveled downward, spotting slim hips and Lana Turner legs.

"Have a seat," she said, stroking the back of a wooden chair with her well-groomed hands. "Give me half an hour. Would you, Maizy?"

"I'll be back at nine-thirty," Maizy answered, and slipped out the door.

I sat down hesitantly. When I scooted back,

my feet wouldn't touch the floor, so I slumped against the chair's spine, maneuvering myself until my feet were situated on the carpet.

"How do you like it here?" Dr. Conroy asked, walking primly behind me.

"Just fine," I muttered.

"Are you sure?" she asked.

"Yes, ma'am," I answered woodenly.

"Uh-huh," she said, touching the back of my dress. "You didn't fasten your two top buttons."

I didn't say anything.

"You must remember to button up and sit up," she said, making no effort to fix my dress.

Immediately I jerked upright, my feet dangling.

"And your hair's a mess," she continued. "Did you braid it yourself?"

I nodded the way a person stutters.

"Still, though, your hair's pretty," she went on. "Like pure gold." She walked around the chair and stopped right in front of me. "Now, what color are your eyes?" she asked, leaning over, studying my face.

I held back for a second; then, before she could answer her own question, I murmured, "Yellow ocher."

"That's an odd thing to say," she said, propping her finger beneath my chin, lifting up my head. "But you're absolutely right! They're yellow ocher."

"And my hair's the color of goldenrod," I added.

182

"Yes, of course it is," Dr. Conroy said. "But where did you hear that?"

"Matanni told me," I said.

"Oh, yes, we met yesterday."

"She's my granny," I said. "She told me all about when I was born. She said that my mama was the one who turned me so yellow. When she was carrying me, she ate a whole bunch of little green crab apples. She ate oodles of them, and they made her sick."

"Crab apples?" Dr. Conroy scrunched up her forehead. "I don't understand."

I began to relax a little. "My little stomach had to digest that sour fruit," I explained. "My baby self had to take it in and grow. Matanni said that by the time I was born, I was so full of kick I burped like a bubble popping. The midwife slapped my bottom, and I croaked so loud she turned around, expecting to see the famous bullfrog from Sweetwater Lake. 'Cold as the bottom of Icy Creek,' she said, as she put me on my mama's stomach. 'Icy,' my mama said, and — according to Matanni — the name Icy stuck."

Dr. Conroy smiled and nodded. "So that's how you got your name!" she exclaimed.

"Yes, ma'am," I said, "my mama named me, but two weeks later she died. Those crab apples killed her, turned her urine yellow, as yellow as my eyes."

For several minutes, Dr. Conroy remained totally quiet, staring at me but saying nothing.

Then she circled my chair and stood behind me, buttoning my dress and undoing my braids. Gently, her fingers combed through the tangled mess. "Would you like me to braid it?" she asked.

I nodded.

"How about French braids?" she said.

"I don't know what they are," I answered.

"Oh, they're beautiful," Dr. Conroy said. "Unique, just like you."

"Yes, ma'am," I replied. "French braids would be nice."

"French braids require a comb and a brush," she said. "Wait here. Will you be all right till I come back?"

"*Oui, madame,*" I said.

"Oh, you are a charmer," she said as she hurried to the door. "But when I come back, we've got to get down to business."

"Business?" I raised my voice, playing with the tip ends of my hair.

"Yes," she said solemnly. "I want you to tell me all about yourself. I want to know exactly how you feel."

I was trying to figure out exactly how I felt when after only a few minutes Dr. Conroy returned.

As she braided my hair, her slender fingers moved rapidly while she spoke. "Icy," she asked, "do you know why you're here?"

I lowered my eyelids and nodded.

"Don't move," she said, gently placing her

hand on top of my head. "Just talk to me. When you move, you mess the braids up. Now, let's try again. Why do you think you're here?"

" 'Cause I did things, said things, that upset my grandparents, Mr. Wooten, and probably Miss Emily, too."

"Mr. Wooten seemed nice," she said. "Do you like him?"

"Yes, ma'am," I said, "and that makes it even worse. I spoke something horrible to him and jabbed him with my elbows when all he was trying to do was help."

"Why did you do that?" she asked me.

"He was ruining everything," I said. "Making a mess of my room at school."

Dr. Conroy's voice was calm. "Well, Mr. Wooten spoke highly of you," she said. "It was obvious how fond he is of you."

"I don't know how," I muttered, "not after the way I've carried on."

"Love doesn't just stop," Dr. Conroy said, gently grabbing a loose strand of hair and bringing it behind my ear. "Who's Miss Emily?" she asked.

"She was my best friend."

"You sound sad, Icy. Why's that? You'll be playing with her again soon."

"If she's not too busy working," I replied.

Instantly, her fingers stopped moving. "Working?" Dr. Conroy said. "How old is this friend of yours?"

"She's a grown-up," I said.

"A grown-up," Dr. Conroy echoed. "Well, then, where does she work?"

"At Tanner's Feed Supply," I explained. "When her parents died, they left it to her."

"Uh-huh," Dr. Conroy murmured, her fingers stirring again. "And what do you like about Miss Emily?"

"I like her 'cause she's fun and smart," I said. "We have tea parties together, and sometimes she reads to me."

"And did she teach you French?" Dr. Conroy asked.

"No," I said, at first shaking my head, then vigorously nodding it. "Miss Gigi teaches me French, but then Miss Gigi is really Miss Emily."

Dr. Conroy laughed. "Hold on!" she said. "You lost me."

"Miss Emily's real funny," I said. "She can throw her voice. Like when a dummy speaks," I mumbled, trying to talk with my lips closed.

"Icy, I didn't understand one word of what you just said."

"She's a ventriquoliss," I said clearly, "like that Charlie McCarthy."

"No, like Edgar Bergen," corrected Dr. Conroy. "He's the ventriloquist. The dummy's the other one."

"Well, it don't matter anyhow," I said, exasperated, " 'cause Miss Emily doesn't use wooden dolls, just stuffed animals."

Dr. Conroy reached around me and with her fingers tenderly brushed my bangs to one side.

"You're lucky to have Miss Emily for a friend," she said.

"I ain't seen her for a long time," I said softly. "I hope she still likes me."

"Oh, she does," Dr. Conroy reassured me. "She wouldn't give up on you. She seems way too nice for that."

"And it don't matter that she weighs a lot," I added.

"Of course not," Dr. Conroy said.

" 'Cause a person might weigh a lot but that don't make her bad," I asserted. "I mean, she stays the same inside."

"That's right!"

"And, truth is, a fat person won't really crush you if she hugs you," I said, nodding. "That's just gossip and lies."

"Lies, huh?" Dr. Conroy said, tugging at my hair.

"Yes, ma'am," I said eagerly, "people in small towns tell tall tales. I guess 'cause there ain't nothing better to do."

"Oh, I see," Dr. Conroy said. "And do you think they lie about you?" she asked, combing the tip end of a braid.

I thought for a second. "I reckon," I murmured. "They probably tell a whole pack of lies on me."

"Like what?" she asked.

"Oh, I don't know," I said, mumbling again. "That me and Miss Emily are strange. Strange like Cousin Acorn." I lifted my eyebrows, slightly parted my lips, and felt the question fall off my tongue. "Are different people scary?"

"Are you talking about yourself, Icy? Or about Miss Emily?" Dr. Conroy asked, plaiting the other handful of hair. "And who is Cousin Acorn?"

I nervously glanced down at my fingers, which fluttered against my thighs. "Cousin Acorn?" I said. "Oh, she don't matter. But now, take a look at Rose, that girl on the mat out there," I continued. "Who would ever want to be her friend? And that one with the big mouth and pink gums."

"Mary," Dr. Conroy said.

"Yes, that one," I said. "Just looking at those sharp teeth of hers freezes my blood."

"Uh-huh," Dr. Conroy said. "I can understand how you might feel that way."

"Well, they're a part of God's creation, too," I said. "God made them. 'Here they are,' He said to the world, then He up and leaves." Hunching over, I hiked up my knees and wrapped my arms around them. "He's the only one who knows what's good in them, but He doesn't stick around. He doesn't say to folk, 'Rose is a good girl. Give her a chance.' No, ma'am, all He does is step back and watch the show."

"God works in mysterious ways," Dr. Conroy said. "Rose has Maizy for a friend."

"But Maizy works here," I disagreed. "She's just doing her job."

Dr. Conroy pulled on the other braid. "So

you're saying if you're different, nobody will like you."

"It's a whole bunch of strikes against you," I said.

"Well," she said, tugging gently on both braids. She went over to her desk drawer and pulled out her purse. "If you don't mind my saying so," she said, walking over with a compact in her hand, "right now you look really different, and right now I like you very much." She flipped open the compact and held it up to my face. "Well, what do you think?" she asked, her eyes dancing.

Letting go of my knees, I rocked forward and planted my feet on the floor. "Oh, it's nice," I said, grinning.

"Well, I just work here, too," she said, before smiling back.

Chapter 17

"You look like a movie star," Maizy had said when I stepped out of Dr. Conroy's office. But when we walked into the dayroom, Wilma — the only one there besides us — sneered at me, licked the mustache above her lip, and walked over to the far side of the room. I was disappointed that no one else would see me and comment on how good I looked. After all, Dr. Conroy was right. The French braids were different. Accentuated by two gold ribbons, the plaits of hair, pulled tightly back, gave me a worldly, unique face.

"Where is everybody?" I asked, looking around.

"Resting in their rooms," Maizy explained.

"Oh," I said, fingering the ends of my braids.

"Why don't you visit Rose?" Maizy suggested. "She'd love to see your new hairdo."

I shook my head. "Oh, no!" I said. "She's probably sleeping."

"If I know Rose," Maizy said, "she's lying in her bed with her eyes wide open, just waiting for someone to visit."

"I don't know," I hedged. "I'm kind of tired."

"Go talk to her," Maizy insisted. "She'd love to see you."

"Knock it off!" Wilma cried. "Clean out your ears! She don't want to talk to that tangled mass of muscle and bone."

"She does, too!" Maizy yelled back. "She just doesn't know it yet."

"She don't!" Wilma bellowed. "If you don't let her be, she'll end up hating you both. Do you hear me?"

Maizy grabbed my hands. "You want to visit with Rose, now, don't you, Icy?"

I looked into her eyes, pleading and earnest, and thought about the loneliness of being different. "Yes, ma'am," I caved in, staring right at Wilma. "I ain't as tired as I thought I was."

"Good! I knew it!" Maizy tossed back her blond curls; her blue eyes sparkled. "Did you hear that, Wilma? Did you hear what Icy said?"

Wilma fumed. "I heard what you — Miss Goody Two Shoes — forced out of her."

Maizy held out her hand. "Come with me, Icy Gal," she said, waggling her fingertips. "I'll take you to her room."

The door to Rose's room was painted dark blue with the number, 8, painted in red above the doorknob. Inside, Rose was dressed in a long green T-shirt and was lying on her back in a large white crib. As I drew near, I noticed that Maizy was right: her eyes were wide open.

"I'll come back in ten minutes," Maizy said. "That'll give you some time to get acquainted."

191

"B-but . . ." I stammered.

"No buts," Maizy said. "She doesn't bite." And with these words, Maizy was gone.

I sucked in air; it tickled my lips. "What are you thinking?" I whispered, inching forward. From two feet away, I tried to find an answer in Rose's face but saw none. "Does it hurt?" I asked, coming closer. "Blink your eyes if it does."

Neither eyelid flickered.

"Speak to me," I begged. "Tell me something."

Rose shut both eyes and groaned loudly.

I pushed myself against the wooden slats of her oversized crib, lifted up on my toes, my head above the railing, and asked, "What is it?"

Rose groaned again; her eyes snapped open.

"I know it hurts." I leaned over and rubbed the inside of her arm. "I wish I could make it go away." My hand rested on her shoulder.

Rose gurgled; her eyes watered.

"Don't be sad!" I said, caressing her skin. "I'm going to be your new friend." I felt the warm flush of embarrassment, cleared my throat, and chanced, "But only if you want me to."

Rose blinked once.

"Does that mean you like me?" I asked.

She blinked again.

"You do," I said. "Even after the way I acted!"

Rose blinked a third time and smiled broadly. Her front teeth — small white kernels of hominy, all of them the same size — gleamed.

"You've got a nice face," I said eagerly, "a sweet smile." When I brushed my fingertips over her lips, she began to laugh.

"Sometimes I do weird things." I was laughing with her. "Sometimes I croak like a frog." I stretched back my neck and croaked. She laughed even louder — so loud, in fact, that her body vibrated and shook the bed. "Sometimes I jerk and jerk and can't stop myself, no matter how hard I try." I contorted my body and made it jerk to the left. "I acted so bad that Mr. Wooten — the principal of my school — asked my grandparents to bring me here. He's my friend, so I don't hold none of this against him." I looked deep into her eyes. "I reckon I got a touch of pokeweed inside me, the poison parts, the roots and berries. People like Mr. Wooten don't have to worry about pokeweed. They're too good." I licked my top lip. "But for the likes of me, it's different. This poison builds up, gets stronger and stronger, until it has to get out. If it don't, it'll eat me up. It'll eat away my good parts, the leaves and stems, and only the bad parts will be left. And I'll be just like Mamie Tillman. My spirit will up and disappear, and only the shell of me will be left behind. So I have to let this poison out. A jerk here. A croak there. A cuss word. A nasty thought. Do you understand?"

Rose rolled her head from side to side, flickering her eyelids. All the while, drool dribbled from the corners of her mouth.

"I thought maybe you might," I said. "You see, we ain't so far apart. I'm different just like you."

Rose moaned.

I groaned back.

She moaned again.

I did the same.

She cackled.

I cackled.

Her dark eyes zoomed back and forth.

I leaned way over the railing. My eyes shot back and forth.

Saliva rolled down her bottom lip.

I gathered up saliva and spit it over my lip.

Rose grinned.

I grinned back.

Then Rose did something incredible. The bedsprings started to creak, and, jerking and sliding across the mattress, she plopped herself at the edge of the crib, much closer to me. Alarmed, I jumped back, stared at her twisted, quivering limbs, and knew, in that instant, that she had deliberately willed her way toward me. Once more, I carefully thrust my arm through the wooden slats and trailed my fingers along her leg. Her eyes grew dark with excitement. She trembled and squealed with delight. "Maizy's right," I said. "You're a sweetie." We smiled silently at each other for what seemed a long time.

"Icy Gal, you need to get some rest now," Maizy said from the hallway. "I'll call you when lunch is ready."

"Bye-bye," I whispered, and blew Rose a kiss. "I'll come back real soon."

Just a few feet from Rose's room, I heard a voice. Loud and gruff, it rumbled from Room 7 and stopped me in my tracks.

"Wilma," the voice said emphatically. "Wilma. Wilma. Wilma."

I peered around the doorway.

Wilma, her mouth distorted and her face red, was standing over a curled-up young girl, the one on the playground that first day, the one with the Brillo pad hair. "*Wil*-ma," Wilma said, stressing the first syllable. "Wil-*ma*," she said, accenting the second. "Wilma. Wilma. Wilma. Wilma," she spat out. "I'm gonna change it. Awful, ain't it?" Fervidly nodding at the young girl, Wilma pried open her balled-up body, unfastened two safety pins, and removed a soiled diaper. "You're a stupid lump," she continued, reaching for a clean diaper. "A stupid lump of shit." She yanked the left corner of the fresh diaper over the girl's hip. "Deirdre," she said, piercing the cloth with a safety pin. "Deirdre, such a pretty name!" she went on, her hand slipping, the pin jabbing the girl's skin.

Deirdre's head popped up like a turtle's, and for the first time I saw her face — blandly registering no discomfort.

"Look at you!" Wilma growled, surveying her charge. "A stupid lump with a pretty name! It ain't fair, I tell you! You get room and board. A cushy life. Ain't a worry in your head." She pulled a T-shirt down over the girl's head, flattening her brushy hair. "All you retards are lucky," she said, the T-shirt in place, the curls shooting out again like bedsprings. Wilma ran her hands through her own dark, stringy hair and grimaced. "Ignorance is bliss!" she pronounced, lifting up the girl, dropping her like a sack of onions into a wheelchair. "Let's brush our teeth," she said, pushing the wheelchair through another door, a private entrance to the girls' communal bathroom.

For several minutes, my hands perspired and my heart fluttered so much that I couldn't move. Then, despite my fear, I wiped my hands on my dress, sucked in my stomach, threw back my shoulders, and cautiously crept into the bedroom. At the bathroom door, I peeked inside.

Standing behind the wheelchair, which stood in front of a sink, Wilma was spreading toothpaste on a green hairbrush. With one fat hand, she grabbed a fistful of the girl's hair, snatched back her head — causing her body, like a noisemaker, to unroll — then forced the thick bristles through her tightly closed lips. "Back and forth. Back and forth," Wilma said, whipping the brush from one side of her mouth to the other. "Back and forth. Back and forth. Even you can grip this. Now you try!" she said, trying to insert the hairbrush into the girl's clenched fist. But rather than take it, Deirdre — once more — snapped shut into a ball. "Try, you idiot!" Wilma yelled, uncoiling her, prizing open her fingers, shoving the brush into her crab-claw hand.

Immediately Deirdre turned her hand over, smearing a path of toothpaste down her T-shirt.

"Stupid shit!" Wilma shouted, smacking the brush from her hand, sending it flying against the yellow-tiled wall.

Again, Deirdre rolled up. Like a caterpillar, she curled into a tight knot.

"Stupid!" Wilma leaned over and turned on the faucet. "Stupid! Stupid! Stupid!" she screamed, cupping up water, tossing it upon Deirdre's back.

Mesmerized, I held in my breath and watched Deirdre, folding up tighter and tighter, burying her head, hiding her hair, until I could tolerate the sight no longer. Then, unable to control myself, I noisily whipped around, scurried back through the bedroom, and bolted out the door. "Maizy!" I said, running toward the end of the hallway where she stood with her back to me. "Maizy!" I repeated, rushing to her, throwing my arms around her waist when she turned around.

Gently, she pushed me back. "What is it?" she said, looking intently into my eyes.

But just as I was about to blurt out everything, I saw Wilma in my mind's eye. Grinning strangely, she stood over me with a hairbrush in her hand. So I took one short breath and lied, "Nothing, Maizy. I missed you, that's all." Then, swallowing my knot of fear, I ran to my room.

"Feeding time for the kiddies," Wilma said.

Through shuffling noises, the clanking of metal against metal, the squeaking cries of wheelchairs, the irritated voices of the staff, the bellows and groans of the patients, I heard every word Wilma said. Even though I was sitting at a table far away from her, I heard her mean voice. Lately, it seemed, meanness followed me. At Ginseng Elementary, meanness had introduced itself in Mrs. Stilton's smile, in the way her Adam's apple quivered when she sang, in the swing of her Ping-Pong paddle against my hands. Here, at Bluegrass State Hospital, sound waves from Wilma's mouth carried meanness. Meanness, I reckoned, was more forceful than kindness. It had a mind of its own.

Immediately I recognized the high, nasal voice from earlier in the morning. It was Delbert's. "Hush your mouth, Wilma!" he said, standing near the side door, wiping off a table. "We're getting sick and tired of your comments."

"Oh, I'm so scared!" Wilma snickered, shimmying all over. "Big, bad, manly Delbert Franklin is gonna get me."

"The devil's already got hold of you," he said. "He's right there in your ugly face and in your nasty voice."

"Shucks!" Wilma said, making a face, holding out her fingers, making them tremble.

Just then, the side door opened as two members of the kitchen staff rolled in stacks of trays on platforms. Maizy had said they drove over in a van from Hickory Hall, where all the meals for Bluegrass State Hospital were prepared. From the back of a van, the food was wheeled down a ramp through our kitchen's back door. The small kitchen, which was kept locked most of the time, had a big gray refrigerator the size of our toolshed, and a little bitty stove. Fruit juices, milk, ice cream, cereals, and snacks could be found there. Meals that had earlier gone uneaten could also be warmed up. But mostly the kitchen housed the carts during mealtimes. I sniffed the air. The acrid odor of vinegar-washed tables mixed with the smell of overcooked ground beef.

"Gordie's having problems today." Delbert spoke to Maizy, who had come in with the carts. She was standing beside him, reading the labels on the sides of trays. "More problems than usual. He's butted me twice already. Almost knocked me out."

"I'll keep an eye on him," Maizy said, coming toward me. "Icy, I think you'll like lunch today," she said, placing the food in front of me.

A hamburger, gray-colored as if it had been boiling in water for hours, an ice cream scoop of lumpy mashed potatoes, a thin, shriveled pickle, and two old candy canes, probably left over from last Christmas, stared up at me.

"Good, huh?" Maizy asked.

I eyed her and shrugged my shoulders, wondering how on earth she thought this meal was good, but her wafer-thin body gave her away;

not once in her life had she eaten good-tasting food. Closing my eyes, I imagined Matanni and Patanni spooning up soup at the kitchen table. During the winter, Matanni made different kinds of soup each week. This week, she would be fixing butternut squash and apple cider soup. The apple cider was made from the tart Winesaps that grew behind our house. She'd measure out three cups of homemade cider then two cups of Essie's whole cream. Then she'd add them to the bubbling, cooked squash. After which she'd plop in three dollops of butter. When the bowls were filled, Patanni would urgently bring his spoon toward him, dribbling soup down the front of his shirt. Matanni, on the other hand, would leisurely dip her spoon away from her. Her mama, she always said, had taught her manners. Sitting in front of this lump of gray meat clumped between two pieces of starchy white bread, I longed for my grandmother, for the steamy mist that clouded my face as I brought a spoonful of her soup to my mouth, for that warm heavy feeling in my stomach after I finished it.

"You're not a real kid," Maizy's voice interrupted my reverie. "All children like hamburgers."

"Come this way," Delbert ordered, clutching a boy's hand — the large, big-boned boy whom I had seen marching in the yard when I first arrived. With his crew-cut, jutting jaw, and seedy black eyes, he appeared older than the rest of us, fifteen maybe. His shoulders rippling like

200

plowed furrows, the boy strutted across the floor, following Delbert.

"Gordie, sit here," the aide said, patting the top of the table. "See how clean it is."

"Did Gordie go crazy when the music started?" asked a large man in a white uniform from several feet away.

"Naw, Tiny. He was just fine," Delbert answered, steering Gordie to his spot at the table. "He didn't butt nobody or nothing. Just me afterwards."

I stared at Tiny — six feet tall, barrel-chested, and potbellied — and wondered how he got his name.

"That's good," Tiny said. "We're making progress."

Gordie sat down rigidly, his spine pressed against the back of the chair. Carefully, he unfolded his napkin, placed it over his knees, and stared, steely-eyed, in front of him. Then a muscle in his face twitched, and the eerie flicker of a smile passed over his mouth.

Now, leaning against a sofa, Tiny nodded knowingly at Delbert, who, in turn, nodded back. I sat up in my chair and looked at the three of them.

"Look at him, Tiny. He's obsessed with Ruthie's forehead." Delbert pointed at a pretty teenage girl, around thirteen, sitting at the end of the table. "I'll be relieved when her transfer comes through."

I turned my gaze to the girl, whose hair was

cut short and curled under like the pictures Miss Emily had shown me of bobbed hair in the Roaring Twenties. She gripped a large spoon in her left hand, mechanically scooped up a mound of mashed potatoes, and shoveled it between her full, pink lips. Yet, even before she swallowed it, she was dipping her spoon into the potatoes again. Gordie, I noticed, was following the spoon's metallic glitter as it traveled from the potatoes to her mouth. Back and forth. Back and forth. Whenever she swallowed, his mouth, opening and closing like a fish's, mimicked hers. Potatoes oozed from the sides of her lips. They were smeared like paste down her chin. Watching her, Gordie glared.

"He's studying her," Delbert said, slowly lifting up the tray. "I'm moving him over there" — he pointed with his little finger at a card table set up in the far right-hand corner of the room.

"That's why I set it up," Tiny said, winking. "Lately he's been going after Ruthie."

Delbert had turned toward Tiny and was turning back to grab Gordie's arm when suddenly the boy jumped up, squared his shoulders, and charged like a bull over the top of the table in a beeline toward Ruthie's forehead.

"Gordie!" Delbert yelled, lunging for him.

But it was too late. With one loud *pow,* Gordie's forehead had already slammed into hers. Like a rubber band popping, she snapped back in her chair. "Owwooooo!" she bellowed, springing forward, pounding the table with her fists. "Owwooooo!" she cried, flipping her plate, mashed potatoes like miniature parachutes falling to the floor.

Frantic, Delbert surged forward, casting his arms like a net way over the table and stopping Gordie's head — which was poised to butt again.

"Gordie!" Tiny skimmed across the polished floor and grabbed the boy's arms from behind. "Cut it out!"

"Owwooooo!" Ruthie cried, before leaning to one side and yanking out a handful of Deirdre's hair.

"Ruthie, no!" Maizy said, dashing over, wrapping her arms around Ruthie's shoulders.

Deirdre remained balled up and silent.

Gordie snorted and pushed against the table. The table rattled forward. All the while, Tiny and Delbert, sandwiched together, were pulling back. Tiny had locked both arms around Gordie's chest. Delbert was now holding on to Tiny's arms.

"Restraints!" Tiny hollered.

"Restraints!" Delbert repeated, his sandy-colored hair plastered over his forehead.

Maizy, still holding on to Ruthie, nodded at Wilma, who, grinning, left the room.

"Thanks, Tiny!" Delbert said, releasing and extending one hand as Wilma returned, sauntering over with the leather restraints dangling from her fingertips.

"Here!" she said, and plunked them into Delbert's palm. "The Bull needs lassoing."

Chapter 18

The odd-looking girl with pink gums, the one Wilma called the Mouth, threw out her bandaged arms and violently lunged forward, unable to move. Howling, she tugged and pulled at a rope around her waist, the end of which was looped through a metal ring attached to a tree. Every so often, while leaning to the front, the rope trembling from the stress, she'd feverishly snap her gums, angrily bring her arm to her mouth, and bite into the thick white bandage.

"Delbert, come get Mary!" I heard Wilma scream, opening wide the door. "Take her back in, or she'll bite through an artery."

Disconcerted, I looked around. The boy who drew pictures was standing in one place next to the building, waving a piece of paper in front of his face. Ruthie, in braces, was hobbling toward the door. Before I saw Stevie, I smelled him, coming up behind me, reeking of excrement. I pinched my nostrils and pivoted. "Come on, Stevie," Tiny groaned, snatching his hand. "You, too. Back inside. You've messed your britches again."

"Maizy, where are those two girls?" I asked when we had finally settled down on a bench beneath the oak tree.

"What girls?" Maizy asked.

"The ones I saw when I arrived," I said. "With curly hair and plaid jumpers."

Maizy thought for a moment. "Oh, yes," she said, "them — the administrator's daughters. Sometimes they play here."

"They don't live here?" I asked.

"Oh, no, sweetie," she said. "They just visit."

Sighing, I stood up and wandered toward the swingsets, where the bird boy was swinging. Bored, I watched as he swished to and fro. When the swing flew back, he'd chirp, his blond hair flying around his head like down feathers. But the minute I came within two feet of him, he stretched out his long legs, plunged his feet into the ground, dirt swirling around his ankles, and came to a stop. I stared at his blond hair, aqua-blue eyes, and long, thin, graceful body; but he didn't look back. In fact, he turned his head away, averting his eyes.

"Reid!" Maizy said, walking over to where I stood. "I'm Miss Cockatoo from Sidney. Don't you recognize me?"

Reid, the bird boy, eased out of the swing, turned his head toward her, and clucked softly.

Perching on her toes, Maizy arched her back, waved her arms slowly, and made tiny guttural noises.

Reid responded, trilling softly.

"This is my new friend," Maizy said, motioning for me to step forward. "Her name is Icy. See the color of her hair?" With her fingers, Maizy fluffed out my hair. "She's a yellow bird."

Reid closed his eyelids, tilted his head to the left, and chirped.

"Reid. Reid. Reid," Maizy sang, creeping closer. "Don't be afraid," she cheeped. "You know me. Miss Cockatoo from Sidney." She inched next to him, extended her left arm, and touched the bottom of his shirt.

Instantly he flashed open his eyes, threw out his arms, and screeched wildly. With bent knees and rounded chest, he swooped around her, circling and circling, cawing and cawing, frenetically waving his arms.

Maizy raised her arms over her head and fluttered her fingers. "See?" she said soothingly. "I've got nothing. No restraints. Nothing."

Then, as quickly as he had begun, Reid stopped screeching. Instead, he raised his leg like a beautiful white heron and — with both arms flying gracefully by his sides — stood perfectly balanced. In this position, he perched and trilled for what seemed the longest time.

Maizy and I, both quiet and thoughtful, backed away from him and sat back down on the grass near the sandbox. Lulled by the moment, enjoying this rare warm December day, I looked at Maizy and, for the first time, really saw her. Blond-haired, blue-eyed, and delicate, she was beautiful. Petite, only five feet two inches tall, she weighed no more than ninety pounds. Like her frame, her hands were small and fragile. So paper-thin was her skin that I could see the dark, threadlike veins beneath. Her nose was tiny yet well defined. When she breathed, her nostrils trembled. Every so often, her eyelids would flutter; she'd seem to drift off. A daydreamer myself, I recognized the symptoms.

"You're daydreaming, aren't you?" I asked.

The muscles around her mouth twitched. She shook her head once and stared at me. "Yes," she answered, blinking her eyes. "I always daydream after lunch," she said. "Full stomach, I guess. How did you know?"

"My daddy was a great daydreamer," I said. "Famous throughout the county, and he passed it on to me."

"Mountain folk are accomplished daydreamers," she said. A faraway look came to her eyes. "I was born in the mountains, in a little town called Lollagag."

"A town of slowpokes." I giggled, clapping my hand over my mouth.

"Funny name, isn't it?" she said. "But I like Lollagag 'cause a person can't get lost there. She can't get lost in a place where everybody knows her mama and daddy, her mamaw and papaw, her aunts and uncles and cousins, her brothers and sisters. Where I was born people know me, and their knowing me makes me real. I'm known for more than just my name."

"It's the same in Poplar Holler," I said. "Except, sometimes, a person becomes known for all the wrong reasons."

But Maizy, with that distant look in her eyes, wasn't listening. "Last year," she said, "Mannie Comfrey, the old man who lives down the road from where I grew up, put up an electric fence. Not around his cow pasture, mind you, but around his house. Can you imagine it? An electric fence around your front yard? What for?"

I cleared my throat, ready to guess, but Maizy broke in.

"It's for keeping people out," she said. "Not for keeping cows in. These days, when I visit with Mannie — rocking on his wide front porch — I can hear that fence buzzing. The noise spins inside my ears, louder than the rocking, powerful like a swarm of angry yellow jackets. The voltage is set so high."

"Good night!" I said.

"Last summer," Maizy continued, "I accidently got caught in that fence of his. The hairs on my right leg sputtered. What I mean is, they sizzled like a match bursting into flame, curling around that wire." Maizy closed her eyes. "Even now, if I'm real quiet and concentrate real hard, I can hear that sizzling sound. I can feel the heat from that deep fire and smell my leg hair burning. It's a nasty, foul odor. The dear Lord sent me that electric fence. I reckon He wanted me to understand what cows go through. God does that, you know. He teaches you lessons."

"I know," I said. "Back home, He taught me a big lesson. He showed me something horrible at Little Turtle Pond. He wanted to see what I would do."

"What did God show you?" Maizy asked.

I opened wide my eyes and shook my head. "I can't tell you that," I said. "But Mamie Tillman sure knows what it is."

"Who's Mamie Tillman?" said Maizy.

"The one God chose to teach me," I said. "She's a strange one, all right! Ain't got nary a friend, living all by herself on that rough patch of land. All she ever done was wait on her daddy. Like a shadow, she was. Then he up and died and left her behind."

"Did you do what God wanted?" Maizy asked, opening her eyes and turning toward me.

"I failed." I shook my head. "No, I couldn't do what He wanted."

"We all fail sometimes." Maizy patted me on the shoulder. "Not one of us is perfect."

"I can't find nothing wrong with you," I said.

A sad smile passed over her face and she said, "That's because you don't really know me."

"I'm beginning to."

Suddenly Maizy laughed. "Then your standards must be real low," she said, shaking her head.

"I know one thing for sure." I boldly wagged my index finger in her face. "This here place is full of mistakes. A person could get dizzy sorting them out," I said. "If I had a mind to, I'd lick a label and stick it on everyone's forehead. One would say the Mouth. Another, the Drooler. Then there'd be Head Butt-er. Maybe even one saying Stupid Lump of Shit."

Maizy caught my finger, jerked it down, and in a serious voice said, "I know where you heard all those names but the last one. It's beyond awful. Now tell me! Where did you hear that?"

I coughed, snatching back my finger. "Which one?" I asked.

"Stupid Lump . . . Stupid Lump of, you know what!" she said sternly. "Who said it? I know you didn't make it up. You don't talk that way."

"How do you know how I talk?" I sassed.

"I just do," she snapped. "Come on. Out with it. Where did you hear those words?"

"I've got a foul mouth," I protested. "Go ask Mr. Wooten. He'll tell you the truth. Principals don't lie. He'll say I can cuss with the best of them."

"You don't fool me for one minute," Maizy said. "I know exactly why you're doing this."

"Shit. Damn. Hellfire," I spluttered.

"Stop it, Icy!" Maizy was trembling with fury. "I don't want you lying, belittling yourself for that mean old hag. I don't ever want that. Do you hear me?"

I clamped my lips together and barely nodded.

"Then tell me, this instant, who spoke those words?"

"I done told you," I said, turning my head away. "Those bad words are mine, all mine."

"Real, honest-to-goodness friends tell each other the truth," Maizy said.

"I ain't lying," I said.

"Okay," she said curtly, "have it your way. But, mark my words, the truth will out."

"Yes, ma'am," I muttered, and slumped away.

Back in my room, on my bed, surrounded by nursery rhyme characters, I thought about what Maizy had said and wondered what "truth would out." Would it be that part of me who longed to be like everyone else, who put on a mask each morning, secured it tightly, and masqueraded for acceptance? Would my secrets eventually pour out of me like water spilling from a broken pitcher? Would I start croaking and jerking until every head at Bluegrass State Hospital turned in my direction? I wondered what truth of mine would out.

Did I, Icy Sparks, consist of two truths — one, the pretty, delicate, golden-haired child; the other, the frog child from Icy Creek? If so, did everyone in this world have two truths, two sides — one, in view; the other, hidden? I asked myself these questions and thought about Reid, the bird boy. Did he have another side, too? What part lay beneath the flapping and chirping? Did he have boy thoughts, or were all his thoughts shaped by images of birds? And if we all had two parts, who was Rose? Was she only a mangled, tangled jumble of parts like the pieces of a jigsaw puzzle dumped upon the floor, or perhaps more? Could Wilma, seemingly so ugly, both inside and out, have another part? Did she have a hidden, sweet side? If so, where was it?

Alone in the silence of my room, I didn't know. I only knew that beneath the silence was the noise, the other part, veiled but as real as the scratching sounds of mice scurrying across the floor at night. Every living thing, I knew, had secrets — concealed and quiet — aching to be seen and heard. Crickets, covered in shadows, their legs contorting deep in the woods, chirped and gave their secrets away. Wildcats cried, mourning over something forbidden. Mamie Tillman had thrown her secret into Little Turtle Pond.

"Matanni always says each mama crow thinks her baby crow's the blackest," I said to Dr. Conroy after my afternoon rest. "What I mean is that she can never find fault with me. And Patanni's even worse. He tells anyone he sees that I'm the prettiest, smartest, sweetest girl in the mountains of Kentucky. To hear him, ain't no other child as good as me. When it comes to me, he ain't nothing but a Blow George."

"A Blow George?" Dr. Conroy asked.

"A boastful person," I explained. "A liar."

Dr. Conroy nodded.

"So it don't matter what they say," I resumed, " 'cause what they say can't be trusted."

"Do you trust what I say?" Dr. Conroy asked,

tapping a pencil against the ink blotter, from the chair behind her desk.

"The other day I did."

"What did you believe?" she asked.

"You said that French braids were unique, just like me."

"Yes."

"And when I saw those braids in the mirror, I believed you."

"Well, Icy." Dr. Conroy put down her pencil. "I have no reason to lie to you."

"You ain't my grandparents, if that's what you mean."

"Regardless, I don't lie," she said firmly. "I try to see things clearly."

"Never?" I said. "Not even a little white lie? Miss Emily says we all lie sometimes, especially when we don't want to hurt another person's feelings."

"Maybe once," she said, "maybe when I was a child, but I try not to. Not even little white lies. I always make an effort to tell the truth."

I lowered my head. "I can't say I always do," I said.

"Tell me about it," Dr. Conroy said.

"Well, once I called someone a big fat liar when I knew that I was the one lying."

"Why did you do that?" she asked.

" 'Cause he was making fun of me."

"How?" she asked.

"He said I had frog eyes, just like Peavy Lawson. He claimed he caught me behind Old

Man Potter's barn, popping out my eyes and jerking. So I called him a polecat and a slimy ole pickle. Got so mad I lied like a tied dog. Then I turned the whole thing around and called him a liar when, all along, I knew I was the one lying."

Dr. Conroy picked up the pencil again. "So you're saying you went behind a barn and popped out your eyes, just like he said you did."

I cleared my throat. "Yes, ma'am," I confessed, "and after that, I dumped my Coke all over his head."

"Coke all over his head?"

"Uh-huh," I mumbled.

Dr. Conroy leaned forward. "Icy," she said, studying me, "why did you feel you had to lie? What's so horrible about popping out your eyes?" She was waving the pencil back and forth, her eyes fixed on mine.

I couldn't answer.

"Sometimes, when I get excited, I pop out my eyes," she said. "Sometimes, when my bones ache, I crack my knuckles. Not very ladylike, is it?"

"But you don't do what I do."

"And what do you do, Icy? I really don't understand what you do." She took aim and pointed the pencil right between my eyes. "You can tell me the truth."

"I . . . I . . ."

"Come on," she urged. "Tell me."

"I . . . I . . . I can act mean," I blurted. "Sometimes I'm mean as a striped snake."

"Explain!" she said, the pencil still pointed at me.

"One part of me is mean," I spat out. "Another part is sweet. The trouble is, I don't know which part is biggest, the mean or the sweet."

"How do you act when the mean part is biggest?" Dr. Conroy asked. "When that striped snake takes over?"

"I pop out my eyes, like Joel McRoy seen me do." I looked right at the lead in that pencil of hers. "I jerk and twitch all over. My arms fly out. Ugly thoughts race through my brain. And sometimes I cuss a blue streak. I say words I didn't even know I knew."

Dr. Conroy straightened up. "Icy, can you tell me why you get so upset?" she asked, calmly returning the pencil to her desktop.

"I don't know," I said, nibbling at my lower lip. "I don't want to be bad. But if I don't let some of the badness out, I'll just explode. That's what I did with Mr. Wooten. I let some of the badness out. And when I did, I scared him. What I'm saying is I'm kinda like Matanni's teakettle. I gotta perk, a little bit at a time, or else I'll spew hot water all over the place."

"That must frighten you?" she asked.

"What?"

"Waiting all the time for that big explosion," she said. "Not knowing when it will come."

"Yes, ma'am," I answered. "I tried being neat and tidy 'cause that's how I wanted my mind to be. I cleaned up that supply room like it really belonged to me."

"Supply room?" she said softly.

"Yes, ma'am," I said. "After I acted up, Mrs. Stilton, my teacher, didn't want me in her room, so Mr. Wooten made the supply room mine. It had a chalkboard, books, and everything, and I could do with it as I pleased. So I got it in order. The oranges with the oranges. The reds with the reds. But I found out that my way of ordering wasn't a bit like his."

"And that made you mad?"

"Mad as a hornet," I said. "When he tried to change back my room, I took a big fit, jabbed him with my elbows, and cussed him like a sailor." I lowered my voice. "I'm scared of the poison parts inside me. The roots and berries. They could get a person hurt."

"What do you mean?" she asked, leaning slightly forward.

"Pokeweed," I explained. "If you eat the leaves and stems, you'll be eating poor man's asparagus. But if you eat the roots and berries, you'll be eating poison. Me and the pokeweed are a lot alike. I got both parts in me, too. Excepting these days, I've got more roots and berries than stems and leaves."

"I don't see any poison parts," she said in a gentle voice. "I've only seen good, healthy green parts."

"What you see ain't always what you get," I said. "If you was to see Mamie Tillman, you'd see a lonely young woman, but she's more than that."

"Hold on, now." Dr. Conroy took a deep breath. "Who's Mamie Tillman?"

"She's the neighbor I was telling Maizy about," I explained. "I got to see way more of her than I wanted to."

"Bad more or good more?" asked Dr. Conroy.

"Just more," I answered. "You can't see poison," I said. "You gotta eat poison to know it."

"Well," she said, "we wouldn't be talking about you again, now, would we?" Before I could answer her, she stared right at me and declared, "Icy, if you think I'm afraid of poison, you got something else coming. I never run from a challenge. The bigger, the better."

"This time might be different," I said.

Dr. Conroy slapped the desk with the flat of her hand. "Absolutely not!" she said. "Not if I have anything to do with it." Then, placing both palms on her desktop, she stood up and said, "And remember, I don't lie."

Chapter 19

"Ace is a genius," Maizy announced, joining us. On the floor in the dayroom in front of the coffee table sat a boy about my age, drawing. Standing beside him, I watched as he drew. "That's a picture of downtown Spiveyville. He lived there when he was little. Every detail is right. I ought to know. Whenever I go back home, I pass right through it."

Ace didn't acknowledge us. He just drew.

I noticed how tightly he gripped the pencil and how he puckered his lips, sucking them in and out with each pencil stroke. When I finally sat down next to him, he didn't seem to mind. He just kept on drawing, his lips working as hard as his hands.

"Look at it," Maizy said. "Main Street with every store in place."

My eyes took in the pencil drawing.

There was a Randall's Department Store with a large SALE sign in the window. LINGERIE SALE, 20% OFF, the sign read. Mannequins, wearing frilly nightgowns and sexy underwear, were meticulously reproduced. A grocery store, called Wilson's, had a window filled with ads for food items — 3 cans of Del Monte Cling Peaches for $.45; Stokley Green Beans @ $.15 a can; bananas, $.19 a lb., and so on. Zippy's Shoe Store flaunted a rack beside its front door. Footwear for men and women — tennis shoes, dress shoes, loafers, and boots — lined the rack. All shoes had price tags attached. Cars were parked in front of meters. People, gathering on the sidewalk, peered into display windows with curious expressions on their faces.

"I've never heard him speak," Maizy said, "but he can draw. If he's hungry, he'll draw what he wants to eat. He talks with his pictures."

"He writes, too," I said, pointing at the lettering on the SALE sign in the window of Randall's Department Store.

"But he doesn't know what the letters mean," Maizy said. "He draws them because he remembers how they looked. He can't read."

"If he can't read, he's not a genius," I said smugly.

"People are smart in different ways," Maizy said. "Ace could pass by your bedroom door, stick his head inside for a minute, and be able to draw everything in it. He'd draw your books. They'd have titles and be stacked in the right order. He's got a photographic memory and a talent for drawing, so he's smart in his own way."

"Really, you ain't ever heard him talk?" I asked.

"Not one word," Maizy said.

"Has Reid ever talked?"

Maizy shook her head. "He chirps and makes little noises, but I've never heard him speak, either."

"How about Head Butt-er?" I wanted to know.

"His name is Gordie," Maizy said, a note of disapproval in her voice.

I nodded.

"He's never spoken to any of us," Maizy said. "But Delbert swears that once he heard him cussing up a storm."

"You don't say?" I said.

"He butted Ruthie. So Delbert made him go to his room and stay there. When Delbert checked in on him, Gordie was standing in front of his dresser mirror, cussing like a sailor. Naturally, he didn't know Delbert was standing there watching him. He spoke that time," Maizy said, "only once, but it wasn't to us, just to himself in the mirror."

"But he could, if he wanted to," I said.

Maizy lifted her eyebrows. "And why do you say that?" she asked.

" 'Cause he's dishonest," I replied.

"How?" Maizy had crooked her head to the left and was staring at me sideways.

"He ain't what he appears to be," I said.

Maizy laughed, jerking her head upright. "You just don't like him 'cause he butted Ruthie," she teased.

"No," I said, suddenly irritated. "That's not true. He's just like Mrs. Stilton, my mean ole teacher. His life ain't nothing but a lie."

Maizy didn't respond. She just stood there — her head straight up and rigid — looking right through me. Then, after several minutes of silence, she glanced down and exclaimed, "The stoplight!" She was pointing at Ace's picture. "He's drawn the stoplight." She grinned. "You see, he never misses a detail."

After lunch that day, I went to Ace's room. He was squatting on the floor, drawing a picture of a beautiful woman. I sat down beside him and watched as he drew the slow curve of her hips into her waist. The outline of her body exuded energy, rolling forward, like a wave breaking against the shore. Her lips, pursed and pouting, teased and licked; and, like an undertow, the curls of her waist-long hair drew me in.

"He thinks that's his mama," Wilma scoffed, shuffling into the room.

"Oh," I murmured, keeping my eyes down, avoiding hers.

"Yes, ma'am, ole Ace here dreams about his mama every night. Don't you, Ace?"

Ace didn't look up; he continued to draw.

"She never visits him, though," Wilma said. "His daddy don't come neither. He'll be in this place till he gets too old to stay. Then they'll put him somewhere else."

Ace held up his drawing and stared at it. I could see his lips twisting nervously.

"He sits in here drawing make-believe pictures of his family," Wilma said. "Once, at the bottom of one, he printed 'Mama's Love.' I got so excited, thinking I was seeing a likeness of the woman who created this." Wilma walked over to where Ace sat and thrust her finger straight down into his shoulder. Stone-faced, Ace didn't react. "But then I found the magazine beneath his mattress. His mama turned out to be Miss August. It was a girlie magazine. 'Can you handle some of Big Mama's Love?' it said." With these words, she threw back her head and guffawed so hard that her face rippled into a great big roll of fat. I pulled air between my lips, focused my eyes on her, and glared. Deep inside my throat, a croak twitched anxiously up my windpipe, ready to leap out.

"Yes, ma'am, his mother was Miss August." Wilma snickered. I balled up my hands, squeezing them so tightly that my fingernails cut into my skin. "Miss August," she repeated, and began laughing again.

Ferociously, I clutched my fists, slammed them against my thighs, and sucked in my lips. I vacuumed up oxygen, but the croak shoved against my teeth.

"Miss August," Wilma jeered. "The Playmate of the Month gave birth to this." Once more, she jabbed her finger into Ace's shoulder. This time his face wrinkled; pain raced through his eyes.

I leaped up. "At least he don't have you for a mother," I screamed, jutting out my chin. "You're ugly as ten miles of bad road. Uglier than a mud fence. Ugly! Ugly! Ugly!" My arms jerked to the left. "Your poor husband flew over the pretty flowers and landed on a cow pile," I yelled. Then I jumped up really high, stretched out my legs into an airborne split, and descended, straight-legged, with a thud — my feet planted squarely on the floor. "Cow pile! Cow pile!" I bellowed, then stood absolutely still for several seconds, rolled back my head, and croaked vociferously at the top of my lungs.

"My Lord!" Wilma gasped, her skin the color of a rattler's underbelly. "You're a nutcase! A crazy person! A lunatic!" she screamed, whipping around and running from the room.

Upset, I croaked some more until my anger dissipated and my voice grew weary and heavy. Looking down, I saw Ace's shoulder, quivering violently. Remorseful, I leaned over and tenderly touched him there.

When I returned to the safety of my room, apprehension and fear flooded through me. Now I've done it, I thought, sitting on the edge of my bed. I've let loose my secret, not to Maizy, not to Dr. Conroy, who are my friends, but to Wilma, the most spiteful person here. I crawled into my bed and pulled up the covers. Breathing rhythmically, I closed my eyes.

In the darkness behind my eyelids, I saw Miss Emily. She was pouring me a cup of tea. "Would you like one or two lumps?" she asked, reaching for a sugar bowl, a spoon in her hand. Hadn't she promised to be my friend forever? "I'll always love you, Icy Gal," she had said. "We're just alike." I once thought Miss Emily never lied. Yet when I had asked her to visit me, she hadn't come. Had her devotion been an act? Perhaps her love had been made of words alone, and words — I realized — meant nothing. Like grains of sand, they flew away, never sticking.

But my words were different. Like glue, all of my curses, croaks, and jerks had stuck, and I had arrived here — at Bluegrass State Hospital — with the label *misfit* tattooed on my forehead. I wondered now what kind of sticking power mean words, spoken to a mean woman, had. A lot, I thought and shuddered, imagining Wilma rocking on her front porch during summer nights, delighting in the crackle of insects flying too close to a kerosene lantern, lit simply because she enjoyed the sound of death. In my imagination, I saw Wilma as a child, smiling gleefully, pulling the legs off grasshoppers. I shuddered again, contemplating what she must have in store for me. I envisioned her holding her brother's .410, shooting sparrows. I saw her drowning kittens, ducking their little heads into a tub of water. In that instant, I knew why she worked at Bluegrass State Hospital. She liked to feel the power of pure destruction; it made her feel like she would live forever.

With these fears on my mind, I slid into a troubled sleep.

Mamie Tillman — a yellow pacifier between her lips — was sinking beneath the surface of Little

Turtle Pond. Frantically, I crawled along the pond's edge, crying out to her, then I turned to face the water, inhaled deeply, and submerged my head. The cold water closed over me. In the darkness below, a golden light shimmered. Closer and closer it came, glowing brighter and brighter, until the murky water was diffused with light. "Mamie!" I cried. "Where are you? Please come back!" At once, I heard the sound of skin sizzling. "Mamie!" I screamed, swishing my head beneath the water, finally seeing the lantern, burning red-hot in the darkness. The flame — like a tongue — flicked out. Mamie wailed. The water began to burn. Huge waves of smoke obliterated the light. In the distance, like a second voice, came the sound of laughter. Through the haze, I saw the figures — a loud, sinister, obscene Wilma snickering in the undertow, and Mamie Tillman, yellow pacifier between her lips, being swept away.

In the late afternoon, to keep my mind off my troubles, I decided to try one of the harder puzzles that were stacked on the bookshelf in the dayroom. It was a map of the state of Kentucky, consisting of 150 pieces, all of which were painted yellow. The fragments came together to form Kentucky's 120 counties. A picture of the state bird, the Kentucky cardinal; the state flower, goldenrod; the state motto, "United we stand, divided we fall"; and the state nickname, Bluegrass State, were the only distinguishing markers. Naturally, I knew some of the counties that slapped up against the Ohio, Kentucky, and Cumberland Rivers and could locate the Big Sandy and Little Sandy Rivers. I could even find the Licking River because it was forever flooding and creating all kinds of problems. Of course, I knew where Ginseng and Poplar Holler were, but I didn't know enough to piece together that puzzle in the two hours I had before supper. I had been working on it for over an hour and had finished only a third of it when I felt someone breathing down my neck.

Alarmed, I twisted around.

Head Butt-er, with a smirk on his lips and contempt in his eyes, was glaring straight ahead.

I nervously picked up a piece.

Head Butt-er tipped dangerously forward.

Terrified, I slid off my chair and ducked under the table. But Head Butt-er didn't see me. Instead, he was focused on the jigsaw puzzle. Every afternoon, he would piece several together. Starting at the top of each puzzle, he'd move mechanically straight across. Like a person writing on notebook paper, from the left to the right, he'd fit the pieces together. He always knew what piece to choose next. He never miscalculated; each fragment meshed snuggly into the other. Although I personally hadn't seen him work on every one of them, Delbert insisted that Gordie could do them all, even the five-hundred-piece ones, although he needed twenty-five minutes to finish each of those. Suddenly he leaned over and with one huge sweep of his arm wiped the table clean. The pieces of the puzzle scattered across the floor. Then he bent down and carefully retrieved each section. There, beneath the table, I waited, imagining him putting the puzzle together, not in my haphazard fashion, but in his own methodical way. He'd snap a piece into place, then grunt loudly. For ten minutes, I listened to one satisfied grunt after another. Then, after a momentary silence, he thumped the last piece into place; and, growling fiercely, he stomped his black-booted feet against the floor. At that moment, I hated him with all of my heart, and as his footsteps faded, I realized that he hated me, too. We hated each other for exactly the same reason. Gordie was smarter than I was. My ineptness bothered him. And as I crawled out from beneath the table, I understood at last that my sloppy way of putting puzzles together infuriated me even more.

I was dutifully heading down the hallway to my own room when — out of nowhere — I got this uneasy feeling. Stopping quickly, I listened for any unusual sounds, but heard nothing. Rather, an absolute, almost eerie silence filled the air. Again, I continued down the hallway, walking quietly and breathing shallowly, when all of a sudden a huge shadow shot out in front of me. Instantly, I stood still. Whipping around, I glanced in every direction, yet saw no one. "Calm down," I told myself, stepping lightly. "Ain't no booger man gonna get you." No sooner had I spoken those words than a loud thud rumbled behind me, and a huge body whizzed by, almost knocking me over. "Merciful Lord!" I cried, sprinting down the hallway, flying by the various-colored doors — their reds, greens, oranges, blues, and yellows splashing against my face. "Hold me in Your hands!" I asked God, flinging my door open.

Fading sunlight was seeping through the nursery rhyme curtains. My bed was rumpled the way I had left it, and my books remained stacked upon the floor. Everything was as it was before supper. Sighing deeply, I stepped inside and started to shut the door when a gigantic, square-edged shadow loomed over me. The words were already formed in my mouth before I turned and saw his shrunken eyes. Swaying firmly forward, his hands braced on either side of the doorway, he deliberately scraped each foot along the floor. Then he charged.

Head Butt-er! my mind screamed.

When I came to, Delbert was holding my hand, sitting beside my bed. "Sugar child, how are you doing?" he asked as I blinked open my eyes.

Groaning, I tried to inch upward, but couldn't because an ice pack weighed heavily on my head. "It hurts," I said.

"Of course it does," Delbert said, releasing my hand. "Gordie packs a wallop."

I groaned again.

"But don't you mind none. We'll have you

feeling better in no time."

I eased down, nestling deep into the covers.

"When you first came to, you was speaking like a crazy person. We had to call Dr. Lambert in Hickory Hall 'cause Dr. Conroy was out. He bird-dogged it over here and checked you over. Said you was hysterical. I been sitting here all this time wondering how a little girl like you gets hysterical. But Dr. Lambert is the ring-leader, a real big shot, so I reckon he knows."

"Uh-huh," I muttered.

"He told me to keep an eye on you and make sure you woke up feeling better. Are you still hysterical?" he asked, leaning over, examining me.

"I don't think so," I said.

"Not even a little?" he asked.

"No, sir," I said. "My head hurts, that's all."

"Good," he said, chuckling. "Not good your head hurts. Good, you're not hysterical."

Using my elbows, I lifted myself up. "Where's Head Butt-er?" I whispered.

"In solitary," he said.

"What's that?"

"In a little room all by hisself," Delbert said.

"Why?" I asked.

"He needs to do some thinking, some straightening out."

"Oh," I said. "One time back in Ginseng, I was asked to do some thinking."

"And look what it got you," Delbert said. "In bed, with a big ole headache." He patted my pillow. "Dr. Lambert wanted Tiny to look in on you before he went home." Delbert went to the door and made a very soft whistling sound.

In an instant, Tiny appeared. "Is she ready for some aspirin?" he asked Delbert.

"I reckon," he said. "Feel her forehead. She's hot."

"I can do you one better," Tiny said, whipping out a thermometer. "Open up, young lady," he demanded, as he thrust the cold stick between my lips. "Almost a hundred," he announced after leaving it in for several minutes. "Dr. Lambert wants you to take these." He bent over me with a packet of children's aspirin in his hand.

"You do what Tiny says," Delbert insisted, pouring me a glass of water. "He's a nurse."

"Swallow." Tiny plucked two pills into my hand.

"Try to rest," Delbert said.

Without hesitation, I swallowed the aspirin before moving back down in my bed, closing my eyes, drifting off.

Looking like a humongous green crab apple, I popped out from between my mama's legs.

"Aye grannies!" the midwife hollered when she saw me. "You have birthed a great big crab apple."

"Oh, Lordy!" my mama screamed.

"Acorns don't fall far from the tree," the midwife said, gripping my stem with both hands.

"Does she have arms?" my mama asked.

The midwife looked down. "No."

"Does she have legs?" my mama shrieked.

"Nary a one."

"Oh, merciful heaven!" my mama cried. "How do we know it's a she?"

"We don't," the midwife said, swinging me by my stem, shaking her head.

At that point, my head began to cry. A long, heart-wrenching sob seeped through my green skin.

"What's done is done," my mama said, then took me in her arms and pressed me against her breasts.

Relieved, the midwife threw up her hands. "Thank God you've recovered!" she said.

Tenderly, my mama cradled my noggin. Rubbing my slick green head, she replied, "Hysterical ain't what you'd call her. Sweet dumpling, you're not hysterical."

"I ain't hysterical. I ain't hysterical," I cried when I awoke in the middle of the night. "Hysterical ain't what you'd call me."

"Calm down, sugar child," Delbert said, grabbing the pitcher from the nightstand and pouring me another glass of water. "You're just having a bad dream."

"What color am I?" I asked.

"You got blond hair, yellow eyes, and white skin," Delbert said.

"I ain't green?" I asked.

"Nary a trace of green," Delbert said, handing me the glass. "Now drink this!"

I guzzled it down. "What are you still doing here?" I asked him.

"That ole Smitty called in sick, so I'm pulling a double shift," he said. "But it's okay, since Dr. Lambert told me to keep an eye on you anyway." He put his hand on my forehead. "Sugar darling, you're still hot!"

"It's all them little green crab apples Mama ate when she was pregnant with me," I said.

"I don't think so," Delbert said, "but I promise I'll wake you up if you start turning green on me. Now turn over and get some rest."

I pulled the blanket up over my head and immediately went to sleep.

Delbert's snoring woke me up. Like a car's engine warming up, each snore sputtered and hiccuped before booming forth and reverberating through the room. I was staring at his plump face, watching his cheeks go in and out, studying the sweet submissiveness of his skin and the neutrality of his camomile-colored hair when suddenly he choked once, gasped for air, and jerked up.

"You spying on me?" he asked, his eyes springing open.

"Delbert, you snore," I declared.

He stretched his arms over his head and yawned. "So what?"

"So, maybe nobody ever told you," I said. "Maybe you been snoring all your life and nobody had the nerve to tell you."

"What's to tell?" he said, rubbing his cheeks with his hands.

"What's to tell is that snoring ends more marriages than fooling around."

"Oh, does it?" He dipped his fingers in the pitcher on my nightstand, then flicked the water on his face. "Who says?"

"My granny," I said with authority.

"Well, my snoring don't bother me," he said, wiping his face with his shirttail.

"If you don't stop it," I warned, pointing my finger at him, "you'll never find a woman."

"I don't reckon I care," he said.

"You'll be lonely and unhappy," I said.

"I don't need a woman friend," he said. "I have a man one, and my snoring don't bother him a bit."

"You sleep with a man?" An incredulous tone was in my voice.

"Goodness no!" Delbert said. "He sleeps in the next room, but he can hear me through the walls."

"And sawing logs don't bother him?"

"Just the opposite," he said. "If I don't snore, he can't sleep."

"How come?" I asked.

" 'Cause when he was little, he lived near the railroad tracks. My snoring reminds him of the Old Ten-forty. The rumble of that train always put him to sleep."

"Well, your snoring does the opposite to me." I touched my forehead and grimaced.

"You got a goose egg," he said, shaking his head, smiling, "but don't worry, sugar darling, it'll get better."

At that moment, the sweetness of his words let me know that I could trust him. Slightly more masculine and all grown up, he was simply another Lane Carlson. "Will you . . ." I hesitated. "Will you keep him away from me?"

"Honey child, I promise I'll try." He reached out and took my hand. "Nobody should hurt a sweet thing like you."

Chapter 20

On the day of my grandparents' arrival, I could taste my joy. Like peppermint, it tingled inside me. Delight square-danced over every inch of my body. From my closet, I — cheerily — selected an evergreen wool jumper, and from my pink dresser, a white cotton blouse. I pulled up dark brown socks and slipped on my brown loafers. In front of my dresser mirror, I brushed my hair. Matanni said that a hundred strokes every day would make it shine. So I brushed and brushed till the strands, electrified, shot up. Then, feeling foolish and silly, I raced to the bathroom and splashed water over my head; my hair flattened like a wet dog's fur. Next I combed out each tangle, twisting each lock around my index finger until it coiled up like a snake, drying in a loose ringlet down my back.

I ate a light breakfast, cornflakes with bananas, and returned to my room. For four hours, I waited; but my grandparents didn't come.

Kneeling on the floor in front of my books, I leafed through *Little Women*; I examined the pen and ink illustrations but was unable to concentrate on the words. When I glanced up, I saw the gray morning through the parted curtains. I rose, and crossed over to the window. The last traces of the fall leaves had long since disappeared; the landscape was dull and cheerless. No patients lingered outside; no cars passed by the iron spiked fence; every so often, a wail pierced through the monotonous daily noise; but then it trailed off, as though it had never been.

I ran into the hallway and stared at the clock on the opposite wall.

I've missed lunch, I thought. It's one-thirty, and they aren't here.

I looked at the patchwork pillows on my bed. Rose, yellow, lilac, tan, green, white, blue, they were so colorful. White ruffles served as borders for both. Matanni had spent hours sewing them.

They promised to take me out to eat, and I've missed lunch, I thought.

I ran back out into the hallway. It was one-forty. Ten more minutes had passed. "Why aren't they here?" I asked myself.

I returned to my room and sat on the edge of my bed.

Closing my eyes, I stretched out both legs, scissor-kicked and fluttered them, and pretended to be swimming in Sweetwater Lake. When I was seven years old, Patanni had taught me how to swim. Cradling me in his arms, he had carried me into the water. "Close your eyes," he had said. "Don't be scared. In a minute, I'm gonna let you go. But remember, my arms are right below you, ready to catch you, if need be." Then he turned me loose.

Relaxed, I had floated with my eyes tightly shut and felt the soft, sweet water caressing my skin.

"Did you like that?" Patanni asked, once more cradling me.

When I nodded, he let go again. Sinking, I felt only the water slapping against me and the warm descent. Instinctively, without a trace of fear, I began to move my arms and legs. The water swirled around me. Caught in the eddy, my body fluttered like a leaf in the wind. Then Patanni had lifted me up, up, and up, until he was holding me several feet above the water. The sun flashed against my eyes, and air swept into my lungs. "Again!" I had begged him. "Let's do it again."

"Again!" I sobbed, now suddenly whipping around and throwing myself across my bed. "Let's do it again!" I said, crying into my grandmother's patchwork pillows.

I was crying like this when I felt a hand on my back. "Icy," Maizy said, gently patting me. "Icy, we've gotta talk."

I turned over. Wet and red-faced, I looked up at her.

"I'm sorry, Icy," she said. "Dr. Conroy told me this morning."

"Told you what?" I asked, afraid of her answer.

"I was coming to tell you," Maizy said, shaking her head, "when Stevie had another one of his accidents. It took me over an hour to clean up the mess."

"What are you trying to say?" I asked.

"They won't be coming," Maizy said softly.

I whimpered, stretched out my arms to push the words away, and fiercely shook my head.

"Dr. Conroy wrote your grandparents, asking them to put off their visit for a little while. She got a call from them this morning and they agreed."

"No!" I said, hitting at the air. "You promised."

"It's only been a few weeks," Maizy said. "We need a little more time. We've got to get to know you."

"But you do know me," I whined.

"Not well enough," she explained. "Give us just a little more time."

"But how much time?" I asked angrily.

"Not too much," she said. "Before you know it, they'll be here."

Clenching my jaw, I shook my head, wiped my face, and yelled, "You're lying! You're all just a bunch of liars!"

"Now, Icy!" Maizy was saying.

"Don't you 'now, Icy' me!" I said. "You, pretending to be my friend. You ain't no better than Gordie. Trying to be someone you ain't."

"Please listen, Icy!" Maizy said, grabbing my hands. "I promise, this wasn't my idea. I told Dr. Conroy, 'Look here, Icy needs to see her grandparents.' " She squeezed my fingers tightly. "But I'm just an aide. No one listens to me," she said, biting at her lower lip. "That's the truth, Icy Gal. I promise, on my granny's grave, I'd never hurt you."

"Just go!" I said, jerking my hands away. "I don't want to talk to you right now."

With a sad look in her eyes, Maizy said not another word. She simply stroked the edge of my mattress, as though it were my cheek, turned around, and walked away.

But I was too hurt to care about her feelings. For weeks I had waited for them to come and get me. In my bed at night, I had looked up at the ceiling and remembered winters on our farm. Matanni always gained weight while Patanni grew thinner. With my covers pulled up around me, I had smelled them both — the sweat and dirt beneath his skin; the flour and yeast beneath hers.

In the thick crack that ran along the wall near the windowsill, I had envisioned the forested hillside that protected our farm from the harsh northerly winds. In my mind's eye, I had imagined our white clapboard house looking like an igloo in the snow, and had seen myself, all cozy in my bed, listening to winter's stillness, hearing a twig as it cracked through the silence. Back home, the sounds of snow were forlorn and disturbing. Coldness, I knew, was not impassive. Ice clinked. A tree limb split and drums resounded.

Every night, I had dreamt about home, knowing that my grandparents would come soon, wrap their arms around me, and take me away. But they had not come. In this sterile blue room, winter was mute. When the snow finally came, it would creep silently. Tree limbs would not fracture. Twigs would not cry out. Like a dense fog, the snow would sneak up and fall upon us, and I would be trapped inside these yellow stucco walls.

Listening to the absolute silence, I cried until I could cry no longer, until exhaustion swam over me, until only rasps came from my mouth. Still, silence was better than speech. Already I knew the truth. Words were just stone-cold syllables strung together. Talking was about as meaningful as Maizy's vow to be my friend, as her promise to never hurt me. Promises, I had learned, meant nothing more than Reid's chirping, Rose's cackling, my croaking after a long, difficult day. Only a deep dreamless sleep — dark, silent, and empty of promises — had the power to calm me now.

"Icy, I know you're in there," Dr. Conroy said, knocking at my door. Having spent a miserable night, I didn't want to see her. After all, she was responsible for the scary dreams that had kept me awake. I wasn't about to ask her inside.

"Whether you want me to or not, I'm coming in." She eased open the door and peeked inside.

With arms crossed over my chest and legs shoulder-width apart, I stood in front of my bed and glared as she ventured through the doorway. "I don't want you here," I said. "If I can't see my grandparents, I don't want to see anybody, especially not you."

Dr. Conroy walked toward me, saying, "Believe it or not, I understand how you feel."

"How could you?" I argued. "They're not your grandparents."

"But I do," she said softly.

"Well, I don't believe you," I said. "You promised my folks could come, then changed your mind."

"I had to," she said, stopping right in front of me.

I kept my arms folded over my chest and said, "I wasn't born yesterday."

"Oh, yes, you were," she said, laughing.

"Take that back," I said, stomping forward, almost stepping on her toes.

She inched back. "Compared to me, you were born yesterday."

I swung my head and snorted, "After all your talk about telling the truth, you ain't nothing but a damn liar."

She walked over to the rocking chair situated in the center of the blue rug and sat down. "Come here," she said, tapping the arm. "I want to talk to you."

"I got nothing to say."

She began laughing again. "That'll be the day," she said. "Now come here."

I trudged over to the blue rug.

"Sit down," she ordered.

I squatted down on my calves at the edge of

the rug, as far away from her as I could possibly get.

"Icy, we need more time with you," she said. "More time before your grandparents come."

"How come?" I snapped.

" 'Cause we need to understand what's wrong with you," she explained. "We need to understand your disorder." She stressed the last word. "We've got to tell your folks something, and right now we don't know what to say."

"There ain't nothing wrong with me," I said.

"Now, you know that's not true," she said, clicking her tongue against her teeth.

"I ain't like Head Butt-er."

"Who?"

"Head Butt-er!" I said.

"Gordie?"

I nodded. "And I ain't like Ace or Reid or Rose."

"That's right." She drummed her fingers against the wooden arm. "That's why understanding you is so hard. You're not like the others."

"So let me go home," I said.

"We can't," Dr. Conroy said. "At least, not yet."

"So let my folks come and see me," I said.

"We can't," she repeated. "Not yet."

"If you act this way," I said, "I'll close up like a turtle, and you won't ever understand me."

"But that would be defeating your purpose," she said quietly. "You want to go home, don't you?"

I bit my lip and glowered at her.

"The sooner you let us get to know you, the quicker we'll be able to help you so you can go home."

"For Christmas?" I asked.

"Maybe," she said.

"I don't believe you," I said. "You'll skin me out of Christmas."

"We've got to get to know you better," she replied.

"What is there to know?" I said.

"Well . . ." she hesitated momentarily, then continued, "I'd like to understand why you spoke so harshly to Wilma the other day."

The muscles in my legs tightened. "What?" I asked, my face drawing up.

"You heard me."

"I wasn't so mean to her," I said.

"Let me see." She squinted her eyes as though she were struggling to remember. "Wilma told me what you said. If my memory serves me, you called her ugly, said that she was uglier than a mud fence."

"I might of," I said.

"Out of nowhere, she said, you lit into her, called her names, and acted like a crazy person."

"I called her ugly, if that's what you mean."

"Why?" she asked. "How could you be so unkind? She can't help how she looks."

"But she can help how she acts," I said. "Pretty is as pretty does."

"What are you saying?"

"I'm saying she's spiteful," I said. "She was making fun of Ace. So I — I got mad at her."

"How was she making fun of him?"

"She came up to him, pointed right at the woman he was drawing, and, real mean-like, called her 'Miss August.' Said that she was just some girl from a girlie magazine, not actually his mama."

"Go on."

" 'His folks never visit,' she said. 'I thought he was drawing a likeness of his mother, the woman who created this.' When she said 'this,' she jabbed Ace in the shoulder with her finger."

"No one's ever complained about Wilma," Dr. Conroy said.

" 'Cause everyone's scared of her," I said.

"Oh?" Dr. Conroy leaned forward; the rocker squeaked.

"Her favorite pastime is pulling the legs off grasshoppers. She shoots sparrows with her brother's .410, and she drowns kittens in a tub of water."

"What else?"

"Once I caught her brushing Deirdre's teeth with a hairbrush. She's jealous of Deirdre. Hates that she has a pretty name."

"Doesn't she like her own name?" Dr. Conroy asked.

"Would you?" I said, cocking my head to one side, opening wide my eyes.

"What's wrong with Wilma?" she asked.

"W-I-L-M-A." I growled out the sound of

each letter. "Listen to it! W-I-L-M-A!" I rocked forward on my knees. "I wouldn't want a name like that."

" 'What's in a name?' " Dr. Conroy recited. " 'That which we call a rose by any other name would smell as sweet.' "

"I don't understand," I said.

"Shakespeare," she answered. "It doesn't matter what something is called. It matters only how something is."

"*Wilma* is something bad," I said vehemently. "She's bad, and her name's bad — low down and ugly."

Dr. Conroy was quiet before putting her hands squarely on the chair's arms, leaning so far forward that she looked like she might tip over, and saying in a stern voice, "Icy, how would you know what Wilma does? Have you ever seen her drown kittens in a tub of water?"

My mouth fell open. "N-n-o, ma'am," I stammered, realizing that I had stated fantasy for fact. "I mean, I ain't seen her do those things, but I bet she does."

"Imagining something doesn't make it true."

"Well, I didn't imagine her making fun of Ace, and I didn't imagine her brushing Deirdre's teeth with a hairbrush. I saw her do those things with my very own eyes."

"Why should I believe those things when you lied about the others?" she said.

" 'Cause they're true," I said adamantly.

"But Maizy's never complained about Wilma,"

Dr. Conroy added. "If she saw Wilma doing something she shouldn't, don't you think she would?"

"Maizy's afraid of her," I said. "Even Delbert's scared of her and so is Tiny."

"Icy." Dr. Conroy shook her head. "Know what I think?"

I shrugged my shoulders.

"I think you're scared of Wilma. Not everybody, just you. That's why you make up stories about her."

I could feel my face burning with hurt and rage. Even the skin on my arms turned crimson. Digging my fingers into the fluffy blue rug, I began to shake all over. Curse words zoomed through my brain, banged against my skull, and demanded to get out. I stretched out my neck. My eyes leaped forward. Sweat rolled down my forehead. "Pot calling the kettle black. Damn liar! Goddamned liar! Shit and piss on you! Shit and piss. . . ."

Dr. Conroy leaped from the rocker. With one large step, she was in front of me, scooping me into her arms. "It's okay, Icy," she said, holding me against her chest. "It's okay."

But I couldn't hush. The curses kept coming — louder and angrier — until, exhausted, I slumped against her shoulder and sobbed.

Sitting on the fluffy blue rug, I experienced the deadening calm which comes after any good cry and the relief of feeling nothing. After five minutes, though, the numbness faded, and the first traces of panic set in. "Lordy sakes!" I said out loud. "What have I done!" I jumped up, nervously wringing my hands. Like a record player stuck in a groove, my mind replayed each moment with Dr. Conroy. I heard myself screaming, "Pot calling the kettle black. Damn liar! Goddamned liar! Shit and piss on you!" I dug my fingernails into my hands. Blood trickled over my skin. Red blood as punishment, I thought, staring at the droplets. Red stains of sin. Oh, God! I thought. What will become of me now? Dr. Conroy will think I'm crazy, and I'll never get to leave this place! "Lordy mercy!" I said. "She thinks I told tall tales on Wilma." What'll I do? I asked myself. What'll I do? I paced around the room; my heart ping-ponged against my chest; my breathing grew shallow. "What'll I do?" I whispered. "What'll I do about my disorder?" Panic-stricken, I paused in front of my stack of books, bent over, and, out of the blue, grabbed the dictionary which Mr. Wooten had loaned me.

Breathing in calmly, I tried to steady myself and focus on the task at hand. "Don't worry, Icy!" I said, reassuring myself. "Everyone here has a disorder, but you're not like everyone here." I wondered about the word's meaning and about how the meaning could apply to me. "Icy, we need to understand your disorder," Dr. Conroy had said. This was the reason they gave for not letting me go home, for not letting my grandparents come to see me. I had a disorder, yet I was not a disorderly person. My room was clean and tidy — not as tidy as Dr. Conroy's office, but tidy, nonetheless.

Resolved, I sat down on the floor, opened the dictionary, and quickly turned the pages until I came to the *d*'s, then I slowly flipped over each page until I located the word I was looking for — *disorder*. According to the *Webster's* in front of me, disorder meant "a lack of order, disarrangement, confusion." None of these words described me. So my eyes followed my finger down the column until they came to the phrases "a breach of order, disorderly conduct, a public disturbance." These definitions, I realized, spelled trouble. Even the following one — "a derangement of physical or mental health or functions" — seemed bad. Determined to find a more positive meaning, I switched tactics and decided to concentrate on *disorder* the verb. "To derange the physical or mental health or functions of," the dictionary said. This meaning sounded worse than the one before it. I was really worried.

Alarmed, I scanned what was left of the column; all at once, the word *synonyms* caught my attention. Miss Emily had taught me all about these words with similar meanings. "Brawl, disturbance, uproar," I read. Gasping, I closed my eyes and saw clearly the writing on the wall. "Pot calling the kettle black. Damn liar! Goddamned liar! Shit and piss on you!" I had screamed. With my eyes still shut, I quietly closed the *Webster's*. "It's true," I whispered, flicking open my eyes. "I can brawl with the best of them." My eyes took in the insipid curtains, the pink dresser, and the flag-painted rocker. "I'll never leave this place," I cried.

At that moment, as if by design, I spotted the heating vent in the baseboard near my dresser. I stood, and with the dictionary in my hands, walked over to the vent and placed the book on the floor. Loosening the screws, I pried open the vent's cover with my fingers. The space behind the cover was large, large enough for my dictionary; so I shoved the book inside, replaced the grated cover, secured the screws, and sighed. Only I would be privy to this damning definition, I thought. My disorder was now hidden away.

On the floor, near the window, rearranging my stack of books, sat Gordie. From the doorway, I watched as he frantically picked up one of the thickest, glanced at its cover, then, exasperated, shoved it between two others. Immediately his hand moved toward another book, wedged in the center of the second pile. It was my book on Kentucky wildflowers, the one which Miss Emily had given me. After he pulled it out, he looked at the title, made a grunting noise, and slammed it back on top. He's looking for my dictionary, I thought, all at once realizing what he was doing.

Then, abruptly, he jumped up, stared at the closet, and headed toward it. Just as he was about to put his hand on the doorknob, I cranked up my courage, strode noisily into the room, and announced, "This is my room, not yours."

He pivoted on his heels, quickly facing me.

Determined, I stared into his angry black eyes, shook my head ferociously, and snarled, "This is my room. Those are my books. You better get!"

He scrunched up his forehead and swayed forward. His face glowed purple. His nostrils flared. His lips jutted outward. His forehead twitched.

"Get out!" I screamed, stepping back.

He grunted loudly and shuffled his feet. Swinging his head from one side to the other, he emitted a skunklike odor. I smelled his stench, felt his knife-edged stare, and knew the butt was coming.

"Get out!" I bellowed, leaping straight up. *"Get going!"* I screamed, then cartwheeled two times across the floor, landing right in front of him.

His eyes grew large. His jaw dropped. His legs bent slightly.

In that instant, I threw back my head, popped out my eyes, opened wide my mouth, and let out a gigantic *CROAK.*

"MMMMMMMMnnnnnnnnnnn!" he grunted, straightening his legs. "MMMMMMMMMnnnnnnnnnn!" he groaned, his eyes darting back and forth. "MMMMMMMMnnnnnnnnnnnn!" he growled, pushing me to the side, heading for the door. Then, mechanically, he turned around, took one last look at me, and strutted out.

"Croak," I enunciated the word clearly when I heard him in the hallway. "Croak! Croak!" I giggled as his footsteps faded. "Croak!" I tittered to the silent, empty space.

Relieved, I collapsed on the floor and began to chuckle. At first the laughter was faint; but before too long, great guffaws ripped from my lungs and tore out of my mouth. I laughed so hard that I could feel my organs shaking, my skin vibrating. I roared so long that when the fit was over, I closed my eyes and fell asleep right there on the floor, at peace with the knowledge that, for the first time since the croaking began, I had called the shots. I had used my disorder and made myself powerful. No actress could have performed better: I had contrived my first croak.

A few days later, I stood outside, savoring my victory. Now, whenever Gordie saw me, he quivered his nose, shrunk his eyes, swiveled around, and marched away. In the distance, I saw Maizy Hurley, bundled up, resting on a bench, all by herself beneath a leafless maple tree. Her hair was fluffed out around her head, and her face seemed to glow with urgency.

"Hey, Maizy!" I called as I ran over to her. "I

want to tell you something." But she didn't look up. "Maizy, you're not listening. It's about Head Butt-er."

"Butter?" Maizy said.

"What are you thinking about?" I asked. "You're not listening to me."

"I'm sorry, Icy," Maizy said. "I'm worried about Rose." Soft, yellow waves of hair framed her face. "I've been trying to feel what she feels."

"How?" I asked, sitting down beside her, forgetting about Gordie.

"The other day, I got down on my bedroom floor," Maizy said, "and twisted my body up like hers."

Astounded, I turned to face her. "Did it hurt?"

"Really bad," she said.

"I bet," I said, shaking my head.

"Picture her arms," Maizy said. "They look like they're strung from a tree." She pointed up at a large branch.

My eyes followed her finger. "Uh-huh," I mumbled.

"Well, I made my arms do the same thing."

I glanced back down at my hands. "Ouch!" I said. "I bet that hurt even more."

She nodded. "But I didn't really look like her. So I tried even harder. I jerked my head one way and my legs so far the other way that I thought my skin would rip."

I made an awful face. "Why?"

"Because I want to understand her," Maizy

insisted. "I want to feel the same hurt she feels."

I shook my head. "I can't figure out what you mean," I said.

"Em-pa-thy." Carefully, Maizy pronounced each syllable. "I want to feel what she feels — completely, utterly, totally. What I mean is, I want to love her."

I was dumbfounded. My jaw fell and my lips parted. "But you do love her."

"Not really," she said. "Not until I feel her pain like I feel my own."

"That won't be so easy." I grimaced. "Her disorder is awful."

"But I can try, can't I?"

"You go right ahead. But Icy Sparks, here" — I pointed my thumb at my chest — "wants no part of it." I eyed her; she wasn't listening again.

Instead, she began talking with that dreamy look in her eyes. "When Reid was a baby," she said, "he ate lead paint, and it made him sick. That's why he's the way he is." She flicked a strand of hair off her forehead. "Last year, I scraped some paint off the trim in my bathroom." She lightly ran her fingernail down her cheek. "I wanted to eat a little poison myself." She closed her eyes and swallowed. "You see, I wanted some of his magic, too. To leave this world. Be reborn as a bird and fly high above it. But I didn't follow through."

"Why not?" I wanted to know.

Her eyes flashed open. "I got scared," she said.

"Lucky for you," I said, breathing easy.

"Maybe," she said, "but in a way it's sad, 'cause I really wanted to understand him. For just a little while, I wanted to be him."

"What about Ace?" I asked, fixing my eyes on her. "Do you understand him?"

"Oh, yes!" she said, clapping her hands. "He's easy. Look at his drawings. They're real. Drawn from love. Ace loves his pictures the way he'd like to love the world but can't."

"Do you ever want to be like Gordie?" I said, cleverly bringing the conversation back to him.

For several seconds, Maizy gazed vacantly in front of her. "No," she finally said, turning around and meeting my gaze. "I don't ever want to be like Gordie."

"Why's that?" I asked.

"His father's a military man, a two-star general," Maizy stated, taking one deep breath. "And Gordie worships order, just like his dad." The air hissed back out through Maizy's teeth. "Everything in his room is perfect," she explained. "All his underwear's in neat little piles. He stacks his briefs in the top drawer. He puts his T-shirts in the second. His socks are last — perfectly matched — black with black, dark brown with dark brown, and so on." Sadly, she shook her head. "All of his shoes are polished and lined up in his closet. He's neater than I am, and he dresses better than anyone here, including the doctors."

"He dresses fit to kill," I agreed.

"He's obsessed with cleanliness," she went

on. "If Delbert wants a trash can emptied, Gordie will empty it. He follows Tiny around, cleaning up what he misses. He hates dust. Before anyone can grab the feather duster, Gordie's got his hands on it. Once, I even caught him going through Tiny's medical cart. The medicines were safely locked away, but he had spotted some cotton balls on top and was sorting through them before Tiny came back. Those that had imperfections, a hint of lint, not perfectly round, he was tossing away."

"Yeah, but what about that head-butting thing? Why does he do that?" I asked.

Maizy tilted her head. "I'm not sure," she said. "Maybe he just wants to feel something. Feeling pain is better than feeling nothing."

"Maybe he just wants to hurt people," I said.

"Or maybe he simply hates disorder and tries to butt it out of the way."

"His disorder and mine." I snickered. "I reckon that was why he was in my room."

"In your room?" Maizy arched her eyebrows. "You never told me that."

"That's what I was trying to tell you. I caught him in my room looking for one of my books," I said. "I stopped him before he got to my closet."

"You stopped him?"

"I told him to get."

"And he got?"

"Yes, ma'am," I said.

"Icy Gal, you amaze me!"

"Sometimes I amaze myself!" I said proudly.

255

Then, amazing myself even more, I asked Maizy the one question which I had been holding back. "Tell me, Maizy," I said forthrightly. "How come you know so much?"

She answered simply. "I read," she said. "Long lists of books that my friend gives me."

"I read, too!" I declared. "Miss Emily helps me. Does your friend help you?"

"All the time," she replied.

"Why?" I asked.

" 'Cause he understands me. He feels what I feel."

"Em-pa-thy," I said, stressing the syllables the way Maizy had.

In the privacy of my room the following day, I thought about empathy. If Maizy felt empathy was important, then perhaps I should, too. Sitting on the edge of my bed, I stretched out my legs, flexing and pointing my toes. Of course, I didn't know if I could really trust her, but she had begun to win me back. Spreading my legs out wide, I rotated my feet. After all, she was just an aide; I was just a patient; neither of us had any power. In this way, both of us were alike. I was pondering these matters, goose-stepping in midair, when someone knocked.

Immediately I sat up.

"It's me," Maizy said. "Open up! I've got something for you."

"Come on in," I said, my feet dangling.

She came toward me carrying a small, rectangular package, wrapped in baby-blue tissue paper, secured with a pink ribbon. "I saw this last night and thought about you." She extended her arms. "Here." The present trembled in her palms. "Well, aren't you going to take it?" she asked, stepping closer.

"Thank you," I said, placing it on the mattress beside me.

"Aren't you going to open it?"

"Now?" I asked.

"What do you think, silly?"

Slowly, I untied the ribbon and loosened the tape, making certain to preserve both. Next, I unfolded the paper. Before me was a box with a sublime yellow heart surrounded by stars on its cover.

"Open it!" Maizy ordered.

Inside were two dozen cards. Outside, each had the same yellow heart and the same blue stars. Inside, each was blank.

"Now you can write to your grandparents," she said. "The golden heart will remind them of you."

The muscles in my throat began to quiver. "But . . ." I began. "But . . ."

"I spoke to Dr. Conroy, and she agreed. Too much time has passed. Your grandparents need to hear from you."

Speechless, I wiped my eyes. "Cross my heart and hope to die," I said, "it's been months since anyone's been this nice to me."

"So why don't you start writing?" she said,

heading for the door. "I'll mail your card for you when you're finished."

"But I don't have any stamps," I said.

"Don't worry," she said. "I got a whole roll in my purse."

Dr. Conroy — her head down, her hands clasped in front of her — walked through my bedroom door unannounced. The minute I saw her, I knew what she was going to say, so I spoke before she could. "I'm lying here thinking about Christmas." I talked rapidly, slurring words together and spitting them out. "Me and Patanni always pick a cedar from our woods. A tall and fat one that goes clear up to the ceiling," I said. "Patanni uses his axe. Just a few swings, it's down. Matanni's got this little angel, dressed pretty in pink and baby blue, that we put on top, and —"

"Icy," Dr. Conroy interrupted, lifting her head, standing stiffly before me. "Icy, we must —"

"Patanni sets it up, away from the fireplace so it won't catch, in the far corner, next to his easy chair. He puts on two strings of lights — every color — red, blue, yellow, white, and green. Matanni buys a bag of cranberries and pops some corn on the stove. We always thread two strings — one out of cranberries, the other out of popcorn — and drape them around the tree, from top to bottom, like icing on a cake."

"Icy, please!" Dr. Conroy insisted. "We must talk about Christmas."

"And we have boxes of ornaments," I went on, ignoring her. "Little knitted candy canes and stars and Santas made out of wood. Matanni and Patanni do it all. They do every little thing. Every little thing for Christmas. To make it special for me, for us, 'cause we're a family, a real family that I need to go home to, to go home to for Christmas. . . . Please!" When I looked at her, my eyes were watering. I gritted my teeth to keep from crying. "Please, don't say those words!"

And for a minute she didn't. She simply held out her hand and with her fingers motioned me to come. Reluctantly, I went to her. "Please don't say those words!" I repeated.

"Icy, you need to be patient just a little longer," she said quietly. "Give us a few more weeks." Gently, she folded her arms around me. "We both have to give some." She patted my back. "It's called compromise."

"But writing ain't the same as being there," I said into her hard, starched shirt.

Chapter 21

December 18, 1956

Our Darling Icy,

Your grandpa and me miss you so much. Right now, there's over three inches of goose down on the ground. The cedars look like they've been dipped in sugar, and the smell of wood smoke is in the air. Christmas is just around the corner, my precious Icy, but without you here it won't be so merry. No, it won't be merry, at all.

Every morning, your grandpa and me go to your room, and he sits on the edge of your bed and talks to you, just like you was here. He says that even Essie and Ellie miss you. Whenever he goes to feed them, he says they look up with their big brown eyes, expecting to see you, then hang their heads real low when they realize you ain't with him. Ain't none of us happy without you.

I'm trying my best to get into the Christmas spirit, like I always do. I'm making us fruit cake. Using some of Patanni's whiskey for flavoring. The alcohol cooks out when the cake is baking so I reckon it's okay. Ain't the same as pure consumption. Ain't the same as your grandpa sneaking out to the barn the way he does, stealing those long, stinging gulps. Tomorrow, I'm gonna make a batch of Christmas cookies. Patanni got me a new mold from Stoddard's. A great big ole star. Won't those cookies look pretty with yellow sprinkles on them? We'll probably send some to Miss Emily 'cause, Icy darling, she has been ailing. I'll let your grandpa tell you about that.

Icy, hope you can make out my chicken scrawl after reading your grandma's prissy hand. Anyway, this here part of the letter belongs to me since it's my doing, truth be told. Sugar, I've a confession to make. Your grandpa, here, never gave your letter to Miss Emily. I never told her your troubles 'cause we knowed she'd get upset, and we knowed you'd get upset if we told you about hers. So, all this time, your grandma and me been keeping our mouths shut, not saying a peep. But seeing that it's nearing Christmas, we wanted to tell you the truth. Miss Emily has been feeling puny, of late. She's down to Florida, we done heard, resting up and taking care of her heart. Was what the doctor ordered. Last week, we got notice that she's feeling better. You're feeling better, too. So, your grandma and me decided it was time to tell the truth. Now, the truth is out. Now, all's right with the world, except you're not here with us. Sugar, come back to our loving arms.

Your grandpa loves you.

So does this grandma of yours.

We're keeping your presents under the tree for when you come home and sending our love your way.

Love & kisses,
Matanni & Patanni

Chapter 22

"That damn Tiny started flapping his gums. Now everybody knows," Wilma said to Maizy over breakfast. "I might as well play Mary."

"I can barely tell," Maizy said. "You're showing a little but not too much."

"It don't matter," Wilma said, smiling suddenly. "I want to be the Virgin Mary. It suits me, don't you think?"

Maizy nodded. "Well, if you don't mind," she said.

I stared at Wilma's stomach, which was puffing out more than usual, and at her mustache, which had become thicker and hardier in the past few weeks, and gagged at the thought of her being pregnant and even more at her being the Virgin Mary. "Poor baby Jesus," I whispered.

Wilma turned toward me. "Did you say something?"

"Nothing," I said, stirring my oatmeal. "It's cold."

" 'Cause you were late," she scolded. "Ain't nobody's fault but your own. Moping and whining since you got the news. For two days straight, you been making everybody around you miserable. If you can't change a situation, you best accept it."

"Maybe, I don't want to," I pouted.

"Maybe you just like misery," she said.

"Maybe I like going home for Christmas," I said, "and not being stuck in some crummy old hospital."

"You best count your blessings!" Wilma pointed a fat index finger at me. "In some far-away country, some little girl is living in the streets, with no roof over her head."

"Yes, ma'am," I muttered.

"Icy'll perk up," Maizy said, walking over, putting her arm around me. "Give her a little time."

I shrugged her arm off. I was tired of mending broken promises with time.

But Maizy was persistent. "Be patient, Icy Gal," she said, touching my forearm. "You'll see them soon. The doctors always give in."

Reid chirped at the end of the table. Arching his back, he held up his bowl and plopped it down.

"He wants more oatmeal," I sneered.

"He's always hungry." Maizy cupped her hands around her mouth. "Delbert!" she yelled. "More oatmeal over here!"

"Reid?" he hollered back.

"Who else?" she screamed.

Delbert strode toward us with a large, two-handled pot in his hands. "Here you go," he said, dipping a ladle of oatmeal into Reid's bowl. Frenetically, Reid began cheeping and flapping his arms, waving his silver spoon like a conductor's baton. "Calm down!" Delbert said. "You're upsetting the others!"

Then pretty Ruthie picked up her spoon, painting oatmeal all over her face and down her blouse.

Wilma passed behind Deirdre and deliberately poked a finger into her back. Deirdre sprung up and out like a jack-in-the-box. A second later, Wilma was standing beside her, spooning oatmeal between her lips. Swallowing, she curled up again.

Ace was painting on his napkin. He dipped the sharp edge of his knife into grape jelly, wildly sketching a purple Santa Claus.

From the opposite end of the table wafted a foul odor. I turned around and spotted Stevie, grinning crookedly, rocking back and forth. "Look at him," I snorted. "Grinnin' like a possum."

"He's had another b.m.," Tiny moaned.

"Phew!" Wilma pinched her nose. "He should eat in his room like Gordie."

"But he's not Gordie," Maizy cut in. "He means no harm." Quickly, she twisted around and popped a fingerful of toast into the Mouth's mouth, who in turn vacuumed it in. "See!" Maizy pointed at Mary's pink gums and four pointed teeth. "If you keep food in her mouth, she's all right."

"That's it!" I yelled, leaping up, waving a carton of milk over my head. "This ain't nothing but a madhouse!" I screamed, the milk frothing rage in the air. "I hate it here. If you think you can make me stay, you're dead wrong!" With these final words, I threw down my milk carton and marched out the door, my feet tingling with fury.

"You'll enjoy it," Maizy insisted. "I'll glue black yarn on your face. It'll look just like a beard. And you'll wear a cone-shaped hat, made out of bright yellow tinfoil. Delbert has contributed his red satin bathrobe 'cause he's gained so much weight, and I'll hem it up. You know, shorten it to fit you. You'll look just like a wise man."

"But I don't want to be a wise man," I whined. "I want to be Icy Sparks; I want to be back home for Christmas with my grandparents."

"Icy," Maizy said firmly, "we can't control that. The doctors have already said no. But we can control what kind of Christmas you have here. If you don't try, you'll make yourself even more miserable."

"Let someone else do it," I said. "Let Wilma be a wise man. She's got a mustache."

"Wilma's playing the Virgin Mary," Maizy said.

"I thought the Virgin Mary was pretty," I said. "Not ugly as homemade sin."

Maizy took one step back. "Icy Sparks!" Both hands clutched her hips. "I've never heard you be deliberately mean."

I screwed up my face. "Then you haven't heard the real me," I said.

"A person can't help how she looks," Maizy said.

I glanced sideways at her. "You know that old saying?" I asked.

"Which one?" she said.

"Pretty is as pretty does."

Maizy glared at me.

"Well, in Wilma's case, it's ugly is as ugly does."

The muscles in Maizy's neck grew taut; she thrust out her jaw. "Icy, I'm disappointed in you," she said coldly.

"Don't that beat all!" I said defiantly, holding my head up high. "You hate Wilma as much as I do," I said, raising my voice, scowling, "but you won't admit it. Wilma's right. You ain't nothing but a Goody Two Shoes."

At once, the fire left Maizy's eyes. She looked down at her feet and sighed. "I didn't realize how much you dislike me."

"I didn't know you liked Wilma better than me!"

"I don't," she answered, then turned around and left.

For two days, I sulked. Christmas felt like it belonged to everybody else, not me. In the dayroom, I sat by myself. When Maizy greeted me, I refused to say hello. If Wilma passed nearby, I pretended she wasn't there. Even Delbert, who had done nothing, received the same treatment. Once, while I was eating, Dr. Conroy came over and placed her hand on my shoulder. Since she was the one I most hated, I sneered at her and shrugged contemptuously. Slowly shaking her head, she walked away.

I sank into the rut of feeling bad. There was no other way to feel. Anger turned into depression. My secrets had cut me off from Christmas, my grandparents, and Miss Emily. That poison part of me had attached secrecy to everything. When Miss Emily didn't visit, I had decided that she secretly hated me. When Maizy defended Wilma, I reasoned that all along she had secretly liked the woman. Feeling low — sinking down further and further — became easier than lifting myself up. Depression grew comfortable and familiar. Not only did my sadness affect me, but it also took a toll on the others. Whenever Maizy brought over a deck of cards and asked sprightly, "Want to play rummy?" I'd relish the urgency in her eyes. Lowering my head, I'd refuse to look at her. Concerned, she'd try again, "Just one game?" After which I'd mumble some insult and feel vindicated. Then I'd sit in my room the rest of the day. If I heard footsteps in the hallway, I'd strike a pose of indifference. My resolve to make everyone, including myself, miserable amazed me. So intent was I on fulfilling this task that impulses to tic, croak, jerk, and curse just disappeared, as though I had never felt them. If I couldn't have a Merry Christmas at home, then — by damn — no one would have a Merry Christmas here.

Yet after two days, the staff's concern began dropping off. At first, I noticed little lapses. Maizy would see me in the dayroom but would just walk by, not saying a word. Dr. Conroy would nod hello. When I didn't nod back, she'd smile, cheerily say, "Good day," then continue on her rounds.

Wilma, who was never worried about me, was now blatantly irritated. "Poor pitiful Pearl," she snarled.

Delbert, too, dismissed me. No longer did he tease me. Instead, he joked with Maizy, held mistletoe above her head, and kissed her every chance he got.

Feeling bad began to feel really bad, even worse than I'd imagined.

Sitting by myself in the dayroom, I studied the smiling faces around me — Maizy singing "Jingle Bells," Delbert sucking on a candy cane, Dr. Conroy wearing a jeweled Christmas tree brooch, Tiny sporting Santa's stocking cap, Wilma tenderly caressing her fat belly — and I couldn't stand myself a minute longer. "Delbert," I said with forced gaiety, "who are you going to be in the Christmas play?"

He ignored me and, turning to Maizy, said,

"Maizy, darling, I want you to be the angel on the top of my tree."

Maizy giggled. "Only if you'll be my star," she whispered breathlessly.

"Are you playing Santa Claus?" I asked Tiny.

"Ho! Ho! Ho!" he roared, stomping over to Dr. Conroy, retrieving a candy cane from his front shirt pocket, and with a flair giving it to her.

Dr. Conroy smiled and waved the candy cane like a wand. "Thank you, Santa," she said, curtsying to everyone — everyone, that is, but me. "Merry Christmas to all and to all a good day!" she said grandly before waving good-bye at the door.

"Merry Christmas!" they all said, waving back.

But I was too busy eyeing Tiny. "Ain't Santa gonna give me one?" I asked.

Tiny took no notice of me. Instead, he approached Wilma and gently pressed a candy cane into her palm.

"Really!" I said, indignantly, looking at candy canes protruding from their mouths. "Where's the Christmas spirit?"

"The last candy cane goes to . . . it goes to . . ." Tiny said, dramatically lifting a candy cane over his head. "Goes to our angel, Miss Maizy — a true Christmas spirit!"

"Humbug!" I snorted.

Maizy deliberately approached me holding the candy cane in front of her. She was walking so slowly she seemed to be floating like a sleepwalker. "An angel of the Lord appeared to Joseph in a dream," she said, with her eyes glazed over. "And the angel said, 'Joseph, thou son of David, fear not to take unto thee Mary thy wife: for that which is conceived in her is of the Holy Ghost. And she shall bring forth a son, and thou shalt call His name JESUS.' "

" 'For He shall save His people from their sins,' " I quoted.

Maizy narrowed her eyes. "But Herod, the king, was jealous," she said, slapping her hands together.

Tiny jumped. "Tell us why!" he said.

"Because," Maizy responded, "wise men from the East came to him asking, 'Where is He that is born King of the Jews? For we have seen His star in the east, and are come to worship Him.' This made Herod furious, so he ordered the wise men to find baby Jesus and let him know where his rival was."

I lowered my voice and began quoting again, " 'Go and search diligently for the young child,' Herod commanded. 'And when ye have found Him, bring me word again, that I may come and worship Him also.' " I stopped, quickly looked around, and saw that all of them — Maizy, Tiny, Delbert, and even Wilma — were listening. I raised high my voice, threw out my arms, and dramatically pushed on, " 'And, lo, the star, which they saw in the east, went before them, till it came and stood over where the young child was.' "

"In Bethlehem of Judea," Maizy broke in.

" 'When they saw the star,' " I recited, " 'they rejoiced with exceeding great joy. And when they were come into the house, they saw the young child with Mary His mother, and fell down, and worshiped Him.' " Smiling broadly, I tossed back my head and caught my breath.

"Well, I'll be damned, Icy!" Delbert joked.

" 'And when they had opened their treasures, they presented unto Him gifts; gold, and frankincense, and myrrh. And being warned of God in a dream that they should not return to Herod, they departed into their own country another way,' " I finished, remembering the verses that Matanni had taught me.

"That was beautiful!" Maizy said.

"What's that stuff, Frankie's scent?" Delbert asked.

"Something that smells good," I answered.

"Gordie's bringing myrrh," Tiny said.

"That's a perfume," I said knowingly.

"You know a lot for a kid," Tiny said, winking.

"Not how to get a candy cane," I replied.

"I reckon you've earned one now," Maizy said. "You did real good."

"Thank you," I said, peeling back the wrapper. "I get a lot of practice. Matanni likes me to quote from Matthew every Christmas Eve." Shoving the candy inside my smile, I waited for more compliments, but they didn't come. Instead, Tiny turned around, looped his arm through Maizy's, and along with Wilma

272

and Delbert started to walk away. "Hey!" I hollered, pink saliva drooling from the corners of my mouth. "What does a person have to do to be a wise man around here?"

"Did you say wise guy or wise man?" Delbert asked over his shoulder.

"We're having our first rehearsal tomorrow," Maizy chimed in. "Be there!"

Chapter 23

"I hear Dr. Lambert's a tough critic," Delbert said as he put his hands on my shoulders and positioned me before an imaginary Virgin Mary.

"Where's Wilma?" I asked. "Ain't she gonna rehearse with us, or is she counting on God to inspire her?"

"Icy!" I glanced over my shoulder. Maizy was frowning. "What's your problem? Poor Wilma can't seem to keep anything down. She's not feeling well, that's all."

"Well, she best start," I said matter-of-factly. "Now that she's eating for two."

Maizy flinched. "How did you find out?" she asked.

"I've heard all of you whispering."

"Ain't it amazing!" Delbert said, shaking his head.

I rolled back my eyes. "It's weird," I said, rolling them again. "I didn't know the ole dirt dauber was married. She ain't nothing but a wasp with a sting. And she's got that nasty mustache kinda looks like a clump of dirt smeared clear across her face."

Running his finger above his lip, Delbert grinned.

Maizy made a scene of stomping her foot. Then she tossed back her head and giggled. "Icy Sparks, without a doubt, the Christmas Spirit has passed you over."

"How come you're always getting on me?" I pouted.

"Why do you think?" she asked.

" 'Cause I say out loud what you might be thinking," I said.

"Sometimes it's best to keep your thoughts to yourself," Maizy replied.

"That don't cut no ice with me," I argued.

"Well, it should," she objected. "Your life would be easier if it did."

"Well —" I began.

But Tiny intervened. Winking at me, he slapped Delbert's back. "We best get to work," he said.

I was getting into my role, transforming myself into a wise old sage, when, ashen-faced and wobbly, Wilma appeared.

"Howdy," Delbert and Tiny said.

"You don't look so good," said Maizy in a concerned voice.

Wilma smiled weakly. "I want to go over my lines," she said. "Just once, to make sure I know what to do."

I attempted to smile back.

"Well," Maizy said, cradling her arms. "It's not too much to remember. When the play begins, you'll be carrying a life-sized doll." She looked at Wilma. "Just like this," she said, rocking her arms. "When the three wise men come up, all you have to do is hold out your arms. 'This is the baby Jesus,' you say. Right after the word *Jesus,* Icy, Tiny, and Gordie —"

Tiny interrupted, "I do the talkin' for Gordie."

"Right." Maizy nodded. "Then, they say their lines and end with 'We Three Kings.' Last, you put baby Jesus in His manger and sing 'Silent Night' with the rest of us."

Wilma put her hands on her stomach. "That's easy enough," she said.

I glanced over at Maizy, took one step forward, and in a loud voice said, "I'm the wise man bringing frankincense."

"And I'll be singing 'Silent Night,' too," Maizy said.

"Dressed in a long white robe," Delbert tossed in.

"Holding up a stick with a big silver star on top," Maizy said.

"The eastern star," I added proudly.

Wilma turned away from me. "What's your role?" she asked Tiny.

"I'm the wise man with the gold," he said. "Plus I gotta watch out for Gordie. He's got the myrrh."

"And I'm the wise man with the frankincense," I stressed again.

"And what about you?" Wilma asked Delbert.

"I'm the peacekeeper," he said. "I make sure everything goes smoothly."

"Good," Wilma said, gently rubbing her stomach, trying on sweetness for the moment.

The Sunshine Building buzzed. A joyful energy whipped through me, and I decided that if the Christmas spirit had been passing me over, it wasn't passing me over today. Even my fingertips tingled with possibility. Maizy and Delbert had hung an evergreen branch, sporting a big red ribbon, above the door to the dayroom. A white linen tablecloth covered the dining room table, and three red candles in glass lanterns were strategically placed along its top. To the left of the bookcase by the door, a spruce fir was decorated with lights, tinsel, and about two dozen red and gold ornaments. The sofas had been moved out and stored away so that Delbert and Tiny could transform the empty space into a stage. Hay, from Tiny's parents' farm in Winchester, was scattered across the floor, and the manger, an old antique flour bin which belonged to Tiny's aunt, stood in the center of the hay. On one side of the manger, cardboard cutouts of farm animals, which Ace had painted, were propped up.

At five in the afternoon, Maizy grabbed my hand. "Come on," she ordered. "It's makeup time. I'm gonna make you look nice."

"But I ain't supposed to look nice."

"Authentic, then," she said.

"Did you bring the yarn, the robe, everything?"

"Everything," she said, pulling me along, through the door, down the hallway, and into the bathroom. On the floor next to the sink was a brown paper bag which she put on the seat of an old metal chair pushed against the wall. Next she stuck her arm deep into the bag, jostled her hand around, and, with a flourish, pulled out the red satin robe.

"Maizy, we're wasting time," I whined. "Remember, Delbert showed me my costume?"

She draped the robe over the back of the chair and stuck her hand in again. This time, she brought forth the golden, cone-shaped crown. "It's magic," she said, holding the crown high above her head.

"Maizy, I've already seen it." Impatiently, I tapped my left foot against the floor.

Unhurriedly, Maizy set the crown on the metal shelf above the sink and, before I could utter another word, dug her arm even farther into the bag. "Now, what do you think I've found?" she asked.

Nervously, I picked at my cuticles. "I don't know," I said, peevishly, "but —"

She cut me off. "Abracadabra!" she squealed. Out came two crimson velvet slippers, the toes of which curled up. "Abracadabra!" she squealed again. Up rose a mass of black curly hair. "Royal slippers and a real, honest-to-goodness beard," she exclaimed.

"Dag nab!" I said. "It's a miracle!"

Outside, three inches of snow covered the earth. Tiny was inside, helping Gordie put on his costume; so I stood by myself in the cold, thirty-degree weather and waited for my cue.

For two days, I'd been rehearsing in front of my floor-length bathroom mirror. Because I wanted to know exactly what frankincense was, I'd looked it up in the dictionary. "Aromatic gum resin," it said. I didn't just want to play a wise man; I wanted to be a wise man. When I walked upon the stage, I wanted everyone to smell the frankincense in the palm of my hand; and, when I sang "We Three Kings" with the others, I wanted my voice — alone — to be heard.

Jittery, I cracked the knuckles on my left hand, then on my right. I tugged at my beard and grabbed the lapels of my coat. The minute Delbert showed his head, I was ready to remove my coat and toss it into the box beside the door. I swallowed five mouthfuls of air, drew a circle in the snow with my red velvet slipper, and tried to get into character. "I'm a wise man from the Far East," I whispered. "I'm a king of the Orient looking for the baby Jesus." Edging my hand against my eyebrow, I pretended to be searching. "I have a gift for Him." Like a flower blossoming, I unfolded my fingers. "Frankincense," I said under my breath, "for the newborn —"
Someone grunted loudly behind me. Abruptly, I turned around.

"Slow down, Gordie!" Tiny said, pulling on

the boy's arm. "They ain't ready for us yet."

"Land sakes!" I exclaimed. "I'm glad you're here!" My teeth chattered. "I've been rehearsing, getting nervous, thinking Delbert would poke out his head and you and Gordie wouldn't be here, and I'd have to do all three parts myself." My toes tingled and burned. "I mean, my knees are knocking. And not just from the cold." I stomped each foot into the snow. "From fear. Plain old stage fright." I wrapped my arms around myself and hopped up and down. "Yessir, I was about to get wilder than a March hare in mating season."

Tiny, still holding on to Gordie's arm, put his free index finger to his lips. "Calm down, Icy!" he said. "You're making Gordie nervous."

My stomach grumbled. My feet felt numb. My hands shook. "You think Delbert forgot about us?" I asked.

"I doubt it," Tiny said. "Any minute now, he'll poke his head out, and when he does, you best be ready to go."

I rubbed my hands together. "I'm ready," I said, wiggling my toes. I rolled back my shoulders, swallowed a mouthful of frost, and declared, "I'm as —"

"Ready!" Delbert said, his head flashing through the door.

This is it, I told myself, tossing my coat in the box. Tiny, with his arm laced through Gordie's, followed close behind. "You're a king of the Orient," I said.

Inside, "We Three Kings" was playing softly. Arranged in a semicircle, the chairs in the dayroom were filled. Dr. Conroy, Dr. Lambert from Hickory Hall, and Dr. Parker, a guest from out of town, sat in the first row. Several kitchen staff members, who prepared our food in Hickory Hall, along with the driver of the van, occupied the remaining seats. Over the manger, Maizy held up the big silver star. Westward leading, still proceeding, guide us to thy perfect light, I thought, my heart pounding, my thawed feet gliding across the stage to stop in front of the manger.

Gracefully, Wilma extended her arms. "This is the baby Jesus," she said, on cue.

For the first time, it seemed, I saw her face. It was Wilma's face, all right, but somehow it had changed. In robes with a shawl over her head, her features were gleaming. Gone were her glasses. Gone was her mustache. Gone was her dead white skin. She had miraculously become the Virgin Mary, radiating only a mother's love.

Scrunching up my face, I transformed myself also. Sweeping forward, I was but one earthly king bowing before the King of Kings. "We, three kings of the Orient, have brought gifts to the Christ Child," I said, rising. "Mine is the gift of frankincense!" I proclaimed.

Magnanimously, I held out my closed hand. My fingers uncurled, and a silver packet spar-kled in my palm.

In robes the color of jade, Tiny, too, stretched

out his hand. A bright gold nugget shimmered against his skin. "See! I've brought gold!" he said in a deep voice.

Then Gordie, wearing royal blue, stiffly extended his arm. "Myrrh!" Tiny said for him. "The sweetest smell on earth."

In that instant, Delbert, who was in charge of the music, bowed slightly, and the measured, heavy tones of "We Three Kings" filled the air. Staring earnestly at the crowd, Tiny and I started to sing. But as we harmonized, something happened to my voice. Wondrously, it began to change. All of a sudden, it was rich and melodious, deep and hypnotic like the notes we were singing. The audience was spellbound. Not a peep could be heard.

When Delbert opened the double doors, the trance was finally broken. Then, to the strains of "Silent Night," the other patients filed in, forming a semicircle around us.

Delicately, the Virgin Mary placed baby Jesus in His manger.

Gracefully, Maizy waved the silver star, sprinkling glitter across the stage.

Glancing around the room, I spotted the faces of the others. Ace, Reid, Rose, Stevie, Ruthie, Mary, and Deirdre. All of them were staring back at me, saying, "Icy, you're the star. You're the star with royal beauty bright. Go ahead, Icy. Sing." And I, taking their cue, with arms outstretched, like Moses walking through the Red Sea, stepped magnificently forward. Breathing in deeply, I felt my lungs expand with loving, hot air; I felt my voice eager to take off and soar through the room. I inhaled again, readied my lips, and was about to begin "Silent Night" when my eyes fixated on Wilma.

Once the pious Virgin Mary, she now had changed. Her features were sharp and seething; her body was oozing hatred. So completely dark was her evil that like a magnet she drew me to her. Her intense eyes mesmerized me, and I was straitjacketed by her stare. Desperately, I tried to close my eyelids, but both were locked open. Next, I tried to step back, away from her, away from her eyes, but try as I might, I couldn't move. Some force held me in place. Trembling, I struggled to break free; but, like before, I stood frozen.

Frantic, I glanced down.

Wilma's battleship foot was anchored squarely on my red satin robe. Fury poured out of that foot. Rage flooded from that shoe. I winced, tugged at my robe, and attempted, once more, to go backward. But Wilma wouldn't let me. Leering at me, she bent over. Then, ever so swiftly, as though she were smoothing out a wrinkle in my robe, her fingers locked into my beard and savagely yanked it. Like an avalanche, the black mass slid downward only to dangle precipitously from my chin.

Laughter thundered through the room.

Leaning as far away from Wilma as I could, I was pulling back even harder when she deftly lifted her foot. At once, I lurched backward and thudded to the floor.

"The best performance yet," a deep voice said.

"A good laugh," said another.

Just as the singing began, I scrambled to my feet. Panicked, I fixed my beard, wanting to sing "Silent Night" with the others. But it was impossible. Tears as big as mothballs rolled over my lip, slid down my throat, and choked me.

In front of me, Wilma was singing. I watched her mustached mouth open and close. I saw her eyes, relishing my misery, and finally recognized the truth. That womb of hers was filled with the devil's child.

As we sat around the dining room table, napkins in our laps, turkey sliced upon our plates, dressing perched upon our forks, I watched Wilma, who was sitting across from me. Back were her glasses. Back was her mustache. Back was her dead white skin. The purplish red scar that zigzagged down her cheek took on the shape of three 6's. Her smile, lurching upward, belonged to the devil himself.

Wilma leaned over and whispered something to one of the cooks from Hickory Hall. The woman glared at me and laughed. Wilma then twisted around and tapped the driver of the van. Immediately he started to snicker.

She's up to no good, I decided.

Wilma tapped her plate with her fork and cleared her throat.

No good. No good. No. Please no! I thought.

Wilma rose and in a loud voice said, "Icy is a star tonight."

I gotta go, I told myself.

"Maybe she's not a star of wonder," Wilma pressed on.

"I gotta go," I whined.

"But she's still a star."

I tried to stand, but my churning thoughts held me back.

Wilma pointed directly at me, smiled, and began to sing, "O, star so clumsy, star not bright."

Rage twitched my eyes.

"Laugh us through this silly night."

My knees slammed against each other.

"Forever falling, always stumbling, into darkness, far from light," Wilma hideously sang out.

The urge to jerk knifed through me. A croak slithered across my tongue.

I jumped up. "I gotta go!" I cried, but my interior voices screamed, *You gotta defend yourself!* "Gottago!" I yelled. *"CROAK!"* I shrieked, violently swinging my head.

Yes! I heard my thoughts say as the jerk tore through me.

Yes! Yes! Yes! they repeated as I slammed against the table.

"Damn you!" I cried, grabbing the tablecloth. "Damn you!" I screamed, as glasses of milk tumbled over, as plates and silverware rattled. "Damn you!" I yelled again, scooping up a handful of dressing. "You cow dung! You sow!" I roared, pitching it, seeing it splatter against Wilma's cheek. Greedy, I snatched another fistful of dressing, flinging it at her, croaking when she ducked. *"CROAK!"* My body twisted as a thousand spasms whipped through me. My arms churned like oars. My legs kicked at the air. "You devil!" I screamed, popping out my eyes. "Devil sow!" I shrieked, twirling around.

"Icy, don't!" Maizy said, jumping up.

"Please calm down!" Dr. Conroy said.

"Delbert, my bag!" Dr. Lambert was pointing.

After that, I heard nothing.

Around and around I twirled. Until colors bled. And odors blended. Around and around. Until faces blurred. Swirling and swirling. Until I was lost in the whirlwind. Whirling and whirling. Until I was caught in the eye of the storm.

Chapter 24

"There ain't no Icy Sparks," I whispered. "She died weeks ago. On the tip end of Dr. Lambert's needle, she up and died." Lying in my hospital bed, following a crack in the high ceiling, seeing where it would lead, I knew that Icy Sparks, this balloon of skin and bones, was no more than just a seed, meant always to float endlessly, to ride the wind. Floating was what I did best. Icy Sparks would never fall, never crater herself in the dark, warm earth, never be reborn. "Once she was a pretty child with hair the color of goldenrod and yellow ocher eyes," I said. "Now she is a smidgen of pollen caught in the breeze."

I closed my eyes and floated. Days passed over me. Days, with long, gray faces, days that never laughed, days that never cried, the sameness of the days glided above. My face remained solid. The dull-edged days, too bored to swoop down, spared the contours of my nose, the glazed expression in my eyes. I was Icy Sparks, the unborn, forever adrift, beginning before the seed, the unbeginning of the beginning. I was Icy Sparks, awash in the never-never. Never to be. Where was the little girl with gold hair and yellow ocher eyes? "Where are you?" I asked. In the fog of your mind, I thought. In the empty space, existing before conscious time.

"In the infirmary, honey," someone said. "I'm Polly, your nurse. It's time for your medication."

I moaned and turned to look at the strange voice. The face to which it belonged was a white blob surrounded by curly red hair.

"Good girl," Polly said as I swallowed the pills.

No longer was any voice recognizable. Maizy's sweet voice had disappeared; her face, lovely as an angel's, had evaporated. In the sparkling of stardust, she had flown away. The only voices I knew were the voices inside my head, muffled and unclear.

"Maizy's proud of you," Polly added when I closed my eyes. "You're behaving just like a little lady."

I turned over on my side.

"Too bad you can't see her," she continued. "She really misses you."

I tucked in my chin and curled up my knees.

"But I'll tell her you're doing better," she said. "Don't worry, honey. I'll tell her all about you."

Like tadpoles, the voices inside the building were indistinct and always changing, swimming above and below my body, in front and in back of me. Fluid-filled and efficient, they cooed comfort and said that soon I would be going home. But go home I never did.

I, Icy Sparks, can't recollect when I was born. That's because I never was. The unborn can't return to a home that never existed.

"Icy! Icy!" someone said from the doorway.

At last, this was a voice I knew. Cautiously, I opened my eyes. The room was not as colorless as it had seemed at first. White curtains with blue rickrack hung from the windows. On one side of my bed was a white cement wall. Right smack in the center of it was a poster of Walt Disney's *Bambi*; with a twinkle in his eyes and his nose upturned, the fawn seemed to be content, spending time in the woods, smelling the colorful flowers lining the pathway on either side of him. I wondered why I hadn't noticed this happy scene before. On the other side of my bed, standing guard, was a cobalt-blue partition. "Icy! Icy!" the voice repeated. Blinking, I saw that the face in front of me was not blurred. For the first time in weeks, the outline of a person's face was clear.

"Dr. Conroy?" I asked between dry, swollen lips.

"Yes, dear," the voice said. At once, her arms engulfed me, pressing me into her white starched jacket. "Icy, sweetness!" she said.

Ever so lightly, I pushed away, looked up at her, and murmured, "I feel better, not so fuzzy-headed."

"I know," she said. "I stopped the pills last night. Dr. Lambert doesn't like what they've been doing to you. He told me it was my call. So I decided. No more pills."

"No more?" I mumbled.

"No more," she said. "No more shots, no more drugs that make you feel bad."

For a minute, I couldn't talk. Then I said, "You promise?"

Dr. Conroy gently hugged me. "Yes," she declared. "Yes. Yes. Yes."

Feeling confused, I broke away. "I ain't sick?"

She cupped my chin in her hands and stared right into my eyes. "I'd rather see you croak, curse, and jerk than be the way you've been. No child should be lifeless. That's no cure."

"But what about my disorder?" I asked.

"Icy, dear, you are your disorder," Dr. Conroy said. "You're a high-spirited young girl." She laughed loudly. "Granted, sometimes too much so. But we'll work on this. I'll show you a few ways to calm down when you start to feel upset."

"Do you think they'll work?" I asked.

"We'll see," she said. "There are no miracle cures, but we'll try. And, of course, we must talk some more."

"How much more?"

"I want you to feel a little stronger," she answered, "a little better before you leave."

My body tensed. "When will I be leaving?"

"The paperwork is ready to go," Dr. Conroy said. "Just two more weeks, Icy."

"And then I'll go home?" I said.

"Definitely!" she said. "No more broken promises."

"Oh, Dr. Conroy!" I squealed, throwing my arms around her.

As though nothing had changed between us, Maizy came up to me while I was sitting on the edge of my bed and said, "Icy Gal, I'm so proud of you."

"Why?" I asked, when she wrapped her arms around me, tipping me forward. "What's so good about being in here?"

Keeping both of her hands on my shoulders, she eased back away from me, looked me right in the eyes, and said, "Because you're doing so much better. Polly has kept me informed about every little bit of progress you've made. Haven't you, Polly?"

Polly's head appeared around the blue partition. "I did my best," she said, smiling. "Icy, though, was no trouble."

I shimmied, and Maizy's hands slipped off my shoulders. "How come it took so doggone long for you to come here?" I asked her, bouncing my calves against the mattress. "I was lonely without you."

"Doctor's orders," she said, frowning. "And you know how that is. Anyway, I'm here now. The minute Dr. Conroy told me I could come, I did."

"Where's Delbert?" I asked. "I want to see him, too. And Tiny? He's my friend, ain't he?"

"They'll be by later on," she said. "Somebody's got to look after the others."

"And Wilma?" I said sheepishly. "I bet she's been dancing a jig ever since I went away."

"Well, if she's dancing," Maizy said, clicking her tongue, "she's doing it at home."

With those words, I popped up off the bed, took one step toward Maizy, and with a gaping mouth said, "She ain't working in the Sunshine Building?"

"Not anymore," Maizy said, her tone perfunctory.

I was about to squeal unbecomingly and dance a little jig myself when Polly interrupted, "Icy, tell Maizy your good news!"

"I'm going home!" I announced grandly, swallowing my squeal like a marshmallow. "Dr. Conroy told me yesterday."

"Well, that's the best news yet!" Maizy said. "When?"

"In just two weeks," I said.

Polly added, "But we'll miss you."

"Of course," said Maizy matter-of-factly. "We'll all miss you, but the most important thing is that you're going home."

"Sure as the day is long," I said. "I'll be seeing my grandparents real soon."

When Maizy escorted me into Dr. Conroy's office, she was sitting calmly behind her desk. "It feels good seeing you two together again," she said, her eyes taking in our locked arms.

"We're pals," I said, smiling broadly.

"Two peas in a pod," Maizy said.

"Twins," I added.

"Enough!" Dr. Conroy laughed. "I get it. Come here, Icy," she said, motioning with her fingers, "and have a seat."

I sauntered over to my old chair, the one in which my feet didn't touch the floor, and plunked myself down.

"Give us an hour, will you?" Dr. Conroy said, nodding at Maizy, who was leaning against the doorjamb.

"Sure thing," Maizy said, walking through, quietly shutting the door behind her.

"So are you excited?" Dr. Conroy asked me.

"About going home?"

"What else?" she teased.

"I'm as happy as a lark."

Dr. Conroy flicked some lint off her coat sleeve. "Well, aren't you a little bit worried, too?" she said.

Nervously, I moved back in my chair and felt my feet leave the floor. "I reckon," I admitted, squinting over the desktop at her.

"How come?" she wanted to know.

I narrowed my eyes even more. "You know how come," I said, staring at her.

"You're absolutely right," she answered. "I most certainly do. But I want you to say it."

I inched forward, sliding my buttocks to the chair's edge so that my feet were again touching the floor. "I'm afraid I'll act touched in the head," I said. "Like Lonnie Spikes, sitting on the courthouse steps with his tongue hanging out of his mouth, or like Peavy Lawson, that frog-catching, tongue-rolling, eye-popping fool, or like Lane Carlson, except I'll turn into the opposite of him and become a rough, tough, mean ole tomboy."

"Icy," Dr. Conroy said, "you know what?"

"What?" I said, wrinkling up my nose.

"You're hedging, that's what."

"No, I ain't," I said.

"Yes, you are, young lady," she said, pointing a finger at me. "You're talking around an issue, instead of talking about it. Now, I'm going to ask you again. What scares you about going home?"

I became really quiet for several seconds, sat very still, not saying a word, breathing in tiny wisps of air, my chest barely moving, then mumbled, "I'm afraid I'll start acting crazy again. Jerking, twitching, and popping out my eyes. I'm afraid I'll start cussing and bring so much shame on my family that they'll quit loving me."

"Icy, I hope you've learned at least one thing here."

I nodded, biting at my lower lip.

"People don't just stop loving people. You've got to do something really bad for that to happen."

I thought about Mamie Tillman, about the bad thing she had done and how I had failed to do what God wanted me to, but I didn't say a word.

"All of us in the Sunshine Building love you. We haven't stopped. Mr. Wooten, Miss Emily, and your grandparents still love you. No one has stopped caring about you. And do you know why?" I didn't say anything, just shrugged. "Because you're a lovable person," she declared.

"Me, lovable?" I said.

"Completely," she responded.

"Even the bad me?"

"We all have good and bad parts," said Dr. Conroy. "Some of us can just hide the bad parts better."

"Even you?"

"Yes, ma'am," Dr. Conroy said, "even me." She leaned back in her chair and smiled. "But I can teach you ways to hide your bad parts, too."

"All the time?" I asked her.

She shook her head. "Probably not," she went on. "But some of the time my ways will help."

"What ways?" I asked her.

"Like breathing in deeply and counting to ten before you let go of your anger."

"But that doesn't work," I said. "Even when I wait, it always comes out in a conniption fit."

"Then try doing something less instead of something more."

I wrung my hands together and whined, "I don't understand."

"If you feel like jerking your arms," explained Dr. Conroy, "change tactics and do something smaller. Wiggle your fingers. No one will notice your fingers wiggling. If you feel like popping out your eyes, don't. Blink them instead. That's less noticeable. If you feel like cursing, choose words that sound bad but really aren't."

"Dag nab!" I said proudly.

"That's right."

"It sounds easy," I said, "but it won't be."

"I didn't say it'd be easy," Dr. Conroy said. "It'll be hard work, almost impossible for you. But if you can do it once, just one time, you'll be able to do it again."

"Swapping one urge for another," I said.

"Yes," she said, clapping her hands together. "Substitution."

"Substitution," I repeated.

"So you say 'Dag nab it' instead of something else," she continued. "You crack a knuckle, instead of swinging a fist. You've got to learn when to suppress your emotions and when not to."

"Yes, ma'am," I said, nodding.

"And right now," she said, "I don't want to suppress my emotions. I want you to know two things." Rising from her chair, she came over to me and tenderly took my hand. "Icy, I'm very proud of you and who you are, and I give you my word that everything is going to turn out just fine."

At that moment, I substituted the doubt and fear I felt about my future for a little bit of hope. Then, smiling broadly, I squeezed her hand.

Red, white, and blue streamers hung from the ceiling in the dayroom. A banner saying WE'LL MISS YOU, ICY was taped to the wall in front of me. A jam cake sat in the middle of the dining room table, and a punch bowl filled with vanilla ice cream was next to it. I was leaving tomorrow, but today I was having a party!

"Everyone's here but Ruthie," Delbert said. "She's been sent back home."

I looked up and down the table and saw that he was right. All of them were there, all of them except Wilma. Like Maizy had said, her behavior at the Christmas party had been the last straw, and finally the staff had taken courage and complained. Standing beside their seats were Delbert, Tiny, Maizy, Dr. Conroy, and Nurse Polly from the infirmary. Rose, Reid, Ace, Deirdre, Mary, Stevie, and even Gordie were seated at the table.

"I made you a jam cake," Delbert said. "Hope it's as good as Matanni's."

"And I snapped the picture," Maizy said. "We don't want you to ever forget us."

Rose gurgled and grinned in her wheelchair at the far end of the table.

Reid was cooing, while Ace was drawing something invisible in the air.

Gordie eyed me and leaned forward in his chair.

"We all love you," Tiny said.

"Even me," Polly said, "and I just met you."

"We wish you the best in life, Icy," Dr. Conroy said. "We wish you the good parts, the leaves and stems." She motioned me over. "Come here and sit down!" she ordered, pulling out a chair. "To the end of striped snakes," she said, and raised her glass.

I strutted over and sat down. In front of me, on the table next to my plate, was a black and white photograph, as big as a piece of notebook paper, filled with the faces of the people around me.

"To the end of striped snakes!" Dr. Conroy repeated.

"To the end of striped snakes!" they toasted, each of them — Delbert, Maizy, Tiny, and Polly — lifting up a glass.

"To the end of striped snakes!" I said, reaching for my apple cider, raising it high into the air. "To pasture roses. To going home!"

As we were drinking our cider, all of us talking and laughing, I glanced around, took in all of their smiling faces, and spotted Gordie. He was standing by his chair, looking straight at me. Then, in one clean, smooth movement, he saluted, grinned widely, and unobtrusively sat down. No one else had seemed to notice.

Part III

Chapter 25

"Icy and me gotta go to Stoddard's for some thread. I need to hem that skirt we gave her for her birthday," Matanni announced one morning, as we passed through Poplar Holler, nothing more than a blink in the road, on our way to Ginseng. Lute's Grocery, a country store with two gas pumps out front, sat across the road from where three lonely country roads met. Peaceful Valley Baptist Church, a white wooden building with a steeple and a bass-toned bell that chimed each Sunday, was situated one-fourth of a mile down the road from Lute's. Its six stained-glass windows — three on each side — were the pride of Poplar Holler.

"You best ask Icy if she's gonna go with you or if she's gonna sit in the truck," Patanni said, turning his head, staring down at Matanni as he drove. "Or, I reckon, she could go to Miss Emily's. You know she don't like to be around folk."

Loudly, I cleared my throat. "You're talking about me like I'm not here."

"Icy," Matanni said, shifting toward me, "are you coming with me?"

I hesitated for several seconds. It had been years since I'd ventured inside a place as public as Stoddard's Five and Dime, years since I'd tried to do what others did, what others took for granted. In fact, it had been two and a half years since Dr. Conroy had talked to me about substitution. After failing time and time again to trade a wiggle for a jerk, I felt all kinds of contradictions roosting inside me. I was afraid of having a spell in front of people, but also afraid of being cut off from the world. I was terrified of the malady plaguing me, yet also frightened by the calm I felt when I was alone.

"Maybe," I said.

"Please, Icy dear, just this once," my grandmother urged. "You been feeling so good lately."

"If all goes well, and it will," my grandfather added, "each outing will get easier."

I drummed my fingers against the dashboard. "I-I don't rightly . . ." I stammered, "I ain't sure it's —"

Patanni interrupted, "Sugar darling, it's the right thing. Ain't nothing ever gained from not trying."

I sat quietly beside Matanni, my mind still dizzy with worries, and turned my thoughts to more positive things: Poplar Holler, a white, cushioned stillness in the dead of winter; toe-tapping gospel music on the radio; Matanni's deep-dish apple pie, steaming hot from the oven, with a dollop of vanilla ice cream on top; and ros'n ears, fresh ears of corn, roasted in the ashes of a fire, massaged with butter, and eaten — teeth nibbling like fingers playing scales up and down a piano. "Okay," I ventured, breathing in deeply.

We rounded the curve and I caught a whiff of Ginseng. It was the smell of coal dust hanging in the air. You could taste it on your tongue. Along the road in someone's front yard, ugly car engines lay on their backs like turtles dozing in the sun. Car seats were sprawling on their stomachs, their spines arched high. Remnants of coal company housing rotted, gray and yellow, beside the road. Every so often, I spotted brandnew black seams of coal in the sides of mountains where roadwork had been done. Occasionally, a tipple, like a huge black mangled grasshopper, dotted the side of the road, and a stitch of railroad tracks was etched into the ground beyond it. Ten-ton trucks, filled high with coal from the new strip mine, groaned as they passed us.

"I'll drop you two off," Patanni said, " 'cause I got some business of my own to do."

"Such as going to the barbershop," Matanni snapped, "and swapping tall tales with that bunch of ne'er-do-wells." Patanni didn't answer her. Scrunching up his eyes, tightly squeezing the steering wheel, he made a display of focusing on the road. But Matanni didn't buy it. "I know what that kind does," she went on. "You'd better not spend all day playing checkers, wasting money on your luck."

"You tend to your business," Patanni said. "And I'll tend to mine."

No one said another word. We sat back and let the sounds of June — crickets snapping through the grass, the breeze whistling through the windows, birds twittering in flight before the midday heat — argue things out.

"Why, they've put a fresh coat of paint on the courthouse!" Matanni blurted, pointing as we drove down Main Street.

"Samson Coal is still doing good," Patanni said, turning right, driving up the narrow street. "I sure hope we'll be spared layoffs this summer."

"Now, don't you go forgetting us," Matanni added, as the truck came to a halt in front of Stoddard's Five and Dime. "We need no more than an hour, you hear?"

Looking straight ahead, Patanni nodded while I opened the door and slid out. "Give me a hand, will you?" Matanni asked.

"You been around Miss Emily way too long." I leaned over, extending my arm. "Since when did you need help getting out of the truck?" I asked. But Matanni didn't answer; she was too busy latching on to me.

The minute I saw all those heads bobbing up and down so early in the morning, my breath caught in my throat and my palms began to sweat. "Dear Lord," I whispered, "please don't let me go making a fool of myself."

Matanni must have heard me, for she grabbed my hand and squeezed it hard. "Just think calm thoughts," she said. "Just like Dr. Conroy taught you. Ain't nobody looking at you."

But just as she said those words, I spotted Joel McRoy at the far end of the store. He was at least four inches taller, but it was him, all right; I could tell from his oval-shaped mouth — the way he kept it open, as though ready to plunge a Chilly Dilly between those wide, thin lips. Ducking my head down, I sidled up beside Matanni and crept forward. At the same time, my head seemed to detach itself from my body and to float three feet above me. My breath whizzed in and out; and although I tried, I was unable to gulp down a single breath of air. Immediately I started to tremble. Every inch of my skin was shivering.

"Who'd use this?" Joel McRoy snorted, appearing all of a sudden just a few feet in front of me. "Clearasil!" He laughed, holding up a tube, waving it above his head. "Only sissies use this stuff!"

Right then, Irwin Leach, with a smattering of pimples across his forehead, appeared. "I don't like my pimples!" he mocked. "Please, Mama, buy me some Clearasil!"

"Matanni!" I whispered, nervously tugging at her dress.

"Irwin, hush up!" came a voice. A woman in a beehive hairdo, thin as a broomstick, scurried forward. "Irwin, put that down!" She snatched the tube of Clearasil from his hand. "I've already warned you that I ain't putting up with nonsense."

"Gosh darn!" Irwin whined. "We weren't doing nothing."

"Matanni!" I repeated. But she didn't hear me, so distracted she was by the scene ahead.

"We was only funning," Joel McRoy pouted.

Alarmed, I slipped behind Matanni's round form and hid there.

"Keep your funning on the farm!" Irwin's mother scolded. Then she stomped forward, brushing past Matanni and me.

"Yes, ma'am!" both boys said, snickering, as she reached the front of the aisle and whisked around the corner.

"We'll behave ourselves!" Irwin Leach said.

"And be good little boys!" Joel McRoy said, giggling.

"Icy?" Matanni said, twisting around.

I held up my finger, pressed it against my lips, and shushed softly.

"Are you feeling poorly, child?" Matanni asked, wrinkling up her brow, bending down.

Frantically, I began to shake my head. "No!" I murmured. "No! No! No!"

"It's okay, honey," Matanni said soothingly. Her face was drawing closer to mine, her fingers stroking my shoulder blade, when all at once the faces of Irwin Leach and Joel McRoy materialized. All I could see were their smirking lips and scoffing eyes.

"Why, if it ain't crazy ole Icy Sparks!" Joel McRoy said, pointing at me.

"It sure enough is!" Irwin Leach chimed in,

the corners of his mouth stretching upward, his yellow teeth gleaming, a laugh spilling forth.

My eyes surged forward like freight trains.

Joel McRoy hopped back. "I'll be damned!" he said, standing there with his hands on his hips. "Miss Frog Eyes herself."

"Pimple on your chin!" I shouted. "Dammit!" I yelled as the jerk tore through me, wrenching my arms to the left, my legs to the right. "Pimple on your mouth!" I felt the muscles in my face twitching. "Can't you just hush up!" I screamed as my eyes zoomed back. "Pimple on your ass!" I cried, jump-jacking upward, before slumping to the floor.

Confused, I lifted my head. Matanni was muttering something I couldn't make out and gently rubbing my arm. In front and in back of me, people had gathered. On either side of the aisle, heads and eyes were emerging.

Irwin Leach stepped forward, his eyes gleaming maliciously, a drop of saliva in the corner of his mouth. "They should keep you at home," he snarled. "Away from us normal folk."

"Shame on you, boys!" my grandmother said. "Now scat!"

"The poor thing! Let's not be witness to this," I heard a woman say.

"Mommie, why'd she do that?" a tiny voice asked.

"I don't know, baby," came the answer.

"Let her pass," a husky male voice said.

"Be glad to," someone sneered.

"Let's go," my grandmother whispered. "I'm so sorry, Icy," she said. "This was a big mistake." Gently, she wrapped her arms around me. "Come on, sugar darling," she urged, easing me upward. "Matanni will make it okay."

In this way, with our arms cloaking each other, we walked slowly down the aisle toward the door. Their voices buzzing, their eyes stinging me, people parted slightly, moving out of our way. I looked up only once. A young mother was fiercely clutching her newborn against her, protecting the baby's head with her hands.

June 17, 1959

Dear Maizy,

I hope that you and Mr. Cunningham are doing fine. Thank you both for my gift! I love it so much I'm using it right now. My grandparents gave me some new shoes and a grown-up, pleated skirt. Miss Emily gave me a sterling silver ink pen, the kind that adults use, and you've given me this pretty stationery decorated with roses. How sweet of you to remember that I like pasture roses! So my birthday was great even though Matanni, Patanni, and Miss Emily were the only people at my party. Patanni kept calling me "his little lady" which made me feel confused, mostly sad because I'm not exactly "his little lady." The truth is I'm not anybody's "little lady" and probably never will be. Of course, he was referring to the fact that I'm a woman now. Thirteen, I reckon, qualifies me as such. And after I blew out the candles, Miss Emily said pretty much the same thing. "Icy," she said, "you're not my little girl anymore. In some countries, when a girl turns thirteen, she's already married with a baby. So, you're rightfully a little woman now."

Matanni didn't say much, just kept crying and carrying on, saying over and over she didn't want me to grow up, that she wanted me to be her golden-haired girl forever. But I will grow up. That's something we all have to do. Considering the alternative, growing up ain't so bad!

By the way, when is your birthday? Compared to you, I'm kind of thoughtless. Since I left the hospital, you've remembered all three of mine, but I haven't remembered one of yours. But you must admit I sent you a great wedding present. I hunted all over Ginseng for that potato masher. Matanni uses hers all the time, and she makes the best mashed potatoes in Poplar Holler, in Ginseng if the truth be known. I gotta ask you, what's it like being married? What's it like having someone to do for besides yourself? Do you like being Mrs. Maizy Cunningham? Are you two still making out those reading lists?

You told me in your letter that you're

thinking about going to college and studying nursing. What college will you go to? Have you started yet? I — myself — think you'd make a great nurse. You're already my own Florence Nightingale.

Anyhow, when I grow up, I'd like to get married, too, but I can't figure out who'd marry me. Even if the tics, croaks, and curses disappeared, I'd still be different. Living way back in these hills, away from people, I'm protected from the real world. These mountains keep me safe. These far-off hills make my life familiar. What I mean is I know every little detail about our farm. I know that Turk's-cap lilies flourish near the woods and that wild garlic grows beside the road leading to our house. At dusk, on a hot summer night, I know where to find pockets of fireflies and where to get a cup of cold springwater. But still I'm lonely.

I guess being thirteen brings out the philosopher in me. Patanni says that I talk everything to death, that all I need to do is sit back and listen. "Ain't no reason to tell everyone all the thoughts in your head," as he puts it. But he doesn't understand my need to speak, my need to draw myself with words. The trees listen, but they don't talk back. The mountains echo my voice, but they can't argue with me. I live in the loneliness of my own conversations and need someone, anyone, to talk to, "to dialogue with me" — as Miss Emily always says.

Still, I wouldn't trade my life here for a farm

in Georgia. That's what Patanni says when he is trying to make a point. "I wouldn't trade my milk cows for a farm in Georgia," he says. So I reckon Georgia must be a good place for farming. Flatland, it seems, is easier to work but not as pretty as these mountains are. Another thing, flatland can't keep a person's privacy. An eye can see clear into the heart of flat country, but mountain country surrounds its heart with bulk and body. In these mountains, I can be me. So what if I'm a yellow-haired gal who sometimes acts queerly! Who's gonna tell on me? Old Mister Moon? These mountains were made for a person like me. I like to rack my own jenny. I don't want prying eyes minding my business for me.

Miss Emily says that I must get prepared for college. She wants me to push myself, go beyond my limits, and soar above these hills. She wants me to further my education — just like you. But how does she expect me — a girl who talks to mountains and trees, to schools of fish in Sweetwater Lake — to get along, instead, with schools of people? Right now, it's only me and her. She brings the books and teaches me. Just like your husband did, she makes out reading lists, and I read all of the books she jots down. I'm a good student, but a student to her alone. She's always telling me that college life is in my future.

I know she means well. But, instead of being encouraged, I want to scream out, "If they

311

won't let me go to school here, here in these mountains where they know me, do you really think they'll let me go anywhere else — where the land is flat, where the heart beats bright red for all to see!" But I don't say anything. I just bite my lip because my mouth starts to quiver. Mostly, I sit quietly on this wide front porch.

Maizy, you should know. Is there a land beyond these mountains? In the great wide world, can a person — so very different — wear her heart on her sleeve?

All I know is that on June 10th, I became a "little woman." Even my bosom had changed, poking out — just a smidgen — like two little powder puffs. When that red patch of blood soiled my panties, I felt scared. I didn't know what was happening to me; so, I showed Matanni the stain. "You got your grannies on," she said. I didn't know what that meant. She said it meant I was a grown-up woman. Then, Miss Emily explained that what had happened was something called a menstrual cycle, a monthly period.

To tell the truth, I still feel like Icy Sparks, that golden-haired, yellow-eyed little girl. I still feel like the Icy Sparks you knew in Sunshine Building. Like her, I still croak, jerk, and curse. The difference is that now Patanni, Matanni, and Miss Emily are privy to the real Icy Sparks. They see me clearly, not only my leaves and stems but also my roots and berries. Still though, only three people in these mountains really know me, really love me.

Maizy, I need to ask you. Can you tell me who'll take their place when the three people I love most in this world are gone?

With all my love!
Icy Sparks,
mountain gal &
philosopher

Since I was growing up, Patanni thought I needed to see my whole self in the mirror. "When Louisa was sprouting up, she always wanted to see how this and that dress looked on her," Patanni said. "It'll be the same for you, too," he added, nailing up a cheap, floor-length mirror on the back of my bedroom door.

"That's right," Matanni said. "Soon you'll be spending more time in front of this here mirror than with us." She squeaked her tiny laugh. "The truth is you're already taller than I am."

"That ain't nothing new," I said. "I've been taller than you for years." I walked over to look at my reflection. With the exception of those acorns of mine called breasts and that peach fuzz called pubic hair, I still resembled a kid no more than ten years old. Naturally, I was a little taller, having grown about two inches, but still I was small — just under five feet.

"Icy Sparks, that simply ain't true!" my grandmother shot back. "While you been growing, I been shrinking. That's all."

"While you been shrinking, Miss Emily's been getting fatter," I said.

Patanni held out his arms, rounded them into a circle, looped together his hands, and puffed out his cheeks. "How much do you reckon she's put on?" he asked.

"About fifty more pounds," I said. "If she's telling the truth."

Patanni rubbed the bald spot on the back of his head. "Whew!" he said. "Three hundred and fifty pounds!"

"She'd better drop some of it," Matanni said, "or else she'll die young."

Angrily, I turned around and faced my grandmother. "Don't you be talking like that!" I fussed. "Miss Emily's gonna live a real long time. Mr. Dooley Sedge's sister said so."

"Geneva Sedge, the janitor's sister?" Patanni raised his eyebrows.

"Why, she's a professional palm reader!" I declared. "The next time Miss Emily comes over, take a gander at her lifeline. It crisscrosses from one side of her palm clear over to the other."

"You don't say!" Patanni said, grinning.

"And it don't matter which hand," I said. "Either one. Both say she's gonna live a long time."

"Does she believe it?" Matanni asked.

"Told me she did," I said. "And I believe her. She's fat, but her heart's getting stronger."

"And, pray tell, how does Miss Emily know that?" Matanni asked.

"Her heart specialist in Lexington told her so.

'You must be doing something right,' he says, 'but that something, I guarantee you, is not massage.' Miss Emily insists that the good doctor won't acknowledge the healthy benefits of massage."

"Moss-hash?" Matanni said.

"Rubbing," I explained. "Rubbing away the hurt places in your body."

"Don't that beat all!" Patanni said, clapping his hands against his thighs. "Miss Emily ain't never gonna change. She's always coming up with a thousand reasons to help her stay the same."

"Wait and see!" I said, pointing my index finger at him. "When Miss Emily took sick and went to Florida, she stayed at a health clinic where they massaged her two hours every single day, and look at her now. I bet she outlives us all."

"I sure do hope so," Patanni said. "I'm getting too old and feeling too puny to be one of her pallbearers. There are worst things in life than death."

"Shame on you!" I said, running over and hugging him tightly. "If anything happened to any of you, I don't know what I'd do."

"Don't you worry none!" Matanni said. "We plan on being here a long, long time."

Chapter 26

"Howdy! Long time, no see," Miss Emily said from her overstuffed lounge chair as we passed through the front door of her store, the CLOSED sign already up, the doorbells tingling. "Somehow I had an inkling you might pay me a visit today." She wiped her face with a red-and-white-checked handkerchief and said, "Tell me, Icy Gal, what's been going on?"

"I need a Coke first," I announced, making a rough, gurgling sound, going over and draping my arms around her neck. "A cold one with ice in it. My throat's parched."

"Icy, don't you beat all!" Patanni said. "Miss Emily wants to know how you're doing, and all you want to do is drink her Cokes. If you want a Coke, you best ask me."

"Well, then," I countered, "will you buy me a Coke, one with ice in it?"

"Here!" He tossed me a quarter. "Now get! I need me some conversation and supplies."

Clutching the coin, I headed toward the back of the store where the Coke machine was, inserted my money, lifted up the lid, and grabbed a bottle with ice clinging to it. Then, using the bottle opener that dangled from a string attached to the lid, I popped off the cap, sauntered toward the back screen door, and settled down into a metal chair tucked into a corner of the porch. I was sipping my Coke, slurping frozen mush through my teeth, when Lena, Miss Emily's tiny orange tabby, slithered against my legs and began to cry. "Yeowwwww . . . yeowwwww . . . yeowwwww!" she meowed, jacking up her rear end, wiggling it around. "Yeowwwww . . . yeowwwww . . . yeowwwww."

Then, out of nowhere, in a blink of the eyes, a long-haired, gray cat appeared. "YEOWWWWW . . . YEOWWWWW!" he bellowed, crouching down, watching Miss Emily's cat from the alleyway.

"Yeowwwww . . . yeowwwww!" Lena droned, purring loudly, ducking down on her front legs, raising her butt up high.

"YEOWWWWW . . . YEOWWWWW . . . YEOWWWWW!" the tomcat screeched. And, flying through the air, he leaped upon the porch; then, with yeowwwww . . . yeowwwww still singing in his throat, he mounted her. Gnashing his teeth into her neck, he jerked back her head, completely lifting her front legs off the floor.

Mesmerized, I didn't move.

The tomcat started to push back and forth, his gray coat engulfing her orange fur, while Lena's yellow eyes continued to glow, until abruptly all movement stopped.

Feeling ashamed, thinking I shouldn't have seen such a sight, I was about to chase the gray cat away and redeem myself when both cats gracefully shook themselves, their coats rippling across their backs, and — like dancers — began to circle each other. For several minutes, they seemed almost woven together; then, side by side, they lay down on the porch. Two cats, one tiny and one big, purred rhythmically while the male tenderly licked the female's back.

During the past two springs, toad-strangling rains had saturated the soil and the possibility of flooding had become a major concern, but this spring had been drier than usual, and I was hopeful that today would be my lucky day, that today I'd happen upon the rose that most resembled my mother. As I hiked, I trailed a stick behind me. Every so often, I'd turn around to see the furrow, like a line of snail's slime, left behind. Dropping my stick, cupping my hand over my eyes, I stared at the underbelly of the cliffs to the right of me. Goat's-beard, those small white flowers that look like snowflakes strung along a spider's web, peeked out at me; and for a second I forgot that it was summer. Then the sun glinted off the rock face, and the goat's-beard glistened brilliantly. "I love it here," I said, and before I knew it, I had stretched out my arms and started to spin. "This is mine," I said, twirling faster and faster. Beads of sweat flew off my face. "All mine," I said, then dug my heels

318

into the ground, rocked clumsily, and stopped.

"This is mine," I heard a voice mimic. "All mine."

"Who's there?" Nervously, I glanced around, but spotted only patches of pink clover and wild garlic with its pinkish flowers. "Who said that?" I asked, suddenly afraid that the voices inside me — silent for so long — were becoming restless again.

"Who's there?" the voice repeated. This time, it came from my left. "Who said that?" the voice echoed.

Immediately I whipped around. "Tell me this instant!" I demanded, but no answer came. Only the breeze, trickling through the pines, replied; and I was on the verge of calling out again when the explanation came to me. "An echo!" I laughed, clapping my hands. "An echo is gonna get me!"

"No, it ain't!" the voice answered.

Startled, I clamped my lips together and stood very still.

"Ain't no echo gonna get you," the voice said. "But your own true love might."

I scrunched up my shoulders. "Who's there?" I squeaked.

"Guess," the voice replied.

"But I don't know," I said.

"Just guess," the voice prodded. "Give it a try."

My eyes darted from side to side. "I don't want to." Nerves, like bedbugs, crawled over my skin.

"If you don't try, you'll never find out," the voice said.

"But I don't know who to guess," I whined.

"I'll give you a clue," the voice said. "You knew me when."

"What kind of a clue is that?" I said. "When, what?"

"You knew me when. We were ten years old and in love."

"Where are you hiding?" I yelled, swiveling around, my heels eating the dirt, my eyes hunting for strangers. "I know you're back there in those baby pines. Why don't you come out and face me like a man?"

" 'Cause you might reject me," the voice replied. "That was what you always did. You always told me no."

"If you don't show yourself," I warned, balling both hands into tight fists, "I'm gonna stomp right through this wild garlic and come out punching."

"You're still spunky," the voice responded. "Ain't no one able to cut a rusty like you!"

"If you mean I'm about to take a fit," I snorted, "well, you ain't wrong!" Bouncing back and forth on the tips of my toes, I leaped forward and, bending down, struck at a mass of wild garlic. Its pink flowers scattered like dandelion fluff. "Come on out here, you big sissy! Face me like a man!"

"Well, if you insist," the voice said politely.

From about eighteen feet away, someone

moved. Olive-green flashed through spruce-green pines. A shock of auburn hair and two green eyes shot up, and a familiar face came toward me. I dropped my arms to my sides; then, blinking my eyes, I spotted the string of freckles — traveling the length of the nose — and blinked again. Bracing my hand above my forehead, blocking the sunlight, I got a better look. Sure enough, the hair was brown with some red in it; the eyes were bright green; and the freckles were plentiful.

When he flashed a thin-lipped grin and lisped, "Icy Sparks," I knew — without a doubt — who was ambling toward me. "If you ain't a sight for sore eyes!" the voice said, coming to a halt about four feet away.

My eyes twitched. "Peavy Lawson," I muttered, then flicked my lashes and stared at this boy rooted broad-legged in the earth. "Well, ain't you all growed up!"

He grinned, looked straight at me, and said, "You ain't changed one bit. You're still the prettiest girl in Crockett County!"

I studied his wiry frame, at least five feet four inches tall, and saw the muscles rippling beneath his T-shirt. No longer did his eyes pop out from his head. Instead, they slanted upward, sparkling emerald green, like the eyes of an exotic animal. Even his hair had changed. The straggly brown strands that once flopped lopsidedly over his forehead had disappeared. Now a luxurious tangle of auburn brown hair replaced them. I mumbled, "Well, I reckon you've changed for the best."

He took another step closer, cleared his throat, and said, "I knowed you lived out here, but I didn't expect to see you."

I could feel the perspiration leaking from my pores. Daintily, I plucked at my blouse. "Sometimes I go for walks," I said, flushing a deep red, lowering my head.

"Every Thursday, I come here," he said. "Old Man Potter hired me to feed his livestock and work his fields. I was on my way back there when I seen you. Like a vision you was, twirling and twirling with your gold hair flying. The minute I saw that yellow hair, I knew it was you."

"And you just stood there, real silent-like, spying on me." I looked up and glared. "Laughing at me, doing what Joel McRoy and Irwin Leach put you up to."

"Never," he said, and his green eyes flashed. "That ain't true! I done ate a bologna sandwich at Lute's Grocery, and I was on my way back, that's all, when I caught you. Like sunlight spinning inside a raindrop!"

"And Joel McRoy and Irwin Leach didn't send you here to spy on me?" I asked.

"No, I promise!" he said. "That's the word with the bark on it! You know I'd never laugh at you!"

"Cross your heart!" I demanded.

"Cross my heart and hope to die!" He crossed his chest with one hand, then held both palms up high for me to see.

Instantly, my face brightened. "I was heading over to Clitus Stewart's place," I said sheepishly. "Matanni told me I could find some pasture roses there."

"I wouldn't know about that," he said, shaking his head.

"Would you like to accompany me?" I asked shyly.

He smiled broadly. "Sure," he said.

Slowly, we walked down the pathway. His stride was unhurried and solid. Self-consciously, I took smaller steps. Once he made a gurgling noise. His bottom lip began to pucker, and I expected him to stop and spit into the milkweed, but he didn't. He simply shuddered, as though jerking to attention, and swallowed hard. "Is Mrs. Stilton, that ole stinkweed, still around?" I asked, knowing full well that she was.

"She's a force to be reckoned with," he replied.

"Is she still ugly?" I asked.

"Even uglier," he said. "And mean as a rattler."

"Next year, you'll be in junior high, far away from her," I said.

"Fine by me," he said.

"How about the others?" Stopping, I pushed a rock with my tennis shoe. "Emma Richards, Lucy Daniels, and that no-'count lying Irwin Leach?"

"Emma's turned into a regular spoiled brat. She's always whining about this and that."

"And Lucy Daniels?"

"To hear tell, she's a big kisser. At recess, she

sneaks behind the garbage cans and plops juicy ones on Irwin Leach."

"Ugh!" I poked out my tongue. "She's just kissing pimples. That's something I don't want to see."

"But, tarnation, I wish you could," Peavy said, " 'cause I miss you."

"Well, you're the only one in Ginseng missing me," I said.

"That ain't true," he said. "Lane missed you real bad. Before he went away, he got real home-sick for you."

Glancing down at my finger, I remembered Lane Carlson and his wart. "How's he doing?" I asked.

"How do you think?" Peavy said.

"Not so good," I said, walking again.

"Mil-i-tar-y school." Peavy emphasized each syllable.

I rolled back my eyes. "I can't even imagine it!"

"Somewhere in Virginia," he said.

"I can't believe . . ." I began. Then, shaking my head, I changed the subject. "Look, over there, at the blue flowers in the thicket!"

"Blue-eyed grass!" we both said, forgetting pasture roses, running toward the patch of blue.

"Next week, same time, same place," he said, picking a bouquet of flowers, gallantly giving it to me.

When I got home, the house was quiet. Softly, I tiptoed to my room, and, in a swoon, I fell on my bed. Crossing my arms over my chest, I closed my eyes and tried to recall every little detail that was him: his deep green eyes, so gorgeous and not bulging — no, not in the least bit bulging from his head! — his auburn hair, not one straggly strand — oh, how could I have been so unfair! — his body, so compact and strong; his mouth, thin-lipped, yes, but sensitive and sweet; his upbringing — hadn't he been polite? Oh yes! Even though he should have spit — for his health, that is — he hadn't; and his voice, the way he said, "Icy," gently lisping the *cy* . . . well, it was simply too noble! Weren't his lips trying to taste my name? With each recollection, I sighed, wiggled my toes, and sighed some more.

"Peavy Lawson!" I crooned. "You were never, never a frog! No, my dear, you were a prince!" I sighed and thought about Sir Lancelot and Queen Guinevere, about F. Scott Fitzgerald and Zelda, about Robert Browning and Elizabeth Barrett Browning, about love, love, love, about Icy Sparks and — maybe, just maybe — Peavy Lawson. In my mind's eye, I saw the future, my future, and it wasn't a long country road, winding lonely through these hills. No, it was a pathway, leading to a tidy little house, surrounded by a white picket fence, covered with moonflowers, shining in the night. Inside glowed the smiling faces of Peavy, our three children, and me. "Icy Sparks and Peavy Lawson," I whispered. "Bread and butter. Toast and jam. Salt and pepper." I breathed in and exhaled a whoosh of hot air. "Love and more love," I said, falling asleep with the clear image of love, Peavy Lawson, and my future etched in my mind.

"Where are my pasture roses?" Matanni asked when I came down for supper. "I wanted a bunch of them for the table."

"What?" I said, looking right through her.

"My pasture roses," she said. "Over by Clitus Stewart's place."

I meandered over to the sink and stared out the window. "I couldn't find any," I said.

"I'm surprised," Matanni said, stirring a pot of pinto beans. "When the weather's good, that field grows them better than any spot I know."

"Well," I said, still gazing out the window, shuffling my right foot along the linoleum rug, "I reckon I didn't try as hard as I could've."

"Oh," Matanni said, taking the spoon out of the beans and putting it on the counter. "How come?"

At that moment, the thought of telling her about Peavy Lawson, of describing how we met on the pathway, so rattled my thoughts that when I turned around I was unable to mutter a word.

"Well, why not?" Matanni asked, perturbed.

I took one step forward, putting my fingers to my lips as though to pull out the words, but instead began to stutter. "I-I-I-I-I," I said, my head bouncing forward like a period after each I. "I-I-I-I-I-I," I stammered, becoming more and more frustrated, sensing a violent tic — the first one since the bad one at Stoddard's — coming on, fearing that every sweet fantasy, every thought about Peavy Lawson would spill forth if I didn't let it loose. Then, before I could sputter again, a spasm — like an earthquake splitting the ground — tore through my body, and I whiplashed like buckling tin.

"Icy, child!" My grandmother rushed toward me. "Icy, child!" she repeated as I corkscrewed and uncoiled my body again and again until, all worn out, I fell to the floor. "What happened?" She knelt down beside me and cradled my head in her lap. "You ain't done this since Stoddard's."

Nestling against her, I felt her fingers on my forehead. "I don't know," I mumbled.

Tenderly, she looked into my eyes. "It's okay about them roses," she said, placing her warm hand on the side of my cheek.

I nodded.

"I didn't mean to upset you."

Sighing, I closed my eyes. "It wasn't the roses," I murmured. "It was something else. I just can't bring myself to tell you."

She leaned over and kissed my eyelids. "When you're ready you will," she said, walking me over to the sofa. "Until then, we won't bother about it." Then, taking my face in her tiny hands, she began to sing softly, "What wondrous love is this oh my soul oh my soul. What wondrous love is this oh my soul. What wondrous love is this that caused the Lord of bliss to bear the dreadful curse for my soul!"

And listening to her sweet voice, I fell asleep.

"Where's my mousey meat?" Patanni hollered as he banged through the front door. "Where's my corn pone? My pinto beans? My poke sallet?"

Matanni and I jumped up off the sofa. Matanni pulled back her shoulders and brought her hands down the front of her dress. She tugged on her apron and straighted it. I wiped my eyes with the backs of my hands, headed straight toward the kitchen, and sat down. "I'm hungry, too!" I yelled back. "Where's my stewed possum? My parched corn? My plum grannies?"

"Where's the cook?" Matanni chimed in. "I haven't been putting the big pot in the little one."

"Well, someone has," Patanni said, poking his head through the door, " 'cause it smells damn good in here."

"Virgil!" Matanni scolded. "Please don't curse around Icy!"

Patanni screwed up his eyes and laughed. "Icy knows words I've never heard before!" he said. "You should be jumping on her, not me!"

"Hush your jabbering!" Matanni ordered, tapping over to the stove. "And sit down."

"Well, is supper ready?" he asked, dragging

out a chair and dropping into it.

"The tenderloin is crisp the way you like it," she said. "I even fried up some sweet onions to put on top."

"I do love mousey meat!" Patanni said, his eyes twinkling, his callused brown hands shaking as he unfolded his napkin and ironed it across his knees.

"Here's the corn pone," Matanni said, putting down a platter. "And the pinto beans and a bowl of poke sallet."

"Sit down, Tillie!" Patanni said. "We can't commence till you join us."

"And you can't commence till grace is given," Matanni added, sitting down beside me and grasping my hand.

"Ask the blessing. Amen," Patanni said, and before Matanni could fuss at him, he had plunged his fork into a piece of pork tenderloin, plunked it upon his plate, chiseled off a healthy hunk, and shoveled it inside his mouth. "Hit ain't fair!" he said. "Several others asked for her hand, but she chose me. While I've been eating the best vittles in Crockett County, they've — all — had to make do."

"Stuffy Barrett doesn't look like he's starving," my grandmother said.

"Stuffy was puffy before he proposed," Patanni said. "Good cooking ain't responsible for his girth."

Matanni nibbled on a piece of pork. "Once he was a looker," she said, "back when he was thin."

"A person can't go that far back!" Patanni huffed. "From three miles away, you could always spot Stuffy. First you'd see this little bitty head." He made a circle with his thumb and index finger. "These little bitty arms." He wiggled both of his baby fingers. "And long, long legs." He walked his middle fingers across the table. "And in between, this fat, balloon belly. From afar, he looked like a great big ball rolling through the air."

"He was a looker, all right," Matanni giggled.

"You-all are mean," I said. "Stuffy can't help how he looks, no more than Miss Emily can."

"Icy, we're kidding," Patanni said.

"Just cutting the fool," Matanni said.

I poked some corn pone into my mouth and, with my mouth crammed, finally mumbled the truth. "I saw Peavy Lawson today." Crumbs spluttered like sawdust from my lips. "And he was beautiful!"

"I couldn't understand a word." Matanni shook her finger at me. "You know better than to talk with your mouth full."

"Probably just another dressing down." Patanni slurped a spoonful of pinto beans. "Icy here has got her dander up. She's loaded for bear."

Chapter 27

I was half-awake when I heard the horn honking and Miss Emily's voice yelling, "Icy Gal, rise and shine!"

"Doggone," I moaned, and rolled out of bed. Slouching over to my dresser drawer, I retrieved a pair of jeans and a sky-blue T-shirt and put them on.

"Icy Gal, rise and shine!" she screamed again. "I need some help!" Once more, the horn sounded.

I could hear Matanni and Patanni down in the kitchen. They seldom greeted her first because they understood that this privilege was meant for me. At least, from Miss Emily's viewpoint it was. "No God-fearing child goes to school in the summer," I said, banging out the front door, heading for her car.

"I can see your lips moving, but I can't hear you," she said, poking her head out the window.

"I was saying that no God-fearing child goes to school in the summer."

"Your going to school ended officially with Mrs. Eleanor Stilton," she said curtly. "As you well know, for some time now, school has been coming to you."

"Whoopee," I sassed.

"I don't cotton to sarcasm," she said, swinging open the car door.

"Sorry," I mumbled.

"Look what I brought you!" She pointed at a stack of books on the seat beside her.

"That ain't nothing new," I said. "You bring me books. I get 'em from Mr. Wooten. Heck, I got a whole roomful of books."

She pursed her lips. "What did you say, child?"

I corrected myself, "That isn't anything new."

"True," she conceded, "except that one of those rectangles isn't a book."

"Really?" I said, scrambling around to the other side of the car and flinging open the door. "Where is it?" I asked, unstacking the pile of books, finding nothing different.

"Look closely," she said. "You're moving too fast."

Once more, I fingered through the books. This time, though, my fingers landed on a red box. "It looks just like a book cover," I said.

"Looks can be deceiving," she replied. "Why don't you take the lid off?"

Slowly, deliberately, I ran my finger around the edge of the box. Next, I picked it up, held it close to my ear, and shook it. It made a thudding noise.

"Take a guess!" she suggested.

"Chocolates?" I said.

332

"Of course not!" she said.

"Well, if they were chocolates, I'd give you some."

"Icy Gal, it's not candy, and you know it." She crinkled her nose and shook her head.

"Peanuts?" I ventured.

"There aren't any peanuts in that box," she snapped, "and you know that, too."

"Well, if peanuts were inside, I'd give you a handful," I said.

Exasperated, Miss Emily plopped her fat hands on the steering wheel. "What on earth do you think you're doing?" she said.

"Teasing you," I said. "And from the looks of your red face, it seems like I'm doing a good job."

"Please, Icy Gal," she pleaded. "You know how excited I get when I bring you something special."

"Oh, all right." Relenting, I slowly raised the lid. A bright yellow handbag — the size of a sheet of notebook paper — was inside. "It's a pocketbook!" I exclaimed, whipping it out of the box. I held it up by its long yellow strap and swung it back and forth. "It's yellow, just like my hair," I said. "And so pretty!"

"Well, it should be. It cost me a pretty penny," she said.

Immediately perplexed, I asked, "But what's it for?"

"For your birthday," she answered. " 'Cause now you're a little woman and should dress like one."

"But you already gave me my birthday presents," I said. "That pretty silver ink pen and all those books."

"The pen's for doing homework, and I always bring you books," she explained. "But the pocketbook . . . now, it's something special. Elvira, down at Dress Beautiful, ordered it for me, and it didn't come till yesterday."

"I love it!" I squealed, leaning over, hugging her quickly, then leaping out of the car. "I'll be right back. I want to show Matanni."

"What about me?" she pouted. "You know I need some help."

"Lickety split I'll be right back!" I said, dashing up the hill with my brand-new yellow pocketbook dangling over my arm. When I reached the front door, I stopped, gathered my breath, and collected my thoughts; then — with my arm thrust out — I strutted through the living room and into the kitchen.

"Have you done hurt your arm?" Patanni asked, saucering his coffee and slurping it down.

I moved my arm from side to side. Like a handkerchief, hanging from a clothesline, drying in the breeze, the pocketbook moved, too.

"Feast your eyes on that!" Matanni said, slapping the table. "Is that our grandchild putting on the dog?"

" 'Pon my honor, I think so," Patanni said.

"I'm not puttin' on airs," I said indignantly. "I wanted you to see what Miss Emily got me for my birthday." Then, before Patanni could question me further, I said, "Miss Emily gives me books all the time, but this pocketbook, here, is something special."

"You look respectable, all right," Matanni said, coming over, fingering my handbag.

"Like that yellow-haired gal who took care of you at the hospital," Patanni said.

"Me — look like Maizy?" I said.

"Yes, ma'am," he said, rubbing his square chin. "Looking at you now puts me in the mind of her."

"Maybe, one day, I'll get married, too," I said, "and be just like her. Maybe I'll even become a nurse."

"We should make Icy a reservation at the Blackberry Inn," Patanni said, winking. "Of course, she'll have to go there all by herself, since Maizy ain't here and they won't let the likes of us common folk in."

"Hush!" I said.

"Let loose," Matanni ordered, yanking at my arm. "I want to carry it, too." With my yellow purse hanging from her arm, she strode leisurely across the kitchen floor to the other side of the room. "It's perfect," she said. "Lightweight and sturdy. Big enough, but not too big."

"Miss Emily ordered it from Dress Beautiful," I said, fluttering my fingers, motioning for my present back. "It cost her a pretty penny."

"I guess so," Matanni said, scurrying over, returning the strap to my arm.

"Icy Gal!" Miss Emily yelled. "Icy Gal! Are you going to make me sit out here all day?"

"This way you got something to carry your pad in," Miss Emily explained.

"What pad?" I asked.

"Your Kotex," she said, raising her eyebrows. "For when your next monthly begins." Leaning forward, Miss Emily pressed her lips together and ceremoniously picked up a brown-jacketed book lying on the kitchen table. "*From Girl to Woman* by Allison Smide," she said, looking at its cover, handing it to me. "Read it for next week." Then, before I could protest, her plump hand plucked another, smaller book from off the table. "*Your Body and You* by Dr. Miriam Wiley," she said. "Read this one, too."

I nodded and made a sour face. "Why don't you bring me some good books?" I asked. "Maizy's husband gives her good books to read. She told me so."

"Well, I'm not Maizy's husband," Miss Emily snapped. "I'm your friend, here to teach you, not coddle you."

"*Little Women* was fun to read," I said. "Jo, Meg, Amy, and Beth teach you about growing up, too. Why don't you bring me books like that?"

"Because Mr. Wooten robbed me of that plea-sure," Miss Emily said, brusquely shoving *Your Body and You* at me. "Anyway, this isn't fun stuff. It's serious business. I want you to know about your body so you'll be able to take care of yourself."

"Good night!" I said, plopping *From Girl to Woman* on top of the table, snatching *Your Body and You* out of Miss Emily's hands, flipping it open, eyeing the tiny print. "This'll take me forever."

"You best get started, then," she ordered. "On Wednesday next week, I'll be here, and we'll talk about what you've read." I moaned. "Oh, by the way," she said, winking at me, "have a list of twenty questions prepared — based on the material in these two books."

"Yes, ma'am," I answered, moaning again. "I'll read both of these doggone, boring ole books. *Your Body and You*," I said sarcastically, thumping it on top of the other. "*From Girl to Woman*. If I'm a woman, why don't you treat me like one and let me read what I want to?"

"Because, Miss Put Upon, you need to learn about your menstrual periods."

"Matanni calls it the curse," I added.

Miss Emily frowned. "Well, I wouldn't exactly call it that," she said. "Menses is a good thing, the natural functioning of a woman's body. You need to understand what's happening to you each month. You need to learn how to take care of yourself, how to keep yourself clean."

"Last time, I used toilet paper," I said.

"Only 'cause that was your first one," Miss Emily said. "Later on, you'll need more than toilet paper. Without a doubt, you'll need one of these." With those words, she stuck her plump hand into her huge handbag and brought out a soft white cotton rectangle. "A pad!" she exclaimed. "Feel it!" she ordered, handing it to me. "It's called a Kotex, and I bought you a box of them. This thing," she went on, shoving her hand back inside her purse, "keeps it in place." Out came a white belt with metal hooks in the front and back. "Give me the pad," she said, gesturing with her fingers. "I'll show you how it works." She took the Kotex, pulled back two paper-thin ends, and fastened each on a metal hook. "See, you put this on," she said, shaking the belt, the Kotex rocking back and forth like a scale. "It goes around your waist, and the pad goes beneath you."

"Ugh!" I said. "Between your legs?"

"Uh-huh," she said. "This belt is small, the right size for you."

"Yuck," I said, "it must feel something awful!"

"Not really," Miss Emily said. "Once you get used to it, you won't even know it's there."

"I don't believe you," I said, making a face. "That thing rubbing between your legs, poking out like a diaper. I don't think I'll ever get used to it!"

"Oh, yes, you will," she said, extending her arm. "Before you start feeling too sorry for yourself, just imagine being me. You'd need a suitcase to carry my pad in. Here, take it!" she demanded, shaking her hand.

Just as I positioned my hand beneath the belt

straps, Patanni stomped through the kitchen door and got a glimpse of the pad dangling like a poor woman's pocketbook. "Dang!" he grunted, did an about face, and marched out.

At once, Miss Emily began to giggle. Clamping my hands over my mouth, I laughed with her, the Kotex dangling below my chin. "Land sakes!" Miss Emily said, shaking all over, locking her fleshy, puffy hands together. "From now on, we need to have our private conversations upstairs in your bedroom."

"If we don't," I said, snickering, "Patanni might get the wrong idea and take to using this Kotex like a spittoon."

"Lordy, we wouldn't want that," Miss Emily went on. "I can already hear the good people of Ginseng. 'Virgil Bedloe's been acting queerly of late.'"

"Quit that cuttin' up!" Matanni hollered from the living room, our guffaws booming, our bodies quaking so much that the table joggled against the floor. "Or else you'll bring the whole house down!"

With red cheeks, Miss Emily quickly composed herself. Breathing in deeply, crossing her arms over her chest, she waited until her skin was light pink again. Then, using the table for support, she heaved up from her chair. "Those aren't much fun, either," she said, making a straight face, pointing at the other books on the table. "Next month, though, I'll bring you some fun books. Vacation reading."

"Finally!" I said, clapping my hands.

"Remember," she said, waddling toward the door, the floorboards creaking beneath her. "Twenty questions."

I made a move to get up but was mesmerized by her huge bulk blocking the doorway. "Just imagine being me," she had said, and, at that moment, I did. There I was with a gigantic garter belt around my waist, a Kotex the size of a pillow squashed between my thighs.

"No, don't bother," she said. "I can make it by myself."

Chapter 28

On Saturday, I decided to return to Clitus Stewart's place. I wanted to find those pasture roses and bring Matanni an armful of them, not only for the kitchen table but also for the living room. On the way, I lingered in the same spot where I had run into Peavy Lawson. There, beneath the cliff covered with goat's-beard, I daydreamed about his tight, sinewy body and his crooked, impish smile. When I recalled the smell of him — a mixture of hay and licorice — I groaned and longed for him to be near me. "My love," I whispered. "My own true love." Tightly, I wrapped my arms around me. "Thank you for the hug," I said, imagining Peavy's strong arms holding me close. I trailed my fingertips down my cheeks and pretended that Peavy was caressing my skin. Then, remembering his sweet and sensitive mouth, I puckered my lips and gently kissed the air. Over and over, I pretended to kiss him. In my mind's eye, Peavy and I were ardent lovers, our bodies aching with each kiss. "Yes! Yes!" I whispered, longingly; and — with my body tingling all over — I slowly began to sing.

"Down in the valley, the valley so low." Again I started down the pathway, my eyes following my feet. "Hang your head over, hear the winds blow." For the first time in a long while, I took pleasure in the sweetness of my voice. The tension inside me began to dissolve as my lips stretched open, and my tongue tingled with relief as my voice massaged the muscles in my mouth and throat. "If you don't love me, love whom you please," I sang on, the notes caressing me. "Throw your arms 'round me, give my heart ease." My singing sounded tender, lilting from my lips like two doves cooing. "Throw your arms 'round me, before it's too late," I trilled, so proud of my voice, as sonorous as an echo in a cave, as hypnotic as a mermaid's chant. "Throw your arms 'round me, feel my heart break," I crooned. "Down in the valley, the mocking bird wings. Telling my story, here's what he sings: Roses love sunshine; violets love dew; angels in heaven know I love you. Know I love you, dear, know I love you. Angels in heaven know I love you." My voice trailed off, delicately, like a sigh. My ears trembled with delight. A sense of calmness spread through my body.

Instinctively, I stopped and looked up. A sea of pink floated in front of me. "Oh, my!" I squealed, recognizing the roses, racing toward them. "Oh, my!" I said, breaking off stems, clouds of pink rising above my hands. Excitedly, I gathered two fistfuls of blossoms. Satisfied, I glanced up — only to see in the distance, half a mile away, Clitus Stewart's old homestead. The gray, hand-hewn logs, silver-colored like the undersides of bluegills in Sweetwater Lake, glowed in the sunlight. And in that instant, knowing exactly where I was, I smiled and promptly decided to take a shortcut, weave through Clitus Stewart's yard, around his thick hedges, between his tulip trees, and end up on the gravel dirt road that led to Icy Creek Farm.

Approaching his place, I heard footsteps and loud clucking noises. From across the clearing, Clitus Stewart, with his tidy, red mustache, was prancing toward me, carrying two red chickens upside down, one in each hand. Their wings flapped savagely. Sprigs of red fluff flew through the air.

"Yessir!" he said at the top of his lungs, turning around and winking at a little yellow-haired boy who was sitting on the porch. "Lincoln Newland's got him some handsome chickens." Immediately I ducked behind a chestnut tree. In an instant, he tied the chickens' legs to a wire strung between two tulip trees. The hens cackled hysterically. "Ain't it funny what a red fox can do!" he said, wiping his hands on his overalls, dipping his fingers into a pocket. "And this here red fox is crafty." Standing bandy-legged in front of me, he spoke grandly, "Yessir, ole crafty red fox killed one on the spot — spreading feathers, blood, and innards all over the ground. Then he went and

343

snatched two more — the plumpest Rhode Island Reds he had ever seen — and, like the wind, he fled with those chickens squawking." Holding his hand high above his head, Clitus Stewart marched toward the chickens, all the while, saying, "Chicken and dumplings on his table." Then his arm swung out. A flash of silver glittered in the sunlight, and a knife instantly appeared. Its sharp blade sliced through feathers, spraying blood over his sun-parched skin. "Two more dollars under his mattress!" He laughed, winking at the boy again.

Gasping, I crouched down. Fiercely clutching the roses against my brownish red shirt, I saw blood trickling down my arms as the thorns ate into my skin. There I dangled as surely as those two Rhode Island Reds.

"Matanni!" I yelled, racing through the front door, the bunch of roses smashed, but still pretty, clasped in both hands. "Look what I brought you!"

Matanni came out of the kitchen. "Heavens to Betsy!" she exclaimed, clapping. "There's enough for the kitchen and the parlor."

"I'll go put them in some water," I said, dashing by her, heading toward the sink. "Can I use the green vase?" I said, plunking the roses down on the counter, turning on the faucet, splashing water over my hands and arms. "The thorns got me," I said. "I'm bleeding." I searched the counter. "Where's the vase?" I asked.

"I'll get it," Matanni said. "It's in the china closet."

"The green vase for the kitchen," I said, "and the clear, crystal one for the living room." I snatched a drying towel from the rack above the counter and wiped both hands. The old refrigerator hummed, and I remembered the lemonade inside. "Do you want something cold to drink?" I asked.

"I just had me a glass," Matanni said, coming toward me with a vase in each hand. "A carpet of pink," she said, winking. "I told you so, didn't I?"

"Yes, ma'am," I answered, filling up each vase with water, then arranging the roses within. "I squashed a few," I said, touching a blossom with several missing petals.

"A body can't traipse that far without losing a few," she said. "Ain't nothing to fret about."

"It's hot and lonely out there," I said. "Like every living thing has gone and dug itself a hole to keep cool in, then jumped inside." I grabbed a glass from the draining board, flung open the refrigerator door, picked up the pitcher of lemonade, and poured. "Hot and lonely out there," I repeated, downing the whole glass, and with it the truthful parts of me. "Ain't nothing out there," I said, swallowing hard, my throat constricting. "The whole time, I didn't see a soul. Not a living, breathing soul." I poured myself another glass, looked up at her honest face, and felt ashamed.

She stared at me for a second, fingered her hair, reinserted the gold combs around her gray knot, and said, "It's too tiresome to chitchat on such a hot day."

"Way too tiresome," I said, blushing, clamping my lips together, stifling a tiny croak.

Chapter 29

I was on the floor in my bedroom finishing the last of my twenty questions when I heard the gnawing sound of tires upon gravel.

"Icy Gal!" Miss Emily screamed as the car door slammed. "Don't bother helping me. I can do it by myself." Her footsteps crunched up the gravel road toward the house. *What is menses?* I scribbled at the bottom of my paper, then leaned against the side of my bed and closed my eyes. Clump. Clump. Clump. She stopped at the bottom of the stairs.

"Icy Gal," she said in a loud voice, "I need your help now."

"You know that the both of us can't fit on those narrow stairs," I answered her. "How in the world do you expect me to help you?"

"Get on out here!" she ordered. "And I'll show you!"

"Tarnation!" I said under my breath.

"What's that?" she asked curtly.

"You didn't hear nothing, I mean, anything," I said.

"Oh, yes, I did," she said. "My hearing is like

Superman's X-ray vision."

"I'm coming," I muttered. "I'm coming." My tone was weary. Slowly opening my bedroom door, I peeked out. There she was — a hot-air balloon in her red-, white-, and blue-striped dress, hovering beside the banister. "What am I supposed to do?" I snapped back. "There's not enough room."

Like a bowling ball rolling into the gutter, her head rolled over to one side. Blinking her eyes, she said, "You could stand on the step below me and prop me up with your shoulder. Then I couldn't tilt back."

I shrugged my shoulders. When she got this way, there was no arguing. "Okay," I said, "anything you want. My life is yours."

With both of her fat hands gripping the railing, she mounted the first step. The whole staircase cried, and she, looking back at me, said, "Wait till I go up another one."

I waited sullenly, watching her crush the second step.

"Now come on up," she said. "Yes, that's right, right beneath me. If I commence to tumble back, push real hard with your head and shoulders."

"If you commence to tumble back," I said, "I'm getting out of here."

"I don't think so," she said, twitching her head from side to side. " 'Cause you can't outrun a falling tree. Your best bet, Icy Gal, is to stop my fall."

"How come my best bet is always taking care of you?" I said.

"Let's not forget that I take care of you, too," she said, glancing over her shoulder, shooting me with her sky-blue eyes. "Our friendship is a two-way street."

I crouched down and positioned my shoulder beneath her armpit. Then I pushed upward. "Ugh!" I moaned as she took another step.

"Whew!" she said, coming to a stop. Then, plopping her hands on the banister, she held on for dear life and shook from side to side. "What it costs me to be your teacher!" she exclaimed, as the staircase swayed and groaned.

"What it costs me!" I said, panting, shouldering half of her weight.

"Stop complaining!" she snapped. "Anyway, I've lost a few pounds."

"As sure as the world is square," I told her.

Up she went again. Up I went with her — the whole staircase shaking as we went.

"My cardiologist can verify it," she said.

"If I keep this up, I'll be seeing him soon," I answered.

"Shush!" Her voice was edged in anger. "Not another word. Let's get this climbing over with. Do you hear me?"

"Yes, ma'am," I murmured, straightening up, squaring my shoulders. "One. Two. Three. Up." Again we panted, waited, and rested. "One. Two. Three. Up." Repeat performance. "One. Two. Three. Up." In this way, we continued until we reached the top, until — like a tank ready to plow through — she stood facing my cracked-open bedroom door. "Go on," I said, gently pressing my fingers against her back. "You first."

With her arms stretched out and her hands held up, she toppled forward and plunged through. Reluctantly, I followed.

"Apparently you did your reading," Miss Emily said. "Those were good questions."

"Thank you," I said from the bed, staring at her. She sat in Patanni's brand-new but rejected rocker, which he had decided to give me. "I like the old one," he had complained. "A rocker should have arms." Even though her fanny was squashed, the rolls of fat rising like dough against the rocker's back, she was smiling. And while the chair moaned beneath her weight, it nonetheless held her up.

"So," she said, pressing her palms together beneath her chin. "Do you have any more questions for me?"

"I don't rightly think so," I said, shifting my weight on the edge of the bed. "Those twenty about cover it."

Squinting at me, she pursed her lips and asked, "What about questions that don't come from the books?"

"What about them?" I asked, kicking out my right leg, pointing my toes.

"Do you have any?" she asked.

"Not exactly," I said, lowering my leg, kicking out my left.

Her eyes began to twinkle and she said, " 'Not exactly' implies that you might have a question or two."

"Well," I hesitated. "Well . . ."

"Icy Gal, spit it out! I can't stand all this hemming and hawing."

"Well . . ." I coughed, cleared my throat, glanced up at her, and said, "what if a person was to meet a fellow?"

"A person meets fellows all of the time," she replied. "What about it?"

"What if — when a person meets a fellow — she thinks he's sort of cute?"

"So?" she said, raising her eyebrows. "Aren't there cute boys in this world?"

"But what if he's the cutest thing she ever did see?"

"No harm in looking," she said.

I felt a knot in my throat. "What if . . ." I said, thumping my chest, "what if she'd like to do more than look?"

"Just what do you mean by that?" Miss Emily asked, her sky-blue eyes opening wide.

"Well, what if she'd like to be touched?" Beads of perspiration were slithering down the sides of my face. "What if she'd like done to her what that gray-haired cat did to Lena?"

An odd expression crept across Miss Emily's face. "Are you saying what I think you're saying?" she asked, fanning her cheeks with her hands.

"Yes, ma'am," I said. Then, alarmed by her look, I thought better about it and rushed in to say, "But I'm not talking about me. No, ma'am! I don't want some ole boy sticking his wiggly up my vagina. That's how you have babies."

"Icy Sparks," she said, putting her hands on her knees, squeezing tightly, "we haven't talked about any of this. I was saving it for later. Where on earth did you hear this stuff?"

"I didn't hear it," I said. "I read it."

"But where?" she asked in a high-pitched voice.

"In that book you gave me," I answered.

"Which one?" she asked, pulling a handkerchief from her dress pocket and wiping her forehead. "I looked them over carefully."

"*From Girl to Woman*," I said.

"Not in the Table of Contents," she said.

"In Chapter Seven," I said.

"Give it to me," she ordered, sticking out her hand.

I grabbed the book from off the bed and handed it to her.

With trembling hands, she turned to Chapter 7 and began to read. As she turned the pages, her face became light pink, rose pink, then deep red. "Just as well," she remarked, skimming the last page in the chapter and slamming the book shut. "I had planned this conversation for next year, but seeing as how you've brought up the subject, perhaps we should broach it now."

"If you want to," I said. "But I wasn't talking

about myself. No, ma'am! Tallywhackers are ugly. I mean, pee-pee comes out of that thing. Nasty, yellow pee-pee!" I contorted my face and shook my head. "Good night!" I said.

"Then who were you talking about?" she asked, wrinkling the corners of her eyes.

"About . . . about . . ." For the life of me, I couldn't produce a name. "About . . . about . . . about Emma Richards," I blurted. "I ran into her a few days ago."

"Where?" Miss Emily asked, pursing her lips.

"At Lute's Grocery, that's where," I said. "I was getting one of those bologna sandwiches, you know with yellow cheese and mustard, and I saw her there. She was visiting her granny on Mill Creek Road."

"And so — out of the blue — you and Emma Richards just started talking about boys. And in the middle of that delightful conversation, she decided to confess her most secret desires to you."

"Uh-huh," I said, nodding.

"Icy Gal, you'll be the death of me!" With those words, Miss Emily pushed herself up and, red-faced, began to lecture me. "First of all," she said, "do you take me for a fool?" She inhaled deeply and pressed her fleshy hand against her heart.

I shook my head; apprehension gnawed at my stomach.

"If memory serves me," she continued in a lawyerly tone, "Emma Richards hates you. If Emma Richards hates you, why on God's green earth would she tell you her secrets? And second" — stretching out her right arm, slabs of fat quivering like Jell-O, she pointed at me — "you don't go to Lute's Grocery 'cause you're afraid. Afraid that you might have one of your spells." She anchored her hands on her hips and glared. In her red-, white-, and blue-striped dress, she was the American flag hanging outside the Crockett County Courthouse, standing for truth, intimidating me; but, merciful God, her face was no longer beet red; her hand no longer massaged her chest.

At once my stomach unclenched itself. "Okay . . . okay . . ." I confessed, relieved. "I was talking about me . . . about me and Peavy Lawson. . . . I met him on the pathway to Clitus Stewart's farm the other day . . . and he was cute . . . not ugly like he once was . . . and he said nice things to me. . . . He thinks I'm beautiful . . . the prettiest girl in Crockett County . . . and I got these tingling feelings all over me . . . like . . . like . . . like nothing I've ever felt before . . . and I just wanted him to touch me . . . gentle-like on the forehead. . . . Honest to God, I didn't want his wiggly near me . . . I just wanted to be touched . . . like how that gray-haired cat touched Lena . . . like how he licked her back." Exhausted, I slumped down; my head hung forward; my chin brushed my chest.

"It's okay, Icy Gal," she said, the floorboards sighing as she walked toward me. "Everyone wants to be touched. Sometimes even I want to be touched." A high, nervous giggle escaped from her lips. "But who would want to touch me, right?"

"Someone would," I said, looking up. "Someone, somewhere in these mountains."

"No, Icy Gal," she said. "You must accept the fact that touch isn't possible for people like us. We might be liked. We might even earn a town's respect. But we're different — too different. We exist beyond the comfort of touch. For us, Icy Gal, touching is dreaming, mere fantasy."

I could feel my cheeks flaming, and despite my efforts, tears began to burn my eyes. Nevertheless, I refused to cry. Instead, I stood up. With the promise of hope riding squarely on my shoulders, I threw them back and faced her. "Maybe for you," I said. "But not for me. Someone will touch me. If not Peavy Lawson, someone else, then. But, mark my words, Miss Emily Tanner, I will be touched."

She stood there, not speaking. She simply stood there on her tree-trunk legs, staring wistfully through me, thinking about God knows what. A faint smile passed over her lips. Her eyelids closed. Her hands rose upward. Then, tenderly and ever so slowly, her fingertips began stroking her face. And, like a blind person, she touched herself until every inch of that round, fat face had been caressed.

I had combed back my hair and fastened each side with one of Matanni's combs, put on the deep purple dress, with its purple-and-white-striped apron and short, puffy sleeves which Miss Emily had bought me; then, because I wanted skin as pale as Snow White's to match my Snow White dress, I had sprinkled some of Matanni's talcum powder on my cheeks. I had even eaten a cherry Popsicle, sucking on it, pressing it against my lips, hoping for a smidgen of color.

Upon arriving at our spot along the pathway, I was even more self-conscious. Any minute he would join me, see me, and judge me. I spotted a boulder, protruding from the rock face, just big enough for me to sit on. The boulder, which was two feet high on one end and sloped down to a foot on the other, was ideal. I transformed myself into a lounging Cleopatra, resting on my side, bending my arm, cradling my chin in my hand. For five minutes I maintained this position, until every muscle in my body started to knot up and quiver. I was shaking and rustling around on top of that rock when all at once, like magic, he materialized in front of me. "Peeeaaavvvyyy," I yelped, rattling like an old woman with palsy, then slid down and plopped into the dirt, my hand still beneath my chin.

Astounded, he stared at me, not speaking for what seemed forever; then, in an instant, like a toy being wound up, with his shoulders thrown back and his head held high, he strutted forward, extended his callused hand, and said, "Ma'am, are you in need of some help?" Thereupon, my head fell forward, jouncing up and down before halting, and my limbs stopped trembling long enough for me to stretch out my hand, grab his, and stand up on wobbly legs.

"You came just in time," I said demurely. "I've been sickly of late. The sun was getting to me."

"Hot spells," he said seriously, like someone possessing full knowledge of such matters.

"Well, I wouldn't think so," I said quickly, my mind focusing on *hot flashes,* a condition discussed in "Menopause and You," the last chapter in *From Girl to Woman.* "I mean, I've just started."

"Just started what?" he said, a puzzled expression on his face.

I flushed crimson before I found the right words. "Just started having hot spells," I corrected. "Before, when I was young, the heat never bothered me. But these days it does."

" 'Cause now you're a young woman," he said, winking. "A beautiful young woman."

Daintily, I took hold of my dress. "Do you really think so?" I asked, twirling around, facing him again.

He nodded slowly and smiled. "You were the girl for me." He reached out and caught my hand. "You still are."

My hand, seemingly not my own, hung limply in his. Nervous sweat seeped from my palm. "You think so?" My voice quivered, and my breath came in shallow spurts.

"Cross my heart and hope to die," he said, squeezing my fingers. "That is, if you'll have me."

Speechless, I inclined my head.

Tenderly, he caressed my skin. "Once, you wouldn't talk to me," he continued. "Once, you wouldn't give me the time of day."

"But that's all changed," I whispered.

"Once, you called me froggy."

"I was awful," I said, shaking my head.

"You told me to jump back into that pond where I belonged." His voice cracked, and his eyes filmed over.

"I acted a fool," I said. "I acted like a sore-tailed cat."

"Then I'm not a frog?" he asked, moving his head from side to side.

"Oh, no!" I said vehemently. "You could never be a frog!" I put my free hand on top of his, the one that was holding mine. "Even if you tried, you could never be a frog."

"Never!" he said, looking deep into my eyes.

"Never!" I replied, and then, before I knew it, I was lifting up on my tiptoes and craning my neck forward. "Never!" I said again. " 'Cause today . . ." My heart thumped ferociously against my chest. " 'Cause today, you are my prince." I puckered my lips and kissed him squarely on the mouth.

At that moment, he rocked backward. Our arms dropped to our sides, and we both stood silently, gazing into each other's eyes. In the depths of his pure green eyes, I was certain that I saw my future. Peavy Lawson and I were holding hands; our lips were pressed together; our bodies were touching.

"I'm in love," I said dreamily as I walked home. "I'm in love. I'm in love." So this was how it felt to be a woman — feeling jiggly and soft inside like Matanni's rice pudding, feeling love spread through your body and into your muscles, blood, and cells, feeling that the world would last forever and that your love would outlast the world. "I'm in love," I said again. "I'm in love with Peavy Lawson, my own true prince."

All the way home, my mind replayed every minute of our rendezvous. I saw him worshiping me and admiring my beauty in my Snow White dress. I envisioned his hand stroking mine. I recalled his lips, tasting the softness of my kiss. Already, I had dismissed my slide off the rock into the dirt below and erased my mistaken notion that he had been talking about menopause. Anything unpleasant was deleted from my memory. Everything else was nurtured. I dwelled on his romantic words, the way his voice trembled when he declared his love for me. "You were the girl for me. . . . You still are. . . . Cross my heart and hope to die," he had said. Yes, without a doubt, his love was rare. He had forgiven the harsh girl of his youth and loved the woman who now stood before him.

When I strolled up, Patanni, rocking on the

front porch, asked, "Girl, what's wrong with you?"

"Nothing," I said, tiptoeing up the steps.

"Since when you been scouting around in that kind of getup?"

"Since I turned thirteen," I snapped. "Since I became a woman."

"Come over here!" He poked out his long arm and waved me over. "Stand still." He rocked forward. Then, with his large-boned hands, he took hold of my face and studied me. After several minutes, he concluded, "You look addled. How come?"

"I ain't addled," I said, pulling away from him, shaking him off like a dog shaking off water. "Some people might call me beautiful, but not you — oh, no, not you — 'cause you're too busy calling me names."

He repeated, "You look addled."

"I ain't addled!" I spat out, grinding my teeth together. "I ain't the least bit addled." I stomped my foot. "This woman standing afore you ain't suffering from a dizzy brain." Angrily, I flicked my head from side to side. "Absolutely not! This woman standing afore you is hurting from the best of maladies. She's suffering from a melted heart."

My grandfather stood up. "A melted heart?" he said, putting his hand on his chest.

"Yessir," I answered, "a melted heart."

"Well, now," he said, rubbing his chin with his fingers. "A melted heart is something special."

"Yessir, I know," I murmured. "For a week now, I've been trying to tell you."

Patanni turned toward the door, cupped his hands around his mouth, and screamed, "Tillie, get on out here! Icy's got something to tell you."

In that instant, I regretted having uttered a word. Filled with dread, I sucked in my stomach and bit my lip.

"What's the fuss?" Matanni said, quickly stepping through the door, wiping her hands on her apron. "I was busy with supper."

"Icy, here, has good news for you," he said, nodding at me.

"What is it, child?" Matanni said.

Like hot lead, embarrassment burned in my throat, making it hard for me to speak.

"Dang, Icy, go on and tell her!" Patanni ordered.

I gagged and several sentences wrenched through my lips.

"I can't understand a word," Matanni said, glaring at my grandfather.

Patanni cleared his throat. "What Icy, here, is trying to say," he intervened, "is that she's gone and got herself a beau."

Matanni threw up her hands like exclamation marks on either side of her head. "Land sakes!" She giggled. "Where — around here — did you find a beau?"

"On the path to Clitus Stewart's place," I volunteered. "We ran into each other."

"Well, who is he?" Matanni asked, slipping

over, putting her arm around me.

"Peavy Lawson," I said softly.

The arm around me dropped. "Peavy Lawson!" she exclaimed. "Ole frog eyes!"

"Not anymore," I said, whipping my head from side to side. "He's changed."

"He'd be Maybelle and Randall's boy," my grandfather said.

My grandmother nodded, and a faraway look clouded her eyes.

"See that?" my grandfather said, winking. "That means she's studying the Lawson family tree."

"Tell me, Icy," my grandmother said, suddenly clear-eyed and eager. "How come he's way over here?"

"Clear across the valley," Patanni added.

" 'Cause Old Man Potter hired him," I explained, "to help with his livestock and fields."

"Well, then," Patanni said, his eyes gleaming.

"That young man of yours is a hard worker," Matanni said.

"Randall's got a good tobacco base," my grandfather said.

"Maybelle's birthed at least nine children," my grandmother said. "I ain't ever heard an unkind word about any of them."

"Decent, honest, hardworking folk," Patanni said.

"The salt of the earth," Matanni said.

"And the boy likes our Icy," Patanni said, rolling his eyes. " 'Cause she's a looker," he went on, "and, mind you, Icy Sparks, if that young man knows what's good for him, he better stick to looking."

"Shush!" my grandmother warned, wagging a finger at him. "Peavy Lawson is our granddaughter's first fella. You'll not tease her. Do you hear me?"

Patanni jutted out his jaw. "Wasn't I the one who called you out here?" he pouted. "Wasn't I the one who let loose the good news? Didn't I tell you everything with a big fat grin on my face?"

"I reckon you did, Virgil," my grandmother said, stepping over to him, patting his stomach. "I reckon I married me a sweetheart."

"Peavy Lawson is sweet, too." I was enjoying my newfound status. "He's as sweet as molasses," I said, wanting to regain the spotlight.

But already it was too late. Patanni was leaning over, way over, because he was so tall, and Matanni was reaching up, high up on her toes, and both of them were kissing, giving each other tiny, little pecks, like two birds grooming one another. None of it was romantic. Nothing like that tender kiss I placed on Peavy Lawson's lips. Their love's wonderful, I thought, watching my grandparents kiss each other. But it was nothing like Peavy and me, nothing like our young love, our Romeo and Juliet love.

My stomach rumbled uneasily. "Aren't we ever gonna eat around here?"

"I don't want you to go back to school," I said, my voice cracking, my white cotton blouse sticking in the heat to my skin, my pink seersucker shorts chafing my thighs. "I'm gonna be so lonely."

"I don't want to go neither," Peavy said, gently tugging at the bottom of my blouse. "But I ain't old enough to drop out."

I tilted forward on the tips of my tennis shoes, already darkened by the dust, closed my eyes, and we kissed. "I'm afraid you might forget me," I said, opening my eyelids, the sun off the rock face blinding me. "There are other fish in the sea," I pouted.

Leaning back on his heels, he widened his eyes and shook his head. "But I ain't going fishing," he said.

"I'm talking about other girls," I said. "You might meet somebody else — some girl at school — and like her more than me."

Peavy stomped his right foot. "Oh, no!" he said as dust rose and settled on his boot and the bottom of his blue jeans like gray talcum powder. "You're my woman. Ain't no cause for you to worry!" he reassured me. "I done seen you all summer. Every Thursday for weeks. Nine sweet times. And once summer comes around, I'll be right back here, helping Old Man Potter, spending time with you."

"What about all the months in between?" I asked, my mouth trembling. "What'll I do?" I bit at my lip and screwed up my eyes and nose. Sorrow lined my brow. The desolation of the trail was depressing me, reminding me of the loneliness to come. The grass had turned yellow and parched; many of the wildflowers had withered. By August, the goat's-beard that had once been so plentiful had long since dried up and disappeared. Only alumroot, its blossoms sprouting like thin beards, dotted the ridges.

"It ain't so long," Peavy said, stepping forward, trailing his pinkie along my forehead. "Maybe I can come see you in the spring, after the snow has melted, when the weather's good."

"You think?" I asked, barely smiling.

"Why not?" he replied.

"And will you write me?" I asked.

"Only if you write me," he said, tapping his chest, leaving behind little dots of sweat on his green shirt. Then he held out his arms.

The minute he folded his arms around me, pressing me against him, my anxiety evaporated. Like a shot of Patanni's whiskey, his presence calmed me. With him, I was free of the urges and compulsions, of the disorder that had plagued me for so long. I want to bottle him, I thought, as he held me close. I want to sprinkle Eau de Peavy all over my body.

Chapter 30

In the spirit of Elizabeth Barrett Browning, I wrote Peavy love poems and letters. "You are my knight in shining armor," I wrote, "my own Sir Lancelot, riding off to school, battling to defend my honor." Tucked between the pages, I slipped in one of Matanni's late-blooming white roses. "White stands for purity — pure, like our love for each other," I went on. "Peavy, my brave knight, pin this rose to your undershirt beneath your cold armor. It will keep you warm and safe." Smiling, I signed the letter, "From Icy, your own golden-haired Guinevere."

Peavy answered. "Roses are white. Violets are blue. You are Icy Sparks, and I love you."

"O, my luve is like a red, red rose," I replied, quoting Robert Burns.

"Roses are red. Violets are blue," he wrote back. "My name is Peavy Lawson, and I love you."

In a book of Victorian poetry, which Miss Emily had given me, I discovered a poem, "Tristram and Iseult," by Matthew Arnold about the tragic love affair between Tristram, one of the most famous knights of the Round Table, and Iseult, wife of King Mark. Filled with longing, I imagined myself as Iseult, separated from my own true love. "Blame me not, poor sufferer! that I tarried," I copied carefully. "Bound I was, I could not break the band. / Chide not with the past, but feel the present! / I am here — we meet — I hold thy hand." I ended the letter with "Your loving Iseult." Below the signature, I drew a cracked heart.

Peavy replied, "Roses are red. Violets are blue. What are you talking about? It don't matter 'cause I still love you. P.S. Is your middle name, Insult?"

Twice a week we wrote to each other. When a letter of his arrived, I'd tenderly carry it to my room, hold the envelope up to the sunlight, and marvel at the curve of his *y* in Icy, at the sensual sweep of his *s* in Sparks.

For Christmas, I sent him a present. "Christmas isn't merry," I wrote, "because you're not here with me. But I made you something anyway. It's an ornament for your tree, a papier-mâché heart. The yellow crack down the center stands for my own heart; it's breaking for you. Do you like it? I put my name on one side and yours on the other. Two halves make a whole, sweetheart. Two halves of our heart beat as one. Hang this ornament from your tree, my brave knight, and when you look at it, be sure to remember me."

"The heart's real pretty," he replied. "I hung

it near the top of our tree. Ain't nobody, but me, knows it's there. Do you like what I sent you? Uncle Ed took it last summer when we went to the hog show at the Crockett County Fair. That smile on my lips is there 'cause when he snapped it I was thinking of you."

"Happy New Year, my dearest, sweetest, handsomest Peavy!" I jotted down on New Year's Eve. "Soon, we'll be seeing each other again. Soon, spring will be here." Then, with the help of Emily Dickinson, I giddily added the following verse. " 'If you were coming in the Fall, / I'd brush the Summer by / With half a smile, and half a spurn, / As Housewives do, a Fly.' I'm always thinking of you, too."

Peavy responded immediately. "Icy," he scribbled, "I thought we were going to see each other in the spring, the Saturday before Easter. Sorry about your fly problem. Tell your grandpa to check under the house for puddles."

I answered him, "At the same place! At the same time!"

"The snow is melting," he replied. "Soon the redbuds will be blooming. That's how soon I'll see you."

We spotted each other at the same time. As soon as I caught sight of him in his brown suit and yellow tie, my heart heaved, and my head seemed to float above my body. "Peavy!" I yelled, racing toward him in my new yellow cotton dress, with my arms flapping, my yellow handbag dangling from my forearm.

"Icy!" he screamed back, running toward me, stumbling once but not falling in his glossy brown shoes.

Simultaneously, we threw our arms around each other, pressing chest to chest. My pocketbook, slipping, hung weakly from my wrist. The tips of my shoes lapped over the tips of his. One of my barrettes, covered with yellow voile flowers, had slipped from the side of my upswept bun, and several strands of hair now hung loosely around my neck. My breath was wet and hot against his shirt. His shirt was stiff from too much starch. I leaned back and gazed at his face. His hair was slicked back, smooth and oily. The freckles across his nose had faded. Two blemishes stood out on his chin. I inhaled a powerful cologne.

"Oh, Peavy!" I gushed, letting my arms drop to my sides. "You've bottled yourself for me."

He smiled broadly. A diamond of saliva plopped from his top lip onto the ground. His eyes, befuddled, clouded over.

"Oh, Peavy! I just love your cologne," I added.

"You do?" he said. "It's called Brut. It's my brother's."

"Are you a brute?" I asked teasingly. My eyes toyed with him. My mouth watered slightly.

Tenderly, he touched his chest. "What do you think?" he asked. From his front shirt pocket, he pulled out a rose, the white rose which so many months ago I had sent him.

"Peavy!" Once more, I wrapped my arms around him and urgently kissed his lips.

"Icy!" he said, kissing me back.

I could feel his teeth, scraping against mine, and his body, vibrating.

"Now," he urged.

"Now, what?" My skin tingled all over.

"Let me hold you." His voice was high and shrill.

"But you are holding me." My mouth was cupped against his cheek; my lips felt drunk and heavy.

"I want to hold you close," he said breathlessly. "Behind those pines, over there." He freed an arm and pointed to the spot where he had hidden that first time we met.

My limbs felt weak. "If you want to." My voice was tremulous.

Tightly, he gripped my hand and, without talking, led the way. In a daze, I followed him. I would have done anything for this young man who carried my rose beneath his cold armor. The spring sun shone down, illuminating pennywort, inches high with its white funnel-shaped flowers, and star chickweed, with its five deeply cut petals, growing in the distance along the wooded slopes. To me, the star chickweed blossoms were guiding lights, fallen from heaven, showing us the way. As we neared the little group of pine trees, Peavy pointed at a clearing five feet away and smiled.

"My Tristram!" I said, suddenly overcome

with emotion. "Blame me not, poor sufferer, that I tarried! Bound I was, I could not break the band. Chide not with the past, but feel the present! I am here — we meet — I hold thy hand." With these words, I firmly squeezed his palm.

Hand in hand, we walked to the clearing, where he began cleaning away rocks and sticks. Thereupon, he ran back to the copse of pine trees, jerked off his coat, gathered up fallen pine needles, and tossed them on his jacket. Then, using his garment like a knapsack, he returned and scattered the pine needles all over the ground. "Our bed," he said, his eyes as green as the new shoots popping up.

"Our bed?" I said. Feelings of ecstasy mingled with those of fear.

Taking both of my hands, he gently pulled me down. On our sides, several inches apart, we stared into each other's eyes.

"Icy." His hand snaked toward me. "Icy." His fingers tugged at one of the pockets on my dress.

"P-Peavy," I stammered, leaning toward him.

"Icy," he repeated in a quivering voice.

"Peavy," I whispered, and felt his fingers slide down my neck.

"Icy," he said, stroking my Peter Pan collar.

My tiny breasts ached. "Peavy!" I moaned.

His green eyes twitched and popped out of his head. "Oh, Icy!" he cried.

Alarmed, I glanced down. His hand was on my bodice, cupping my breast. And although I liked his touch, it also terrified me, so much so that in that instant, I envisioned my real future — Peavy Lawson's wiggly inside me, spewing forth pee-pee and sperm, babies leaping from my stomach, yowling and crying, a brown-weathered shack clinging to the side of a mountain and the bitter stink of coal fouling the air. I saw all of my hopes and dreams lying dead, lined up side by side, in the happenstance of one touch. "P-Peavy," I stammered, feeling a croak building up in my throat and a jerk collecting in my muscles.

"Oh, Icy!" Passionately, he squeezed my breast. "It feels so good!"

Fiercely, I clenched my teeth and forced my lips together.

"Icy! Oh, Icy!" he said, his eyes popping from his head.

The croak shoved against my mouth. My eyes flew out.

Blinking and breathing heavily, he clutched my breast. "My sweet Icy!" he groaned.

At that moment, for the first time in a long time, I saw his froggy green eyes gazing at me and felt his muscle-hopping body pressing against mine. Disgusted, I stared at his amphibian, dead white skin and at his thin-lipped, fly-catching mouth, and I panicked. A convulsion of sheer terror shook me, and my whole body — arms, legs, neck, and torso — began to jerk.

"Icy?" Peavy said, arching away from me. "Icy?" he said loudly.

"*C-R-O-A-K!*" I roared.

"Icy!" he said, jerking back.

"*C-R-O-A-K!*" My body whipped to the left.

"What the heck!" he said, leaping up.

"*C-R-O-A-K! C-R-O-A-K!*" My limbs surged to the right.

"By damn!" he said, looking down at me. Then, staring a hole right through me, his eyes bulging, his lips grinning, he guffawed like a thousand frogs disrupting the night. "You do beat all!" he yelled, slapping his thighs.

"*C-R-O-A-K!*" I bellowed, jumping up-ward, landing solidly on the ground. I shot out my right leg and twirled around on my left. "*C-R-O-A-K!*" I screamed, turning around and around. "*C-R-O-A-K!*"

"You're crazy!" he said, laughing nervously. "A nutcase!" he added, scrambling backward.

On a dime, I stopped spinning.

"A loony person!" He snickered, pointing at me. "Just like everybody says!"

In that instant, I breathed in deeply, gulped down all of my anger, and spewed it back out. "You frog-eyed piece of slime!" I snarled. "Why don't you jump back into that pond where you belong?"

There we stood — face-to-face.

Out popped his eyes. "Monster!" he growled.

"Frog eyes!" I cried.

"I don't need this!" He smacked his hands to-gether.

"You need a pond to swim in! You need some lily pads to hop on!"

"I need me a normal gal," he said angrily. "A gal people like. Someone like Emma Richards."

"Well, you can have her!" I shouted, my voice shaking. "Just get out of here!"

"Don't mind if I do," he said, plucking his coat off the ground. "You've made your blister." He clicked around on his heels and began to walk way. "Now sit on it!"

Chapter 31

For weeks, I refused to discuss with my grand-parents what had happened with Peavy Lawson. How could I tell them that Peavy and I had been kissing? How could I tell them that we had lain on the ground, side by side, and that I had let him touch my dress where my breast was? I couldn't. I just couldn't; so I didn't tell them anything. Whenever either asked about him, I'd shrug and say, "We broke up."

I walked around the house with a perpetual scowl on my face, with my shoulders humped over as though I were a shriveled-up old spin-ster. At meals, I had no appetite. Mouthfuls of food got caught in my throat. I couldn't swallow and lost weight. But none of this bothered me because I knew that the next phase — an even worse one — would soon come.

Eventually, the emptiness in my life would beg to be filled; and, unable to control myself, I would begin to eat. In fact, just like Miss Emily, I'd live to eat. If Matanni cooked an apple pie, I'd eat all of it — each slice with a double scoop of vanilla ice cream. Patanni would get a worried look in his eyes. Like scavenging dogs, on Thanksgiving and Christmas Day, Patanni and I, our eyes darting back and forth, would slyly compete for food. Meanwhile, I'd grow larger and larger. Patanni would have to buy me a bigger bed. Matanni would sew me huge revival-tent dresses. When Patanni got a haircut, he'd hear the men at the barbershop say, "No God-fearing man will marry Icy Sparks. If she took to hugging him, he'd be squashed." Whenever I'd pass, people on the streets of Ginseng would hold their hands to their mouths and snicker. This scenario would be my future. I only had to look as far as Miss Emily Tanner to see it unfolding before my eyes. Yes, she had been right all along.

Upstairs in my lonely bed, the bitterness of Miss Emily's life, forever living without another's touch, overwhelmed me. And because in Miss Emily's moon face I saw my own — the empty landscape of limbless, faceless people — my heart tore away from the rest of my body, and, like the uprooted stump of a tree, it floated inside me, disconnected from my soul. Lonely, desolate, my heart pumped only for itself and let me be. "Oh, Lord!" I cried, staring at the vacant ceiling. "God help me!" And closing my eyes, tenderly and ever so slowly, I began to stroke my face.

"There ain't no reason to celebrate my birthday," I pouted, sitting on Matanni's new oval-shaped braided rug, the corners of my mouth pulled down like someone suffering the aftermath of a stroke. "Even Maizy forgot about it this year," I whined, "and she never does."

Miss Emily frowned back. "There is no reason to celebrate my birthday," she corrected me.

"Whichever way you say it," I said, "it means the same."

Patanni tipped forward in his frayed easy chair and shot me a look.

Grinning, Matanni turned and nodded at Miss Emily, who was sitting beside her on the sofa.

Miss Emily nodded back, positioned her square hands on either side of her body, and, huffing, tried to hoist herself up. "Icy Gal," she began, falling back onto the sofa, the cushions whooshing with her weight. "Give me your hand!"

I crooked my head to one side. "Why?" I asked.

"Shush!" Miss Emily pressed her fat index finger against her lips. "Your hand, please!"

Cautiously, I thrust out my arm, slowly turned over my hand, and exposed the pink flesh of my palm. Looking around, I noticed that all three of them were leaning forward expectantly. Smiles as wide as watermelon slices cut into their faces. "What are you-all up to?" I asked.

Dramatically, Miss Emily slipped a piece of paper between Matanni's fingers. "Just this!" she said.

"Just this!" my grandmother repeated; and, reaching over, she flamboyantly placed the slip of paper in my palm.

I stared at the cream-colored paper, no bigger than a three-by-five index card, the top of which read, "Crockett County Telephone Cooperative," typed in bold print. Then, in a neat, cursive hand below it was the message: "Dear New Customer, we will be installing your telephone during the week of June 7–12. Thank you for your order!"

"A telephone?" I asked, anxiously glancing at Patanni.

"Just for you," he said grandly.

" 'Cause you're a modern gal," Miss Emily said.

"A regular teenager," Matanni added.

In that instant, my arm began to quiver; and, like a maple leaf in the breeze, the piece of paper trembled in my palm. A regular teenager, I thought. "A regular teenager!" I said aloud. "A regular teenager!" I sneered, watching my hand shake, seeing the paper shimmy back and forth.

"Icy!" Patanni said, alarmed.

"Icy Gal!" Miss Emily said.

"What's wrong?" Matanni asked, rising.

"Are you blind?" I asked as the slip of paper quaked spasmodically. "Can't any of you see?" My hand lurched upward, and the paper fell to the floor below. "Don't you understand?" I cried, restraining my arm with the other. "Who . . . who . . . in this great, big, wide world . . . is ever going to call me?"

The minute I heard the car door slam, I thought, Lord, please don't let it be Miss Emily! I was in no mood for another one of her lectures, especially the one about ingratitude, but when I looked out the parlor window, it was Mr. Wooten I saw, crunching over gravel, heading toward our house. "Geez!" I moaned, seeing the usual armload of books. I cranked on a smile, pushed myself up off the sofa, and dawdled over to the door.

"Well, ain't you a sight for sore eyes!" he said with a toothy grin. "With every birthday, you get a little bigger."

"Yessir," I mumbled, moving to one side, letting him saunter in.

"Where can I put these?" he asked.

"Just drop them on the couch," I replied. "I'll tote 'em to my bedroom later."

"Whew!" he said, as the books fell from his arm, thudding against each other when they plopped upon the sofa. "Mostly, these are math books. Miss Emily says you're having some trouble with geometry."

"According to her, I'm always having some trouble with something," I said, sighing, lowering myself into Patanni's easy chair.

"Where are your grandparents?" he asked, looking around, sitting on the sofa beside the books.

With my index finger, I flicked a strand of hair out of my eyes. "In town — shopping," I said. "I didn't want to go."

"Well, now." He leaned forward, cupping his hands over his knees. "How does it feel being fourteen?"

"Same as thirteen," I quipped. "Ain't no difference as far as I can tell."

Mr. Wooten turned sideways and began to finger through the books. "I bought you this," he said, slipping one out, proudly holding it up so that I could see the title. "It's for your birthday."

"*The Dollmaker*," I read aloud, "by Harriette Arnow."

"She's from the mountains of Kentucky. A real Kentucky author," he explained.

"Thank you," I said, none too convincingly. "I'll enjoy reading it if I ever get through those math books." I pointed to the landslide on the sofa.

"What did Maizy send you this time?" he asked me. "I always liked that young woman."

"Not a thing," I snapped. "Not even a card. I reckon she's too busy tending to her husband and going to college."

"People do get busy," he said, his voice serious. "She's always remembered you before. Why are you so hard on her now?"

Annoyed, I crossed my ankles and ignored him.

"How about that telephone!" He opened up his mouth as though surprised.

I glared back at him. "It's ringing off the hook," I sassed. "My calendar's so filled up I don't have time to do another thing."

Mr. Wooten coughed into his hand. His nose had started to run, and the rims of his eyes were turning pink. "It's the pollen," he apologized, pulling a handkerchief out of his trousers pocket, blowing hard. "You got neighbors, Icy," he said, wearily blowing again. "You don't have to be so alone."

Angrily, I lunged forward, my weight lodged in the balls of my feet. "And who are they?" I demanded.

"Let's see," he said, rubbing his temple. "The McRoys are nearby, and the Lutes are down the road. Then there's Clitus Stewart. And right over the ridge," he added, smiling, "the Tillman girl."

"Some neighbors!" I shot back. "First of all, don't even mention Joel McRoy's name around me! Second, that Clitus Stewart is nigh nothin', and Mamie Tillman . . . well, she's . . ." My voice shook. "Queer." I felt my hands trembling. "If you knew these people, you wouldn't be telling me to visit them. No, sir! You'd be telling me to run in the opposite direction."

Mr. Wooten started to laugh. A scratchy laugh that itched from his throat. "I didn't know your neighbors were such a sorry lot," he said.

"Not worth a hill of beans. Not worth two cents. Not worth a hoot."

"Well, I'll be," he said, looking right at me, narrowing his eyes. "All this makes me wonder what you think of me."

Clamping my lips together, I lounged back in

my chair. If he was fishing for a compliment, I wasn't about to give him one. "Would you like something cold to drink?" I finally asked, my mouth tired from the strain of pressing my lips together.

"A refreshing cup of springwater would be nice," said Mr. Wooten politely. "That is, if it's not too much trouble."

"Ain't no trouble at all," I said, rising. "The spring's right behind the house."

"Wouldn't that put you a tad closer to the Tillman place?" he teased, his eyes sparkling. "You be careful, now, or you might just run into those bothersome neighbors of yours."

My grandfather was yelling — "Goddammit! Goddamn thieving fox!" — as I strolled up the dirt driveway. Veering to the left, I ran toward the barn. In the distance, through the dusk, I could see his large, bulky form, his left arm raised high above his head, a dead chicken grasped in his hand. "Goddamn fox!" he screamed, swinging the chicken back and forth. "Goddamn fox!"

Waving my arms, I raced toward him. "Patanni!" I yelled. "What's wrong?"

Looking up, he caught sight of me. Then he lowered his head and dropped his arm. The chicken slipped from his fingers and plopped in a haze of dust on the ground. "Icy," he said, wilting in front of me, "I didn't mean for you to hear that."

I walked over and picked up the mangled, plump red hen who never failed to lay an egg every day. "Poor Zelda," I said.

"Some thieving fox," he said wearily. "Zelda, Henrietta, and Bonnie."

"Not Bonnie!" I shook my head. "She was so pretty."

He wiped his forehead with the back of his hand. "I had to lock the rest of them up," he said. "They was carrying on so. Buster was stark-raving mad."

"I'm sorry, Patanni." I heard Buster still squawking loudly. "I know how much you loved them."

"The varmint carried off Bonnie and Henrietta, that stupid, scrawny hen, but left Zelda all over the place." He looked around the yard. "He didn't even have the courtesy to eat her — and her being the plumpest and the juiciest. He left the best one here. Left Zelda right here in the yard. Almost like that fox was laughing. Being spiteful. Saying, 'Wake up, old man. I can come back any ole time and gobble me down a fat one.'"

Scanning the ground, I spotted only a scattering of thin-lined strokes. "Where's the tracks?" I asked.

"I can't find nary a one," Patanni said. "Odd, ain't it?"

"You sure you didn't stomp through them?" I asked. "I mean, you was upset."

Patanni shook his head. "Nope!" He was vehement. "I watched myself and looked where I was stepping. I tell you, there weren't no tracks."

"That's 'cause . . ." I hesitated and breathed in. "That's 'cause . . ." I stopped again.

"Speak up, child!" Patanni said, narrowing his eyes. "Tell me what's on your mind."

I walked over to the zigzag lines. "Look at these here marks." Squatting down, I ran my index finger through the dirt. "Looks like someone took a twig and made them."

My grandfather joined me. Bending over, he said, "Why, I declare, I hadn't noticed!"

"Maybe this varmint walks upright," I said. "Maybe what we got us is a two-legged varmint."

"Yes, buddy!" Patanni said. "He cut himself a brushy twig, swished through his footprints, and left poor ole Zelda behind."

"To throw you off," I said.

"Don't you know, he did!" Patanni stood up. "But who?"

"A neighbor?" I ventured.

"Oh, no!" Patanni said.

"Why not?" I asked.

" 'Cause no neighbor of mine would do something like that," he said.

I stood up, placed my hands staunchly on my hips, and asked, "How can you be so sure? No one knows what another person is up to. Everybody's got secrets."

" 'Cause I know my neighbors. Nary a one of them would rob me blind."

"Well, this time you're wrong, 'cause one of them already did."

Patanni scowled. "Who, then? Poor old Mamie Tillman?"

"Someone you'd never guess."

"Spit it out, girl! Say who you mean!"

I pressed my fingernails into my hips. "Clitus Stewart, that's who. He's the varmint stealing your chickens."

Patanni made a fist and smacked his palm. "Icy Sparks!" he said, in a voice so full of rage that it cut through the air like wind wheezing around a taut, thin wire. "Why are you lying about my good friend's son?"

"I'm not lying," I said, my voice also swelling with anger. "I'm telling the truth. If you're too deaf to hear it, then that's your doing, not mine!"

Patanni fisted his palm again and, red-faced, fumed, "Lately you been spreading your misery around like jam on bread, but never . . ." Fiercely, he shook his head. "Never, in my wildest dreams, would I have imagined you'd do this!"

"Do what?" I growled back. "Clean the wax out of your ears and make you hear the truth?"

"You got no right badmouthing neighbors. You got no right slandering a friend of mine!"

"Clitus, Jr., ain't no friend of yours," I said. "Your friend was Clitus, Sr., and he's long since been dead and buried."

"You better watch it, young lady! Just watch your tone with me!"

I removed my hands from my hips, pointed

angrily at him, and said, "You best quit worrying about me and turn your energy to someone else. To that dear friend of yours who's about to cook your hens!"

"Why, you've lost your head!" my grandfather shouted. "Spreading such stories!"

"My head's on straight as ever!" I declared, thrusting out my chin.

"Young lady!" My grandfather glowered at me. "I'm getting sick and tired of your nastiness. Darkness is the only thing you see."

My voice shook, but, determined, I didn't cry. "I saw him with my very own eyes," I said. "I was out walking and saw him. All high and mighty. Tying two plump chickens from a wire stretched between two tulip trees. All the while, he bragged to that son of his how he had stolen two of Lincoln Newland's plumpest hens, how he had killed one on the spot and left the innards behind. All the time, he went on about himself, called himself a crafty ole fox. Then he swung that knife of his and cut their throats. As sure as God is my witness, he sprayed the yard with blood. That's the truth."

"If you're so honest, why didn't you come right home and tell me?" Patanni asked. "How come you've been so quiet?"

"If you want to believe a thief, that's your privilege and your right!" I cried. "If you think Clitus, Jr., is so good and I'm so bad, so dag nab different, so be it! If you feel that way, I don't want to be your kin!" And with those words, I broke down and began to cry.

Patanni made a guttural sound, took one step toward me, snatched my hand, and said, "Come on. We're gonna settle this thing. Once and for all."

When Patanni drove up to Clitus Stewart's place, it was still light. No vehicle was parked in the back, and the house seemed empty. "I don't see anyone," my grandfather said, slowly opening his door. "No people and no dead chickens."

"They'd be in the front yard," I said. "Away from the road."

"Open your door," he ordered. "Let's go and see."

I wiped my nose with my palm, unlatched the door, pushed it ajar with my foot, and stumbled out. "The tulip trees are in the front," I said, "away from the road, overlooking the valley."

"I hear you," he said coldly, walking quickly toward the front yard, way ahead of me.

When he rounded the corner, I heard him. Even before I saw him, I heard him. A sad, low groan, like the bellow of a sick cow, came to my ears, and I knew then that he had seen them, that he had seen Henrietta and Bonnie dangling from that wire, blood — like droplets of rain — scattered over the ground. Quietly, I came up behind him. "That's them, all right," he said in a shaky voice.

But I didn't say a word, just turned around and briskly walked back to the truck.

Chapter 32

"I've always been a yaller dog Democrat," Patanni said, when he heard President Eisenhower speaking as we listened to the evening news on the radio in the parlor. "Old Ike helped us whup the Germans, and I respect him for that, but he's still acting like a general, not a president, and in all this time, he ain't done nothing here at home. Eight years of doing nothing is eight years too long."

As he spoke, he nervously tapped his large foot against the floor, all the while stealing looks at me, all the while turning into a stranger. I saw him changing, once grabbing his arm, shaking it like it had died on him. I heard him complaining of dizziness, of punishing headaches. He was laying low, not working as hard, getting thinner, but I couldn't make myself be kind to him. Some fierceness of pride had come over me. The more I wanted things to be like they were, the worse I behaved. The worse I behaved, the more I hated myself and the nastier I became. In my grandfather, I saw every person who had ever hurt me. He became Mrs. Eleanor Stilton.

He was Wilma. He was Peavy Lawson. He was every snicker I had ever heard and the million staring eyes that excluded me from the flatland. He stood for judgment and intolerance, the aisles of townspeople parting. He was a red heart pumping normalcy; he was a Bedloe. I was a Sparks.

"If Ike don't like that vice president of his," Patanni went on, "why should I cast my vote for him? Anyhow, that young fella Kennedy did just fine when he was politicking in West Virginia. Even took it upon himself to go down deep into a mine shaft where he almost got himself kilt on a high-voltage line. Story goes he talked to the miners like they was family, never puttin' on airs, never preaching at them, just asking them about their work."

"None of that excuses the fact that he's a Catholic," Matanni added, "and I don't want some Pope telling me what to do."

Surprised, I perked up. "A Catholic?" I declared, turning to look at my grandmother.

Matanni bit her lip, nodded, and continued to crochet.

"He was baptized in the Catholic Church just like you was in the Baptist," Patanni said, fixing his eyes on her. "That's all it means. Ain't no one taking orders from the Pope."

"Mercy me, I hope not!" Matanni shot back.

Patanni cleared his throat, pulled a handkerchief out of his shirt pocket, and spit into it. "Why are we always badmouthing someone who ain't like us?" he asked. "Ain't we learned nothing from our own trials and tribulations? We, who are poked fun at and judged harshly every time we leave these mountains."

I thought for a minute about what my grandfather was saying, but I had been brooding too long to care. "Mrs. Stilton's mean as a rattler," I declared, disregarding his words, "and I'll tell you why." I enlarged my eyes, raised my eyebrows, and pointed my index finger at nothing in particular. " 'Cause she's a Catholic," I stated, "and the Pope is always telling her what to do."

Patanni scowled at my grandmother. "Tillie, you know that's plumb foolishness!" he snorted. "Mrs. Eleanor Stilton is mean 'cause she's mean. If she was a member of the Baptist Church, she'd still be mean. People have their natures. Hers happens to be ornery."

"Well, I guess that's my problem, too," I said to Matanni. "Being born a Sparks, I ain't able to shed that ornery part of me."

At that moment, my grandmother jumped up, glared at me, then at Patanni, and exclaimed, "God help me! I can't take this bickering anymore!" Then, flinging her needle and thread upon the sofa, she stomped out of the room.

"Look what you did." I leaped up from my chair and faced my grandfather. "You and your Pope-loving heart have upset my granny!"

"No, missy! Your false pride is the culprit."

"That ain't true! I only want you to love me,

to believe me when I tell you something."

"But I do believe you," Patanni insisted.

"Not till I showed you," I said, shaking my head. "Not till you saw the truth with your very own eyes."

"But for weeks you was acting up," Patanni said. "Carrying on like a sick hornet." He pressed his hand against his forehead, then looked up and anxiously caught my eyes. "Icy, honey, you had me all confused. I didn't know what to believe."

"And you been sulled up," I said, "not talking to me. Treating me like I ain't nothing, just because I got Sparks blood in my veins." I lowered my head. My shoulders heaved. "If you don't love me, I don't want to be a Sparks anymore." My voice quivered, and I began to sob. "If I don't have you," I moaned, swiping at a string of mucus that dangled from my nose, "I —"

My grandfather rose quickly from his chair. "Icy, my sweet child!" he protested, taking a step toward me. "Why, you're the only grandchild I got!" His fingertips touched my shoulder. "You got gallons of Bedloe blood in you." Putting his hand beneath my chin, he lifted my head. " 'Cause you're stubborn, every damn bit as hardheaded as me."

Awkwardly, I reached out to him. "Oh, Patanni," I said. But just as he leaned over to hug me, a tic rippled through my body and jerked me to one side.

Surprised, he pulled back, and we both looked

at each other. Then, cocking his head and squinting his eyes, he folded his arms over his stomach; and, with a confused expression on his face, he walked away.

October 5, 1960

To Whom It May Concern:

I, hereby, leave all of my earthly belongings — the little bit of money I've saved, Icy Creek Farm, and every animal on it — to my dearly beloved wife, Tillie Fields Bedloe. Because I left the church long ago, I would be no more than a double-faced, smooth-tongued hypocrite to demand a church service now. All I ask for is a pine-planked coffin and a burial place beneath Louisa's crab apple tree. I want to look up, see the white blossoms every spring, and taste the wild, sour apples when they fall to the ground to become once more a part of the earth. I want to be near my dear wife and sweet grand-daughter until they are called to join me. Caught between heaven and earth, I'll be basking in my daughter's golden light and cooling beneath the shade of her fruit tree. So Tillie, my sweetheart, don't you fret none. Dearest Icy, don't you sprinkle the soil with one tear. Your Virgil is still near the both of you, with Louisa and Josiah, with his own Mama and Daddy, with everyone he has ever loved. I've gotten shed of my broken down body, and my spirit, as light as a kite, soars free.

My heart in heaven,
Virgil Bedloe

As had been his habit, Patanni had hidden each new will in their bedroom in the wardrobe behind Matanni's dresses. When my grandmother found the two pieces of folded-over yellow paper, scrunched into the toe of one of his bedroom slippers, she put on her glasses, dangling from a silver chain around her neck, unfolded his last will and testament, and before reading his words aloud, said, "Virgil enjoyed doing this. It was a game to him."

Then she walked over to the huge oak bed and tentatively fingered the quilt. "It's called Eight-Pointed Star," she said. "Your grandpa picked out the pattern. In all our years together, we never slept apart. No, we always slept with each other — right here in this big old bed." She touched the wooden carving on the headboard. "It belonged to my mama," she explained. "Her daddy was a furniture maker, and he fashioned it."

A week earlier, I'd found a woolly caterpillar, and when I saw it, I had known what to expect. A very cold winter, deep snow, the dark trunks of frozen trees.

Now, as I looked at Matanni, I saw the true

coldness that awaited us. I remembered how I had called out her name when I heard glass breaking and her screaming down below. In my mind's eye, I could still see myself skidding down the stairs, rounding the corner. She had been standing by the stove, whimpering, "Virgil! Sweet Virgil! Virgil, my love!" A jar of canned apples lay broken and smeared on the floor at her feet. Cautiously, she had walked toward him. His body was slumped over in his chair; his hands, still neatly clasped on the table. "What have you gone and done?" she'd said.

I had stared at the two of them — at my grandfather, swaying in my grandmother's arms. "Please, Patanni, don't leave us now!" I'd begged. "Please!" Then pressing my chin against my chest, I'd wrapped my arms around my body and fiercely hugged myself.

Matanni sighed. Looking beyond her, I saw Patanni's unfolded will in the center of the bed. "What are we going to do?" I asked, my voice trembling.

"Right now, I don't know." She put her hand on my shoulder. "But as the saying goes, 'Time heals all wounds.'" Wearily, she closed her eyes. "With time, then, the answer will come."

"I wish the hours would fly," I said.

"Me, too," she said, behind closed eyelids, "but backwards, way back to the beginning, to when Virgil and I first met, to when we were courting, before time had the chance to hurt us."

On the first of November, three days after his death, we buried Patanni. Not many people came. Distant relatives, living in West Virgina, sent condolences but thought the trip too long to make, and most of Patanni's old friends had already passed away. Of course, Miss Emily, Johnny Cake, and Principal Wooten were present. Sam and Martha McRoy, Joel's parents, who lived down the road from us, and a few of Patanni's buddies from the barbershop in Ginseng also attended. Dennis Lute, the owner of Lute's Grocery — where Patanni always bought supplies when we couldn't make it into town — likewise decided that he owed it to my grandfather to come. All of us paid our respects to my sweet grandfather on that cool yet sunny November day. All of us stood beneath the crab apple tree and bade a fond farewell to Virgil Bedloe — loving husband, caring father and grandfather, good, loyal friend. All of us watched as the coffin was lowered into the ground and the rich soil of Icy Creek Farm was shoveled on top. But as each of us turned to go, Matanni, pulling on the tail of Dennis Lute's coat, was determined that we should stay. "Dennis," she said in a clear, strong voice, "would you please read Psalm Twenty-three?" Then, before I could protest and remind her of Patanni's last wishes, she handed Dennis her Bible, looked me straight in the eyes, and said sternly, "Virgil had his ways. Now, I have mine."

Thereupon, Dennis Lute, in a loud, booming voice, began to read. And as I listened, I recalled what Patanni had written: "I've gotten shed of my broken down body, and my spirit, as light as a kite, soars free"; and, in that instant, I felt comforted, for it seemed to me that Patanni's words and the Twenty-third Psalm meant exactly the same thing.

"I thank you for this," Matanni said, as she slipped onto the front seat beside Miss Emily, who had come to pick us up to drive us to the voting booth behind Lute's Grocery. "Lately, I don't have the energy to drink a glass of water, let alone walk two miles to the grocery store."

Miss Emily touched my grandmother's forearm. "Grief can make you sick," she said. "But as the months go by, you'll feel better."

"Right now, I keep thinking a part of me has died," Matanni said, "and wondering how long it'll take to grow it back."

"Time passes and the pain eases," Miss Emily said. "One miraculous morning, you'll wake up and be ready to greet the day."

"God willing," Matanni said.

For the good Lord's sake, I hope so, I thought, feeling the familiar pain — its sharp teeth clamping down. No amount of sympathy seemed to ease it. Miss Emily had tried to comfort me; so had Mr. Wooten and, of course, Matanni. Even Maizy had written me a sweet letter of condolence. "There is a life beyond," she had said. "God's empathy is greater than ours. So have faith, Icy. You'll see your dear grandpa and all your loved ones again."

At first, I'd gasp to ease the hurt. But soon the gasping wasn't enough. That's when the croaking began. Low, despondent croaks would come from my throat like the moans of a dying person. Puffed up with grief, they grew like fetuses and cried as they were born. Same as a wild dog's loneliness, they howled through the house, then wailed in the woods. And, still, I hadn't cried.

"We best get going," Miss Emily said.

"Before that shed gets full up," I added.

"Before a long line of people fills the voting booth," Miss Emily corrected me.

So the three of us, cramped together on the front seat of Miss Emily's car, headed over the bumpy road toward Lute's Grocery. Ten people were standing in line when we arrived.

"I'm a Democrat," a bald-headed man at the end of the line said. "My daddy was a Democrat and his daddy was one, too. I come from a long line of them, and I ain't about to break the chain just 'cause the fella running is a Catholic."

"It don't matter anyhow," another man said, " 'cause Johnson's one of us."

I squeezed my grandmother's elbow. "You gonna vote for Kennedy?" I asked.

My grandmother, without turning around, nodded. "This vote belongs to Virgil," she explained. "If your grandpa liked this Kennedy fella, he can't be too bad."

"Well, you could do worse," Miss Emily chimed in. "I voted early this morning, and I don't mind saying that I cast my vote for John F. Kennedy. Oh, no, I don't mind telling you one bit."

"They say in Harlan County, there are no neutrals there. You'll either be a union man, or a thug for J. H. Blair," the bald-headed man said, recalling the words to the old song.

"Yessir," Miss Emily said as she patted the man's arm. "Whose side are they on? Without a doubt, I know that Richard M. Nixon isn't on mine."

"As far as I'm concerned," the bald-headed man said to anyone who might be listening, "there ain't much difference between a Catholic and a Quaker. Both are strangers to these here parts."

The following day, after we heard that Kennedy had won, Matanni, standing next to the crab apple tree, looked down on the plain granite marker that bore her husband's name and the years he lived and died, and said solemnly, "Virgil, we won." Then she broke down and cried.

"What's wrong with you, Icy Gal?" Miss Emily asked, putting down a huge stack of books. "You've been acting strange for over two months now. I can see it in your eyes; they're dull. In the way you walk, slouched over, with

398

no energy. All this reading. It's not right. You read like I eat."

I fingered the stack and pulled out *The Strange Case of Dr. Jekyll and Mr. Hyde* by Robert Louis Stevenson. "Maybe this," I mumbled, scanning the dust jacket and sliding the novel across the kitchen table toward her.

"I don't understand," she said. "You haven't even read it."

"But I can guess what it's all about," I said. "A split personality," I went on, "one good and one bad. I'm acquainted with the disorder."

"Oh, so that's it." Miss Emily propped her dimpled elbows on the table. "You think you have two people living inside you. One good and one evil."

"Yes, ma'am," I said. "Except I'm not able to hide the bad me, at least not the way other people can. No matter how hard I try, I can't make my fingers flutter when my arms want to jerk. So the bad me croaks, jerks, and curses while the good me stays hidden. She ain't, I mean, she hasn't been around for a very long time."

"In other words," Miss Emily said, and licked her upper lip, "the bad part of me eats and eats and eats while the good part of me just eats." She smiled.

"All I want is to be happy," I said. "Happy and normal. Like I told you Maizy was. You know what I mean."

"But I don't," she insisted. "And unless you

tell me why you're acting so weirdly, I won't. I *know* you're sad because your grandpa died. When my parents died, I felt exactly the same way. As if there was nothing left. As if I was all alone in the world. And, the truth is, I was. But, Icy Gal, you're not alone. You have me, your granny, Principal Wooten, Maizy. We all care about you."

"But I get scared," I moaned. "When I see Matanni sitting by herself at the kitchen table, barely eating her food, I feel afraid. Sometimes, when I hear a creaking sound, I think Patanni is still around, sitting in his old rocker, and then I remember . . . I'll never see him again . . . and a dark, frightful feeling takes hold of me."

"It's natural for you to be sad about your grandpa," Miss Emily said, leaning forward. "You're grieving the way you're supposed to."

"But Patanni doesn't want me to be sad," I said. "He said so in his will. 'Don't you sprinkle the soil with one tear,' he wrote, and I'm trying to be like he wants. I try to act strong and brave, but there's a darkness inside me. One part of me is angry; the other part is hurt. Ain't neither part any good."

Miss Emily held up both of her hands. "But both parts are normal, Icy Gal." She sliced the air with one hand, then with the other. "Even necessary if you're going to work through this. Your grandpa doesn't want you to hold on to death. That's all. Some people nurse death the way others nurse babies."

I thought about Mamie Tillman. "Some mothers don't like their babies," I said.

"That's not what your grandpa meant," Miss Emily said. "He just wants you to hang on to life and be happy. But first, you've got to purge the grief out of your system. You've got to do this, so that new emotions can take root and grow."

"What if Matanni leaves me? What happens if you leave, too?" I asked. "I'll be left with all these holes, deep as Sweetwater Lake, and nobody to help me fill them in."

"Every month that passes," Miss Emily said, bringing her hands together, "your grandma gets stronger and stronger. Every day, she feels a little better. Don't you go kidding yourself! Your grandma intends to live her life because this is what your grandpa wanted."

"What about you?" I asked. "You've been so sick."

"You better not waste a minute worrying about me," she said, her eyes sparkling, " 'cause I plan on being here a very long time."

I looked directly into her light blue eyes and said somberly, "One thing I've learned is that a person's plans don't always match up with God's."

"Icy Gal," Miss Emily said, covering my hand with her own, "stop fretting about all of this. Soon you'll be going to school, where you'll make so many friends. You'll see."

"See what?" I said, jerking my hand away. "Not long ago, you said, 'We're different. We exist beyond the comfort of touch.' Now you're telling me something else." I chewed at my bottom lip. "Now you're talking about the friends I'll make at school. What school?" My voice was turning shrill. "What friends? My phone's not ringing. No one is asking me to parties. I don't do anything. And why?" My fingers grasped at the air. "Because people are afraid of me. Whenever I go to Lute's, the customers pull back. Molly pushes my sandwich at me like she's afraid she might catch what I have. No one asks me anything. No one says, 'How are you doing, Icy?' The minute I step through the door, everybody gets quiet. And I'm not even out the door before the talking commences again. 'Did you see her?' someone'll say. 'She's always taking a fit.' They don't stone a person around here, but they do worse. They shun you to death. Just pretend you away."

"But at college, no one will know," Miss Emily protested, making a fist of her right hand, punching the air when she said the word *college*. "You can be whoever you want."

Like Miss Emily, I balled my hands into fists. "And the first time . . ." I said, thumping my fist against *The Strange Case of Dr. Jekyll and Mr. Hyde*. "The first time I croak, the first time I twitch, the first time I jerk, that'll be the end of me," I said, bringing both fists down on top of the dust jacket. "How many friends do you really think I'll make? 'Crazy as a loon,' they'll gossip. 'Crazy as a jaybird,' they'll say behind my back. Just how long do you think I'll last?"

Miss Emily's mouth contorted, and her eyes opened wide. "But it won't happen like that," she said, urgently shaking her head. "I've seen the future, your future, and it won't happen like that."

Suddenly weak, my arms dropped to my sides. "For a person like me, 'touching is dreaming, mere fantasy,' " I quoted. "That's what you once said. Well, Miss Emily, I believe you now. Just like you, I'm all alone. And the sad thing is, I don't even like the me I'm left with. Why would anyone want to touch me when I don't even want to touch myself?"

"When the going gets tough, the tough get going." Miss Emily centered her hands on top of the table and pushed up. "I understand what you're saying, Icy Gal, but it's not going to be that way for you. Like I said, I've seen your future, and it'll be filled with people and friends."

I rolled back my eyes. "That's not what you said before."

"Pay no mind to what I said before." Miss Emily wiped the table nonchalantly with her hand. "Back then, I was talking about romantic love, and that kind of love is something altogether different. But I could be wrong about that, too. I'm not too proud to admit that Miss Emily Tanner can be wrong. I've been wrong before, but I'm not wrong now. One thing I know for certain is that your life will be rich. You'll feel what I've never felt, see what I've never seen, be touched like I've never been."

"But how can you know?" I asked, lifting my eyebrows.

"I just do," she said with total conviction. "God put me here on this earth to do one thing, Icy. And that one thing is to show you the way." Still standing, she pressed her palms together. "But right now the best thing for you to do is to get out of yourself and do something extra special for your grandma. Your grandpa would want that."

"Yes, ma'am," I said. "But —"

She cut me off. "But sometimes you don't want to . . . but sometimes you're just too selfish, right?"

The word *selfish* should have felt like a slap, but yet the love in Miss Emily's eyes made me lean toward her. "Yes," I said, nodding.

"Welcome to the world, Miss Sparks," she said. "We're all too selfish sometimes. This is how the world is. Life's a trial, Icy. We're always fighting against our natural-born selfishness, always having to work hard to do what's best. It's hard to care for others, but this predicament makes us more human, not less."

"Maizy told me the same thing," I added.

" 'Cause she knew you were good enough and fine enough to make use of what she had to say," Miss Emily said.

I lowered my head, and my lips began to tremble.

"And I do, too," she asserted. With those words, she slowly wheeled around and waddled out the door.

Sitting at the table, I stared at the Stevenson novel. My fingers rested beside the binding, but I was still too afraid to pick it up, too fearful of what I might find inside. "Lately, you been spreading your misery around like jam on bread," Patanni had said. "Darkness is the only thing you see." And although I hadn't lied about Clitus, Jr., my grandfather was right. That day near the chicken coop, I couldn't wait to tell him the truth. A part of me wanted to break his heart, to show him how bad it felt to be friendless, to be hurt and all alone. Two people did live inside me. One was a golden-haired, sweet little girl; the other was, at fourteen, already an embittered old maid.

"No," I said vehemently, "the world will never welcome me." And with a loud thud, I knocked *The Strange Case of Dr. Jekyll and Mr. Hyde* off the table.

"Matanni?" I called from outside her door. "Matanni?" She moaned and mumbled. "Matanni?" I repeated.

"Icy?" Her voice was drowsy and tired. "I'm coming," she said. "Just give me a minute."

"No, Matanni," I said. "I made breakfast for you this morning."

"Well, then, come on in," she said.

I twisted the doorknob and pushed the door open with my foot. She was sitting up and smiling with two pillows propped behind her. "Look what I brought you!" I walked over and carefully placed the tray on her lap. "It's oat-meal, the way you like it, with lots of milk, cooked a long, long time."

She picked up her spoon, dipped it into the oatmeal, then ran her tongue around the spoon's edge and swallowed. "Mmmmmm," she said. "I didn't know you knew how to cook."

A wide grin covered my face. "I learned from watching you." I looked down at the tray, and my smile fell. "Oh, no," I said, "I forgot your juice."

"Why, it don't matter!" she said. "While you get it, I'll be eating."

"It's already poured," I said. "I just forgot to put it on the tray." I leaned over and kissed her forehead. "I'll be right back."

She ran her fingertips down the side of my face. "Where's my coffee?" she asked.

"Coffee's hard," I muttered. "Mine looks like weak tea."

"It don't matter one bit," she said tenderly. "I like it knowing I still have a job."

After Matanni got out of bed to make herself some real coffee, I decided to take a stroll. As I walked, my toes went numb. Whenever they did, I'd stomp my feet until they began to tingle again, until it felt like ants were crawling over them. February had never been so cold. The longer I walked, the colder the day seemed, with its edges growing sharper, as silver-white auras glowed around the blades of grass and trees.

With each step I took, my thoughts, also, began to crystallize, and for a minute, I felt hopeful. I wanted to believe Miss Emily's latest prophesy: Your future will be filled with people and friends. Even though she had been equally forceful the first time, it was this new prediction I longed to hold on to. "Your future will be filled with people and friends," I said aloud.

I inhaled the frosty air, and a chill spread through my chest. As fast as I could, I trudged through the woods. My heart panted. My chest burned. The taste of blood coated my mouth. I walked beyond the old field into the copse of pine trees that stood at the edge. Energized, I went on, desperately trying to believe what I couldn't the day before, when suddenly a blaze of sunlight shimmered in front of me, and I realized that I was back at Little Turtle Pond, that small, dark green pond, with its little round pool of water and its eyelike rock. Trembling, I moved slowly to the water's edge and recalled that cool November day — how Mamie Tillman had cradled the burlap bag, gently rocking it to and fro — how on the far side of the pond she had extended her arms, leaned over, and placed it in the water. In the silence, it had floated for a second and slid under. Standing there beside Little Turtle Pond, I remembered how she had fallen to her knees and tenderly kissed the water.

I lifted my head and gazed up the hill. In the distance, I saw a funnel of smoke. She heats with wood, I thought, watching the smoke rise upward and beckon me forward like a huge arm. Mesmerized, I turned and moved toward it. The bright sunlight drew a line around Mamie's house, and the sight of it soothed me. In the woods far beyond, something silver was shining. Through the pines, I saw it gleaming. Strangely, I felt no fear. Frozen twigs snapped beneath my feet as I drew closer. A cold wind blew, and in the background, shimmering, stood a large metal cross. Just five feet away from me was a little mound of earth. In the center of the cross was a small silver plaque, glowing with the epithet "My Sweet Baby."

I knelt down beside the small grave, for now I understood that buried beneath the cold, green water of Little Turtle Pond were only some painful memories — perhaps a blue baby blanket which Mamie had knitted, a stuffed teddy bear, her bloody clothes — things too heartbreaking for any good mother to keep.

Tenderly, I touched the metal cross. At that moment, the sadness of Mamie Tillman's being brushed against the sadness of mine; and, pressing my hand against my chest, I began to cry. A painful, whining sound issued from my throat, the world around me nothing more than a tomb of ice. Then, bursting with such loss and longing that I thought my chest would split, I threw back my head, opened wide my trembling mouth, and all of the grief inside me gushed forth, spilling onto the ice-cold ground, letting the hope of a new me grow.

Chapter 33

Matanni and I were eating country ham, redeye gravy, biscuits, and fried eggs when she put her napkin to her lips, wiped her mouth, and declared, "Tomorrow, I'm going to church."

"What?" I looked up from my plate, my eyes searching the room. "Who said that?" I joked.

"Your granny," my grandmother said. "She's lonely, living way out here all by herself."

"What about me?" I said, leaning forward.

"She needs the company of people her age," my grandmother said. "She needs someone to talk to."

"But she has me." I shifted back in my chair and drummed my fingernails against the table.

"She needs something more," my grandmother said.

"Well, I don't have nothing more," I snapped. "I don't have any friends my age to talk to."

"And that ain't right." Matanni placed her napkin beside her plate. "I didn't realize how not right it was, till now." She put her hands on the table and pressed down. "Your grandpa and me always thought we were enough, that if you had us, you wouldn't need nothing else. That thinking was wrong. We had no right to expect so little for you."

"It don't matter nohow," I said. My fingers grew limp upon the table. "I'm the way I am. Peculiar. Different. No one wants a friend like me."

"Church people might," Matanni argued.

"That's not what Miss Emily said," I grumbled. "Don't you know she's gone to a few churches!"

My grandmother raised her eyebrows but said nothing.

"She has been to almost every church in Ginseng. Old Vine Methodist. Second Street Baptist. Ginseng Full Gospel Baptist Church. Union. Even the Episcopalian. I can't remember all their names, but she has been to every one of them. None of their pews were wide enough — and guess what those righteous, churchgoing Christians did about it."

My grandmother shrugged.

"Nothing!" I said. "They didn't do a doggone thing — just sat back on their pious behinds and stared. Her, trying to squeeze between two narrow rows and sit down on a bench way too small for her. No one lifted a finger."

"Some people ain't into practicing what the good Lord preaches. They go to church, all right, but for all the wrong reasons," Matanni said. "But if I talk myself out of everything just because that thing ain't perfect, then I won't be doing nothing. Ain't one of us perfect, Icy darling. But still Jesus loves us. We're all part of His creation."

"If you say so," I said.

"So, why don't you come to church with me?" Matanni asked.

"And what church is that?" I asked her. "Peaceful Valley Baptist," I answered before she could, "the church where you were baptized."

"No, I'm changing to Poplar Holler Pentecostal Holiness Church," Matanni replied.

"Poplar Holler Pentecostal Holiness Church!" I shrieked. "Not that church, it's full of crazy people!"

"If you came with me," Matanni said, "you'd see just how wrong you are."

"I got no need to," I shot back. "The world's my church, not some mess of people crammed together on little bitty wooden pews."

"Icy, please!" Matanni said, rising. "I've been studying this for some time now. I even went to a few of their prayer meetings."

"When?" I asked. "You didn't tell me."

"Those Wednesday evenings," she said, "when Miss Emily took you out driving."

"Well, I'll be!" I said, tightly clutching my hands.

"Icy, honey, hear me out!" Matanni said, pacing back and forth anxiously. "Darrel Lute is strong as three men and able to work our farm all by hisself. He don't need any help from me. I don't even get to fix his lunch. He brings it from

411

his daddy's store." She stopped pacing and held out her palms. "I got time on my hands, too much time. Icy, I'm lonely. One day soon, you'll be gone, too. Married with a family of your own or, according to Miss Emily, away to college. Then what'll I do?"

"You'll always have me," I said, standing up, walking over, and putting my arms around her.

"I know you love me," Matanni said, gently pushing me away, "but I've made up my mind. I'm going to church. I'm going to Poplar Holler Pentecostal Holiness Church. And if you really want to show how much you love me, you'll let me go in peace."

"Patanni had his ways," I said, kissing her cheek, "and you have yours."

"It's April," she responded. "Time for new beginnings."

I kept an eye on Matanni and noticed that throughout April and May, she came home a little happier each Sunday afternoon. The lines in her face began to turn upward, not down. Her cheeks bloomed pink with color. She started sewing again, new dresses for church and prayer meetings. Every Sunday, she'd rise early, make us a light breakfast, soft-boiled eggs and toast, which we'd promptly eat. Then she'd fry a chicken for dinner, put it in an iron skillet, cover it, and slip it into the oven. Afterward, in her bedroom, she'd read the Bible for an hour and get dressed. At ten o'clock, she walked to the Poplar Holler Pentecostal Holiness Church, just half a mile down the road, much closer than Peaceful Valley Baptist. By one in the afternoon, she was always home. Over a dinner of fried chicken, mashed potatoes and gravy, collard greens, pinto beans, and biscuits, she'd sneak tidbits of religion into the conversation.

"The Catholics are altar-centered," she said over dinner one Sunday. "The Baptists are pulpit-centered, but we — we Pentecostalists — are pew-centered."

"Well," I chimed in, "I hope your Pentecostal pews are wide enough for Miss Emily's broad behind."

"If they weren't," Matanni said, "we'd make some that were. We want to bring people to God, not turn them away."

I licked my fingers. "This chicken's good," I said. "Real tender."

"It's easy to satisfy your physical hunger," she said, "but you also need to feed your hungry spirit."

"Miss Emily's spirit is starving," I said. "But the Christians around here are too busy judging her fatness to see how hungry she really is."

"Then they aren't true Christians," Matanni said. " 'Be of sin the double cure, save from wrath and make me pure,' " she sang out. "We are all caught in original sin. If we truly believe in the Lord, Jesus Christ, and in what He preaches, then we'll take care of everyone. We won't turn nary a soul away."

"Around here, I don't see too many true believers," I said.

"Open up your eyes, Icy Sparks. Good Christian people are all around you. All you gotta do is see."

I stabbed a drumstick with my fork. "Well, right now all I'm seeing is this good meal afore me." I bit into the tender chicken and added, "And I sure would like to eat it in peace."

Matanni didn't say another word about religion; she simply sat beside me eating Sunday dinner and going on about Darrel Lute, bragging on him, saying what a hard worker he was. All the while, she glowed with health, and her voice lilted as though she were about to sing.

Chapter 34

As I awoke on Saturday, June second, the daylight breaking through my curtains seemed different. I yawned, propped myself up on my elbows, and watched the sun sculpt blocks of glass against the sheets. Buster, our rooster, was crowing loudly. His deepbellied, ecstatic squawking filled my ears. And even though it was June and the humidity was high, the air was dry like talcum powder on my skin. I stretched out my legs, wiggled my toes, and inhaled. I sniffed again. Roses, all right. The smell of deep red roses sweetened the air. Down below, I could hear the pitter-patter of Matanni's little feet scurrying about the house. What on earth! I thought. Cabinet doors slammed and pans banged. The whooshing sound of water came from the kitchen.

"Rise and shine!" Matanni yelled from the bottom of the stairs. "Get up!"

"I'm coming!" I screamed, popping up like a jack-in-the-box, slinging my legs over the side of the bed. "Give me a minute!"

"Big day! It's a great big day!" Matanni yelled

again, then scampered away.

As I jerked on a pair of blue jeans and a tattered denim shirt, I thought about the revival, and a tight-fisted knot began to form in my stomach. Under that big tent, in front of the whole of Crockett County, Matanni, my own flesh and blood, was going to embarrass me. I could see her right now. Tonight, she'd shout out to God, sway back and forth — holding her hands high above her head — then fall into a dead faint upon the sawdust-covered floor. Thereupon, she'd rise again and speak in tongues. Patanni, up in heaven, would be horrified; the Bedloe/Sparks name would be ruined forever. Already I could hear the snickers.

Emma Richards would be first. "Tsk . . . tsk . . . tsk," she'd say. "Problems on both sides of the family. Josiah Sparks . . . afflicted with eye popping. Tillie Bedloe, well . . ." She'd point to her head.

Joel McRoy would throw in his two cents. "She's touched," he'd say. "Addled." He'd shake his head.

"A nutcase," Peavy Lawson would sigh. "With that family of hers, she didn't stand no chance."

From the bottom of the stairs came another one of Matanni's screams. "Breakfast is ready!"

"I'm coming!" I yelled back, shuffling to the foot of my bed. "Let me put on some shoes!" I grabbed my tennis shoes, moseyed over to the window, and looked out. Old-fashioned chrysanthemums, little blotches of yellow, were blooming around the edges of the yard. Coral bells, which resembled delicate pink seashells, bordered the rose garden near the house. In the distance at the edge of the woods, Turk's-cap lilies were nodding regally in the breeze.

"I don't have all day!" Matanni shouted. "Get on down here!"

"Yes, ma'am," I murmured, remembering Patanni. "Yes, ma'am," I repeated, feeling sad.

"Sausage and pancakes with warm maple syrup!"

"Dammit!" I said, but not loud enough for her to hear. "Stupid revival!"

"Icy!" she started again. "Hurry up afore it gets cold!"

"Dammit!" My muscles twitched nervously. "You're gonna make everything worse!" I mumbled. "Everybody's gonna laugh at us tonight."

"Steam is still rising!"

Out of nowhere, for the first time since Patanni's death, I sensed a jerk coming on. "Hush!" I said through clenched teeth.

"Cold pancakes taste bad!"

I clapped my hands against my ears; the tennis shoes dangled from my fingertips. "Please be quiet!" Tightly, I closed my eyes. "Just go away!" I said, hearing Matanni's footsteps scurry across the floor, away from the stairs. Softer and softer they grew, before fading altogether. Miraculously, the urge to jerk fizzled. "Thank heavens," I sighed. "Finally some peace." Relieved, I dropped my hands and sat down on the floor.

"Mine's good!" came the scream from the kitchen. "Mine's real good!"

Fiercely, I tugged at my tennis shoes. "That does it!" I fumed, tying the laces. "You're making me crazy."

Nervously, I rocked forward. My mind was in a frenzy again. "Why on this day?" I asked aloud. "Of all days?" I pressed my hands against my stomach. Anxiety had tightened the muscles there. Slowly and methodically, like Miss Emily had taught me, I massaged my belly.

"It took you long enough," Matanni said testily when I came into the kitchen. "Don't expect me to cook up some hot ones for you."

I snatched out my chair and plopped down. "I ain't expecting nothing from you." I gave her a nasty look, picked up my fork, and stabbed a piece of sausage.

We ate this way — in silence — for five minutes. Every so often, Matanni would swallow a mouthful of pancakes. After which I'd bite my bottom lip and glower at her. Finally, though, tilting her head to one side, she eyed me curiously and asked, "What on earth is troubling you?"

Holding up my finger, I shoveled some pancakes into my mouth and chewed. "Well," I said after swallowing, "if you really want to know, I'm bothered by this revival thing we're going to."

She put her napkin beside her plate. "How come?" she asked.

" 'Cause," I said, "people might act weird. They could have fits, jump up and down, and holler. I mean, it could get embarrassing."

"Praising the Lord," Matanni said, "ain't shameful. It's one of the finest things a person can do."

"It ain't the praising part I'm worried about," I said. "It's how the praising's done."

"If love comes from the heart, it'll come out all right," Matanni said, gulping down the last of her tomato juice. "You don't have to worry none. You'll act just fine."

Stunned by her words, I snapped upright in my chair. "You ain't heard a word I've said, now, have you?"

"To be truthful," Matanni confessed, "I been thinking about what I might put on tonight." She picked up her napkin and daintily patted her lips. "What are you wearing?"

I stamped my foot against the floor. "Something that don't stand out!"

"And why's that?" Matanni asked, perturbed.

" 'Cause I don't want to be noticed," I stressed. "I don't want a soul to know I'm there."

"Well, then," Matanni responded, "whether you want to or not, you'll soon be walking down the glory path!"

"I ain't walking down any path," I warned her, "where people act hysterical, where some crazy man jumps up and down and calls it preaching."

Matanni tossed her napkin on top of the table

and pushed back with her chair. "Right now, I'm sorry I ever asked you."

"And don't you be expecting much better from Miss Emily!" I sassed.

"Shush!" Matanni scolded. "I don't want to hear another word. This is the Lord's night, and you'll act accordingly. Do you hear?"

"Yes," I mumbled.

"Yes, what?" she demanded.

"Yes, ma'am," I said. "I'll act right."

"That's all I ask." Rising from her chair, she carried her plate to the sink. "Now, missy, come over here and do these dishes. I've got to fix my hair."

"How do I look?" she asked me.

I stepped back and eyed her from head to toe. The blue, pin-striped dress was modest. A white lace handkerchief popped up from a pocket on the bodice. She wore black leather shoes, "nurse's shoes," I called them, except they were black instead of white. Her long gray hair was puffed up on top, bouffant style — with two little curls, dangling like commas, near her earlobes — and twirled into a bun on the back of her head. "You look very proper," I commented. "Very churchgoing."

"Good," she said, walking back and forth across the living room floor, stopping right in front of me. Then, turning her head from side to side, she asked, "But what about my hair?"

"Very respectable," I said, nodding. "I like

those curlicues." I pointed to my own face beside my ears.

Her face reddened. "Vanity ain't the Lord's business," she said in a serious tone. "But I wanted to look nice."

I stared at her soft, plump figure, with her huge bosom, at her sweet round face, and relented. "You look real nice."

She beamed.

"But remember," I said, pointing my finger at her, "a respectable woman don't go lolling around on the floor, babbling nonsense."

"A respectable woman should come to the Lord with an open heart," she rebutted. "Ready to receive from Him what He wants to give."

I gave up. "Lordy massie!" I said, throwing down my arms. "There ain't no chance of turning you around."

"Of course not," she answered, " 'cause I'm walking with the Lord."

In my bedroom, I pondered on what I would wear. A dark gray skirt, full with an elastic waist, and a light gray shirt, with tiny, dull gray buttons would do the trick. Both were nondescript, nothing flashy, made of cotton. At the back of my wardrobe, I spotted my black patent-leather pumps with heels no higher than matchboxes. Of course I'd wear them, too. I ran my fingers through my hair, my best feature. There was no other choice but to pull it back and clamp it on both sides with pewter hair clasps. I would make certain that no part of me would beg for attention. No part of Icy Sparks would stand out. My debut, this time, would be different. I'd become invisible, erased not by my strangeness, but by my commonplace dullness.

However, when Miss Emily drove up, I realized that all of my toning down would amount to naught. There she sat, proudly filling up the front seat, covered in a jade-green polished cotton dress with church bells for sleeves. When I saw her sitting there, her fleshy hands upon the steering wheel, a smug grin on her face, my heart skipped a beat.

"Oh, no one will notice you!" I said from the back seat of the car. "I might as well walk in with Beelzebub himself."

"This time, I decided to give them something to snicker about," Miss Emily said with a laugh.

Twisting around, Matanni glared at me. "Maybe this time no one will snicker," she said. "Maybe this time the Lord will take center stage."

It was almost dark when we drove onto the fairground, but I could still make out the golden sand-dollar clusters of yarrow peeking out among the weeds and grass. A sliver of yellow moon and a scattering of stars hung above, while an electric string of lights, stretching behind the tent, glistened like a huge aura in the heavy mist that now filled the air. Cars of every make, randomly parked everywhere, sent a tremor of alarm down my back, while the arklike, dark green tent stood like an oasis smack in the center of them. Old-timers and young boys alike leaned against trucks and beat-up automobiles, sucking on cigarettes, spitting out tongues of smoke. Ladies in long dresses with their hair pulled back into buns stood in separate corners talking softly and excitedly. In the background, I could hear the deep, slow strains of an organ warming up. Near the top of the tent, a cluster of fireflies twinkled like stars, lighting up the entrance. Two oily-looking men, one on each side of the doorway, gave out fans and programs and greeted worshipers as they entered. I was looking out the window, feeling both curious and horrified, when I heard Miss Emily unlatch her door.

"Aren't you gonna help me?" she asked. "I need a little help."

Quietly, Matanni pushed open her door and squeezed out. I was slipping out the back seat when my grandmother threw up her hands and waved enthusiastically. "It's Gracie Vanwinkle," she said, looking back at me. "You don't know her, but she's a friend of mine. I met her at church."

"I'm boiling in here," Miss Emily complained. "Icy Gal, have you forgotten me?"

I came around to her side, grabbed the door handle, and pulled back. "Help me some," I grumbled. "Push it with your feet. It's too heavy." With a huge groan, Miss Emily pushed, and the door flung open, only to expose bunches of fat, like fallen socks around her ankles, and bright green shoes, glowing like gigantic beetles. "Merciful heaven!" I exclaimed. "Why did you wear those?"

"They match my dress," she said, folding her dimpled arms across her stomach, throwing back her head, and guffawing.

"I know you," I said. "You're just showing off."

"Now, who's sounding like a Second Street Baptist?" she quipped, holding out her arms and wiggling her fingers. "Give me your hands."

"Have mercy on me!" I moaned as I lunged backward and hoisted her up.

Up she rose like a big green submarine. "Whew!" she exclaimed, steadying herself by extending her arms, using them like an acrobat's pole. "That was a close one!"

I felt scornful. "It's always a close one with you."

"Well," she huffed. "I don't have to go to Old Vine Methodist or Union Church to get mistreated. All I need is some Christian kindness from you."

"I'm nervous," I said.

Miss Emily glanced over at Matanni. "Look at her!" she told me.

My eyes landed on Matanni. Under the slit of moonlight, she stood very still. Only her fingers gave her away — moving constantly, anxiously twisting her white lace handkerchief, wringing it tighter and tighter, over and over, before letting it go.

"Looks like the whole county is here tonight," Miss Emily said, grabbing my hand, trudging toward the tent's entrance. "We're all nervous. Now come on. Let's go."

"You go on," I said, jerking my hand loose, letting the two of them precede me.

A painting of Jesus Christ on light blue velvet was hanging behind the stage. In colors as bright as the Sunday comics, a sweet-smiling Jesus, with long brown hair and flowing beard, extended His palms to a circle of children, who looked up at Him adoringly. On an old upright piano, a woman played "Rock of Ages." The air was stifling, thick with the smell of sweat, talcum powder, and aftershave. Tall, erect fans stood like sentinels, but their twirling blades barely mixed the air. Overhead, the electric lights cast a yellow glow. At least five hundred jaundiced-faced worshipers sat crammed into metal folding chairs. Women were cooling themselves with fans that had JESUS SAVES stamped across the front. Whining children were straddled over fathers' knees; crying babies were cuddled in mothers' laps. The pianist, a plump, blond-haired woman with two chins, stopped playing, quickly stood up, wiped her hands on her dress, and exited off the stage through a back entrance. The stage, a raised wooden platform about eight feet long and twenty feet wide and a foot off the ground, was now completely empty. Microphones stood voiceless and alone. The drums remained mute.

Every so often, a voice cried out, "Praise the Lord!" After which another answered with, "Amen!"

As I walked down the center aisle, my head fluttered, and beads of perspiration dotted my skin. A toothless old woman smiled at me when I passed. Another middle-aged woman with a glass eye whispered, "May God bless you." I raised my head. Up front, near the stage, strung together on the first row were old people with walkers, blind people with canes, and children on crutches.

A young woman in a wheelchair babbled something, and the woman next to her called out, "It's too hot in here!" At once, men in royal blue suits began lifting up tent flaps and snapping them into place, creating portholes through which humid air would flow.

Anxiously, I followed Miss Emily, waddling down the center aisle in front of me, the green brushing against her ankles. No one, it seemed, was put off by her size. "Here," Miss Emily said, slowly turning around, tugging at my skirt, pointing to Matanni, who was weaving through the fifth row from the front of the stage, one of the few rows that had a cluster of empty seats. Sighing and apologizing, Miss Emily went next. "I'm sorry. I'm so very sorry," she said to every person she passed, finally positioning herself across the tops of three chairs next to Matanni, who had settled down in the center of the row. "Thank you so much," she said, smiling.

I stood at the end of the row and watched. After Miss Emily folded her hands in her lap and became still, I glanced down, smiled at the face of a wizened old man, and uttered, "Excuse me." Then, breathing in deeply, I maneuvered around outstretched legs to the space beside Miss Emily. Relieved, I slumped down.

Three elderly women in front of us turned around and said, "Hello." The young woman next to me welcomed us with, "It's so nice to have you here."

In response, the three of us nodded slowly.

"We welcome all of God's children," one of the elderly women said.

Then, much to my horror, my grandmother responded, "One church. One God. One Jesus."

"Amen," the young woman said.

"One church. One God. One Jesus," the elderly women echoed.

My grandmother amened and added, "Praise Jesus!"

"Praise Jesus!" they all said.

Aghast, I wiped my forehead with the back of my hand. All the while, I kept one eye on Matanni, the other on Miss Emily, looking for signs of support. But reassurance wasn't forthcoming, for the placid curve of Miss Emily's mouth warned me that she was settling in.

"Welcome, my brothers and sisters!" came a deep voice from the entrance of the tent.

Immediately I turned around.

A tall, large-boned man with a head full of

black hair was marching down the center aisle, wearing a navy blue, pin-striped suit, a white shirt, and a narrow black tie. "My name is Brother Thomas," he announced grandly. "And I'm a Christian soldier. All of us here are soldiers, and I welcome you. It don't matter from where you come. If you're a Methodist, I welcome you. If you're a Baptist, I say, 'Come on in.' It don't matter 'cause, just like me, you're a Christian soldier, fighting for God."

Sounds of "Onward Christian Soldiers" blared from the stage. I twisted back around. The fat, blond-haired woman played the piano; accompanying her were two pencil-thin men on guitars and a man with long arms and big hands on the drums. Two pretty women — in identical purple silk dresses — stood to the right of the microphone, shaking tambourines, leaving the space in front of the microphone empty.

"No, children! I didn't study religion in a classroom!" Brother Thomas shouted, prancing down the aisle. "No, children! I didn't learn about God from some stiff-necked man in spectacles. I learned about Jesus the right way — in the little brown church in the vale."

Instantly, the music changed. "Oh, come to the church in the wildwood. Oh, come to the church in the dale," the women with the tambourines sang. "No place is so dear to my childhood as the little brown church in the vale."

"Oh, come, come, come, come," the crowd began to sing.

"Oh, come, come, come, come," Brother Thomas sang out, marching forward. "Oh, come, come, come, come." When he reached the edge of the stage, he leaped up; then, swirling around, he vigorously held up both of his hands. Abruptly, the music stopped. Brother Thomas grabbed the microphone from its cradle. "Jesus Christ, our Lord, died on the Cross of Disgrace," he preached, "and left us with a Cross of Glory. He died on the Cross of Pain but gave us a Cross of Joy. His Cross of Death became our Cross of Life." With the microphone still in his hand, Brother Thomas threw out his arms, fell down on one knee, and bowed to the audience. "Christ gave us a Cross of Glory," he shouted, throwing back his gleaming head of hair.

"Amen!" the crowd cried.

"Christ gave us a Cross of Joy."

"Amen! Amen!" the audience shouted.

"Jesus Christ, our Savior, died on the Cross, but He gave us something back. He gave us the sweetest gift."

"The sweetest gift," the tent repeated.

"And what gift is that?" he demanded, jumping up, pointing directly at the people.

"The gift of everlasting life!" they replied.

"The gift of everlasting life!" Brother Thomas screamed.

"Amen! Amen! Amen!" the tent roared.

"Amen! Amen! Amen!" Brother Thomas said, hopping backward. "Amen! Amen! Amen!" He stopped on a dime in front of the velvet backdrop, turned to one side, looked up at Jesus, and shouted, "Praise God!"

"Praise God!" someone in the audience yelled.

"Praise God!" everyone screamed.

"Jesus, our sweet Savior, gave up His Holy Breath so that we could breathe it in," Brother Thomas said in a cracked voice. "He breathed forth the Holy Ghost so that we could . . ."

"Receive the Holy Ghost," the crowd shouted back.

"Praise God!" Brother Thomas sang out, waving his hands, wildly shaking his head. "Praise God!" he cried, twirling around on one foot.

"Praise God!" the people answered.

Matanni closed her eyes. "Praise God!" she cried, tightly clenching her fists. "Praise God!"

"Praise God!" the elderly women sitting in front of us said.

"Praise God!" the young woman beside me screamed.

Fearful, I looked over at Miss Emily. To my relief, she wasn't praising God, though a strange gleam seemed to glitter in her eyes.

"Children, first we are baptized with water!"

"Amen!" the tent resounded.

"Then with the Holy Ghost!"

"Amen! Amen!" the crowd clamored.

" 'For John truly baptized with water; but ye shall be baptized with the Holy Ghost not many days hence.' "

"Amen! Amen!" the tent cried out.

"And our sweet Savior told us that when we receive the Holy Spirit we will be filled with power. The power of His love!"

"Amen! Praise God!" the crowd screamed.

"The second blessing!" Brother Thomas shouted as he leaped up and down upon the stage. "You shall receive the second blessing!" Zooming straight up, twisting around in the air, he landed in a split, then shot upright again. "Gifts of Inspiration," he said. "Tongues, Interpretation, Prophesy. Gifts of Revelation," he went on. "Knowledge, Wisdom, Perceiving Spirits. Gifts of Power," he concluded, "Faith, Healings, and Miracles."

"Praise God!" the crowd thundered.

"Because He is good," Brother Thomas boomed.

"Because He is good," the crowd reverberated.

"Because He has been good to me," Brother Thomas cried. "When I was a drinker, He said, 'Drink Me.' When I was a doper, He said, 'Take Me.' When I was a skeptic, He said, 'Believe in Me.' When I wanted death, He said, 'I gave you life.'"

"God is good!" the crowd screamed.

"God has been good to me!" Brother Thomas said.

"Amazing grace, how sweet the sound that saved a wretch like me," the women with the tambourines sang. "I once was lost, but now am found, was blind, but now I see."

Brother Thomas stretched out his arms,

raised them upward, popped out his eyes, and cried, " 'Cause our Lord, Jesus Christ, is good!"

"Yes, when this flesh and heart shall fail," all of the musicians sang out. "And mortal life shall cease. I shall possess, within the vale, a life of joy and peace."

All around me people were singing. The woman beside me was swaying, clapping her hands, and singing. In front of me, the elderly women were singing. "This earth shall soon dissolve like snow," the whole tent sang. "The sun forbear to shine. But God, who called me here below, will be forever mine."

I turned toward Miss Emily and saw that her thin-lipped mouth was singing, too. "When we've been there ten thousand years. Bright-shining as the sun. We've no less days to sing God's praise, than when we first begun."

"God's been with us forever," Brother Thomas said. "Can't we give Him the few years we have here on this earth?"

"Amen!" the church responded.

"Can't we let the Holy Ghost come in? Can't we purify our souls and be sanctified?"

"Amen!" the woman beside me yelled.

"Amen!" Matanni shouted.

"It don't matter about our outsides," Brother Thomas preached. "Only that our insides love Him."

"Amen! Amen! Amen!" the crowd thundered.

"Does it matter if we're old?" Brother Thomas asked.

"No 'cause God is love!" the tent shouted.

"Does it matter if we're wrinkled?" Brother Thomas frowned and pressed his fingers against the lines that ran down from the corners of his mouth.

Heads in the audience began to shake. "Hallelujah, no!" they roared.

"If we're tuckered out?" Brother Thomas said. "With our bodies bent over?"

"Praise the Lord! No!" the tent screamed.

"Does He care if we worship Him in raggedy clothes?" Brother Thomas asked.

"No! No!"

"If we're too tall?"

"No, not at all!"

"Too short!" Brother Thomas cried.

"No! Praise God!"

"Does it matter if we're bald?" Brother Thomas inquired, running his hands through his thick, black hair.

"No! No! No!"

"If we're thin?" he kept on.

"No! No! No!" the crowd yelled. "It matters only that we love Him."

Brother Thomas strode over to the edge of the stage and stood silently for several seconds. Then, leaning way over the side, balancing precariously on the tips of his toes, he bellowed, "Does it matter if we're fat?"

Quickly, I twisted toward Miss Emily. Her mouth was trembling. Her fat hands were frantically rubbing circles against her legs. Her eyes were moist. Her skin was flushed.

"Does it matter if we're fat?" Brother Thomas repeated.

All of a sudden, Miss Emily jumped up. Light, like a cat, she was on her feet. "No, 'cause God is good!" she cried, lifting her hands high over her head. "No, 'cause God is good!" she shouted, rocking from side to side.

"No, 'cause Sweet Jesus is good," the tent resounded.

"No! No! No!" Brother Thomas preached. "It don't matter, 'cause all God cares about is our insides. All God wants is our love, our hearts, our souls."

"Hallelujah! Sweet Savior!" the crowd yelled.

"All God cares about is our souls," Miss Emily sang out. "All God wants is our love," she said, her mammoth hips swaying, her fingers splayed open, trembling for a taste of the Holy Spirit, like mouths of baby birds, opening for the taste of worms. "In God's eyes, I'm not fat." Miss Emily was shaking her head. Her eyes were closed tightly. Her body was moving gracefully back and forth. "In God's eyes, there's just more of me to love. More of me to love Him."

"Sweet Jesus is good!" the people declared.

"More of me to love!" Miss Emily began drawing imaginary circles in the air, swirling her palms around and around, the circles growing larger and larger. "More of me to love Him," she said, gingerly lowering her body, then springing upward, painting circles all the while.

Astounded, I stared wide-eyed at her while sliding my chair closer to the woman beside me. But Miss Emily didn't notice. She just stood there, now perfectly still, her hands clutched, her eyelids closed, her lips puckered as though she were kissing the air.

"Come on up, sister!" Brother Thomas urged, as she stood there with tears streaming down her plump cheeks. "Give your heart to the Lord!" With those words, Brother Thomas extended his hand in her direction.

The musicians began to play.

"What a friend we have in Jesus," the tent sang. "All our sins and grief to bear! What a privilege to carry, everything to God in prayer!"

Brother Thomas insisted, "Please, sweet sister, give your heart to the Lord!"

"O, what peace we often forfeit. O, what needless pain we bear. All because we do not carry everything to God in prayer!"

Miss Emily's eyelids fluttered open. My arms reached out to her. But her arms reached out to the stage.

"Are we weak and heavy laden, cumbered with a load of care? Precious Savior, still our refuge, take it to the Lord in prayer."

"Come, sister! Come!" Brother Thomas begged.

"No!" I mouthed, shaking my head. "Don't go!"

"Come to the Lord!" Brother Thomas requested.

"Please, Miss Emily," I entreated, "don't go!"

"Do Thy friends despise, forsake thee? Take it to the Lord in prayer."

Miss Emily took a step forward.

"Don't!" I begged her. "Don't do this!"

"In His arms He'll take and shield thee. Thou wilt find a solace there."

"I'm coming!" Miss Emily cried. "I'm coming to the Lord!" With those words, she took another step. People seated in front and in back of us slid back their chairs, and Miss Emily began to move easily between the two rows, past me, toward the center aisle. "I'm coming!" she declared, with her arms stretched out in front of her, with her fingers flailing the air. "In His arms He'll take and shield me," she sang out. "I wilt find a solace there."

I buried my face in my hands and felt the beginnings of a jerk ripple along my stomach. "Please, Miss Emily, not you!" I moaned. Horror-stricken, I caught sight of Miss Emily's massive form, gliding like a hula dancer down the aisle, her arms undulating gracefully to the music. As she moved, she effortlessly lowered her body — inch by inch — bending down, closer and closer to the sawdust-covered floor, until she was resting on her haunches directly in front of the stage. Then — like a huge emerald whale — she rose upward, through the mist and heat, onto the platform.

"Standing on the promises of Christ my King.

436

Through eternal ages let His praises ring," five hundred sweet voices rang out.

"Come to me, sister!" Brother Thomas implored.

Surrounded by the rhythmical clapping of hands, Miss Emily stood before him with her head tossed back, her mouth opened wide.

"Give your heart to the Lord!" he said, offering her his hands.

"Glory in the highest, I will shout and sing. Standing on the promises of God," the tent sang out.

With her face turned upward, Miss Emily ever so slowly, finger by finger, put her hands over his and gently squeezed. Thereupon, Brother Thomas folded her into his huge arms and pressed her against him. "This is a holy hug!" he announced, fervently patting her back, stroking one shoulder, then the other. "Touch sanctioned by God!"

"Oh, merciful Lord!" Miss Emily cried, her fingers tentatively brushing against her shoulders. "Oh, praise God!" she shouted, turning to face the congregation. "I've been touched!" she sobbed. "Touched! Touched! Touched!" At once, she started to vibrate. Waves of fat rippled and rolled down her body. A smile covered her lips. Ecstasy shimmered in her eyes. "Touched! Touched! Touched!" she cried. I began to see smiles. Smiles, it seemed, were forming all over Miss Emily's body. Creases of fat had turned upward. On her elbows. Around her ankles. On her earlobes. Smiles were in her chin. They chased each other, giggling down her neck. They danced on the palms of her hands. Around her knuckles. All over her. But I could not smile back.

"Touched! Touched! Touched!" her voice lilted.

Smiles were whiplashing around her. Outlining her girth. Swimming near the lights. Like giddy earthworms, they pirouetted across the stage. Smiles were everywhere. On everyone's face. Yet my face was frozen.

A commotion came from the back of the tent, and I turned to look behind me. The middle-aged woman with the glass eye vaulted up and started babbling, "Ajja . . . Nasha . . . La . . . La . . . La!" Rivers of sweat poured down her face. Looking directly at me, she chanted, "Talla . . . Salla . . . Ta . . . Ta . . . Ta!"

"And they were all filled with the Holy Ghost, and began to speak with other tongues, as the Spirit gave them utterance," Brother Thomas quoted, holding aloft the Bible.

"Driiii . . . Sriiii . . . Mriiii . . . Triiii . . ." the wizened old man at the end of my row trilled.

"God's power is here tonight!" Brother Thomas screamed, shaking the Bible like one of Moses' tablets. "Don't turn your backs on Him!" he warned. "Just open up your hearts!"

"Mi corazón! Mi corazón!" Miss Emily shouted.

The jerk, once in my stomach, now yanked at my heart, then slammed against my chest. "Matanni! Matanni!" I whined, my eyes scanning the row. But she was gone, too. "Matanni! Matanni!" I called out, whipping around in my seat, frantically searching for her. "Oh, Matanni!" I cried. In front of me, one of the elderly women jumped up, tossed out her hands, and shrieked. I covered my ears with my palms. The men in the royal blue suits who earlier had opened the tent's flaps were now moving methodically up and down the center aisle, offering their hands, and escorting people toward the stage. Worshipers were contorting and falling down on their knees. I removed my hands from my ears. Twisting from side to side, my eyes continued to hunt for her small form. Then I spotted her. In the side aisle, on the arm of Gracie Vanwinkle, the two of them were walking, floating toward the stage. "I'm all alone!" I muttered. "Here, in this place, all alone."

"Just a closer walk with Thee," the musicians sang, swaying from side to side. The women in purple were shaking their tambourines. The drummer's sticks were gliding over the drums. The guitars buzzed like bees.

The jerk ripped through my head. My neck lurched spasmodically to the left. *You're alone!* my thoughts declared.

"Grant it, Jesus is my plea!" the tent boomed.

You got no one, my mind said. *No Patanni. No Matanni. No Miss Emily. No Jesus. No God.*

In front of the curtain, Miss Emily's humongous body was oscillating. Beside her, Matanni and her friend were swaying, too. So was the woman with the glass eye and the wizened old man. Fifty people were weaving back and forth on the wooden platform. All of them were singing, "He leadeth me. O blessed thought! O words with heavenly comfort fraught!"

"What'er I do, where'er I be, still 'tis God's hand that leadeth me," Brother Thomas sang back, tightly gripping the microphone, which once more was fondling his lips.

"Oh, merciful Lord!" I whispered, folding my arms around me, hugging myself tightly. "Please, don't leave me now!" I begged, realizing that the people I loved most in this world were separated from me by a gulf much wider than the distance I had to travel to get to that stage.

Panicked, I stared straight ahead at the swinging backdrop of Jesus and at Miss Emily swaying in front of it. Energy rippled through the curtain and through Miss Emily's body. Back and forth. Back and forth. Like frames in a movie, the backdrop began to flicker to life. Miss Emily moved to one side, and a blond-haired boy looked up adoringly at Jesus. Miss Emily moved back, and Jesus smiled down at him. Miss Emily swayed again. Now a little girl with dark hair was sitting on the ground, worshiping by His feet.

"He leadeth me. He leadeth me. By His own hand, He leadeth me. His faithful follower I would be. For by His hand, He leadeth me."

No one! I thought. Another jerk throbbed in

the tips of my toes. *No one!*

Miss Emily shifted again, and all of the children at Jesus' feet turned around to look at me.

"Sweet Jesus!" I sobbed, gazing at the curtain, staring at the children who were staring back at me.

Once more, Miss Emily swayed; and between each of her movements, I saw either Jesus or my grandmother standing behind her.

"Sweet Jesus!" I repeated, looking straight ahead.

Back and forth. Back and forth. It was Jesus. Then Matanni. Jesus. And Matanni. And then Jesus changed.

Startled, I jumped up.

"Patanni!" I cried.

All alone. All alone, my thoughts insisted.

"No!" I said out loud. "No!" I repeated.

The backdrop pulsated, and my grandfather held my grandmother.

"Patanni, I'm back here!" I yelled, stretching up on my toes.

And, breaking into a smile, my grandfather nodded, then reached out his arms to me.

The backdrop waved again; instantly, Patanni disappeared.

You see, he's dead, my thoughts said. *You're alone.*

"No!" I groaned as a twitch tore through my arm. "It's not true!" I protested, my fingers clawing the air. "No! No! No!" I cried, breathing in deeply, feeling hot tears. "No! No! No!" Then, clutching my forearm, I bowed my head and began to plow through legs, pushing toward the center aisle. "No!" I sobbed, tripping over a woman's foot, stumbling to the floor.

"Don't you worry none," a voice whispered, soft fingers taking my hand. "I'll help you up," the soothing voice said. And, turning my head to the side, I watched silently as Mamie Tillman wove her strong arm through mine and eased me off the sawdust-covered floor. Unsteady on my legs, I nodded to her and smiled. Nodding back, she lifted her head and, with eyes opened wide, looked toward the stage.

Hovering above the platform was a golden light, and everyone illuminated beneath it was as still as a mannequin. Only the curtain moved, floating like a cloud above the platform.

Alone! my thoughts reminded me.

Exasperated, I covered my eyes with my hands.

"Don't let your heart be afraid," I thought I heard Patanni say. "If you're waiting for darkness, you'll never see the light."

I held in my breath and parted the fingers over my eyes. Yellow rays of light slipped through. Like a curtain opening, my hands slid to the sides of my face. There, shining bright before me, was Jesus Christ, His form dancing across the backdrop. At His feet, gazing upward, was the dark-haired girl. My eyelids blinked, and Rose's knotted body was fighting against itself. Jesus was looking down at her, His eyes brimming with tears, His hand trembling with hesitation. Sweet Rose lay twisted beneath Him.

Suddenly her lips turned upward, and her arm corkscrewed outward. Tenderly, she touched His fingers; whereupon He brought that same hand to His heart and smiled. Rose touched Jesus, I thought. She willed it just like she willed her way toward me.

I closed my eyes again, and when I opened them, the blond-haired boy was singing along with Jesus. In the chirps that sprang from Reid's throat, sweet Jesus was singing but one song. You must love yourself!

"You must love yourself," I echoed.

At once, the five hundred churchgoers began to sing. "All my heart to Him I give. Ever to Him I'll cling," they sang out. "In His blessed presence live, ever His praises sing. Love so mighty and so true merits my soul's best song. Faithful, loving service, too, to Him belongs." I glanced around me. Five hundred faces were flushed; a thousand eyes were beaming. "Love lifted me! Love lifted me!" all of those who were lost but looking were singing. "When nothing else could help, love lifted me!" all of those already saved sang.

Standing there beside Mamie Tillman, with my arms spread out, my yellow hair an aura around my head, determined to cross that distance and reach the ones I loved, I began to sing. I felt love radiating from me and massaging the airwaves. As I sang, Mamie Tillman gently guided me toward the stage. "All my heart to Him I give. Ever to Him I'll cling." The love inside me penetrated my skin, muscle, and bone, nourishing not only myself but every red, open heart which beat inside that tent. "In His blessed presence live, ever His praises sing." I was singing white-shining lullabies that have existed since the beginning of time. "Love so mighty and so true merits my soul's best song." In each note I sang, love was being born. "Faithful, loving service, too, to Him belongs. Love lifted me! Love lifted me! When nothing else could help, love lifted me!"

"L-o-v-e! L-o-v-e!" I sang out. The pure chords of my voice rang true. My voice became the voice of every animal. The voice of every tongue. The voice of every human. The language of God. "When nothing else could help, l-o-v-e lifted me!"

Tightly, I closed my eyelids. Singing blindly but with full sight, I was drawn to the light. Divine, holy, and inspired, my voice came from somewhere beyond me, from a blessed place that embraced everyone I had ever loved. And for once, my life cradled possibility. Slowly, I opened my eyes. While the people behind me were still singing, those on the stage were quiet. With faces filled with wonder, they were listening to me.

Chapter 35

Upstairs in my bedroom, Miss Emily, rocking back in Patanni's chair, asked, "What's a prayer meeting like?"

"Matanni's church is different," I answered her. "Not like the churches we've gone to in Ginseng."

Miss Emily formed a church and steeple with her hands. "And how's that?" she asked.

Sitting Indian-style in the center of my bed, I explained, "It's more like the big tent revival — only smaller."

"Oh, I see!" Miss Emily chuckled, turning her hands over, exposing her interlocked fingers, wiggling them. "They get the Holy Spirit."

"Here's the church," I said, imitating her. "Here's the steeple. Open the door." I, in turn, opened my hands. "And here's the people." Frantically, I jiggled my fingers.

Miss Emily eyed me and asked, "Do you like it more?"

"I like the smallness of it," I said. "Everybody knows everybody. It's real friendly. No one is in charge. Whoever gets the Spirit stands up and speaks what's in his or her heart. When the Holy Spirit comes upon them, they don't hold back. I mean, they all shout and praise God. Speak in tongues. No one's left out."

"Holy Ghost bedlam!" Miss Emily said, clapping.

"And I've felt it, too," I said. "Even stronger than at the revival."

"Tell me more," Miss Emily said. "I'm still thinking about the revival."

Carefully, I unfolded my legs and swung them over the edge of the bed. "It'll be hard," I said, clumping to the floor.

"Give it your best shot!" Miss Emily urged.

Thoughtfully, I began pacing. "Of all the preaching, the one who sticks in my mind the most is Brother Emmit. In the beginning when he spoke, I couldn't feel what he was saying. You see, I was listening with my mind," I explained. "I was hearing his words, but not feeling them in my heart. But then I left my mind at the door and let my heart take over. The minute I did, the fire of God's love began burning through my body. The Holy Spirit bubbled in my blood and blazed in my soul. All of a sudden, I wanted to shout. I wanted everyone to know about the power of God. And before I knew it, I was singing, my voice stronger than ever before.

"I sang out in English, in Spanish, and in French. Then in tongues I'd never heard. My voice was like a hundred bells sweetly ringing. It became a chorus of voices. A one-person heavenly choir. As I sang, everyone became quiet, and every head turned to look at me. Not once did the jerks come. Not once did I feel a croak creep up into my throat. God had unblocked my energy and set it free. It was the power of His touch, Miss Emily. God gave me a massage. A massage of love."

"Touched?" she said, bringing her index finger down her cheek.

"God was the One Who touched me," I said solemnly.

As I walked to Mamie Tillman's farm that day with the blue birthing blanket draped over my arm, I felt the June sun, already hot on my back, and thought about the changes Matanni, Miss Emily, and I had gone through. That morning, I knew what I was about to do was right. In fact, the rightness of it was urging me on. The day before, I'd asked Matanni to give me one of the birthing blankets my mama had made for me.

At first Matanni hadn't said a word. Then, as if she hadn't heard me, she asked, "One of your birthing blankets?"

"Yes, ma'am," I said. "They're mine, aren't they?"

But before I could continue, Matanni was reciting her story, the one I had heard so many times before, about how my mama grieved three times before I was born. "God took three of her babies," Matanni had said. "The longest one she carried five months. Your mama knitted ten birthing blankets, five blue ones and five pink ones." She had held up her tiny hands and wiggled her fingers. "After so much pain and sorrow, she weren't taking no chances with you. 'My lucky charm,' your mama called you 'cause you was conceived the night of the shooting star when Poplar Holler was sprinkled with stardust."

After which Matanni ran her fingers through her hair, straightened her apron, looked me straight in the eyes, and asked, "May I ask what you want it for?"

I cleared my throat and explained that I couldn't give particulars because that would be breaking a trust, but that I could tell her the blanket was for a friend.

Her eyes welled up with tears. "Once you give a thing away, you can't ask for it back," she said. "It'll be lost to our family."

Nodding, I walked over, put my arm around her, and told her I was doing the right thing, this was something my mama would want. "I'm starting a ritual," I had said. "A blanket every year for my friend. Each one of those blankets has some of Mama's spirit in it, enough to give my friend courage."

As was her way, Matanni had moved briskly to her bedroom, where the birthing blankets were stored in a trunk at the foot of her bed.

All around me now, along the roadside to Mamie's house, the wildflowers were blooming.

Patches of chicory with their lovely lavender-blue flowers greeted me, and I greeted them back; for by noon their blossoms would be withered; only their stalks would remain. My future will be filled with books and college, I thought, dreaming while I strolled along. Books, college, and friends. Since the big tent revival meeting, I could feel some direction in my life and could sometimes imagine my future. And it was a future filled with possibilities.

"I'm going to make you work hard this summer," Miss Emily had said at my fifteenth birthday party. Books were in piles on the floor: Shakespeare's *Hamlet*; Chaucer's *Canterbury Tales*; *Leaves of Grass* by Walt Whitman; *The Prophet* by Kahlil Gibran; Huston Smith's *The Religions of Man*; textbooks on algebra, biology, botany, world history, and even philosophy. "In two years, you're going to take your high school equivalency exam," she said, "and, of course, you'll pass." She had drummed her fingers urgently against the sofa's armrest. "Right after that, the college entrance exam. Then we'll apply to colleges. Berea College is a good choice. And I'm not just saying that because I went there. It's for smart kids who can't afford school. They help you work your way through."

"Please," I had groaned. "I'm fifteen, now! Can't we have some fun?"

Huffing and puffing, Miss Emily had stood up. "Fun?" she said, ambling out of the room. After five minutes, completely out of breath, she had returned. "Here," she'd moaned. "It's a Smith-Corona. For your studies." Before I could utter a word, she had said, "This year, we'll write term papers — footnotes and all. But first you must learn to type."

Yes, I thought as I walked along, Miss Emily's prophesy might come true. Every so often, I spotted rocket larkspur, those purple petals growing in a sunny, rocky field. Squirrels chattered in the trees; they always made me laugh. Blue jays flitted and fought. "Yes!" I said at the top of my lungs. "Yes! Yes! Yes!" And even though I knew that I'd still want to croak and sometimes jerk, I wasn't afraid. After all, hadn't Dr. Conroy told me what to do? I now realized that if I met the urge halfway, nourished it with a flutter of my fingers and consoled it with a song, then maybe, just maybe, college would be possible.

"Here," I said, gently placing the blue blanket in Mamie's arms when she met me at the door. "In memory of your baby."

She asked me in like I'd been coming every Saturday for the last ten years. She didn't seem surprised by my words, nor did she ask how I knew about her baby. It was simply understood that I knew. In the living room, we sat in silence.

After a few minutes, she spoke. "I buried him in the woods out back." Softly, she stroked the blanket. "He was born dead. Never got a chance to live. But — oh — he was so pretty!" she said, flickering her eyelashes, throwing back her head. "He looked just like his daddy. A cap of black hair. Tiny beautiful fingers. Perfect. Not a mark on him," she said in a quiet voice, gazing into my eyes. "Why did God take him? I couldn't understand why. On account of me, I thought, on account of my sin."

I reached out and touched her arm. "It's not so," I said.

"No, it's not so," she said, and held the blanket up to her nose, breathing in. "I know that now. God loves me. He loves you. His heart is big enough for all of us. Ain't one of us alone."

Matanni and I were savoring freshly sliced peaches covered in cream when she asked, "Icy, when will you join the church?"

"I won't be joining any church," I stated without hesitation. I had been expecting this for a week.

"Why not?" she asked, swallowing hard.

" 'Cause I like them all," I said.

"But you can't like them all," she said.

"But I do," I said. "I've been visiting a whole bunch of churches these past few weeks," I went on. "I've been reading books all about the world's religions. And, to tell the truth, I've grown to like bits and pieces of them all. When Miss Emily took me to the Episcopalian church in Ginseng, I liked the ritual. It was beautiful. Even Old Vine Methodist with its high-steppin' congregation was charming, especially when they forgot to put on airs, when they showed their true feelings and reached out to the Lord. And Matanni, I reckon if I went to a synagogue, I'd find God there, too. Even the Catholic Church, I imagine, holds the promise of glory. What I'm saying is, you have your ways. Patanni had his. And I — being the strange mixture of so many things — will have my own."

Later that day, I was fingering the pile of books on the kitchen table which Miss Emily had brought me when my fingers suddenly stopped on the benign-looking slim volume *Leaves of Grass* by Walt Whitman. Opening it up, I was instantly amazed. There, before me, was a poem — a very long poem, with no hint of a rhyme scheme in sight. Curious, I began to read:

Swiftly arose and spread around me the peace
    and joy and knowledge that pass all the art
    and argument of the earth,
And I know that the hand of God is the promise
    of my own.
And I know that the spirit of God is the brother
    of my own,
And that all the men ever born are also my
    brothers, and the women my sisters and
    lovers,
And that a kelson of the creation is love,
And limitless are leaves stiff or drooping in the
    fields,
And brown ants in the little wells beneath them,
And mossy scabs of the worm fence, heap'd
    stones, elder, mullein and pokeweed.

"Even the pokeweed is a part of God's creation," I whispered. "So God must love the pokeweed inside me." No one is perfect, I told myself. Everything is flawed. Just look at the moonflower, blooming only at night, not wanting to share its beauty. Patanni liked himself, I thought. If he liked himself, then he must have liked me, 'cause I'm every damn bit as hardheaded as he was. Hadn't Mamie Tillman eased me off the sawdust-covered floor; hadn't she been my friend when I was feeling so alone? Wasn't she my sister? And didn't I have a valley of sisters? "Ain't one of us alone," she'd said.

"Matanni," I yelled, "get in here!"

"Land sakes, child," she said, slamming the screen door, coming in from the porch. "What is it?" she asked, wiping her brow with her hand.

"Ain't one of us perfect," I said, jumping up from my chair. "But still the good Lord loves us. We're all a part of His creation."

Matanni cocked her head and said, "Haven't I said those same words to you?"

I nodded vigorously. "From the highest to the lowest," I said. "From the hand of God to ants, to mossy scabs, stones, and even pokeweed."

Matanni was grinning. "I know where you heard the other, but where did you hear that?" she asked.

"From the great American poet Walt Whitman," I replied.

"Well, he must of been a good boy," she said. "Sounds like he went to church."

Chapter 36

"Is this Union Church?" I asked.

"Yes, it is," the voice on the phone replied.

"May I speak to Miss Gooch?" I said.

"She's not in right now," the voice said. "Would you like to leave your number and a message?"

"Yes, ma'am," I said. "Would you please tell her that Icy Sparks wants to try out for the Union Church Chorus?"

"For the celebration on the Fourth," the voice added.

"Yes, ma'am."

"Best choral group in these free mountains," the voice sighed. "Wouldn't that plaque be nice?"

"I been dreaming about it," I said.

"Well, then, Icy," the voice said, "I'll give Miss Gooch your message and have her get back to you. Your number, please."

"Poplar Holler 0541," I answered.

"Good luck!" the voice said.

"Thank you," I said, before politely hanging up, readying my fingers to dial the next number. After all, I thought, a person couldn't trust

Aggie Gooch. Too much communion, Ginseng folk said. Too much of last year's apple cider, they would add to be polite.

I telephoned three more churches which I had been attending and asked if I could audition for spots in their choral groups. Poplar Holler Pentecostal Holiness Church had already asked me to sing with them, and even though I had consented, I knew better than to count on Matanni's church. At the last minute, something always happened to that old bus and their choral group never showed up. I would not take any chances. I reasoned that if many pathways led to God, then singing for a handful of churches was the most righteous thing I could do.

"You've got yourself a heavenly voice," Miss Gooch said, hiccupping, bringing the glass of cider to her lips, swallowing. "Union will be glad to have you. How long have you been singing?"

"Since childhood," I said, relieved that I was auditioning for Mr. Leedy next.

"Clear as a bell," Mr. Leedy said. "Second Street Baptist welcomes you."

"It's an honor," I said, "since you already have so many fine voices in your group."

Persnickety Mrs. Reece, strutting in front of the piano at Old Vine Methodist, had praised me effusively. "Why, my child, you sing like an angel!" she said. "Your talent is a blessing from God."

Pleased with myself, I smiled and said, "Thank

you, Mrs. Reece. Coming from you, that means a lot." But she could be fickle and had a habit of changing her mind.

Even decrepit Mrs. Fiedler at Ginseng Episcopalian appreciated my voice. "You're amazing," she said, her voice quivering. "And you sing as pretty as you look." Of course, I was afraid she might die by the Fourth of July. Then what would I do?

So altogether I had five auditions, hedging my bets, so to speak. Each choir had wanted me; and, by the third of July, I was signed up to sing for all five churches.

Upstairs alone in my bedroom, with the windows open and a rose-scented breeze wafting through, I stood in front of my floor-length mirror, the one that Patanni had hung for me, and practiced. "Mine eyes have seen the glory of the coming of the Lord," I sang out in a deep, rich voice. "He is trampling out the vintage where the grapes of wrath are stored. He hath loosed the faithful lightning of His terrible, swift sword. His truth is marching on." As I pranced back and forth in front of the mirror, singing with as much gusto as I could muster, the veins in my neck started to pop out and turn a dark blue. What power! I thought, singing on. "Glory, glory, hallelujah! Glory, glory, hallelujah! Glory, glory, hallelujah! His truth is marching on!" With my hands on my hips, in front of the mirror, I ordered my reflection to sing as if auditioning for God. This time my voice held even more power; I sang as though my soul were on fire. "In the beauty of the lilies Christ was born across the sea. With the glory in His bosom He transfigures you and me. As He died to make men holy, let us die to make men free. His truth is marching on."

"Icy, what on earth are you doing up there?" I heard Matanni yell.

"I'm practicing!" I yelled back.

"Time for bed!" Matanni cried, tapping up the stairs. "I'll get you up early," she said, cracking the door, poking her head through. "You can practice some more then." Before closing the door behind her, she cocked her head to the side and said, "Icy Sparks, you're going to make me and my church real proud."

In the silence of the night, I could hear the night birds calling and the crickets singing. Just minutes before, I had been singing, too; and when I sang, every nerve in my body relaxed. Like everyone else, I was normal. No grotesque twitches overwhelmed me. No unnerving sounds jumped from my throat. My voice simply washed them away. Only my essence remained — simply that of a yellow-haired girl with a golden voice.

Stretching out my arms, I breathed in the sweet fragrance and felt the sticky night air on my skin. "Five churches have accepted you," I whispered. "Five churches have said, 'Icy, you have a heavenly voice.'" Five acceptances, I thought. I was about to repeat the words out loud when my breath got caught in my chest. I gasped, sat up, and clearly understood what was facing me. Like a bat blinded by the sun, I had been blinded by the glow of acceptance. For the past two weeks, I had been maneuvering rides into Ginseng with Darrel Lute. I had been sneaking around, rehearsing with five choruses of loving people who had grown to accept me. Swallowing my apprehension as if it were stone, I had easily substituted small twitches for big ones. I had gloriously fluttered my fingers — not flapped my arms — and simply sung. Filled with hope, I had wanted to make it all work, resolved to transform my hope into happiness, and, in my delirium, mapped out my future — one which would be filled with people and friends. At the big tent revival meeting, God had shown me the way to acceptance. Then He had shown me how. But in my wild excitement, I had overlooked one important thing. Tomorrow, in front of the Crockett County Courthouse, in front of all five groups, I'd be forced to choose just one; and when I chose, everything I had been working for, any respect I had won, would vanish. In that split second, all of my hopes would disappear.

Later, combing my hair in front of the mirror, I remembered Matanni's words: *"Icy Sparks, you're going to make me and my church real proud."* A twitch started in my arm; my hand snapped up; my fingers spasmed. "Merciful, Lord!" I said aloud, shuddering as the comb hit the floor. "What have I done?"

Chapter 37

People lined the streets of Ginseng as Darrel
Lute drove through. Red, white, and blue crepe
paper decorated the shop fronts. The Darley
Theater was showing a double feature. The
marquee read LAST OF THE MOHICANS with
Randolph Scott and THE BUCCANEER with Yul
Brynner — neither of which, according to Miss
Emily, was about the American Revolution. In
front of the Samson Coal Company, vendors
were selling fireworks. Two little girls were
twirling around with sparklers in their hands.
Even the post office had been draped in red,
white, and blue. Colorful plywood cutouts of
Paul Revere on his famous ride were positioned
out front. The year, 1776, was hung above the
door. In the distance, I could hear the sounds of
the Ginseng High School Band warming up.
Soon the parade would begin, but first the
church choral groups would compete. Darrel
stopped right in front of the courthouse and let
us out. Immediately the smell of popcorn, hot
dogs, and peanuts filled the air. A little boy with
a cherry Sno-Kone coloring his lips swooped by

me. Little old ladies wiped the sides of their faces with embroidered white handkerchiefs. Farmers in overalls chewed tobacco and spit the brown juice into the grass. Local businessmen in blue suits smoked quietly. Mothers, cradling babies, sighed in the noonday heat.

"Hey! Hey!" Miss Emily yelled. I spotted a fan with TANNER'S FEED SUPPLY stamped across the front. "Hey! Hey!" she cried, waving it back and forth. "I'm over here!"

I tugged at Matanni's dress. "She's over there," I said, pointing at Miss Emily among a throng of people. "Beside the bench."

"Well, I'll be," Matanni said, scurrying forward, weaving around people in lawn chairs and stepping over legs sprawled out on blankets on the grass. "She's saved us the best spot."

When my eyes caught sight of the courthouse, a low groan escaped my lips. In front of the building, just behind the stage, among all the competing choruses and their singers, I spotted my groups. Much to my horror, all five of them were huddling behind and to the left of Mayor Anglin, who, sporting an Uncle Sam top hat, stood in the center of the platform. Directly behind him was a small band. In the background, the U.S. flag and the Kentucky flag proudly flew.

"Here! Here!" Miss Emily screeched.

My eyes couldn't avoid her. There she was, wearing her red-, white-, and blue-striped dress, every bit the spectacle I knew she'd be.

"There's your group over there!" Miss Emily exclaimed, pointing at the mass of singers.

I shrugged and wiped my sweaty hands on my blouse.

Mrs. Reece, strutting by at that moment, grabbed my hand and pulled me along, saying, "Come along, Icy. We've got to get you robed."

"Hey, there!" Miss Gooch said, waving the minute she saw me.

"How ya doing, honey?" Mrs. Fiedler declared when I brushed against her.

"Clear as a bell," Mr. Leedy roared when his eyes caught mine.

Miranda Williams, one of the singers from Poplar Holler Pentecostal Holiness Church, yelled, "There's Icy!"

All of them, all five of them, are counting on me, I thought, swallowing hard, feeling the muscles in my throat tighten.

"Testing," Mayor Anglin said as the microphone buzzed. "Testing. Testing."

From behind the platform came the disjointed notes of a band warming up. Guitars hummed. An electric keyboard whined. Drumsticks coughed.

A young man in front of me bent over and retrieved a stone from off the ground. He cupped it, then shook his hand like a rattle. My heart skidded, and I ducked my head. What if love won't set me free? I thought.

"Ladies and gentlemen!" Mayor Anglin announced when the band stopped. "Welcome, each and every one of you, to our great Fourth of July celebration!"

"Please, God!" I prayed, my hands gripping each other beneath my chin. "Please give me strength," I asked.

At that moment, Mrs. Reece tossed a choir robe over my shoulders. "Oh, no!" I said when I saw it, shimmering green in the sunlight. "Bullfrog green," I moaned, my hands dropping to my sides. "I'll be a frog child forever." Nervously, I surveyed the crowd. There was Miss Emily, smiling and pointing hysterically. Here I was, covered in green, looking every bit as green as she did the night of the big tent revival. "Merciful Lord!" I pleaded. "Help me."

"Our local churches have gathered here today," Mayor Anglin continued, "to compete for the highest honor given on this day of celebration." Grandly, he opened up his arms. *Best choral group in these free mountains.*

The band let out a few more chords. Whoops rose from the crowd. The townsfolk clapped. Beneath my green robe, sweat oozed from my body.

"These will go first," Mayor Anglin said, pointing to my five groups. "Thelma, will you and yours please come on up?"

Thelma Reece nodded politely.

"Lord, help me!" I said when the group moved forward.

"Old Vine Methodist!" Mayor Anglin shouted, stepping aside as we squeezed onto the platform.

"Mmmmmm," Mrs. Reece hummed, turning toward the band. " 'Battle Hymn of the Republic,' " she said primly. Then, with a flourish of her hand, she turned back toward the crowd while the band began to play.

"Mine eyes have seen the glory of the coming of the Lord," the others sang. "He is trampling out the vintage where the grapes of wrath are stored."

Afraid, I hung back, away from the microphone. My voice froze. It was lodged in my throat like a block of ice.

"He hath loosed the faithful lightning of His terrible swift sword. His truth is marching on."

A jerk started in the toes of my left leg. "Ouch!" I squealed, grinding my foot into the stage, curling my toes against the wood.

"Glory, glory, hallelujah! Glory, glory, hallelujah!" the group sang.

"Ooh!" I whimpered, as the muscles in my leg tightened, the way they always did before a jerk.

"Glory, glory, hallelujah!" the group continued.

Up went my leg. It snapped straight out from my body at a ninety-degree angle. Alarmed, Mrs. Reece looked at me. "Lord, help me," I prayed.

"Hold on, honey," Mrs. Reece whispered as she took a step toward me.

My leg began to shake in midair.

"Don't worry, sugar," Mrs. Reece said, stroking my cheek. "I'm right here."

"His truth is marching on!" the group sang.

I felt the warmth of her touch. The heat from her fingers sizzled through my throat. "Yes, His truth is marching on!" I said, the block of ice melting away. "His truth is marching on!" I repeated, forcing my foot down in front of the microphone, liberating myself with a twitch of the toes instead of a jerk. "His truth is marching on!" I shouted ardently. My arms were moving; my legs were stepping high. With the aplomb of a Buckingham Palace guard, I marched. Up and down, I marched, parading back and forth. Grinning widely, Mrs. Reece motioned to the band, who had quit playing; once more they began to play. "In the beauty of the lilies Christ was born across the sea!" I belted, my voice bursting from my body. "With the glory in His bosom He transfigures you and me." The music was finally engulfing me, mesmerizing me, holding me close. "As He died to make men Holy," I sang in a deep voice, "let us die to make men free. His truth is marching on."

"Glory, glory, hallelujah! Glory, glory, hallelujah! Glory, glory, hallelujah! His truth is marching on!" all of us sang until the crowd, clapping loudly, drowned us out and we could no longer hear ourselves. So, joining hands, we formed a semicircle and silently bowed.

Looking up, I stared at the townspeople, at all of those faces. Some were perplexed. Confusion twisted their features. Others were annoyed. They were shaking their heads. But many, it seemed, were happy. And, suddenly, the impact of their smiles flowed like warm water all over me.

"Old Vine Methodist," Mayor Anglin shouted, pushing through our arms. "Good citizens of Crockett County, how about giving them another hand!"

Then, before I knew it, while the audience was still applauding and I was still basking in the heat of approval, royal blue robes began floating across the stage. "A little angel," came the withered old voice of Mrs. Fiedler as she extended her arm and offered me a robe. Dizzy and disconcerted, I blinked once, inhaled deeply, then composed myself. Quickly, I took the blue robe. On it came, washing away the green. Immediately, the choral group from Ginseng Episcopalian pressed forward. A slight twitch tingled in my arms. For a second I felt the urge to flap them, but then the music started. "Onward, Christian soldiers, marching as to war," we all sang. The melody seeped into my arms and calmed me. Its measured tempo soothed me. And when I ordered my arms to substitute flutter for flight, they did just as they were told. Daintily, I fluttered my fingers. A touch of love. A bite of cake. And next — full-throated and grandly — I was lifting up my voice in song. "With the Cross of Jesus going on before!" My heart liquefied. The music washed over me. ". . . Through the night of doubt and sorrow. On goes the pilgrim band, singing songs of expectation, marching to the promised land," I sang. We all sang. And the crowd went wild. They marched, pounding their shoes into the grass, all the while chanting, "Onward, Christian soldiers," over and over again. At the same time, the choral group from Poplar Holler Pentecostal Holiness Church was marching toward the platform — shaking it with the thumping of their feet.

"We didn't know you were singing with everyone." Miranda Williams giggled, edging against me. "That's nice." She handed me a white, discolored robe. "You've already got on two," she said. "Now it'll be three." Instantly, a wave of white, like a blanket of foam, splashed forward. At once, ten people burst out singing. "Up to the bountiful Giver of life. Gathering home! Gathering home!" they sang in rich, melodious voices. "Up to the dwelling, where cometh no strife. The dear ones are gathering home." With arms locked around each other, all of us started to sway. Like a huge wave, that soft blanket buoyed me up and exposed me to the sun. The Holy Spirit burned through me, and I began to sing alongside my brothers and sisters. "Gathering home . . . gathering home," I sang out. "Never to sorrow more, never to roam. Gathering home . . . gathering home. God's children are gathering home." My face was wet; my eyes were filled with tears. "Up to the city where falleth no night. Gathering home! Gathering home!" we all sang together, rocking from side to side. "Up where the Savior's own face is the light. The dear ones are gathering home." Releasing our arms, we raised them upward and looked toward the sky. "Gathering home . . . gathering home," we ardently chorused. "Never to sorrow more, never to roam. Gathering home . . . gathering home. God's children are gathering home." Thereupon, each of us joined hands, and like a big net, we swung our arms outward. "Up to the beautiful mansions above. Gathering home! Gathering home!" we all harmonized, bringing our arms back to our sides. "Safe in the arms of His infinite love. The dear ones are gathering home," each one of us sang, our arms still swinging. "Gathering home . . . gathering home. Never to sorrow more, never to roam," our voices sang out. "Gathering home . . . gathering home. God's children are gathering home."

"Here we come!" Miss Gooch said, as we finally stood still on the stage. "For you," she said, grabbing my arm, pulling me over, and wrapping a gold robe around me. "You gotta stay. We need you," she said, as the group from Matanni's church stepped down and the group from Union Church took their place. "Oh, beautiful for spacious skies. For amber waves of grain," her strong soprano voice rang out.

"For purple mountain's majesty. Above the fruited plain," we all joined in. Like wheat blowing in the breeze, our gold-draped bodies leaned from side to side. Our voices were ripe and hearty. "America, America, God shed His grace on thee. And crown thy good with brotherhood. From sea to shining sea."

"Oh, beautiful for patriot's dream," we were singing when Mr. Leedy bellowed, "Make way!" And with his words, in a flash of red, the choral group from Second Street Baptist Church materialized. "This is yours!" Mr. Leedy shouted, throwing a red robe high into the air, where it opened up like a flower before falling to my shoulders. "Now sing!" he commanded, theatrically shaking his arm like a baton.

Whereupon all of us began to sing, "My country 'tis of thee. Sweet land of liberty. Of thee, I sing. Land where my fathers died. Land of the pilgrims' pride. From every mountain side, let freedom ring!" Mayor Anglin, who had been frowning, was now lifting his voice in song. And soon, in a transfusion of sound, every group was singing, and every person in front of the courthouse was singing, too. "My native country, thee. Land of the noble free. Thy name I love. I love thy rocks and rills. Thy woods and templed hills. My heart with rapture thrills, like that above."

I was sweating profusely beneath all five robes — the green, the blue, the white, the gold, and the red. "Our Father's God to thee. Author of liberty. To thee we sing," all of us sang. I was singing rapturously when suddenly my eyes met Matanni's; and, for an instant, my heart froze. Her arm shot up, waved, then she smiled. "Long may our land be bright. With freedom's holy light. Protect us by Thy might. Great God, our King!" At that moment, a handwritten sign shot up like a crown above the heads of the crowd. Dressed in red, white, and blue, Miss Emily was tilting on top of the bench like an unfurled, massive flag, propped up by the sturdy shoulders of Darrel Lute. WELCOME TO THE WORLD, the sign read. Right then and there, I believed in my future. In front of the whole of Ginseng, beneath that mountain of cloth, my heart was finally beating bright red and strong for all to see.

Epilogue

"Tourette Syndrome is a reason for your behavior,"
the doctor had said, "but it's not an excuse."

That was four years ago at Berea College. I'm
twenty-one now.

I got an education and a diagnosis all at the same
time — the reason why I am, the reason why I jerk,
croak, and tic. A neurological disorder, neurotransmit-
ters gone haywire, lid off the id, computer overload. I
suffer from a disorder. A disorder with continental
flare. First described in 1885 by Gilles de la Tourette.
The good doctor was glad to make my acquaintance.

But why did I say suffer? Let's say, grow. I have
found order in my disorder. I have embraced my dif-
ference.

In rocky soil, I, Icy Sparks, have blossomed. My
difference has allowed me to flourish. Without it, life
would have been easier, but I would not be me.

Look around you. Nowhere in these mountains
will you find a stronger family. The photograph on
my mantel says it all. Me in my cap and gown.
Matanni and Miss Emily dressed in smiles. All of us
wearing a legacy of joy.

Nowhere in these mountains will you find a better

friend. Just ask Mamie Tillman, or Mrs. Mamie Combs, I should say. For six years, through six birthing blankets, we've been fast friends, and now, with my own hands, I'm knitting her a seventh. A blue and pink one for the baby on the way. The rest of Mama's blankets I'm keeping for myself and my daughter.

Look closely. You'll never find a more loyal friend. Maizy Hurley Cunningham will tell you so. We talk about nursing, about music therapy. We still talk about empathy.

Just write Peavy Lawson and Lane Carlson in Vietnam, and they'll tell you about getting a letter from me every week.

Look around you. In this country of coal mines and curves, you won't find a more openhearted woman — to her old friends and to her new ones.

I'm a caring therapist. Children silent as stone sing for me. Children who cannot speak create music for me.

"And why, frog child or saint?" you might ask. "Why are you so special?"

In just two words, I'll answer you. In just two words, I'll give you the reason why. Tourette Syndrome. At first, a curse. Now, a blessing. Frog child and saint. Matanni always says, "The good Lord works in mysterious ways."

So what do I care if — in these genes of mine — I also carry croaks, curses, and jerks?

So what do I care if I'm led to speak in tongues and in the voices of animals, if I have the urge to flap my arms and fly?

If I sometimes let my feelings show and expose the pokeweed inside me, I say, "So be it," because in these genes I also carry nourishment, a voice so sweet that it can soothe the angriest spirit, and eyes that not only pop out to look at the sun but also are curious and eager to learn.

So if in these genes of mine I pass down all of these traits — the jerks, croaks, curses, and repetitions — I will not care because my children will be blessed.

And if someday the townsfolk say to my daughter, "You is your mama's child," I'll rejoice knowing that no one can forget the memory of a golden-haired girl who throws back her head, pops out her eyes, and croaks loudly into the dusk of a hot summer day.